SHUTEYE FOR THE TIMEBROKER

To Cathy,
Mario
&
Zach!
Love,
Paul

SHUTEYE FOR THE TIMEBROKER

STORIES

PAUL DI FILIPPO

THUNDER'S MOUTH PRESS

NEW YORK

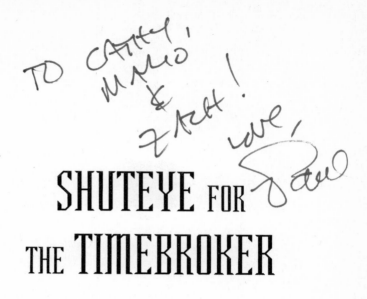

SHUTEYE FOR THE TIMEBROKER
Stories

Published by
Thunder's Mouth Press
An Imprint of Avalon Publishing Group, Inc.
245 West 17th Street, 11th Floor
New York, NY 10011

AVALON
publishing group incorporated

First printing May 2006

Copyright acknowledgments: "Captain Jill" has not previously been published. "Billy Budd" has not previously been published. "Slowhand and Little Sister" first appeared in *Miami Metropolis*, 1990. "Underground" first appeared in *bOING-bOING*, 1991. "Going Abo" first appeared in *Aberrations*, 1996. "Distances" first appeared in *Pirate Writings*, 1997. "We're All in This Alone" first appeared in *Interzone*, 2002. "Walking the Great Road" first appeared as a chapbook accompanying the novel *Harp, Pipe and Symphony*, Prime Press, 2004. "The Mysterious Iowans" first appeared in *The Mammoth Book of New Jules Verne Stories*, 2004. "Shadowboxer" first appeared in Amazing Stories, 2004. "Shut-eye for the Timebroker" first appeared in *Future Shocks*, 2005. "The Days of Other Light" first appeared in *In the House of Poe*, 2005. "The Secret Sutras of Sally Strumpet" first appeared in the *Magazine of Fantasy and Science Fiction*, 2005. "Eel Pie Stall" first appeared in *Adventure*, 2005. "The Furthest Schorr" first appeared in *Interzone*, 2006.

Library of Congress Cataloging-in-Publication Data is available.

ISBN: 1-56025-817-9
ISBN 13: 978-1-56025-817-9

9 8 7 6 5 4 3 2 1

Book design by Maria E. Torres
Printed in the United States of America
Distributed by Publishers Group West

For Deborah, who never, ever, ever gets enough shuteye.

And to the memory of Ginger Newton, 1990–2005:
"A little dog would get tired living so long."

CONTENTS

Readers of my Neutrino Drag *collection will perhaps recall the presence there of two early stories of mine: "Rescuing Andy" and "Yellowing Bowers." As I explained in those pages, these stories were the start of an abortive series set in the mysterious New England seaside town of Blackwood Beach. Two other installments were written but never sold.*

On a whim recently, I went into my cave of memories (a large closet in my office full of moldering boxes) and dug out the manuscripts of those two tales, which I had not looked at in nearly twenty years. I was amazed to see they were at least as readable as the two that saw print, and so I determined, rather nostalgically, to give them a long-delayed life.

Following the seasonal motif established by "Rescuing Andy" (summer) and "Yellowing Bowers" (autumn), the third story, "Captain Jill," illustrates the events of a typically atypical Blackwoodian winter. The knitting motif herein traces its origin to the vocation of my mate, Deborah Newton, who at the time I was embarking on my career with this story was starting her own as a knitwear designer.

Captain Jill

Someone was singing in the cellar.

T. Clayton Little, sitting stiffly in his ornately carved canopy bed, the still-strange room around him darkly full of the accumulation of two hundred years of other people's lives, wondered if he should investigate.

Perhaps, he thought, *if I simply lie here, Granny will go and check it out. And if she doesn't get up, then it can't be anything serious.*

For a moment, that train of reasoning reassured him. Its derailment, however, was almost immediate. Granny Little was partially deaf and suffered from arthritis in several crucial joints. Additionally, she would never see the blithe side of ninety again. Weren't these very facts the reason why Clayton had let his father convince him to come live with her and manage her affairs, not the least of which was the Little Mistletoe Farm of Blackwood Beach? *Have to drive out there early tomorrow and show some extra attention to Ethel,* thought Clayton with absurd irrelevance, before dragging his mind back to the problem at hand. What was he thinking of, hoping the frail old woman would save him the unpleasant task of venturing out of his warm bed at four in the morning, padding down three flights of steep stairs into a cold, damp basement, and finding out just who—or what—was making that cacophony?

Ashamed of his selfish trepidation, Clayton tossed back the thick comforters and swung his long, gangly legs over the side of the bed. Midwinter moonlight shafting through a leaded-glass window revealed one of Clayton's best-kept secrets: a fondness for old-fashioned nightshirts most unfashionable in a young man of thirty-two. Catching sight of the dim ghost of his reflection in a mirror, he winced, recalling the derision Marianne had heaped upon him back in Asheville when she had discovered this gaucherie. Her insensitive laughter had been one of the prime causes of their breakup, freeing Clayton from his last tie to the town of his birth.

He shook his head in wonder at the inexplicable twists and turns of life. Had he not been so enamored of being unromantically comfortable while sleeping, he might never have broken up with Marianne. Consequently, he would not have been inclined to move north, to this strange New England town of his ancestors. And therefore, he would not, at this instant, have been shuffling from one frozen foot to another, postponing the inevitable moment when he would have to descend to locate the source of the mysterious singing.

Chafing his big, rawboned hands together nervously, Clayton left his bedroom. Out in the long third-floor hall, he turned left and proceeded cautiously past Granny Little's room—whence gentle old-lady snores issued—to the head of the stairs. The noise was more easily heard here, drifting up from the depths of the large house like the notes of an infernal symphony. Although Clayton could not make out any words, the lusty soprano seemed to convey unpleasant intimations of villainy and unholy glee.

Down the stairs, with their threadbare woven runner, to the second floor, Clayton slowly made his way. Pausing, he sought to discern at least the refrain of the song, hoping to recognize a pop tune and thereby draw the reassuring conclusion that the radio had somehow shorted itself into activity. No luck.

On the ground floor of Clayton's new home, tiny fragments of the song became recognizable. Standing in the kitchen, with its massive wood-gas stove and cantankerous icebox, Clayton thought to make out the words "dead man," "treasure," and "rum." Not exactly the components of any current Top 40 hit he could recall. And anyway, the innocent radio sat quiescent on its shelf.

Now Clayton began to grow intrigued, despite his fears. Who could be responsible for this bellowed chantey? Some drunk who had wandered into their cellar to escape the cold, no doubt. Emboldened, Clayton took a long-handled flashlight from its resting place and moved to the locked door leading to the stone-walled cellar.

The rickety stairs leading down were lined with old galoshes, empty Ball jars, broken crockery, and other relics of life led by generations of Littles. Clayton descended cautiously, reaching the dirt floor without barking his bony ankles, a minor triumph.

Here the song welled up in its full glory, only slightly muted. Clayton recognized it now for a version of that beloved boyhood favorite, "Fifteen Men on a Dead Man's Chest." Odd, he hadn't thought of that song for decades. He wondered that anyone still sang it. And the voice! Was it that of a throaty woman, or of a high-voiced man?

The familiarity and innocent connotations of the song lifted Clayton's spirits even further. Some teenager it had to be, bent on mischief.

Flashing the beam of his light around the web-shrouded, unpartitioned space, cluttered with generations of offcast miscellany, Clayton looked for an open window that could have granted the intruder access. But as far as he could see, the small, dusty casements were all fastened securely with rusty hooks and eyes. Perhaps elsewhere, out of sight, a window had been breached. Clayton pictured the inconsiderate singer, supine and drunk, lying facedown on the damp earthen floor, bellowing in his muffled manner. Not wanting even an annoying vagrant to catch a cold, Clayton moved away from the foot of the stairs and walked down irregular aisles of cartons and loose junk, furniture and Flexible Flyers.

A thorough investigation of the capacious cellar, however, revealed no open window or supine drunk, but only more assorted trunks and boxes, a gigantic furnace with its pile of coal boxed by three wooden walls, and a dilapidated sleigh covered with cobwebs and smelling of musty leather.

The unseen singer had switched tunes by the time Clayton had completed his search. The new song was unfamiliar, but of the same genre, detailing unsavory depradations and plunderings, accompanied by graphic bloodshed.

Clayton returned to the foot of the stairs and stood there, baffled. Where the hell was this intruder who had disturbed his sleep?

He cocked his head. Was the sound issuing from below?

Suddenly he was ten years old again. Gran'pa Little, long dead, stood beside him. "Yup, Clay, this town is wormier than Swiss cheese. Laced with tunnels dug by the old freebooters and smugglers. Why, one of them surfaces right here."

Perhaps the old man hadn't been joshing. Clayton went to the southwest corner of the cellar. There, shifting a box or two, he uncovered the trapdoor set in its wooden frame. He pried up the rusty ring set in its top and heaved. The door opened with a ghastly creak, and surprisingly fresh, sea-scented air rushed out in a puff. A set of rungs led straight down into the black hole.

Flashlight in one hand, its lonely beam directed uselessly upward, Clayton took the first step downward.

His return to Blackwood Beach was proving a bit more arduous than he had anticipated.

* * *

Once upon a time, Blackwood Beach had been, for young Clayton, a place of no responsibilities. In those days he had never had to contend with late-night caterwauling; nor had he had to manage family businesses.

Every summer for thirteen years, from the age of six to eighteen, Clayton had left behind the mundane for the miraculous by means of a simple sixteen-hour drive north with his parents. Departing hilly Asheville, North Carolina, where his father was the curator of the Vanderbilt mansion, Clayton always felt as if his soul were being freed from the bondage of his schoolwork and his paper route and reformed into a purer, more marvelous thing.

The feeling would persist until his father would yell at Clayton and his sister, "Get your goddamn feet off the back of my seat, you two depraved young monsters, and count out-of-state license plates!" Reality reasserted itself then, informing Clayton that he was not entirely free. Still, something of the sense of emancipation would remain with him through the long months of June, July, and August, spent amid the straggling, elm-shaded streets of Blackwood Beach.

For the first few trips, Clayton was never quite sure of how they arrived at the old seaside town. Pestering his father to tell him the precise directions, he got back such instructions as "follow a dark star" or "turn left where normality turns right." By the age of ten, though, he knew the route as well as Mr. Little, though he could not put it into phrases any less opaque than his father's.

Although it took some getting used to, Blackwood Beach eventually became Clayton's favorite place. (What child could fail to fall in love with a village where, for instance, the town coordinator possessed scales, webbed fingers, and a penchant for raw herring?) When, in his teens, he came to read the works of Asheville's most famous native son, Thomas Wolfe, he found a sentiment that tallied with his feelings for Blackwood Beach:

"America is the only place where miracles not only happen, but happen daily."

Throughout his teens, Clayton continued to enjoy his yearly stays with Granny and Gran'pa Little, especially the visits to the Little Mistletoe Farm, which lay a few miles out of town. As the years passed, however, other interests naturally grew to assume equal importance. When it came time for him to enter college, he regretted that having to work during the summers would mean that he could not keep up his visits. After a time, the town and its weird doings shrank to relative insignificance, a parcel of happy, youthful memories wistfully untied and examined during the more stressful moments of adult life.

At the age of thirty, Clayton had returned to Asheville to live with his parents. His own business—a video-rental store specializing in recordings of various elderly actors reading the works of Romantic poets—had gone bankrupt, thanks to an appalling lack of taste on the part of the general public, and he needed some time to recoup his inner resources.

Somehow, two years had drifted by while he held a succession of odd jobs. A wan romance had developed with an old friend, now divorced. Its ending had almost ruined the pleasure of nightshirts for Clayton, leaving him bitter and confused.

Then had come the letter from Granny Little, written in her familiar crabbed script, which looked as if a drunken spider dipped in ink had wandered across the paper. Requesting help with the family business, the letter was too plaintive to go unheeded.

And so Clayton had taken the well-known road north, finding that he hadn't forgotten the final, crucial passage into Blackwood Beach, and feeling as if the tawdry years were dropping off his back like a snake's too-small skin.

* * *

The splintery ladder had left its calling cards in the soles of Clayton's bare feet and under the base of one thumb. Standing beside the ladder, he tried to aim the flashlight at his injury with the same hand with which he was attempting to remove the sliver in his digit. The whole procedure was both ineffectual and frustrating, so he gave up and concentrated on taking in his novel surroundings.

The ladder vanished above into a deep black square that was the cellar trapdoor casement. The tunnel ceiling around the hole was braced with wooden planks and beams, mossy and green with age. The rickety ladder hung down like a dipstick in an oil tank, not far from the earthen wall of the passage, so that one might almost have missed it without moving slowly through the subterranean shaft and carefully shining a light.

The passage—obviously part of the extensive network underlying Blackwood Beach—was wider across than the span of Clayton's outstretched arms, a not inconsiderable distance. From behind Clayton came a moist breeze meandering in from the sea. Ahead, the beam-ribbed tunnel stretched cold and damp.

It was from this direction that the singing came. So much was clear. Also apparent was the nature of the voice. It was a woman's, reminiscent of that of the young Lauren Bacall. (Clayton still got shivers when he recalled the neophyte actress telling Bogart how to whistle.) Had this woman wandered in from the seaward end of the tunnel and gotten lost? She certainly didn't sound frightened, unless she was singing solely to keep her courage up. Clayton doubted, however, that someone who was terrified could put so much almost palpable joy into lyrics about maiming, looting, and burning.

Down the tunnel, flashlight probing ahead, Clayton cautiously advanced.

He was not ready for what he encountered.

The young woman sat on a big crate. Her hair was a wild mass of red curls, like a bank of roses in spring. Her skin was white as country snow, save for random freckles and ruby lips. Her green eyes seemed to catch the flashlight's rays; they shone like a cat's. Her small nose managed to imply an impudent archness.

She was dressed rather unconventionally. A white shirt of masculine cut, big balloon sleeves tight at the wrist, its buttons half-undone, causing it to hang off one shoulder. A short black skirt with a jagged hem, revealing long, exquisitely tapering bare legs, which were encased below the knees in high boots. A wide leather belt, from which depended a sheathless sword.

Swigging from a bottle, she let one leg dangle; the other was bent sharply, the heel of her boot caught against the upper edge of the crate. The whole effect was exceedingly indelicate, and had Clayton's mother ever caught his sister sitting in such a fashion, the girl would have gotten the walloping of her life.

An icy drip started to fall from the root-tangled ceiling of the ancient, beam-braced tunnel, directly above the befuddled Clayton. It seemed the very essence and distillation of frigidity, a succession of pure arctic droplets, each stinging like the Ice Queen's kiss.

Clayton didn't even feel them. He stood barefoot—his robe twitching halfheartedly in the tunnel's mild breeze, his collar growing wetter by the minute—unable to believe what he was seeing.

Bellowing out the final refrain of her chantey, the woman paused to drink long and heavily from her bottle, afterward wiping her mouth with the back of one hand. Clayton noticed then that one board of the crate had been pried off, revealing numerous bottles packed in straw within. When she lowered her head, her gaze at last fell upon Clayton.

"Company!" she shouted. "'Sblood, but I do hate drinking alone! Haul your carcass over here, man, and help me hoist a few."

She patted the empty spot next to her invitingly, with a lascivious twinkle in her eyes that Clayton found disconcerting, to say the least. He gulped, coughed, and found his voice.

"Uh, sorry, ma'am, but I make it a policy not to mix spirits with spirits."

"Ah, a regular tavern wit, I see! Very glib, indeed. But your caution is overnice, in this case. I'm no ghost, you mooncalf! Look at me! Does this flesh look less than solid?"

Subtly shifting her position, allowing her skirt to hike up in an apparent attempt to meet her downward-trending blouse halfway, the woman offered herself for inspection.

"Ma'am, please!" Clayton begged, averting his reddening face.

"Have some spine, man! Are you a eunuch? Why, the scurvy potboy, lowest of my crew, would have known how to react to such an invitation by Captain Jill Innerarity, Hellcat of the East Coast, known from Cape Cod to Cape Hatteras as a mortal terror and expert wench. All right, you can look again. I've composed myself all ladylike for your eyes."

Clayton swung his head back around. Captain Jill had spoken true, going so far as to demurely cross her legs at the knees. Still, Clayton didn't trust her.

"If you're not a ghost," he demanded, "then what are you? And what are you doing underneath my house, howling those awful songs and keeping me awake?"

"I'm a woman and a pirate, any fool could see those two things. And as for my singing, I'm celebrating my release. After three-hundred-odd years of entombment, you'd bloody well feel like singing too, bucko!"

Clayton's bafflement must have been obvious. Jill boosted herself off the crate, dusting her skirt neatly. "Follow me, you poltroon, and I'll show you."

She headed off down the tunnel, and Clayton cautiously came after her.

By a tumbled pile of bricks partially filling the way, they stopped.

"My home for these past three centuries," Captain Jill said, indicating with a wave of her hand where Clayton should look.

He swung the flashlight to reveal a brick-lined cubicle set into the earthen side of the tunnel, its fourth wall a knee-high remnant flush with the passage.

"How—" began Clayton.

Captain Jill interrupted. "This Blackwood Beach of yours was a wizardly place even in my day, and I steered clear of it as long as I could. But after raiding up and down the coast for years, I ran out of towns to sack. And I was always looking for new challenges. So at last I convinced my men that we could deal with any dastardly tricks this hamlet could offer. One stormy evening, we hazarded a landing on the beach, thinking no one would be expecting us. But they were. A queer one-eyed sorcerer by the name of Goodnight led them. My men he bewitched into hermit crabs, who promptly buried themselves in the sands. Me he bricked up here, filling the loathsome box with a strange blue gas that left my senses intact, saying he might have a use for me in time."

Clayton contemplated the coffin-sized space. Three hundred years in a closet? He would have gone mad.

As if guessing his feelings, Captain Jill continued. "That devilish blue phlogiston, or whate'er it was, left my poor body suspended, but my mind all arace, like a chip in a millstream. At first, I thought I'd be a bedlamite ere long. I couldn't understand why the warlock had gone to such trouble to preserve me, only to drive me mad. Why hadn't he just extinguished my thoughts for the nonce, as one caps a flame? But then I noticed the gas gave me certain powers. To wit, I could see and hear what was happening outside my petty cell—all over the world, in fact. I suspect that the scheming Goodnight wished me to keep abreast of history as it happened, so to speak, perhaps in preparation for whate'er obscure use he had for me. At first, I was chary of using my supernatural vision and hearing o'ermuch. But I soon came to enjoy amusing myself, watching the folly of mankind."

Clayton had a sudden frightening thought. "Welcome Goodnight, the magician—did he just free you tonight?" Clayton had no wish to intrude on any of the mysterious Goodnight's projects.

"Hah! That rascal did no such merciful thing. Yesterday a tremor of the earth opened a crack in my prison. The gas seeped out, and I came to, my old self. With my sword, I gradually chipped away this old mortar and made my escape. If luck be with me, that bastard Goodnight knows nothing of my escape, and I'll soon have my revenge."

Talk of taking revenge on the powerful Goodnight, still living as one of Blackwood Beach's most eminent citizens, sent gooseflesh crawling up Clayton's wet back, and he sought to change the topic.

"Uh, your visonary powers—do you still have them?"

Captain Jill scowled fiercely. "Blast it, no! They've vanished with the gas. A handy talent those would have been, now that I'm free! Luckily, I remembered watching some men hide that crate of whiskey not far from me some sixty years ago—during a time called Prohibition, I wot—and I knew where to head as soon as I was free. All those years built a powerful thirst, my lad." Captain Jill passed a silky tongue over her lips. "As well as certain other yearnings."

Nervously, Clayton replied, "Well, yes, I'm sure that's true. We'll see about attending to those when we get you back up to the surface and make you presentable."

"Who says I'm following you back up aboveground?" Captain Jill demanded.

"I naturally assumed—"

"You've assumed wrong, my fine fellow. Your modern world makes me nervous, at least for the nonce. I've everything I need down here. Whiskey, song—and now you."

While she talked, Captain Jill had managed to inch closer without Clayton's noticing. Now she was within a foot of him. Realizing this with a start, he began to back away.

"Uh, that's very flattering, Miss Innerarity, but I'm afraid I have no intention of staying. I have duties up above, a saintly old grandmother to attend to—"

"Grandmother be damned!" Captain Jill yelled. "I've got blue fog in my veins that I've got to work off. It's left me cold after that long sleep, and I need some mortal warmth!"

Captain Jill extended one slim finger to touch the back of Clayton's hand. A preternatural bolt of ice shot up his arm, and he hastily jerked back.

"I'm sure a doctor can cure that condition better than me," Clayton argued. "Perhaps a day in the sun would work wonders—"

"I'll pick the nostrum for what ails me, you snivelling whelp, and it'll be a cure that's never failed me yet!"

With this, Captain Jill leaped upon Clayton with alarming speed. Her embrace transmitted a fearsome chill through his nightshirt and throughout his entire body. He felt her breasts as two soft mounds of snow tipped with nubby little stalagmites. (Or was that stalactites? he wondered absurdly. He could never keep the two straight. He supposed it depended on whether she was lying on her back or on her stomach.)

Clayton's mind began to fail under the onslaught of the cold radiated by Captain Jill, who now wrapped one leg around one of his and toppled him to the ground. Much to his alarm, he detected certain umistakable stirrings below his waist, as her actions combined with the supernatural chill began to rouse him to an icy erectness.

Before blanking out, Clayton had time to wonder if "Roger me silly, you varlet!" meant what he suspected it did.

* * *

Why was he thinking of John Keats? Surely there were more pressing matters to fill his mind as he lay there on the damp, packed earth of the tunnel floor. Such as finding the power to get to his feet.

Ah, that was why thoughts of Keats had occurred to him. Those lines in "La Belle Dame sans Merci": "And I awoke, and found me here / On the cold hill's side." Certain parallels were undeniable. Was there any record of how the knight in that poem had dealt with the morning after?

Summoning energy from previously unplumbed depths, Clayton woozily got to his feet. His flashlight was sending out a yellow beam indicative of drained batteries. Captain Jill was nowhere to be seen.

Somehow Clayton made it back to the ladder leading up to his cellar. His energy was dribbling back in small increments, and he used some to ascend the rungs.

In the basement, he dropped the trapdoor and weakly shoved boxes atop it. He jumped as a noise sounded behind him. Jill? No, only a whiskery rat scrambling across some cardboard.

The cellar stairs were another obstacle, but he conquered them like Hillary taking the last hundred yards of Everest. In the kitchen, he slammed the door shut and locked it, wondering if he had the strength to move the refrigerator in front of it.

"Clayton?"

He nearly shot out of his skin. Turning around slowly, he found Granny Little seated at the breakfast table. His loud sigh of relief obviously puzzled her.

Granny Little was about four feet five inches tall. Her silvery white hair was caught up in a large bun partway back on her head. Thick bifocals in gold frames rested on her hawklike nose. Her knobby, arthritic hands were clasped clumsily atop the table. She wore her unvarying outfit: a gingham dress covered with a homemade cardigan.

"Where have you been, Clay? I checked your bedroom and found it empty at six. It's nine now. I was so worried."

Clayton began to explain. The singing, his descent to the cellar, and then to the tunnel, his conversation with Captain Jill. When it came time to detail how he had been rendered unconscious and taken advantage of, Clayton paused, unsure of how to phrase it delicately. At last, he bulled ahead, knowing Granny had led no sheltered life.

Granny nodded knowingly. "I was afraid something like that had happened when I saw the cellar door open." Granny's cherubic face assumed a look of worry and sadness. "Oh, I'm afraid it's all my fault for not warning you, Clay. And once I suspected where you'd gone, I still couldn't help. My joints, you know."

Clayton felt awful that Granny was blaming herself. All his self-pity quickly vanished. What did he have to worry about? At least he was young and healthy. The woman lurking under the house could surely be evicted by someone of his ingenuity and abilities. When he smelled the coffee Granny had perked, he felt even more hopeful.

"I had completely forgotten about this Jill person," Granny continued, her look of concern partially overlaid by one of calculation. "There was an old legend about her, but after so many years, no one gave it much thought. It seems now we'll have to do something about it. Tell me, Clay, what exactly did that chill of hers feel like?"

Clayton thought a moment, then strove to capture the preternatural sensation in at least a simile.

"Like being squeezed by a polar bear during an Antarctic midnight while simultaneously having a spinal tap."

Granny shook her head in sympathy. "It sounds, son, like you could have used a nice warm sweater between you and that witch."

At that instant, having placidly uttered the non sequitur, Granny began to knit.

Clayton put a hand to his forehead and eyed her uneasily—for the woman had neither needles nor yarn in her hands.

For almost seventy years, Granny had been a compulsive knitter. Even her arthritis had not slowed her down. The output of her flickering needles had clothed, covered, and comforted dozens of Littles and their neighbors with sweaters, blankets, slippers, mittens, socks, and gloves of every description and size. Nor was Granny a purist. She would knit with wool, rayon, acrylic, even string. She knew every pattern in the books, and dozens that were unique to her. Clayton had worn garments made by her all his life.

But just recently, Granny had developed a disconcerting habit. Although as capable as ever, she had forsaken the conventional implements and materials of her craft, apparently having exhausted their potential after seven decades of activity. Instead, she seemed content to make busy knitting motions with her empty hands, knitting sheer air, apparently working in a medium invisible to the eye.

Clayton suspected and dreaded that Granny was gradually succumbing to something awful like Alzheimer's. Yet she seemed so competent in every other area. Her only eccentricity was that ghastly miming of knitting. It gave Clayton the heebie-jeebies.

"Have something to eat, Clay," Granny said, "before you drive out to the farm." Then she repeated, as her hands ceaselessly shifted, "Yes, we'll definitely have to do something about this."

* * *

When was the state ever going to pave this stretch of highway? They neglected Blackwood Beach shamefully, and sometimes it didn't help that the town repaid them in kind.

Of course, the ride was not enhanced by the fact that Clayton's red '59 Ford pickup had no shocks. Clayton always meant to get around to installing some, but both time and money conspired against him. By now, he was coming to feel that any vehicle that had served as faithfully as the Little Mistletoe Farm delivery truck for so long deserved respect for its innards, and should be allowed to keep all its original, Detroit-given organs right up until death.

Still, it made for a bone-shaking ride.

Driving along Middenheap Mile (so called because the town dump had existed there since the seventeenth century), Clayton alternately steered and chafed his gloved hands together. Another deficiency of the truck exhibited itself in the heater department. But was it worth the effort to fix something that was needed only two or three months out of the year?

Heading out of town, tire chains rattling and crunching over the snowy gravel road, Clayton considered the problem of the excitable and lickerish Captain Jill. Although his concerns were many, his solutions were few. Eventually he gave up.

Middenheap Mile forked onto Holsapple Meadow Road. A ways down the latter, a sign appeared on the left, supported by two tall wooden poles above a driveway:

THE LITTLE MISTLETOE FARM OF BLACKWOOD BEACH, JEROTHMUL LITTLE, PROP.

Jerothmul was Gran'pa Little. Despite Gran'pa's demise, Clayton saw no reason to impose his own name on the sign. He was not the true proprietor, any more than Gran'pa had been.

That office belonged to Ethel.

Pulling into the plowed driveway, Clayton checked the picnic basket beside him, which Granny had prepared as usual. He hoped Ethel appreciated the fact that he trekked out here every day despite all his own problems. Perhaps he would get a civil response today.

Engine killed, Clayton climbed out, his size thirteen Timberland boots biting into the snow. He turned to enter the grove.

Clayton experienced another slippage of time. He was a child again, visiting the farm for the first time. It had been summer.

"Where's the mistletoe, Gran'pa?" he had asked. "I don't see anything but a bunch of oaks."

"Look closely, boy. Use your eyes."

Clayton had stared and stared, until at last he spotted the mistletoe. "It's woven all among the branches, Gran'pa. How come?"

Gran'pa Little had explained then that mistletoe was a parasitical plant, growing on many different kinds of trees, not able to take root on its own. Without pruning, it would eventually kill its host. As it was, the life processes of the mistletoe infected the host, causing bizarre growths—so many, in fact, that the branches of mistletoe-bearing trees came to be called "witches' brooms."

So, here was another essential paradox of Blackwood Beach: one of the town's prime exports was barely visible on its own, a mere straggler hiding among the commercially unimportant, but more impressive, oaks.

However, when he was just thirteen, young (but, at nearly six feet, not little) Clayton had not been particularly aware of paradoxes as such. He had simply been enthralled with the fact that his grandparents ran such an intriguing, Christmassy business.

"Gran'pa," Clayton had asked, "how did you ever decide to grow mistletoe, of all things?"

Gran'pa Little stopped to load and tamp a charred briar pipe before answering. "Did you ever hear of Druids, Clay?"

Clayton nodded.

"Well, we Littles trace our family tree back to Druidic times. Although we were never Druids ourselves, we were of their religion, serving as acolytes. In Germany, one branch of the family was called Klein. In pre-Christian France, we were Petite. In old England, Lytle. Apparently, part of our duties was attending to the sacred groves of oaks and mistletoe so important for Druidic ceremonies. Eventually, as our religion was superseded and replaced by Christianity, the keeping of the groves was transmuted into a strictly commercial enterprise. In a nutshell, that's how I inherited this business."

Clayton had studied his grandfather, standing there stalwart, with the summer sun burnishing his silver hair, and had been suddenly swept by a chilly awe and respect for their lineage.

Returning to the present with a start, Clayton realized the chill was real. It was not summer now, and the mistletoe was plainly visible, the oak's own leaves having dropped. Among the widely spaced trees, Clayton sought to gauge the progress of the crop. The berries seemed to be flourishing, promising a bountiful crop in the summer. (Paradox two: although a symbol of winter and Christmas, mistletoe was harvested in midsummer. Clayton had learned to accept such ironies with a shrug.)

After a walk of some minutes' duration, Clayton came at last to the largest oak in the grove. A massive, gnarly-rooted giant, it thrust its branches up toward the deep winter sky and rattled its few dead leaves as if in supplication for the sun's return.

Between two thick roots that formed a rough circle, at an angle of forty-five degrees, was set a door of planks bound with iron straps.

Clayton knocked politely on the door and called, "Ethelred, sir. It's me, Clayton."

After an interval, a rude grumbling came from behind the door, which swung reluctantly open, revealing Ethel, standing on a flight of steps leading down below the tree.

Naked save for immense quantities of hair that hung down to his feet, Ethelred the Druid was a spindle-shanked, wizened being even smaller than Granny Little. His mad eyes and pointy nose were the salient features of an otherwise hirsute face.

"Oh, it's you, is it?" said Ethel, squinting belligerently at Clayton. "What do you want now? Can't a fellow even read his runes in peace, without these constant interruptions?"

Clayton stooped from his height to politely regard the mannikin on his own level. "Sorry, sir. I meant to show up earlier. But there was some trouble back at the house. I've just brought your food for another day."

"Here, give me that then, and begone." Ethel seized the basket by the handles. "Unless you've brought those magazines I asked for."

Damn, thought Clayton. He had forgotten again. The Druid was essential to the success of the farm, and was worth the cosseting he demanded.

"Sorry, Ethelred. I haven't had a chance. Next time, for sure. *Penthouse, Playboy, Gallery*—and what else?"

Ethel shook his head ruefully, as if nothing human could amaze him. "Can't you remember anything? A volume of stories by that fellow named Duke or Knave or Queen or whatever, stories to chill the blood. Just the reading for a cold winter's night. And don't forget again, Mister High-Pockets. Such neglect makes me mad! In fact, I don't know why I stay with your family. All these generations since the Romans drove us out of Gaul. Why, if it weren't for my grove—" Clucking his tongue, Ethel left the implications of his remarks unvoiced. He turned his back abruptly on Clayton, slammed his door, and then could be heard retreating to his burrow.

Straightening his spine with a groan, Clayton turned to go. He heard the door open again behind him, and immediately felt the not negligible impact of an empty picnic basket striking his back.

Clayton wondered if there weren't easier ways to earn a living.

***

The next few weeks were among the most tiring, irritating, exasperating, and downright crazy Clayton had ever experienced.

First, there were the continuing depradations of Captain Jill, now transformed from the Hellcat of the East Coast to the Subterranean Scourge of Blackwood Beach.

The tunnels she inhabited—and which she had apparently learned to navigate in the dark with the utmost ease—penetrated everywhere in the town. Captain Jill made a point of spreading her attentions far and wide along their length and breadth.

One of the first things she did—as Clayton learned later, while enjoying a beer at Emmett's Roadhouse—was to plunder Rackstraw's Market, laying in a hoard of food, which of course her reanimated body now required. Whiskey she had aplenty, Clayton knew.

Next, she began snatching bodies—the bodies of healthy young men, to be precise. She nabbed Piers Seuss at dusk one day, while he was digging for quahogs with a bullrake by the mouth of one of the tunnels. His wife, Andy, was furious, and uttered various futile curses upon his chagrined return. Other men and boys soon met with similar fates, some willingly, others with the same distaste Clayton had exhibited. At swordpoint, however, distaste becomes eagerness. And of course, there was Captain Jill's power of benumbing coldness to contend with, too.

The singing was another sore point. People were losing sleep all over town. Captain Jill's voice, oiled by liquor, was apparently inexhaustible. And her choice of songs was highly objectionable, consisting of gory ballads and bawdy ditties. Mothers began sending their children to bed with earmuffs on.

Bad as these town-wide mutual sufferings were, Clayton found a personal burden more irksome. It was Granny's invisible knitting.

Clayton had now been living in Blackwood Beach for over a month. During the first week of his transplanted existence, Granny had mimed knitting only once or twice, for short periods, and Clayton had been able to live with it. But ever since the day Captain Jill had appeared, the phantom knitting had been a nerve-wracking constant in his life.

Granny persisted at it day and night, wordlessly moving her clumsy fingers in the old familiar patterns. Clayton found that when he was in the same room with her—which was often—he could not take his eyes off her, captivated by the senseless motions as a rabbit is hypnotized by a snake. (Desperate to end it, he even tried leaving yarn and needles around in conspicuous places, hoping Granny would pick them up and resume normal knitting. But she never took the bait.) After a while, Clayton felt his mind disappearing into the same elderly abyss Granny seemed to inhabit, for he swore—no, it couldn't be.

Was there something invisibly accumulating in Granny's lap, depressing her gingham dress into a valley across her thin legs?

Added to the disturbing actions of Captain Jill and Granny was the disgruntlement of Ethel. The Druid, whom Clayton had to deal with daily, was growing more and more crotchety. Even the girlie magazines had produced no more than a temporary respite from his caustic comments and surly behavior. (Clayton had learned to sidestep the picnic basket after developing a permanent bruise in the middle of his back.) Somehow, the Druid hung constantly at the back of his mind, as if there were a tenuous connection between the problem he represented and the dilemma of Captain Jill.

Finally, something Captain Jill did persuaded Clayton that he had to act to stop her. No one else seemed to be taking the initiative, and he couldn't stand by and see Jill's foolish bravado place the whole town in jeopardy.

Captain Jill had begun to make moves toward her revenge on the puissant Welcome Goodnight. Somehow, she must have gotten into his dark, high house one night. The town awoke to their raging battle. Colored lightning split the blackness, arcing from Goodnight's house and falling to scorch the town. Cries and bellows shook the winter air, balls of sulfurous gas rolled through the streets, and all of the town's cats lost their tails. People cowered beneath their beds. The earth shook like a carpet the gods had decided to beat. A rain of golf balls—Titleists—fell and bounced down the hilly streets, as if Mr. Moose had finally decided to kill Captain Kangaroo.

Then, as suddenly as it had begun, the battle stopped. All night, though, people huddled in their houses, waiting for it to resume.

In the morning, the sleepless Clayton was sure Captain Jill had overstepped herself and gone to her long-delayed final rest. Hoping to learn more about the outcome of the battle, he went to Emmett's Roadhouse for breakfast.

Walking through town, Clayton marveled at the patches of melted snow where Goodnight's bolts had landed, churning the frozen earth as if it were chocolate pudding. The tails of cats lay here and there like the popular car-antenna squirrel-tails of Gran'pa Jerothmul's youth. A smell of sulfur still hung in the frigid air. One house—he wasn't sure whose—had burned to the ground, the volunteer firemen apparently having been too scared to come out and fight the fire.

Inside Emmett's Roadhouse—with its wooden booths and long counter bearing pie cases, ketchup bottles, and sugar shakers—Clayton found a goodly number of Blackwooders gathered. Most of the town's inhabitants were not much given to the drinking of alcohol, and especially not this early. But today was different. The whole town had narrowly escaped destruction. Everyone knew that if Goodnight had so wished, he could have leveled the village. So Barry Emmett had opened the bar, and many men and women sat clutching drinks and muttering, their ham and eggs growing cold.

Clayton sat down with Ed Stout, the friendly if unsmiling handyman, and his perpetually silent son, Jack, who had never in his life uttered a sound, even when the doctor first slapped him.

The elder Stout nodded and said, "Clay. Have a beer."

Not averse to the suggestion, Clayton ordered a 'Gansett. When it came, he sipped thoughtfully, and then asked, "What should we do about Goodnight?"

Stout looked long and level at Clayton before replying. "Leave him be. That's what best. He don't need our help none. After last night, either him or that ornery bitch is done for. Maybe both."

Jack inclined his head sagaciously in agreement, making Clayton feel as if he had witnessed Buddha blessing a petitioner. (What went on in that guy's mind? Clayton wondered. Silence was so suggestive.)

As Clayton raised his beer mug to his lips, he heard the door open behind him. He turned—

—and spit out his beer.

The cadaverous form of Welcome Goodnight filled the doorframe. His normally impeccable, if fusty, black suit hung in sword-slashed tatters on his rachitic frame. From behind his eye patch came an even more malevolent glittering than usual. His lined face wore a look of somber defeat.

Silence filled the restaurant like clammy Jell-O as Goodnight strode to the bar, behind which bearded Barry Emmett cringed.

"My brand," croaked Goodnight.

Although the wizard seldom deigned to drink with the hoi polloi, a bottle of his private label—Old Newt—was always kept ready for just such rare occasions as this.

The neck of the bottle clattering against the shot glass, Emmett poured with shaky hands.

Goodnight grabbed the glass and hoisted it to his dry, withered lips—

From beneath the roadhouse came a hearty female laugh, followed by the first verses of "Do You Believe in Magic?" by the Lovin' Spoonful.

Goodnight roared and hurled his glass at the wall. The spilled liquor sizzled when it hit the wood. Raising his arms, Goodnight began to gesture.

"Down!" someone shouted.

The patrons hurled themselves to the floor and covered their heads. An immense explosion rocked the building.

Clayton was among the first to recover his senses. He stood up shakily and looked around.

The warlock had vanished. Where he had stood was a ragged hole. Peering within, Clayton saw a corresponding gaping mouth in the floor of the cellar. And in that hole, he caught the fleeting sight of a head full of red curls disappearing down the tunnels revealed by the blast.

Apparently, Jill was immune to Goodnight's awesome powers, having absorbed three centuries' worth of the sorcerer's own mana like a storage battery, via the blue gas.

Someone had joined Clayton. Looking up, he saw Pug Lasswell, the town's entire police force.

"Pug," said Clayton, "you've got to stop this woman, before she gets us all killed. Get down there and arrest her for unprovoked assault and disturbing the peace."

Lasswell's sleepy features registered a slight uneasiness, which, for him, passed for the emotions a man about to be hanged might feel. He removed his badge from his shirt and pinned it on Clayton.

"I used to get paid every other Tuesday," said Lasswell. "Next check'll have your name on it."

By the following morning, Clayton had decided what needed to be done. And he knew that only he could carry out the plan. Although he had finally convinced Lasswell to take his badge back, the policeman had made it plain he was going to do nothing to apprehend Captain Jill. So Clayton had spent a second night with little sleep, speculating over various possible ways to trap the captain. At last, one barely feasible solution occured to him. And, as his subconscious had been trying to tell him, it involved the family Druid.

In his antiquated truck, Clayton drove the familiar road to the farm, so drowsy he was barely able to keep his eyes open. There, he met Ethel at his root-framed door. The grumpy Druid looked in vain for a picnic basket, then opened his mouth to complain.

Clayton cut him off, incapable of any niceties today. "Listen, Ethel—how would you like to come home with me for the day? Just a friendly visit."

Ethel was dumbstruck. He resumed his surliness with an effort. "Do you have any of those special magazines at your house?"

"Yes."

"Ones I haven't seen?"

Clayton was growing impatient. "Yes, yes. All brand-new girls. Now, are you coming or not?"

After a few seconds, trying to maintain his normal curtness, Ethel said, "I suppose the grove could survive a few hours without me."

In the truck, Ethel exuded a not unpleasant odor of loam and acorns. He stared with wonder at the passing scenery.

Back at the house, Ethel consumed two apple pies, a steak, three baked potatoes, a quart of ice cream, and a quart of Colt 45, in that order. Then he fell asleep on the couch next to Granny, who was busily knitting nothing into nothing. Clayton used the quiet interval to catch a few winks himself.

At around 6 P.M., Clayton heard the opening strains of a song from the sub-basement. Arming himself with a flashlight and a can of Mace, he descended to the tunnels.

He found Captain Jill atop the nearly empty crate of bootlegged whiskey, already well on the road to inebriation.

She spied him and raised her bottle in salute. "It never fails. In the end, anyone who has tasted my love returns. It was why my crew was so loyal. Ye've doubtless heard the phrase 'iron fist in a velvet glove.' Well, I ruled with velvet, too, a velvet—"

"Stop right there!" Clayton said quickly. "I don't want to hear such talk. I've come to ask you to cease and desist this juvenile hell-raising of yours and come to your senses. Despite all the damage you've caused, no one's actually been hurt yet, and Blackwood Beach will gladly accept you as a citizen, if you would only surface and behave civilly."

Captain Jill did not deign to answer, save by depositing a loathsome wad of chewing tobacco on the floor at Clayton's feet.

Disgusted, Clayton returned upstairs to unleash his secret weapon.

He roused Ethel from his stuporous sleep on the couch. The Druid stumbled sleepily under Clayton's direction to the basement trapdoor.

"Ethelred," Clayton urged, "there's a woman down there who's making an extreme nuisance of herself. Please go subdue her with your Druidical arts."

Ethel woozily descended the ladder.

Clayton waited for the fireworks.

Minutes passed.

A sudden torrent of whoops and laughter issued from the tunnel. There were cries and shouts and various banging noises, hoots and hollers and gasps. Clayton waited patiently for Ethel to emerge, dragging the subdued Captain Jill by the hair.

Several hours later, Ethel alone surfaced. All his hair stood on end, causing him to resemble a human porcupine, and what little skin was visible appeared suffused with healthily renewed circulation.

Smiling broadly, Ethel said, "I take back every bad word I ever said about you as an employer, Mr. Little. You're a saint to treat an old fellow to such a night."

* * *

If I don't get at least one good night's sleep, Clayton thought, and if I have to watch even one more invisible purl stitch, I'm going to crack up.

Sitting at the breakfast table, red-eyed and itchy-faced with three days' stubble, Clayton held his head in his hands. Across the way, he knew, Granny was patiently knitting, a look of blissful happiness and concentration on her seamed face.

Could he go home to Asheville? No. Who would manage the farm and the household while he beat such an ignominious retreat? What would he tell his parents? "A female pirate and Granny's eccentricities were driving me out of my mind, so I ran." That would hardly do. But what good would he be around the place if he lost his mind? A dilemma indeed.

Sensing somehow that Granny had amazingly ceased her knitting, Clayton looked up.

Granny was smiling happily. "Do you remember, Clay, that first day of our troubles, when I said we'd have to do something about it?"

"Yes, Granny," Clay replied politely. "I do."

"I know you've been thinking I had gone around the bend, Clay. No, don't try to deny it. Seeing me sitting day after day, knitting in this newfangled way of mine, which I learned not long ago—why, anyone would suspect I had a few bats in the old belfry. But I had to keep it secret, Clay, for I didn't want our girl down below to learn of it. But I'm done now with my knitting, and our troubles are at an end. Come around to me here."

Wearily, Clayton complied.

"Take this," Granny said, scooping an invisible mass out of her lap. "My goodness, you don't know how hot and weighty this thing is while you're working on it."

Expecting nothing, thinking only to humor his grandmother, Clayton held out his hands. Into it, Granny dropped—

—a soft, warm garment!

Clayton almost dumped it on the floor. "What—what is it?" he asked finally.

"It's a protective union suit that will cover you from neck to wrists to ankles. I would have been done sooner, but you're a darned tall drink of water, Clay! When you wear it, that Jill minx won't be able to paralyze you. You'll be able to handle her then."

Clayton regarded the nothing he held. "What's it made of?"

Granny shrugged. "Oh, the usual materials in a case like this. Moonbeams, dream threads, sea spume, bleached milkweed fluff."

Clayton considered his choices. Either he had already gone mad—in which case it made no difference if he went along with a charade—or he was still sane—in which case, maybe Granny's suit would work.

"I'm going upstairs to change," he said.

Granny nodded her approval.

* * *

All he had to do was follow the snores.

He came upon Captain Jill stretched out on a plundered mattress. Stopping a few feet away, he studied her in the flashlight's beam. She was indisputably beautiful, he had to grant. And he supposed her lack of morals was attributable to the era and circumstances of her upbringing. Were she not so vile, one could almost imagine enjoying her company on a daily basis—

The light on her face awoke the pirate queen, and she sat up, sleepily rubbing her eyes. When she recognized Clayton, she said, "Zounds and Snails, you lubberly lout, what the hell do you mean by disturbing my sleep like this?"

Clayton's soft-heartedness evaporated instantly, as Captain Jill's rude manner reminded him of all the grief she had caused him and the rest of the town.

"Get up," he said. "You're coming with me."

Captain Jill shot instantly to her feet, drawing her sword. "No one orders Jill Innerarity about like that!"

Moving quickly, with his long reach, Clayton plucked her sword from her hand.

Captain Jill smiled ferally. "Been eating your oats, I wot. Well, I admire spunk—to a point. But this will cost you dearly, my lad."

Advancing sinuously, Captain Jill grabbed Clayton's biceps. A long moment passed. Clayton stood there grinning. Captain Jill squeezed harder, to no effect. She stepped back in awe, her jaw dropping.

Clayton moved to grab her.

Jill launched a booted kick that landed on Clayton's stomach and blasted the air out of his lungs. He dropped his flashlight and doubled over.

When he recovered, Jill was not to be seen, but the sound of her running feet echoed down the tunnel.

Picking up his light, Clayton jogged off after her.

Several hundred yards down the dank passage, Clayton came to a branching. He stopped to ponder. Silence filled his ears like cotton. Cautiously he peered down one alley, shining his torch.

Out of the other branch resounded a piercing battle cry: "Yaaaah!"

Captain Jill landed like a hod of bricks on Clayton's back, wrapping her legs around his waist and her hands around his unprotected neck.

The choking was bad enough, for Jill was frightfully strong. Worse was the cold. Clayton's invisible suit stopped just above his collarbones. Jill's enervating chill was seeping in, numbing his muscles and brain.

Left with no alternatives, Clayton threw his whole weight backward, landing atop Jill. He heard her head smack the hard floor of the passage.

Her grip relaxed, and Clayton got to his feet.

Jill's eyes were still open, although she gasped for breath, evidently fighting unconsciousness. She seemed to be making an effort to get up and fight some more.

So Clayton slugged her on the jaw.

He felt just like Bogie.

Clayton picked up her unconscious form. He retraced his steps to the ladder to his cellar. There, he slung Jill over one shoulder and climbed up easily.

In the living room, he stretched her out on the couch. When the passing minutes drew a beam of moving sunlight across her face—where a bruise was appearing on her jaw—a transformation seemed to occur, an ineffable softening of her marble flesh. On a hunch, Clayton tentatively raised her limp hand to graze his unprotected face. There was no accompanying blast of chill.

Granny shuffled in as Jill began to stir. "I've fixed up a spare bedroom," she said, "if you want to carry her up."

Clayton nodded, entranced by the sparkle of the light in Jill's green eyes.

"I can unravel that suit now, I suppose," said Granny, "for my next project."

Back when I wrote this story, I was on a Herman Melville kick. I mentioned in my 2005 collection, The Emperor of Gondwanaland, *how one of my earliest sales was made by taking the template of Melville's "Benito Cereno" and using it to produce an SF adventure. It amused me afterward to co-opt one of Melville's titles for a story that bore no thematic or conceptual links to his masterpiece. I'm not sure now if such a joke isn't ultimately confusing and off-putting, but I'll let it stand.*

Twenty years ago, Hollywood had barely begun to scratch the surface of computer-generated imagery. Nor had the reign of the megafilm been fully inaugurated. But I could already see that both trends would come to dominate the film industry and offer ripe material for satire. Hence Billy's tangle with the composite Luke Landisberg.

I thought that my "spring" story, completing the seasonal cycle in Blackwood Beach, should, naturally, focus on growing things. Thompson and Morgan is a real seed company, but I've yet to find them offering such extraordinary seeds as they do here.

Billy Budd

Billy Budd didn't find it hard being green.

Despite what that stupid cloth frog always sang.

How distressed Billy had been when that song had infiltrated the airwaves. How grateful he had been when it had vanished. Although the citizens of Blackwood Beach were, of necessity and habit, quite understanding of each other's quirks, foibles, and unavoidable eccentricities, Billy had not enjoyed having his particular uniqueness the constant focus of everyone's attention. During this period, while walking the twisty streets of his queer New England hometown, Billy felt that everyone's eyes were upon him. The story of his strange birth, he imagined, had been resurrected among the townspeople, just when he had hoped it was forgotten. But after a time, other, more demanding events came to displace Billy's temporary notoriety, and in the end he claimed no more attention in town than anyone else.

Perhaps the reason Billy was usually so comfortable with the shade of his skin was that it was such a lovely, subtle hue.

Picture the earliest spring leaf buds of a lilac, or the tender innermost layers of an artichoke. Lighter than a blade of blanched grass found beneath a mass of wet leaves in April, Billy's skin was perhaps the lightest color that could still be called green. It was as if Billy's veins ran not with blood colored by hemoglobin but with sap tinged by some exotic chlorophyllous substance, suffusing his skin from crown to feet.

Which was, in fact, the case.

Because Billy's hair was a thick, unruly thatch of bright yellow, some said he looked, on the whole, rather like a dandelion. It was rumored that there was even a family connection between Billy and the dandelions, and one mentioned *Taraxacum officinale* in Billy's presence only gingerly.

This bright May morning, however, as Billy took his regular walk from Eva's Boarding House to his business, he felt charitable even toward the dandelions that dotted the untidy front lawns of the houses in Blackwood Beach. The source of his good-natured happiness was a certain special plant growing in a secluded and laboriously chosen spot on the outskirts of town. This plant, sown from seed just a month ago, was already half as tall as Billy. In another eight weeks or so, it would reach its mature height and full growth, and Billy would gently harvest it, achieving a dream that had recently come to dominate his thoughts.

But for now, all he could do was tend the plant lovingly. Fertilize its roots with 5-10-5, keep it free of mites and fungus, fence it diligently from gnawing rabbits and rodents, water it thoroughly but not over much—and read aloud to it from as wide an assortment of books as he could find.

Billy, thinking warmly of his pet project, wished he could visit it this morning. But his greenhouse—Budd's Plant Emporium—had to be opened and his more conventional stock there seen to. He would have to content himself with visiting at noon, and again after closing time. Those two trips should be enough attention at this stage, although as growth progressed, he might have to fit in a third each day.

Walking beneath the greening trees that overhung the streets of the village, Billy, his thoughts running in such channels, soon came to Budd's Plant Emporium.

The greenhouse—the only one in Blackwood Beach—dated from the 1920s. It had not been run by the Budds all that time; Billy had only recently bought the business from its ancient proprietor and founder, who wished to retire. It had been quite a run-down structure then. After Billy's restoration, it looked as it must have looked when new. White stucco walls supported a roof of Spanish tiles, forming the retail and office portion of the building. Attached to this was a long, one-story shed, whose few courses of brick upheld the framework of painted metal and sparkling glass beneath which thrived Billy's stock.

Pushing open the unlocked door, Billy went in. He flipped the CLOSED sign to OPEN and turned on the lights.

The front of the store exhibited a counter, a cash register, a roll of wrapping paper on its upright cutter-spindle, a wrought iron table holding various cards that customers could inscribe, and numerous plants on display. What it lacked was refrigeration units. These Billy had torn out, for he refused to sell cut flowers of any type.

It was just too much like a surgeon setting up a shop to sell bloody organs he had removed from helpless patients.

Only live plants left Billy's store, and he had to be convinced that their new owners would treat them right before he let them go.

Business wasn't great, but he somehow eked out a living. And nothing pleased him more than matching up a happy plant with an appreciative human.

Going to a glass-paned wooden door leading to the actual greenhouse,

Billy could feel the emanations of the various plants within. Cyclamens and clivias, azaleas and hyacinths, orchids and violets, all radiated their individual personalities, welcoming Billy back for another day.

Throwing open the door, Billy stepped into the warm, moist, richly scented embrace of his growing charges. Time for another day of work.

But what a pleasure it was!

The morning passed in a busy flurry of repotting, watering, mulching, clipping, dividing, misting, and sowing. A few customers came in and had their needs met, but generally Billy was alone with his eager green friends.

Around noon—Billy could tell the time to within a few minutes by the position of the sun—a commotion sounded out on the street. Laying down his trowel and wiping his hands on the apron he wore, Billy headed out to see what could be happening.

Out on the sidewalk, he looked down the elm-bordered street toward the noise.

A garish madman was leading a parade.

This was Billy's first thought, while the crowd was still at a distance. As they approached, he saw no reason to modify it.

The stranger at the head of the procession was dressed like no native. He had on a multicolored Hawaiian shirt that stretched across his big stomach like a jungle scene distorted by non-Euclidian geometries. He wore pale orange pants equally tight and thick-soled shoes obviously intended to compensate for his shortness. His bald pate was trying to hide beneath a few reluctant strands of hair. A great deal of gold jewelry festooned his neck and fingers. He chewed aggressively on an unlit cigar, around which he occasionaly uttered a heartfelt exclamation as some new sight caught his roving eye.

"Wunnerful!"

"Jesus, whoda thought it—"

"What a find!"

"Lookit that old house, fer Chrissakes!"

"Where the hell've they been hiding this town? It's just perfect!"

The fat stranger waddled past Billy where he stood at the entrance to his store. When his glance alighted on Billy, it rapidly bounced off, perhaps refusing to acknowledge that he had actually seen the light-green man.

Following some distance behind the man were scores of citizens of Blackwood Beach. They shared a look of immense curiosity and puzzlement, apparently finding this intruder as much of an improbable spectacle as he found their town.

Billy hailed the man nearest him, who happened to be Tom Noonan, owner, publisher, editor, reporter, and typesetter for the town's newspaper, the *Blackwood Beach Intelligencer.*

"Hey, Tom. Who's this character?"

The burly Noonan stopped beside Billy. As he frequently did when nervous, he unconsciously stroked the three stubby fingers on his left hand, whose upper joints he had lost when first learning to operate his cantankerous, antediluvian printing press.

"Can't rightly say, Billy. He pulled up in a fancy foreign car half an hour ago, and he's been wandering through town ever since, gaping like a mooncalf. When the kids got out of school for lunch they started following him. Then the adults joined in. Pretty soon, I reckon, he'll have the whole town trailing along."

Billy was about to ask why no one had stopped the stranger and inquired his business when Noonan said, "Can't stand and talk, Billy, he's getting away."

Noonan rejoined the parade. Billy stood still a moment, then did the same.

The horde of Blackwooders continued to follow the meandering stranger. Each house he passed seemed to add its trickle of inhabitants to the flow, until Noonan's prediction was almost fulfilled, and hundreds of citizens obligingly trailed the loudly marveling and still-oblivious man.

Gradually working their way up the slope of the natural amphitheater in which the town lay, the procession wended its way toward the western outskirts. As Billy noticed where they were heading, he began to grow nervous. They were approaching the very spot where his most important plant grew. It was generally known to the natives that Billy had something going up near the old Mowbray house, but they were too respectful to intrude verbally or physically on his project. Certainly this stranger couldn't know about it also? No, it had to be coincidence—

At last, houses growing sparser around them, they reached the Mowbray manse.

Andrew Mowbray was a sorcerer who had lived during the early 1700s. Unfortunately, he hadn't been a very good one. When it came time for an inevitable showdown between him and Welcome Goodnight, the other resident mage, Mowbray lost. The climactic battle—during which the figures of the two men could be witnessed one night as gigantic white shadows against a cloudy sky—had been the last time anyone had ever seen Mowbray.

After his disappearance, his house had stood vacant for many years. Eventually, new inhabitants dared to move into the desirable property. They didn't stay long, however; nor did any others who tried over the next two hundred years. Finally no one could be found who would dare dwell in the house. It had been vacant for fifty years.

Now the many-gabled house stood in the center of its weedy lot, surrounded by a picket fence from which the paint had all weathered off and most of the pickets had fallen. Thick woods began at the rear of the property, and it was not far within those trees that Billy had his little plot of special land.

The stranger came to a halt before the shuttered, decaying house. With his back to his neglected audience, he placed his hands on his wide hips and stared for several minutes at the stark building. The crowd waited with its breath held for the next startling actions of this anomalous figure.

He didn't disappoint them. Throwing up his pudgy hands he shouted, "This is it!"

The crowd jumped as one.

The fat man whirled around and, for the first time, directly addressed the expectant Blackwooders.

"Freddie Cordovan," he said, pulling a wallet from his rear pants pocket and flashing an official-looking gold badge. "State Film Bureau. Friends, you are in luck.

"We're gonna make a movie here!"

* * *

Florence Budd was an old maid. An old old maid. She lived alone in a small, one-room house on Nightshade Lane, far from the physical and social center of Blackwood Beach. Her house resembled a pack animal that had been overburdened for too many years: a prospector's donkey that had ascended the Grand Canyon one time too many; a nomad's camel that had been mercilessly driven back and forth across the Sahara; a peasant's water buffalo bent from years beneath the yoke. Her little cottage had slanted walls that were threatening to pop out of their window frames like seeds squeezed from a grape. Her roof of wooden slates, where soil had lodged over the years, was full of weeds and wildflowers. The ivy climbing over the exterior of the shack seemed to be the only thing holding the building together.

Florence had no running water or electricity. Having been born about 1870 (she wasn't quite sure of her birth date), she considered such things modern affectations. Oil lamps and a well supplied her basic needs. As for luxuries—she had her books.

Besides a bed and a cupboard and a chair, Florence's house held little except books. Piled high from floor to ceiling, they were the musty ramparts that shielded her from the outside world, which she had never been too fond of anyway. Every day, in the flickering light of her lamps (the books blocked whatever sunlight might have crept in through the dirty windows), Florence read her favorite volumes over and over, finding new pleasures in their familiar faces and voices.

The books Florence read were those of the American authors who had been popular during her youth. She had seldom cracked the spine of a twentieth-century novel. There was enough earlier genius to occupy her for more than a lifetime. Just to recite the names was to tell all: Hawthorne, Howells, Thoreau, Emerson, Alcott, Cooper, Twain, James, Melville, Longfellow . . . . The list went on and on.

Florence's favorite author was Melville. Although she greatly admired his writing, her partiality toward him stemmed from personal, rather than critical, reasons.

Melville was the only author she had ever met.

When she was twenty, her father had taken her to New York on business. It was the one and only time she ever left Blackwood Beach. She didn't care for the city at all. In fact, the noise and stink and filth of New York City just prior to the advent of the twentieth century was probably what fully soured Florence's already fussy attitude toward life. But one thing she did enjoy was meeting an author. True, the bearded Melville was somewhat crabby and remorseful, due to his lack of criticial and financial success, and didn't pay much attention to his young female visitor (except to comment that she had "an interesting name"). But still, he was a real author, one of those glorious figures who produced the books that Florence even then relished more than life.

Florence's father lost all his money soon afterward, in the Great Cathay Bubble of 1901 (which involved investors trying to convince the Chinese population to adopt johnnycakes as their dietary mainstay rather than rice). When his creditors came to attach his house, he thwarted them by setting fire to it and perishing in the flames. Florence barely escaped. After that, she took up residence in the shack on Nightshade Lane, the only property left to her by the creditors.

For forty-five years, Florence lived her bookish, solitary existence without any compunctions. She supported herself by selling herbs and simples to the population of Blackwood Beach. There was much call for such things, and Florence made enough to supply her spartan needs.

In her seventies, Florence suddenly and inexplicably became lonely.

She felt it would be rather nice to have someone to talk to every day, someone to draw the water when her joints were acting up. But who would ever consent to share her eccentric life?

One day, Florence was studying a plant catalogue. This particular catalogue came from England, and was called the Thompson and Morgan Seed Catalogue. It was a compendium of the strangest plants she had ever seen. From it, Florence had gotten many of her best-selling seeds, which she grew in a small plot behind her shack. She thought she knew the contents of the catalogue from cover to cover. This day, though, her eyes fell on an entry—without an accompanying picture—that she had never noticed before:

> *Homo sapiens mandragora:* This rare cultivar, commonly called a mandrake, is offered exclusively by Thompson and Morgan to those discerning customers whose orders over the years have shown their interest in the unusual. PLEASE DO NOT SHOW YOUR COPY OF THIS CATALOGUE TO ANYONE ELSE.
>
> The mandrake is a vegetal cousin of humanity, of a commensurate size and intelligence. It should be sown in early April, in slightly alkaline soil. After three months, it may be harvested at that stage of development resembling a human five-year-old. (Certain of our correspondents report achieving an accelerated development by various methods. However, we cannot recommend such forcing.) Upbringing after harvest is the responsibility of the individual.
>
> Germination rate: 100 percent. Price: £1 the packet. (Please specify sex.)

Florence filled out her order at once, and walked out to the Blackwood Beach post office.

The package arrived on the last day of March.

Florence sowed the single big seed with trembling hands, and then settled in for the three months of waiting.

The plant shot up with remarkable speed. It resembled a huge cabbage, taller than it was wide, with many dark green leaves wrapped around a hidden core. By May, it was as high as Florence's knees. That was when a thought occured to her.

If from the mature plant emerged a five-year-old, would its mental development parallel its physical? How would the poor thing, even granting certain inborn knowledge, be the equal of its human peers, who had interacted with the world on a daily basis? Was there some way, Florence wondered, that she could help her son (for so she already thought of the mandrake) catch up to its peers?

Why not, Florence thought, try reading aloud to it?

And so began a most unusual course of prenatal care. Each day, Florence would sit beside the plant and read her favorite books to it. At first, it seemed to exhibit no response to the tutelage. But in June, when the plant was three feet tall, it began to sway gently whenever the climax of a story was reached. Florence was sure her reading was having some good effect.

And on that long-awaited day when Florence awoke to find the outer leaves of the plant fallen away and her naked son standing with closed eyes, still attached by his soles to his stalk, she received confirmation that her efforts had not been misdirected.

As Florence crouched near her son, his eyes opened and he said, "Call me Billy Budd."

So she did.

* * *

The knife pierced the table just inches from Billy's hand—which had been reaching for a dish of scrambled eggs—and vibrated in place like a tuning fork. Billy hastily withdrew his offending member and mumbled his apologies. What had he been thinking of, trying to serve himself before the Skandik twins? This unsettling affair of the stranger, with his talk of movies, combined with Billy's normal anxiousness about his special project, must be disordering his thoughts more than he realized.

It was the morning after the day the stranger—Freddie Cordovan, was it?—had made his apparently aimless peregrinations through the town. Billy sat at the communal breakfast table in Eva's Boarding House. He had called this generally amiable residence home ever since his mother had died and he had sold her property so as to raise the money to go into the nursery business. The ancestral homestead had meant little to Billy, since he really preferred the open air to any dwelling, and in any case the ramshackle shack was on the point of almost total collapse.

Eva's Boarding House was a large Victorian structure not far from the seaside. Its interior was as immaculate as its exterior was weather-beaten and flaking. The individual rooms Eva Breakstone let out to her tenants (whom she tended to regard as irresponsible children, no matter how old) were high-ceilinged repositories of massive pieces of old furniture bearing bric-a-brac as a whale hosts barnacles.

The sunny dining room, with its lace curtains, sideboards, and long oak table, was the center of the house. Here the inhabitants met for two meals a day, over which Eva presided like the matriarch of an exceedingly heterogeneous family.

Thin as a spar, blue-eyed and gray-haired, her skin like leather—from years spent in Montana on a ranch—Eva sat at the head of the cloth-covered table. She had witnessed the assault on Billy and had been ready to step in to settle it. But as it played itself out without her intervention, she said nothing.

The twins Billy had inadvertently run afoul of were Gunnar and Gothard Skandik. They were identical trollish brothers with flaming red hair and beards. One day they had shown up in Blackwood Beach, rusty picks over their brawny shoulders, and demanded of the first passerby, "Where we dig?" They had been directed to the limestone quarry outside of town, where they had been employed ever since, having displaced two bulldozers and a steam shovel. Naturally, their work required that they stoke themselves like furnaces at breakfast, and woe betide those who dared serve themselves before the Skandik brothers took their share.

At the proper time, Billy filled his own plate with eggs, home fries, toast, and ham. (Billy had once tried living on a diet of sunlight and water. Although it was possible for him to subsist on such ethereal food, such a diet reduced his thoughts to an arboreal slowness, and he much preferred normal human fare.) He ate rather absentmindedly this morning, not paying much attention to the talk of his fellow diners. His mind was busy with his own problems.

Toward the end of the meal, as people were shuffling about before departing, a stray phrase seeped into Billy's awareness and made him take notice.

"—at the town meeting."

Billy looked up from his half-eaten food. The speaker was Max Myrtlewood, a tall fellow with a paunch that testified to the allure of Eva's cooking, who washed dishes at Emmett's Roadhouse.

Billy caught Myrtlewood's attention and asked, "What's this about a town meeting, Max?"

"Was in the paper this morning," said Myrtlewood. "Musselwhite's called one for noon today." Milo Musselwhite held the post of town coordinator for Blackwood Beach. "Topic's gonna be this movie business, and what's to be done about it. Hear that stranger's gonna give his side of the story, 'fore we vote on anything."

"Thanks," Billy said. "I'll be there."

Myrtlewood smiled somewhat suggestively. "Well, don't get so busy with your project up at Mowbray's that you forget."

Billy's tinted blood suffused his face, causing him to blush verdantly. Damn it, that was the trouble with living in such a small town. Everyone knew all your business. This was the first time anyone had mentioned it aloud to him, though, and he felt suddenly like a pervert of some sort, just for finally yielding to his natural urges.

The room had cleared before Billy could compose himself sufficiently to make a retort, and so he got to his feet with words bottled frustratingly up inside him and headed out.

The gibe had made Billy more concerned than ever about his prize plant. He realized that with all the excitement yesterday, he had made only one visit to it, in the evening. On the spur of the moment, he determined to delay opening his shop and visit the month-old growth first thing.

Out on the brick sidewalk, Billy sniffed the delightful spring air. May was such a lovely month! Billy's pulse quickened with the aura of vegetable entities resurging after the trauma of winter. He inhaled deeply, savoring the loamy green fragrance of the cool air.

Billy's sensitive nostrils detected a slight tinge of something rotten in the air. Irrationally, he attributed it at first to the presence of the Film Bureau man, until he remembered the whale. Looking in the direction of the hidden beach, Billy shook his head. Something was going to have to be done about that. Perhaps he would bring it up at the town meeting.

Setting out for the old Mowbray house, Billy tried to ignore the disturbing component of the gentle May breezes.

At the shabby fence surrounding the deserted manse, Billy paused. The forlorn old house looked different today, as if Freddie Cordovan's exclamation "This is it!" had somehow invested the mundane structure with new significance whose full extent was not yet apparent. What could have so excited Cordovan about this house? Billy wondered, gazing at the many-gabled roofline of the building. Something tugged at the back of his mind, but refused to fully present itself.

Giving up on the puzzle, Billy went through the sagging gate, across the weedy yard, and straight to a spot in the rear where the fence had completely fallen down. Here a path led away into the bordering woods. Moving down the faint trail, Billy recalled how he had first found this special site.

The whole thing had started when Billy decided he wanted a mate.

Billy had always known of his origin. His mother had been quite frank with him, and waking up sentient and attached to a root had been indisputable confirmation of her story. When Billy, in his maturity, some years after his mother had died at the fine age of 112, had felt certain natural stirrings, he had known just what catalogue to turn to, to purchase the seed that would eventually, he hoped, become his bride.

But there was one seemingly insurmountable problem. The mandrake subspecies had a certain development cycle that thwarted Billy's plans. Planted in early April, the mandrake (or should that be womandrake?) plant would grow until late June or early July, whereupon it would open and give forth a child. Billy didn't want a child; he wanted an equal. He didn't care to spend a dozen or so years raising someone who in the end he would probably come to regard more as a daughter than a bride.

Studying the catalogue description, he read the sentence about forcing, and grew hopeful that here was a solution. Writing to Thompson and Morgan, he begged them for information regarding the methods involved. He received this reply:

Dear Mr. Budd:

We are happy to hear from one of our products and learn that your life has been so successful. We regret the passing of your mother, who was an esteemed customer, but take comfort in the length of her life.

As for your question concerning the forcing of *mandragora,* we are unfortunately unable to aid you. The information we have on the process is so fragmentary and contradictory that we hesitate to impart it to you, lest we cause your mandrake to be born with a malformation of some sort. We are afraid that we must leave you to your own devices in this matter. Be sure to inform us of any successes so we may help others in your situation.

Sincerely,
Thompson and Morgan
Enc: one (1) seed packet

Billy's despair grew upon his receiving this reply. The fat mandrake seed sat unplanted on a shelf in the greenhouse, and Billy took to walking in the woods for long stretches, seeking consolation amid the wild growths. One day, he came upon a patch of ground, not far from the Mowbray house, which was covered in the wildest profusion of tangled greenery Billy had ever seen. So luxuriant was the mass of plants that Billy was moved to take a sample of soil from the plot. This he sent to the state university for testing. While he awaited the results, he enquired among the older citizens of Blackwood Beach to see if they had any information regarding the strange soil. After much futile questioning, he finally found out that the small plot had once held the cauldron wherein the wizard Mowbray had boiled his potions. The cauldron, like Mowbray, had been fatally cracked, invariably leaking its contents out, permeating the soil with an unpredictable mix of potions, apparently still active at this late date.

The results came back from the university soon after Billy learned this. They were simple and direct.

> Mr. Budd:
>
> The soil you sent us cannot exist. Please do not send us any more. We are still trying to find a cage big enough for the lab rat that accidentally ingested some.

Billy made up his mind then and there. When April came, he laboriously cleared the ground and planted his seed.

Now, walking down the path he had worn over that time, he fervently hoped that he had done the right thing.

The path debouched into a small clearing. At the center was Billy's pride and joy.

Surrounded by a shoulder-high gated fence of wood and chicken wire, the womandrake plant stretched as high as Billy's waist. It looked sleek and healthy, and Billy felt happy. Its dark outer leaves were wrapped protectively around its hidden core, at which Billy had not dared yet peek. (His own nurturing plant had taken three months to get this big.) That recent freak April snowstorm—called "poor man's fertilizer" by some—seemed to have agreed with the womandrake.

From the back pocket of his jeans, Billy took an ever-present paperback. Billy's taste in literature derived from his mother's prenatal tutoring. But whereas her favorite author had been Melville, Billy, as he matured, came to prefer Hawthorne. Currently, he was reading *The House of the Seven Gables* aloud to his charge, as he sought to educate her for the life she would face when she awoke.

Settling himself down on a stump that served conveniently as a chair, Billy began to read, picking up where he had left off the night before. The plant seemed to quiver noticeably as Billy spoke.

"Possessing very distinctive traits of their own, they nevertheless took the general characteristics of the little community in which they dwelt; a town noted for its frugal, discreet, well-ordered, and home-loving inhabitants, as well as for the somewhat confined scope of its sympathies; but in which, be it said, there are odder individuals, and, now and then, stranger occurrences, than one meets with almost anywhere else."

* * *

The town hall of Blackwood Beach was a Gothic structure of rough-cut stones, with a square tower at one corner that gave a splendid view of the Atlantic to the east. Town coordinator Musselwhite had his office on the top floor of the tower, where, so it was said, he spent a good portion of each day gazing with faint nostalgia at the ever-changing sea.

Now, however, Musselwhite sat at a table on a dais, at the front of a big room filled with wooden folding chairs. The chairs were occupied by a good portion of the population of the town, including Billy, who had shown up early and claimed a front-row seat. People stood at the back, in a whispering crowd, although there were a few seats still untaken. These empty chairs, however, formed a protective zone around the chilling figure of Welcome Goodnight, the town's capricious mage, who had surprised everyone by showing up.

Billy regarded the town coordinator. The man appeared nervous, swallowing raw smelts at intervals from the bowl beside him and occasionally twining his moist webbed fingers together. (The Musselwhite family had interbred at some distant time with the fish-god who dwelt beneath Big Egg, the lonely, sea-girded rock out in the bay.) The source of Musselwhite's nervousness sat beside him.

Freddie Cordovan wore a new outfit generically similar to yesterday's. His unlit cigar remained caught between the mangle of his teeth. He appeared confident, despite facing a strange and hostile audience.

At last Musselwhite seemed to realize that the entrance of anyone else was impossible, and that he had better call the meeting to order. Standing up, he banged his gavel and said, "This emergency meeting of the township of Blackwood Beach is hereby convened. Our only order of business today is the proposal put to us by Mr. Cordovan, of the State Film Bureau. I now turn over the floor to Mr. Cordovan, who will explain the exact nature of the proposal."

Musselwhite sat and Cordovan stood. The heavy-set outsider regarded the assembled Blackwooders like a confident lawyer about to deliver what he knew was a potent summation to a credulous jury.

"Friends," Cordovan said. "Your state government wants to help you."

A burst of derisive laughter filled the room. Unfazed, Cordovan continued.

"My agency has the job of scouting out possible locations for filming, and convincing studios to come to *our* state, rather than another. As you mighta guessed, your town has qualified as such a site. Now, the money these people inject into the economy is not to be believed! You people are going to be floating in dollars pretty soon."

"Who says we're going to let these Hollywood types in?" someone shouted.

Cordovan's good-natured mask slipped a trifle, and his voice grew sullen. "Listen, you people are a part of this state, and owe the government this favor."

"The state never does anything for us!" another heckler yelled.

Cordovan lifted up his meaty hands. "We can change that," he soothed. "Whadda ya need? Ya need some roads paved?"

People were silent, as they recalled the bone-jarring, rutted stretch of Middenheap Mile, and envisioned it macadam-smooth.

Cordovan saw that he had them leaning toward him. He played a trump card. "What about that whale that beached himself and died last week? You'd like him removed, wouldn't you? Well, we can get the Coast Guard in here tomorrow, and haul him away."

Billy, who hadn't been swayed by the promise of paved roads, found this offer as tantalizing as the rest of his fellows seemed to. Still, he felt put upon by this stranger. Why was he coming here and disrupting everything? And what connection did the Mowbray house have with all of this?

Without intending to, Billy got to his feet. All attention focused on him, and he felt his mouth grow dry.

"The state should be doing these things for us anyway," Billy managed to say. "Why do we have to let ourselves be taken over like this?"

Murmurs of agreement rose up, and Cordovan fixed a baleful look on Billy.

"Don't get riled, folks. You're not seeing it like it is. Maybe the state has slighted you some—but you've turned your backs on us, too. Now we need each other—just for a little while. It's inevitable, and temporary. So let's try to work out a mutually beneficial arrangement. Now you, son, seem to worry about being taken over. Suppose we appoint you as official liaison between the town and the film company? You'd be responsible for making sure that no one oversteps their proper place. Smooth everything out, like. All for a good salary. How's that sound?"

Billy was taken aback, and couldn't say anything. The crowd made grateful noises, as the burden of watching out for their interests seemed to be falling on someone else. Pretty soon, shouts of "Yeah, let Billy handle it!" filled the hall.

Cordovan smiled craftily, and Billy got mad. "Wait one darn minute," Billy shouted. "We haven't settled anything yet. We don't even know what this film's all about."

The room quieted, and Cordovan spoke.

"This is the best part, folks. I'm not bringing you a two-bit PBS special. No, we're talking the most famous director in the world, with a thirty-million-dollar extravaganza! We're talking Luke Landisberg, people! And how's this for stars?

"Ol' Patton himself, George C. Coates, as Judge Pyncheon."

Billy flinched at this revelation of one character's name. Could it possibly be true—?

"One of the prettiest babes in films, Natasha Kaprinski, as Phoebe Pyncheon. A real classy old gal, Dame Peggy Shabbycough, as Hepzibah Pyncheon. For comic relief, Murray Roydack, as Holgrave the daguerreotypist. And last but not least, Walter Matthew as Clifford Pyncheon.

"Yes, I can see by your faces that you recognize the tale, like the literate types you are. But you can't possibly envision the shoot-'em-up, special-effects, rollicking good-time version Landisberg has in mind. Folks, you've never known this *Hellhouse of Seven Gables* before! And you've got the perfect house for it—that old Mowbray place."

Billy almost fainted. Swarms of strangers clambering over the Mowbray grounds, trampling his plant, ending his hopes—

At that moment, silence descended like a pall. Welcome Goodnight had unfolded his cadaverous frame and risen to his feet. In his fusty archaic suit, his eye patch barely concealing the glinting object socketed beneath, he looked like some specter come to dissuade.

"We cannot endure publicity," Goodnight intoned. "I myself will not permit it. I know measures to ensure our privacy."

Those who knew Goodnight began to quake. Cordovan, armored in his ignorance, stood firm, however. Courageously, he responded.

"There won't be any publicity," he said. "Landisberg wants absolute secrecy on the set. He'll come and go and the outside world won't even know about it. No tourists, I promise. We won't even mention the name of your town in the credits."

Goodnight seemed unmollified, and was about to utter some further warning when Cordovan dared to interrupt.

"I didn't get to say that there's quite a few bit parts uncast. Also one crucial one. We need just the right guy to play the Pyncheons' arch-enemy, the wizard Maule. Now, I can't promise anything, but you look like just the man we need, Mr., Mr.—"

The sour old mage was utterly disarmed. The thought of appearing in a film seemed a stronger magic than any he could muster in defense. He weakly said his own name aloud, like one sorcerer surrendering his most prized possession to another.

"Goodnight. Welcome Goodnight."

Cordovan seemed to gloat. "Hey, Welcome, welcome aboard."

After such cavalier treatment of the town's most forbidding figure, the vote was a foregone conclusion.

* * *

Luke Landisberg had a big shock of aggressive black curls that foamed above his youthful unlined brow like a perpetually breaking wave. Aviator-style sunglasses hid his eyes, and a sparse beard less successfully concealed his face. He wore a denim shirt with pearly buttons, jeans, and sneakers. He dominated the organized confusion at the Mowbray house like some Toscanini demon conducting the Pandemonium Symphony Orchestra.

Billy watched Landisberg's crew scurry about the property, obeying the director's mysterious and sometimes contradictory orders. They reminded Billy of worker ants under the control of some domineering hive-mind. One by one, they were harmless. But together—

Who knew what they contemplated, or could do?

The town had been invaded shortly after the decisive vote had been cast. Cordovan had disappeared back to the state capital, and the citizens of Blackwood Beach, as if recovering from a spell, had begun to consider what they had done.

Billy, now official liaison, had been perhaps more concerned than anyone else. His duties remained nebulous, his worries many—chief among them what would happen to his future mate when the strangers arrived. Billy dreaded the questions and intrusions that would doubtless accompany the discovery of his secret.

This period of nervous anticipation was mercifully short. One day, without warning, the assault began.

Huge trucks rumbled in first, carrying all manner of lights, cameras, props, and outré devices. Following these were pickups pulling trailers that were to be the living quarters for those involved. (Billy had wondered where everyone would stay. He had visions of sharing his room at Eva's with a dozen assorted strangers.) Following the sleek silver trailers were several black stretch limos, behind whose smoked windows lurked the director and the stars.

Hearing the first trucks, the townspeople lined the streets, watching the parade as if it were an invasion of Martians. The vehicles passed through the center of the town and headed for the Mowbray place. The Blackwooders solemnly followed.

At the decrepit mansion, the vehicles formed a half-circle around the building like a wagon train under attack. The citizens hung back, cast in the role of reluctant Indians, and waited for someone to emerge.

A limo door swung open and Cordovan bellied out. Landisberg, instantly recognizable, followed. The crowd was silent.

"Here it is, Luke baby," the Film Bureau man said. "Isn't it just what you asked for?"

Landisberg studied the scene for a moment, inscrutable behind his sunglasses. Then he spoke, his voice a youthful but assured soprano.

"Not bad, but where's the elm?"

"The elm?" Cordovan repeated, as if he had never heard the word before.

"You didn't pay attention to the script, Freddie. There's supposed to be a three-hundred-year-old elm—the Pyncheon elm—in front of the house. I don't see it, do you?"

Cordovan trembled, as if expecting the crack of a lash whistling toward his back. He stammered, "Gee, Luke, I just—that is—couldn't we—"

Landisberg waved a hand imperiously. "Forget it, Freddie. We'll let the SFX crew handle it. You did good."

Turning toward one of the trucks, leaving Cordovan to wipe sweat from his brow, Landisberg yelled, "Turnbull!"

A small man emerged. He looked like a hunched gnome with indigestion.

"Turnbull, give me a three-hundred-year-old elm in front of the house, shading the doorway."

"Will do, chief," said Turnbull. The gnome assembled helpers from within the truck. Clutching numerous tools and raw materials, they swarmed to a spot before the house. Moving so fast that no one could see what they were doing, they hammered and sawed, yelled and swore, rasped and drilled. Staging and ladders were assembled and dismantled in seconds, the workers clambering over them like blurry ghosts.

When their rapid motions finally ceased, a forty-foot elm, its gnarled trunk so wide three men couldn't circle it with their arms, stood in plain view.

Billy, who had been watching the whole operation with the rest of the town, walked with vast bemusement to the tree. Close up, he could sense its life aura, indistinguishable from that of any real tree. Over Billy's head, the leaves of the tree rustled gently, dispersing shade like gentle balm.

Billy walked up to Landisberg. "How—how did you do that?"

Landisberg smiled cryptically. "Special effects." He sized Billy up. "You must be Budd, the delegate for the town."

Billy nodded. Landisberg shook his hand, then said, "Well, let's get busy. We've got a film to make here."

Following that, nothing was too clear.

The trucks disgorged more workers, the limos spat forth the stars, and chaos was under way.

After two weeks of filming, however, Billy was almost used to the craziness.

Listening to Landisberg shout orders now, he even dared to hope that things might turn out all right, for both the town and his special plant. Miraculously, no one had yet—to the best of Billy's knowledge—stumbled upon his secret. These outsiders seemed too incurious and jaded to bother poking around much. Since Billy was continually on the set of the movie—save for a few hours begrudged to sleep—he had been able to keep constant tabs on his maturing womandrake. There were never any signs that anyone had disturbed the thriving plant, and Billy was happy with its progress. Now three weeks into May, with only five weeks left in its accelerated growth, the plant was already four feet tall, glossy and healthy-looking, its hidden core bulging the outer leaves in a suggestive fashion. Billy continued to read aloud to it, hoping that the texts he chose would somehow counterbalance the debased dialogue that drifted over from the filming. The liberties they were taking with one of Billy's favorite books—! It made him almost nauseous at times.

Landisberg's calling of Billy's name shattered his reverie. "Hey, Budd, we're ready to shoot! Where the hell is Goodnight?"

Billy sighed deeply. Keeping Welcome Goodnight appeased was his most delicate and dangerous chore. The resident sorceror had indeed been cast as the wizard Maule, and also as Maule's descendant, Matthew. (Due to the generational nature of the tale, almost everyone had dual roles.) He chafed under the rigors of filming, resented having to obey the director's orders, and was constantly on the verge of blowing up.

Billy found Goodnight at last sulking in the dreary basement of the

Mowbray house and convinced him to come up to the parlor, where the current scene was to be filmed. There, Natasha Kaprinski, a smoldering, dark-eyed beauty dressed in eighteenth-century clothing, awaited her costar among the imported furnishings. When Landisberg saw Billy and Goodnight, he began to issue instructions.

"All right, Natasha, remember that in this scene you're not playing Phoebe, but her ancestor, Alice. Goodnight has just propositioned you, and you're suitably shocked. Got it?"

Kaprinski looked offended, her lush lips twisting in a pout. This moue of distaste was her favorite expression, and she was seldom encountered without it. "This isn't my first movie, Luke. Of course I know my part. I just hope these amateurs do."

Goodnight bristled at this aspersion and seemed ready to retaliate in some dreadful way, until Billy managed to calm him down. He convinced him to stand a few paces away from the actress.

Landisberg shouted, "Places, everyone! OK? Roll!"

Kaprinski assumed a look of shock and horror. Her expansive bosom heaved in righteous indignation. "Sir! How dare you!" she exclaimed. Then, without warning, she slapped Goodnight across the face.

Landisberg had said nothing to Goodnight about this. His theory was that certain reactions would be truer if the actor was not forewarned. Once he had dropped a snake on an actress without first alerting her. That time, he had gotten the results he wanted.

Today, his luck wasn't holding.

Goodnight reared back in angered disbelief. From beneath his eye patch a malevolent glow diffused, sickly blue in color. Before anyone could stop him he raised his arms and gestured. A searing radiance flared, blinding everyone.

When Billy's vision cleared, Goodnight was gone. So, it appeared, was Kaprinski. Then her voice could be heard, a few inches from the floor.

"Oh, Luke," the once-sultry voice moaned, "I don't feel so good . . ."

Billy looked down. All he saw was a big slimy newt.

Then he noticed it was pouting.

* * *

Free for the moment from the exigencies of his new job, Billy was reading aloud to the womandrake when he sensed someone entering the clearing behind him. At last, he thought, they've decided to intrude. With a feeling of mixed sorrow and relief that the wait was over at last, Billy shut his book and turned to face whoever was coming.

It was Landisberg. The man smiled, his eyes unreadable behind his mirrored lenses.

"Hey, Budd, I need you to hold Goodnight's hand for another scene."

Since asserting himself in the incident with Kaprinski, Welcome Goodnight had, surprisingly, become more tractable, as if exhibiting his power had been enough to mollify him. After he had restored Kaprinksi to her old self, he had cooperated fairly well with the director and his demands. Still, he needed cosseting now and then, which it was Billy's duty to supply.

Landisberg seemed to spot the plant for the first time. "What's this?" he demanded.

Before Billy could do more than stammer a few words, Landisberg had gone to the gate in the chicken wire fence and opened it. Billy rushed to his side, but he was too late to stop the director's eager hands from gently parting the outer leaves of the tall plant.

Revealed was the beautiful, pale green, heart-shaped face, framed with long blonde hair, belonging to Billy's mate. Her eyes were closed, but as the sunlight hit them the long-lashed lids trembled and her lips quivered.

Billy knocked the director's hands away.

"Don't!" he said. "She's not ready yet!"

Landisberg seemed stunned by the revelation of what Billy was growing. He allowed Billy to conduct him out of the enclosure.

"Wow," Landisberg finally said. "What's this all about, Budd?"

Reluctantly, Billy explained.

Landisberg gradually recovered his normal aplomb, until once again he seemed in control of the situation. He took Billy's hand and shook it. "This place is freakier than Hollywood! Well, let me be the first to congratulate you, Budd. I'm sure it'll be a happy marriage. But let's get going. You're needed on the set."

The two departed from the clearing. The director seemed once more mentally immersed in the technicalities of his project, as if he had never seen the startling sight in the hidden dell.

But Billy observed the strange and covetous glance Landisberg cast back over his shoulder as they left.

* * *

Sitting once more on the stump in his clearing, Billy breathed deeply, then coughed at the obscene odor he had inhaled. Damn that Freddie Cordovan, he thought. When was he going to keep his promises?

It was now June. The Landisberg film company had been shooting for over a month, and the town still had not received its promised rewards from the state. Middenheap Mile was unchanged, a long stretch of rutted clay. More disturbingly, the beached whale was an inescapable rotting presence on the town's shore. The smell was now so inextricably intertwined with the presence of the movie stars that everyone in the town was calling it "the Landisberg aroma."

Billy shifted uneasily on his uneven seat. June sunlight filtered down at an angle through the full canopy of leafy trees that surrounded his future bride. His frequent visits to his prospective mate had once been his only source of pleasure, amid the pressures of keeping both the townspeople and Luke Landisberg happy. Now, however, even these visits had become something to worry about.

And like everything else wrong in the town, this trouble could be traced directly to Landisberg.

Ever since the brash young director had dared to look upon Billy's bride, Billy had noticed—or imagined he noticed—a change in the womandrake. Whenever he read aloud to it, it seemed to stir restlessly, as if in discomfort. Whereas before it had seemed to appreciate his readings, now it reacted to them as if they were boring or actually distasteful. Billy chalked it up to growing pains of some sort—after all, he had really sped up his mate's normal development. But what he feared was contamination from the movie set.

What they had done to one of Billy's favorite novels was really a horror story in itself. Gone were all the original work's meditative passages on society and ethics. In their place, the supernatural happenings never explicitly endorsed by Hawthorne had been blown up to gigantic proportions, and now made up the bulk of the action. Murders, chokings on blood, supernatural sexual thralldom, and fits of insanity now ensured that *Hellhouse of Seven Gables* would be another Landisberg triumph.

Billy looked wistfully up from his copy of Melville's *The Confidence Man,* which he had been about to read to the womandrake. It hardly seemed worth it now. The beautiful words would probably only cause the plant to wince and shudder. He would just have to wait out these last couple of weeks of filming—which coincided with the last weeks of the plant's development—and hope that when the strangers left, his bride would be OK.

Getting to his feet, Billy headed back toward the Mowbray mansion, wondering what troubles today's filming would bring.

Entering the manse, he wasn't even surprised when he nearly stepped on the newt that was shrilly screaming at Landisberg, "This is the last time I do *anything* you tell me to, Luke!"

* * *

Billy had survived. He prided himself on that. Although he couldn't have said how he had done it, he had outlasted the filming, which had wracked Blackwood Beach with unprecedented turmoil.

He had endured the countless shouts of "Hey, Weed," which was what the cast and crew had begun to call him toward the end.

When Goodnight—prevailed upon to summon up actual ghosts for one portion of the film—had accidentally brought back the spirit of his rival, Andrew Mowbray, and begun a titanic magical battle with it, punctuated by loose bolts of green lightning, Billy had emerged unscathed, although he had been caught right in the middle of the fighting.

When the Viking-like Skandik brothers—they of the immense appetites—had kidnapped both Natasha Kaprinski and the ancient Dame Shabbycough, and Billy had been called upon to effect a rescue, he had somehow accomplished the release of the ravaged actresses without getting his head split by one of the Skandiks' picks (which they always kept by their sides).

When the tempermental and anti-establishment veteran actor, George C. Coates, had learned that the Film Academy was considering him for an Oscar for the role of Judge Pyncheon—on the strength of rumors alone—and had disgustedly stalked off the set, it had been Billy who had found him consoling himself with a bottle at Emmett's Roadhouse and convinced him to return.

And when Murray Roydack, in a pranksterish mood, had, despite repeated warnings, swum out to Big Egg and been plucked from his perch by the angered humanoid fish-god beneath it, it had been Billy who had run for Milo Musselwhite and ferried him out in a rowboat, whereupon the town coordinator had convinced his distant ancestor to release the actor unharmed.

Yes, taken all in all, it had been quite a rough two months. Billy doubted if he would ever enter another spring with exactly the same idyllic feelings he had once brought to the season.

But now it was over at last. The stars had all left as each finished their scenes. Today, the crew had restored the Mowbray manse to its former decrepitude (no one could figure out how they took down the big elm) and departed. Finally, Landisberg himself had been chauffered off, with Freddie Cordovan blusteringly accompanying him, as the fat man tried to weasel out word of the director's next project.

As for the town's payment for hosting the filmmakers—well, it had come, after a fashion. The whale, after being reduced mostly to bones by the elements, had finally been hauled out to sea by the Coast Guard. The aroma still lingered, though, and there was talk of having to replace all the sand on the beach. Middenheap Mile had been paved, but in such a shoddy manner that it was already deteriorating, and everyone knew that by the end of the next winter the road would be almost as bad as before. And regarding the money the newcomers had, as promised, injected into Blackwood Beach's few stores—as any Blackwooder would tell you, it was only money, and could hardly compensate for seven weeks of mass confusion.

Luckily, thought Billy, his special project had not fared as badly as the town. The womandrake was now over five and a half feet tall and fully mature, as Billy had discerned from many timorous peeks. It seemed psychologically whole, too, no longer reacting so violently to Billy's readings. He hoped that it would recall nothing of the filming that had been such a pernicious prenatal influence.

And today—today was the first day the plant might be expected to open. Billy was ecstatic. He hardly believed his longtime dream was about to come true. Since planting the seed, he had been careful to distance himself, thinking of his mate as "it," never knowing if something would go wrong and prevent the expected birth. But now, he dared to mentally say the crucial pronoun. *She* was almost ready!

Striding happily through the once-again deserted yard around the Mowbray house, Billy came unexpectedly upon a familiar figure.

Luke Landisberg stood there alone, a smile on his enigmatic features.

"What are you doing here?" Billy asked, trepidation knotting his stomach. Had the film been lost or destroyed? Was the entire project about to start all over again?

"I just wanted to be in on the climax, Budd. From the moony way you've been acting, I knew your lady friend was about to emerge, and I wanted to see her. After all, I helped keep the rest of the crowd away from her, you know. I issued strict orders about staying out of the woods, right after I learned what was going on. Although I must admit, I did visit her a few times myself, when you were otherwise occupied."

A pang of inexplicable jealousy shot through Billy when he heard this, but he suppressed it as unworthy. Instead, he chose to concentrate on Landisberg's good deed of helping to keep his secret.

"Well, why not?" Billy said, forcing himself to be generous. "Come on, then."

Together, the two men walked to the clearing.

Just as they entered, the birth occurred.

The big glossy leaves, heretofore encapsulating the growing woman, lost all their rigor and fell away into a flaccid pile at her feet. The woman was revealed in all her naked green and golden glory.

Billy's breath caught in his throat. She was just as he had pictured, yet more than he had ever dreamed of. He completely forgot the presence of Landisberg in the exaltation he felt.

The woman opened her eyes. With a tentative motion, she snapped her pedal umbilical stalk and stepped out from the collapsed leaves.

Billy held up one hand toward his garden-girl. She focused on the movement and took a step forward. Then, without a moment's hesitation, she sprinted and launched herself—

—into Landisberg's arms!

"Oh, Luke," she exclaimed in a melodious voice, "all those scripts you read me sounded so thrilling! And the contracts! Not to mention your reviews! Take me with you to Hollywood!"

Landisberg encircled the waist of the green woman with one arm. "Sure thing, honey. I've got just the vehicle for the start of your career. It's an old book by some sci-fi guy named Williamson. *The Green Girl.* You'll love it."

"I can't wait," said the treacherous womandrake. "Let's go!"

And so they did.

When Billy was finished crying, he started to think.

An outsized tubful of this special soil brought to his greenhouse, where conditions could be more carefully controlled; another letter to Thompson and Morgan; a few months' work after receipt of the seed—

Happiness was just a retake away.

I am uncertain how younger people today regard pop stars. Are they seen as mere shills for the various products with which they are commercially associated? Are they seen as clowns and jesters fulfilling a societally mandated position? Are they seen as commodified rebels? Are they seen simply as working stiffs doing a job like any other? Are they seen as "artists," special beings aloof from the masses of fans? I suppose any and all of these guises could be applied to different performers at different times nowadays.

But what I do know is that back in the 1960s, for a brief shining moment, certain rock stars were veritable louche and embraceable demiurges to their listeners, manifestations of larger cosmic forces at play, conduits through which glory flowed.

That's the mythos I've tried to capture in this tale of an unrecorded meeting between Eric Clapton and Janis Joplin.

Slowhand and Little Sister

They called him Slowhand with a certain irony, because when he played his demon half-alive guitar ("This weapon kills fascists" was burned on the neck) his fingers disappeared in a blur, pealing out squalling notes at the speed of light, and because those same string-ripped and -calloused fingers had kept many a woman on the edge of coming for up to three and a half hours.

That record had been set nearly a hundred years ago, back in '69, with the world-famous groupie Pamela Des Barres. Slowhand's roadies had started selling tickets during the second hour of the digital engagement. By hour three, there was a crowd of fifty people in the tiny motel room where it was taking place. Slowhand was holding a joint in his free hand, taking an occasional slow toke, and staring up at the ceiling. The hand between Pamela's legs barely moved. But she was writhing and groaning nonetheless. All the spectators could tell she was trying desperately to climax. But Slowhand wouldn't let her. It was kinda mean, his toying with her that way. The girl was overmatched. But she knew what she was getting into, and anyhow it wasn't like Slowhand was abusing her. Midway into hour four, the joint burned down between Slowhand's pinched thumb and index finger, he swore, jerked away, and set Des Barres off. And that was all she wrote.

Slowhand's skin was pasty white, from playing all night under deficient illumination in seedy smoke-curdled clubs and sleeping all day.

He had had a major drug jones for twenty-five years, had Slowhand. Heroin and coke were his substances—not of choice, but of necessity. They helped him endure life when he wasn't playing. He could handle more smack and blow than any human had a right to, and still live. Everyone knew it was due to his guitar. The creature in the shape of a guitar sustained Slowhand and siphoned off the drugs from his system.

One legend said that the guitar had been crafted by Les Paul under the influence of LSD as he sat inside a pentagram. Other legends made it older than time. Some said it had belonged to Django Reinhardt, the gypsy genius. Others said that it came out of Africa with the slaves, and could only be possessed by a sharecropper's son. Then there were supposedly witnesses who had seen Slowhand sell his soul to the devil at a crossroads at midnight, in order to be rewarded with the instrument. The legend on its neck seemed to link it to Woody Guthrie. However, if the guitar had existed in acoustic form, it had somehow mutated to fit the new era, since its body was now clearly solid.

Whatever its ultimate provenance, when Slowhand strapped on the instrument he visibly grew stronger. Some nights he'd be so weak and shaky-legged he'd have to crawl onstage or be carried on by his roadies, an oxygen mask pressed to his face. But no matter what condition he arrived in, as soon as he clamped the guitar against his midriff and jacked in, he'd stand tall and swell up all godlike, looking to the audience like some earth-visiting deity from the same heaven that had supplied Van Morrison's vocal cords.

There was one school of thought that claimed the guitar actually extruded feelers into Slowhand's body. Whether that was true or not, Slowhand's style onstage was not to flail around like other famous guitarists, but to stand composed in one place, with the golden-stringed instrument held tightly against him.

At age forty-five Slowhand showed few or no signs of growing older or tired, or of stopping. A lot of people said the guitar was supplying him with eternal life. Others claimed it just wasn't done using him yet. Oh, some sour folks swore they could detect Slowhand resting on his laurels, taking it easy, not pushing himself, using fellow players to carry the weight, letting his fingers rest, thus making his name not ironically antithetical to, but sadly synonymous with, his skill.

To these detractors Slowhand would usually turn a disdainful blue gaze cold as a Detroit winter on the unemployment line and rip off a chord or two that would reduce them to jelly . . .

* * *

They called her Little Sister because she was anything but. Oh, maybe one time she had been somebody's actual little sister, but that period was lost in the past she had never cared to hold on to. We could picture, if we wanted, a scrawny twelve-year-old always tagging along with her big brother when he went over to play the drums for a friend's garage band. Pigtails and a pudgy sunburned face (even then she had a tendency to put on weight), overalls whose bib front covered a flat chest, untied sneakers, and maybe a bandage on her elbow. Told to sit in the corner and keep quiet. Unnoticed until one day, when the boys were striving to master some old blues standard they'd heard secondhand off an old 78, Little Sister, unbidden, opened her mouth and started to wail.

Turned out Little Sister had been spinning all her big brother's records in secret, absorbing all the intonations and phrasings of the departed great ones—Smith and Holiday, for example—and of the still living soul-belters, Big Mama Thornton and Wanda "Fujiyama Mama" Jackson, say. (We're reconstructing, remember.)

But she was no mere copycat, even from the start. This Little Sister had a fire in her belly, a hardscrabble soul, loads of pure talent. Even on that first day, the boys could sense it. They nearly dropped their instruments at first, when they heard that voice pour out of Little Sister. But give them credit, they recovered and continued playing. Little Sister's voice urged them on. (Two decades later, those boys, now men, would often wake up sweating in the middle of the night, their wives asleep unsuspecting beside them, remembering Little Sister's wordless yowl, which had gone straight to their crotches, or wherever it was they kept their souls.)

The only thing missing that day was experience. Little Sister's voice was still too new, untouched by real sadness or doubt, pain or heartache, to make her a real queen of the blues.

But that soon changed. Right about the same time as Little Sister's body.

Little Sister seemed to grow up overnight. The singing must have released all her hormones in a surging flood. Somatic changes followed hard on the musical ones. From out of nowhere, as if her body were absorbing substance from the music, she developed Earth Mother hips and tits, an ace pair of the latter, visions of which would send more than one spurned high school classmate home to hump the bed.

There was a famous picture of Little Sister from later in her life, wearing nothing but several long chains of beads, her glasses, and a goofy smile. Her belly was like a pillow beckoning you to rest your head on it. And maybe it was only sweat, but there seemed to be a drop

of moisture exuding from each big dark nipple that looked suspiciously like Southern Comfort. But that part comes later . . .

Well, as soon as Little Sister quit looking so little, boys began to do her wrong. She had a trusting heart and a bottomless need to be loved. The guys could never see Little Sister as an individual. To most, she was sheer cosmic archetype, a red-hot small-town mama who liked sex and could sing the paint off the wall. Her musical talents added some cachet to her girlfriend credentials. At first, so did her libido. But after a while, whatever guy was currently squiring Little Sister around would begin to make excuses not to see her anymore. It seemed Little Sister had made the cardinal mistake of liking sex too much for a woman. She scared guys with her appetites. They'd try to get out of bed after an all-night marathon and Little Sister would haul on their shirttails or some appropriate portion of their anatomy and drag them back. Guys only took this treatment for so long, and Little Sister couldn't change. After a while, there got to be a saying in her hometown: "I got these blisters from Little Sister." No one would go out with her anymore. That was when she decided to split.

Little Sister had started smoking by this time. It had roughened her voice in an intriguing way. But that instrument still hadn't reached the peak it would soon attain.

Little Sister was living in a midsize nowhere city, singing in a dive for fifteen dollars a night, when she met Bobby M. Handsome and affable, he was the bartender of the joint. He and Little Sister hit it off. There was more chemistry in their relationship than there was at Dow Labs. Little Sister was happy.

One night between sets, Little Sister, hanging with her man while he worked, noticed Bobby pouring amber liquid from a curious bottle. No matter how many shots came out, the level of booze in the bottle stayed the same. Little Sister asked for an explanation. Bobby had none. He told her it was an anomaly he had discovered one day, an inexplicable thing, a quirk of the cosmos, like the one factory-standard lightbulb that just wouldn't die. The bottomless bottle had simply arrived one day from the distillery with the rest. He saved it for special customers. Now he poured Little Sister a shot.

She had never tasted anything so good. Despite the familiar label, this wasn't the same liquor she had tried once before. It seemed to sit in her belly like molten love.

Bobby noticed right away how Little Sister reacted, and put the bottle away. But it was too late; she was hooked. And, after a few months, the magic liquor had cured her already formidable vocal apparatus into an instrument that could produce a unique, head-turning, heart-stopping sonic barrage. When she got up onstage to sing, it didn't matter that she had spent most of the day in an alcoholic haze.

And when Bobby tried to wean her from the bottle, she slid it into her bag one night along with her few clothes and left him, not without a tear or two that would later show up, transmuted, in her songs.

After that it was a short ride to the top.

Once, Little Sister almost died from an overdose of some meaner drug. But a last instinctive pull on the magic flask had brought her back, to keep on shouting and hollering her soul out in great raw gobs . . .

* * *

Now, despite parallel careers in the same business, Slowhand and Little Sister had never once occupied the same stage. It was said that they simply couldn't. Not out of competitive mean-spiritedness, but simply because they were each too huge, too titanic a natural force. People still spoke about a famous incident, when their tours had accidentally intersected at O'Hare airport. The rivets had begun to pop from both planes before the pilots were alerted to taxi farther apart . . .

It didn't seem likely, given this natural barrier, that Slowhand and Little Sister would ever knowingly work together. There was too much at risk.

But unknowingly—well, that was another story . . .

* * *

Slowhand was sitting alone at the dark bar of a sleazy cavern of a club called Crossroads, waiting to go on during an open-mike night. He was clean of junk for once, he had shaved his beard, and he was without his entourage. No one, not the owner or the patrons, knew who he was. Or if they guessed, they were all too polite or awed to speak to him. Careful to keep his dark glasses on, he hoped it was true ignorance. Because Slowhand had reached a point he had reached several times before. He was sick of himself, sick of being Slowhand, sick of mounting the stage with his enthusiastic reception guaranteed. It was all a tremendous bore sometimes, a royal pain in the ass. You wondered if they even heard the playing, or if it was just a reaction to his legendary presence. And then there was the money. The money distorted everything. Every now and then he had to get away, to find out if he could still cut it as an unknown, to discover again what the music had once meant to him.

Nursing a beer, Slowhand waited for the inept act onstage to finish. He spotted the owner coming across the floor toward him. There was a woman on his arm.

Slowhand's guitar, resting on the floor and leaning against his leg, let out a raw amplified squeal without being touched. Slowhand felt a quiver in his gut. He knew who that was holding the owner's arm. And he knew that even across the room, she knew, too.

Little Sister had shaved her head like a punk, and substituted contacts for her trademark wire-rims. Always known as a natural chick, she had put on too much makeup, black encircling her eyes and orange on her lips. But there was no hiding her identity as it came roaring down an invisible channel into Slowhand's groin.

The owner and Little Sister came up to within a yard of Slowhand and stopped. It was as close as they could get. Slowhand felt like he was being torn apart, atom by atom. Judging from her face, he knew that Little Sister was going through the same thing.

It was all Slowhand could do to pay attention to the owner's voice.

"We had more performers show up tonight than we counted on," said the owner, looking a little baffled at his inability to get inside the maelstrom of forces surging between Slowhand and Little Sister. "You two are gonna have to go on together. Work something out. Be ready in half an hour." Then he left.

"Funny meeting you here," said Slowhand between gritted teeth.

"Just had to get away," said Little Sister. "This seemed like a place I could be free. You know how it is."

"Yeah," said Slowhand, "I know." He clutched the neck of his hellish guitar for comfort. It squirmed like an electric eel in his grip. Little Sister took a bottle out of her rear jeans pocket, uncapped it, and swigged. The level didn't diminish.

Glasses were starting to hop around on the bar, and bottles to shake, rattle, and roll. A lightbulb flared and popped. Drinkers clutched their drinks nervously, picked shards of glass from their hair, and resolved that this would be the last belt for the night.

"Well," said Slowhand, "I guess we'd better blow. So much for a night out."

"I ain't ready to leave," said Little Sister defiantly. "I come for some release."

"What else we gonna do?"

Little Sister hooked her thumbs in her belt loops and tugged the waist of her jeans down a little. "Maybe we can defuse some tension before we hit the stage. A little before-play foreplay, if you know what I mean."

Slowhand held his right hand up, fingers outspread, then slowly cracked all five knuckles without obvious effort. "I'm game if you are, Little Sister."

There was a dressing room in the back of the club, its walls covered with graffiti, its floor littered with empty bottles. The stained couch with springs poking through its cushions was occupied by a few local guys and girls when Slowhand and Little Sister entered.

"Clear out, kids," said Slowhand. "Me and the lady want some privacy."

"Who the fuck are you?"

In answer, Slowhand lightly strummed his guitar, evoking a piercing wail of feedback that went on and on. Simultaneously, Little Sister opened her mouth and released a raw Valkyrie's scream. When the kids took their hands down from their ears, there was blood on their palms.

When Slowhand and Little Sister were alone, Little Sister said, "We don't have time tonight for no three hours of your diddlin'. Not that you could do it to me anyway."

"Well, that remains to be seen," drawled Slowhand. "But I'll just have to settle for making you come harder than you ever done before."

"You just better be grateful you don't pick that guitar with that big boner you're showing, 'cuz it's gonna be mighty sore soon."

Slowhand set his guitar down on a shelf, and Little Sister put her bottle down beside it. The talismans were wreathed in a mutual nimbus, a heavy corona of visible manna.

Separated from their familiars, the two performers found they could make contact.

"I put a spell on you, woman."

"You won't be too proud to beg in just a minute, boy."

Then Slowhand and Little Sister were out of their clothes and on the couch.

When Slowhand entered Little Sister, the club's entire electrical system went up in frying insulation and sour smoke.

That's why no one ever saw exactly what went on in that dressing room, nor who, if either one, could be called the winner of the contest, if contest it was.

When they were done, and lying still a minute, Little Sister said, "Sometimes I get real sick of keepin' on keepin' on."

"I hear you, Little Sister."

"But if I was ever gonna go out of this world, it would have to be with a bang."

"Like with me, tonight."

"Yeah, like with you, tonight . . ."

* * *

Half an hour later, well after midnight, the demigods emerged. The club called Crossroads had filled up by word of mouth. Their faces lit by candles, the crowd waited breathlessly. When Slowhand and Little Sister appeared, there was a muted whisper that grew to a rafter-rattling roar. Slowhand and Little Sister ascended the stage. Slowhand beckoned imperiously to a couple of the musicians who had been playing earlier. Timorously, the drummer and piano player climbed onstage.

Up front, Little Sister said, "Welcome to our farewell concert, folks. We're gonna play you a few little numbers now." Even without a microphone, Little Sister's voice filled the club.

Slowhand pretended to tune up, trying to reassure the other musicians. The drummer's sticks shook in his hands; the keyboard man was wiping sweat from his brow.

Deferentially, Slowhand launched first into one of Little Sister's standards, and she began to sing.

The two mortals sitting in were instantly infused with borrowed skill. They began to play better than they ever had in their lives.

Rust began to flake off the ceiling. No one noticed.

Little Sister finished singing. The crowd clapped for five minutes straight. Then Slowhand launched into one of his own tunes, Little Sister taking over the vocals he had so often sung. They locked eyes across the dim stage. Both felt completely fulfilled, for the first time in their lives. There was nowhere else to go.

A ceiling beam crashed to the floor at the rear of the room, mashing a dozen mesmerized spectators. Slowhand and Little Sister knew it was time.

From the depths of her bowels, Little Sister pulled up the roots of her sad life and distilled it all into a wordless ululation. Slowhand's fingers accelerated until the strings on his living guitar grew red-hot and glowed in the dimness, before snapping. Plaster crumbled, steel snapped, bricks popped.

And that's how, together, by the combination of the two, Little Sister and Slowhand brought down the house.

In the mid-1980s, my partner, Deborah Newton, got an interesting job: she became a freelance editor at Vogue Knitting *magazine. This assignment took her into New York City three days a week; I tagged along. While poor Deborah slaved away, I used the time to roam the city, familiarizing myself with its every nook and cranny, at least insofar as humanly possible. My map of Manhattan in particular was soon threaded with inky lines charting my aleatory progress on foot. And of course, I rode the subways often as well.*

I generally never tried to write in the hotel room or in cafés, preferring my home environment, as I still do. But the story that follows is the lone exception to that statement. This tale seemed most susceptible to composition while still environed in that haunted city.

Underground

The girl came hurtling out of the faraway blot of darkness and down the radiant tiled corridor at me, crucified on a dirty white square of light.

The air was filled with a roaring like the bellows of slaughtered mechanical gods.

Before I had time to register more than a flash of her frightened face and awkwardly contorted form, she was past me, and the train ground shudderingly to a halt.

I was standing at the very end—and edge—of the platform, so I was even now with the first car. My wingtip shoes overhung the stained concrete by less than an inch, but the train actually brushed them lightly before I could pull back. I was that startled by the apparition of the girl pressed up against the grime-smeared window of the lead car.

While I stood transfixed by what I had seen (or imagined I'd seen), the doors nearest me—and along the length of the train—opened with a noisy rolling clatter.

I've often thought—in years of subterranean travels—how much this opening of doors resembles the way impulses propagate down a nerve, as if the subway were the fibers of something sentient, thinking vast and inconceivable thoughts, of which humans are merely the chemical messengers.

Everywhere down the long, impatiently waiting bulk of the train, people exited. Everywhere, that is, except for the first car, the car I stood beside. No one came through any of the three sets of doors set into its length—most certainly not the girl I had briefly seen.

I thought this was odd. True, the first car always had an inexplicable tendency to attract fewer passengers than the others. But it shouldn't have been entirely empty at this hour of the morning. Was there something the matter onboard? Was I going to be putting myself in jeopardy by getting in? What about the girl I had seen? Was she the victim of some assault whom everyone had abandoned? Or—and why did I imagine this?—was she the reason the car was empty?

All these thoughts rattled through my head in the time it took the hungry train to disgorge its old riders and swallow new ones. Then I heard the doors begin to roll shut, saw them inching out of their slots, and I knew the train was chafing to be gone.

If I didn't move now, it would leave without me.

How would I ever learn the story of the girl pinned to the window like a dead butterfly?

Did I even want to learn it?

Yes, I thought, I did.

I tossed myself through the narrowing doors, feeling them snap at my coattails.

Inside I caught a pole with my free hand (briefcase swinging in the other), spun around halfway, and fell into the gray plastic bench against the inner wall.

As the train roared off, I saw that the car was indeed empty, except for one small figure at the front end (and, I assumed, the driver, ensconced in his little coffinlike cab up front; however, I had not noticed him in his window when the train pulled in, since the drivers tend to keep their cabs dark for better tunnel vision, and also since I had been so shaken by the sight of the girl; for all I knew the cab could be empty and the train a driverless rogue).

The other person in the car with me was, of course, the girl I had seen as the train surged into the station.

From my new perspective, the girl was even more dramatically positioned. Only now the window was obsidian black, shot through with an occasional blue tunnel-light.

Her arms were raised over her head as she gripped the narrow ledge above the door. (I knew her fingers would come away filthy from such a hold, since I had often stood that way myself.) Her legs were braced wide apart, to accommodate the unpredictable rocking of the train. The X of her body seemed pasted to the graffiti-sprayed wall. As I watched, she pressed her young loins against the door as if to burn a hole in it with the force of some fervid desire compounded not of sex, but of some even more primal urge.

She was dressed like a million others girls: flat shoes, black stretch pants, a white shirt hanging out to below her slim hips. Her shoulder-length hair was an unusual color, though: icy blond, almost platinum. The black headband she wore across the top of her skull and down underneath her fall of hair only accentuated the startling color, and I could picture her choosing it for just that reason.

With that confident—and usually false—sense of certainty that we sometimes get as we consider strangers, I felt that she had to be a student, either late high school or first year of college. Why she was standing in such a strained and dramatic fashion, though—that I couldn't say. Was she high, I thought, so early in the morning? Or was she only emotionally distressed? Perhaps she stood as she did just for the hell of it. As I said, I often stood and gazed out the front window myself, watching the lost, dark miles of track go by, wondering when the last time was anyone had set foot on any particular spot. I especially liked watching as the train pulled into the stations, seeing the assembled commuters sprawled chaotically like chess pieces shaken out of their box.

Now that I had seen how bizarre a person framed in the lead window could look, however, I doubted I'd be doing it again soon.

Deceleration tugged at me as my thoughts wandered all around the girl in this fashion. The train was slowing for the next stop. I looked intently at the girl—whose face I had not seen well from the platform—wondering what she would do now, if this was perhaps her stop, and would I learn any more about her.

But as the train ground with screeches and shivers to a halt she remained immobile, a martyred saint out of some medieval triptych, still glued to the wall.

The doors rumbled open, and I waited for fellow passengers to stream in, since this was usually a busy stop.

But no one else got into my car.

By the time the doors closed and we got under way again, I had decided. I couldn't just sit there and not ask if the girl was okay. Her whole posture bespoke some tremendous agony or anxiety, which was obviously communicating itself to everyone on the platform and keeping them out of this particular car. (Everyone except me, of course. And why was that? Some special affinity for the girl, since I had so often been in her position? I found it hard to say.)

I stood up in the swaying car, clutching my briefcase in one hand and a strap in the other. (What an anachronism, to call these metal, shovel-grip arms "straps"—but the city is made up of many such layers of new reality over old terms.)

I moved awkwardly down toward the front of the car.

The girl didn't turn until I was right behind her.

Then she swung around stiffly, as if she had to fight to make her muscles obey her.

I saw her face.

Maybe it could have been beautiful under different circumstances. Now it was distorted by a mixture of emotions: fear, rage, terror, grief, uncertainty.

Her skin was blotchy from crying. Her lips were tightly compressed, her chin dimpled with the effort. A lot of my uncertainty about her looks stemmed from the sunglasses she wore. (Yes, now I remembered her visage striped with blackness through the window.) Darker than an abandoned station, hugging her pronounced cheekbones, they concealed her eyes entirely, making her face largely a mystery.

"Leave me alone," she said grimly, barely moving her lips to utter the warning.

"Listen, miss," I said. "I don't normally bug people on the subway—no sense pushing the wrong button and getting shot. But you look like you could use some help."

She barked, a noise I hesitate to call a laugh. It was more like a hysterical, indrawn sob.

"You can't help me. I'm dead."

Her words hit me like a runaway train. The fetid underground air seemed to thicken as she spoke, until I felt I was going to choke. The train passed over a gap in the power rail and the overhead lights went out for a second, like a candle in the wind, leaving the wan glow of the emergency bulbs to fill the car with a sickly orange hue. The noise of the train's enormous passage suddenly changed to a sitarlike whine, and I heard in my head, of all things, the Beatles singing: *She said, she said, I know what it's like to be dead.*

The memory of the familiar song restored me a little to myself, serving as a reassuringly mundane touchstone. What kind of person would say such a thing? She didn't look crazy, so she had to be really distraught.

"Don't talk like that," I said, "even as a joke. It's wrong. You're no more dead than I am."

Again, she barked, a sound too harsh for such a young throat. When she'd turned, she had dropped her arms to her sides, and now one hand wrung the other, as if it were a washcloth that had to be squeezed dry.

"All right," she said bitterly. "If it makes you feel better, I'm not dead. Maybe I was just never born. That would explain it. I feel like part of this train anyway. I've been riding it since I was a kid, going one place or another. Sometimes it seems I'm down here more often than I'm not. Do you know how that can be, mister? Is time different down here, maybe? You think that's it?"

She seemed to be calming down a little—or was I just deluding myself? She still stood taut as a bowstring, almost ready to snap. Perhaps if I humored her, I could get her to sit down, at least.

"I don't know," I said. "I never thought about it that way before. Perhaps you're right though. Sometimes you read a page in your book, look up, and you're halfway across the city. Other times to go a few blocks down here can take forever."

She nodded rather too violently, as if what I had said confirmed her worst fears. A tear leaked out from under her glasses and crawled slowly down one cheek. I wished I could see her eyes.

"Forever," she said after a few seconds, looking as if she wanted to spit. "Jesus, how I hate that word. It's so fucking big and cold. It's like a stone in my stomach."

She left off wringing her hands and laid them both across her stomach. She bent forward violently, as if someone had gut-punched her. It was as if she were the magician's assistant in the sawed-woman trick and something had gone wrong and now she was feeling the toothed blade pulled back and forth across her soft flesh.

"Hey," I said, really concerned now. "Why don't you sit down for a minute?"

She unfolded herself gradually—as if the pain were receding, or perhaps had been only remembered—with an immense effort of will and energy. She looked straight at me. At least I think it was straight at me. Those damn glasses made it almost impossible to tell. She could just as easily have been looking over my shoulder at some nightmare vision conjured up out of her own brain.

Suddenly I felt that maybe, in looking at her, I was doing that also.

"No," she said, now somewhat more self-possessed. "No, I don't want to sit down. I want to stand here and look where we're going."

With that she turned again toward the window set in the door and practically mashed her face up against it, as much as her glasses would allow. I wanted to say: *If you've ridden this train so often, surely you know where you're going*. But something kept me from speaking.

I wondered what the driver beside us—if he could hear us through the closed door of his cab—thought of our crazy conversation. I wondered what I thought of it. Was it worth pursuing? Shouldn't I just leave this poor distressed kid to her private sorrows and move to another car? What right did I have to intrude?

I was just turning to go when her voice brought me back.

"Hey, mister, it's lonely in this car. Won't you look out with me?"

I hesitated. Then I heard myself saying, "Sure. If you want me to."

She didn't say anything to that, so I assumed it was OK.

I moved beside her and she shifted to give me some room at the window. It was a tight squeeze and our hips ended up touching.

Her clothed flesh was as cold as the water that dripped from the station ceilings in winter. Her touch seemed to suck the living heat from my body.

But I couldn't find it in myself to desert her.

Together we stared at the scene hurtling by, as if it were some television broadcast from hell.

Just beyond the door was a small platform extending out a few inches. Three or four weak-looking chains were strung across the edge of this precarious ledge. They were all that would hold you back from falling onto the tracks if you stepped out.

But I had no intention of stepping out. Why had I even briefly considered it?

Beyond the nose of the car the tunnel was a claustrophobic, stygian alley, relieved here and there by puny lights outlining emergency exits to the surface or certain inscrutable valves and switches. The train's own headlights barely diminished the overwhelming darkness that continually rushed forward at us. The track was littered with random rubbish: paper cups, spikes, boards, pipes, rags. I wondered how the drivers could stand to confront this senseless, monotonous, utterly ugly vista hour after hour. What must it do to their souls?

And to the souls of the passengers?

Suddenly, without warning, my perceptions of the scene flipped ninety degrees. The tunnel, instead of being horizontal, became vertical.

It was an endless pit. And we were plunging straight down it.

I witnessed our heart-stopping fall for countless seconds, sweat beading my brow, my pulse racing. My hand clutching the handle of my briefcase ached.

A portion of the tunnel on both sides suddenly flared brightly, and I knew we were pulling into another station. The spell began to lift. But for a long moment I saw the station as a vertical slice of the pit, all the people hanging at right angles to gravity's inexorable pull.

I yanked back at last from the window with an involuntary grunt as the train pulled completely into the station and the illusion shattered. My palms were wet and my heart was pounding. Still the girl stood by the door, apparently unfazed by—if she had indeed shared—my dizzy vision.

I waited for other passengers to board the train so that I could shuck off the responsibility for this girl onto them.

But no one dared step in with me.

The doors rattled shut.

We pulled out, acceleration tugging my limbs like an angry demon.

The girl was—looking?—at me again. The lower portion of her features was wreathed with mixed puzzlement and anger.

"Why underground?" she demanded.

"What?"

"Why did they have to build these damn tracks underground?" she nearly yelled. Her lowered hands were balled into fists. "Why couldn't they have left them out in the sun and air, out with the living?"

"Well," I said, my voice sounding much too sane for the circumstances, "some of the tracks are aboveground. You know that, I'm sure. But as for the rest—it saves valuable space to bury them."

Even to my ears this explanation sounded lame and inane. To her, in her crazed condition—and by now I was beginning to feel reluctantly convinced that whatever my initial estimation, she was indeed crazy—my words must have sounded positively insulting.

"So it saves space," she shouted above the noise of the train's swift rush. "Is that the most important thing? Cremating the dead saves space, but mostly we bury them, don't we?" That rough bark escaped her throat again. "Oh, yes, we bury them, although they don't always rest easy, even with such a blanket."

Now I definitely felt that it was useless to continue to try to help this girl. She was beyond any aid I could render. I made as if to move away.

She laid a hand on my arm.

Through suit jacket and shirtsleeve, it felt cold as her hip.

I found I couldn't leave.

Her goggled insect eyes fixing me, she said:

"I want to feel the breeze once more. Open the door for me."

I wanted desperately to say no. I struggled to. But it was beyond me.

Instead I found my free hand moving toward the latch.

I pulled the latch up and back.

The front door of the front car slid back like the well-oiled jaw of a snake.

A wind that stank of decay and piss, of grease and electricity, flooded into the car. It caressed us like a skeletal lover.

"Step out with me," she said. "It's easy—I've done it before."

I did.

Out on the tiny rocking platform everything happened both fast and slow.

The driver saw us through his window. His face cracked in amazement and he brought a walkie-talkie to his lips.

The girl—still gripping my arm—reached up to her face and removed her glasses.

She had no eyes. Where they should have been were only two pools of underground blackness.

"Come with me," she said.

Then she jumped.

But she never screamed.

Her grip on my arm, before it came loose, upset my balance. I came up hard against the chains and the top two snapped. I let go of my briefcase and it fell beneath the wheels of the train. The lower two chains caught me in the back of the knees. I started to topple over and out, following my briefcase down.

My flailing hands found one of the thin poles that supported the chains and clamped on. I kept falling. My right leg swung out to dangle in midair in front of the train. My left leg got snared in the chains, both the ones that had broken and the ones that remained.

Hanging like some obscure figurehead, I kept my eyes shut as the train slowed.

At last it stopped.

When I was done talking with the cops and transit officials, they let me go out into the daylight and fresh air. They were still looking for the body of the girl.

Outside I blinked wetly and looked around like one reborn. The familiar street scene struck me like some new paradise.

There was a newsstand at my elbow. The daily tabloids were propped up so passersby could see the headlines. Automatically I read them:

COED IN MIDNIGHT SUBWAY SUICIDE

I had a moment of supreme disorientation, as I imagined that what I had just lived through had already been miraculously digested and excreted by the media. But when I bought a copy and read the story, I knew that it was only a coincidence. The incident the papers referred to had happened as I slept. I realized then that that was what one of the cops had meant when he muttered something about "another one."

I went off to work, outwardly normal but inside strangely numb after what that had happened. All day I listened to the radio, expecting each minute to hear that the authorities had found the second girl's corpse.

But when I saw the first girl's picture on the six o'clock news that night, I knew they never would.

As I recall, this story owes its inception to my reading of Jack Williamson's great story from 1930, "The Cosmic Express." In Williamson's tale, two ultracivilized decadents end up at the mercy of nature in their quest for a more "primitive" existence. The same essential riff informs my tale as well. But whereas Williamson's protagonists are able to fall back on their wits and educated sensibilities, I saw fit to tamper with that mental refuge, trying to amp up the terror.

Going Abo

"I really need to get away from all this." Brian used his full glass of fine white wine to indicate with a broad sweep the whole scene around them.

Cindy Rose looked up from the prime rib and vegetables on her plate. Usually she ignored Brian's penchant for melodrama. But tonight was different. She could tell by his tone that he was unusually serious.

Across the room the waiters moved with elegance and precision. Fellow diners chatted wittily. Crystal and china chimed. Chandelier light fell buttery on wainscoting and wallpaper.

Deliberately choosing to misconstrue her husband, Cindy Rose said, "What's wrong with this place? I thought it was your favorite restaurant."

"You know perfectly well that it's not just the restaurant I'm talking about. It's everything. Work. The city. Civilization."

"That's a lot to escape."

"With good reason. I'm really feeling burnt."

Cindy Rose sipped at her own wine. "I suppose this means you'll want to go camping again."

"Camping is OK. I know you weren't crazy about it. But it's the closest I've ever come to forgetting my responsibilities. Yet it's still not enough. With these new satellite phones, the office can reach you in the middle of Yosemite or the Yukon, for God's sake. And you're made to feel practically unpatriotic if you leave the unit at home. 'What if there's a family emergency?' 'What if negotiations fail?' 'What if the market plunges?' Jesus, I know all those things are important and affect my future. But they're precisely what I want to leave behind!"

"You could forget all those things right here in the city, without leaving the apartment, if you only knew how to relax."

"Easy enough for you to say. Your job is low-stress."

"Yours could be, too. If you let it."

Brian threw his linen napkin on the table. "Let's quit comparing angst. I'm determined to take some serious time off. But I'm not going to waste my vacation the same way we always do. I'm going to find a really unique place, somewhere that offers total escape from this twenty-first-century morass."

"Good luck."

"Oh, I'll find it, believe me. And despite your jeers, you're still welcome to come along when I do."

Cindy Rose stabbed the meat on her plate and began to saw it. "Don't I always end up going with you?"

She did not add, *Whether I want to or not.*

* * *

"No harmful side effects? None at all?"

The travel agent regarded Cindy Rose with a complacent look that radiated complete confidence. "You're free to consult any of our past customers. They'll all assure you that the drug acts just as I've stipulated. The FDA is not in the habit of approving dangerous substances for recreational use. And the AMA endorses Devotemp without any reservations. It's all here in the brochure, including file codes to download further information. You can even access the molecular formula for Devotemp if you wish."

Cindy Rose snorted. "Not that I could understand it."

Brian was growing impatient. "What's the trouble, Cindy? Either you assume the man knows what he's talking about and is telling us the truth, or else he and everyone else connected with this program is lying. For my part, I buy it. It's just what I've been looking for."

The travel agent spread his hands in an attitude of openness. "Thousands of satisified devolutionists are our best advertisement. As I mentioned, you can speak to any of them."

"We already have," said Brian. "That's how we learned about your trip."

"Hmph. Janet and Peter. Hardly the smartest people in the world to begin with. It would be hard to tell whether they'd come back from the trip or not."

"Ignore her. I trust that the drug will work as you say. I want to hear more about the physical aspects of the vacation."

Fanning out several glossy leaflets, the travel agent dove deeper into his spiel. "Devotemp Incorporated leases several thousand square miles from four different cooperative Third World governments. The locations of these preserves are kept secret, even from our customers, in order to frustrate trespass or intervention from the curious or the malicious. Each preserve features a different motif. Rain forest, savannah, Polynesian, or semi-arid. The vacation zones are telemonitored twenty-four hours a day by a trained staff alert for any possible large-magnitude inconveniences to the customers."

Cindy Rose interrupted. "So much for escaping modern gadgets, Brian. It sounds like a high-tech concentration camp. And what's 'large-magnitude inconveniences'? It wouldn't be a synonym for something harmful or, perish the thought, even fatal, would it?"

Now the travel agent looked a little nervous. "To provide the realistic ambiance which our psychological staff insists offers the most cathartic possibilities for the Devotemp user, the preserves are essentially wild and unregulated ecosystems. So, yes, bodily harm is possible, and accidents might happen. But the same is true of, say, a snorkeling vacation in the Caribbean, a hundred yards offshore. Not to mention the streets you walk down every day. In fact, statistics show that the average urban environment is a thousand times more deadly than one of our preserves."

"A little risk is just what's missing from our lives, Cindy. C'mon, what's the matter? Don't you have any adventurous bones in your body?"

"Yes, and that's just where I'd prefer to keep them."

The travel agent focused on Brian. "I can guarantee you that a Devotemp vacation is like nothing you've ever experienced before. You'll return with your psyches fully soothed and reintegrated. As our slogan goes, 'It's like visiting Eden.'"

"I never looked good in snakeskin."

Ignoring his wife's gibe, Brian took out a pen. "Where do we sign?"

* * *

The copter stuttered off into the cloudless African sky. In the end, with Cindy Rose sighing as she signed, they had chosen the savannah preserve. A patch of thorny, scraggly trees surrounding a watering hole had been the landmark to which they had been delivered, after a long transatlantic flight deliberately shrouded in an atmosphere Cindy Rose could only compare to a cheap "mystery-theater dinner" production.

Rubbing an arm still sore from vaccinations, Cindy Rose watched their transportation disappear with a feeling of utter desolation. Then she turned to her husband, who was busy fooling with the supplies that were part of the Devotemp vacation package.

"Before we get stupid, Brian, I just want you to know that I'll never really forgive you for this."

Brian was wrestling with a tall, slim unit that vaguely resembled the traditional Christmas tree packaged in fishnet to confine its branches. Finally, he managed to trigger a catch somewhere inside it. The unit popped open, and internal aluminum rods unfolded and locked into position, resulting in what appeared from the outside to be a crude handmade hut or tepee of plastic palm fronds.

Standing back and surveying the shelter with evident satisfaction, Brian addressed Cindy Rose without looking at her. "I don't believe that, dear. I think that after this week, you'll be glad I talked you into this adventure."

"If that should ever be true—which I very much doubt—it won't be because of these new clothes you bought us."

Cindy Rose fingered the hem of her outfit with distaste.

They man and woman were dressed in authentically ill-cured skins from which bits of noisome gristle still hung. Hers was a cheetah shift; his a zebra loincloth. There were also fur capes provided against the evening chill. The barbaric clothes were theirs to keep afterward—at a price, of course—as souvenirs of their week in the prehistoric past.

Their only other adornments were transponder patches pasted to their skin behind their left ears.

Cindy Rose was grateful for the comforting steady throb emitted by the microcircuitry of her patch. It felt like civilization.

Brian faced his wife. "You look beautiful. Admit it. Doesn't it feel good to leave all your makeup and pantyhose behind?"

Cindy Rose regarded Brian as if she had never seen him before. "Judging by the stupidity of that remark, the drug must've started working in you already."

With a hurt look on his face, Brian said, "I've told you a dozen times. Devotemp doesn't make you 'stupid.' And it's not going to hit us all at once, either. Because it's time-encapsulated, it'll trickle into our systems slowly, so that we have a chance to adjust to it. The effect will be cumulative, until the last day. By then we should be thinking just like our remote ancestors."

"I hope I'm not as dumb as your father was on the day he decided to have you."

Brian scowled. "Our primitive ancestors were not exactly dumb, dear. They survived for hundreds of thousands of years under the challenging conditions we're going to face. I admit that certain parts of their brain were less developed than ours. The so-called higher centers. Though I can't say what good those extra bits really do, looking at the way we live today. But other parts of their brains were perhaps even more sophisticated than what we inherited. The parts for processing sensory input, or sensing the passage of time, for example. The reptilian brain dominated. All of this is what Devotemp is supposed to simulate in us."

Cindy Rose curved her spine and scratched under an armpit, hopping and chittering like a chimp.

"Oh, just forget being sensible then." Brian returned to unpacking their supplies. "They told us to make sure everything was out of the containers before we forgot how to open them."

Straightening, Cindy Rose staggered a bit; she was off-balance and felt all at once all over odd. Her vision seemed to sparkle at the edges.

"Don't worry," she said, frowning. "I'm forgetting all right."

* * *

Their patches woke them by dying.

That first night they had eaten a semicharred yet still tasty supper, watched a beautiful equatorial sunset, and seen the multitude of stars emerge. Brian had added the Everglo element to the fire to insure that it would remain permanently burning throughout their big forgetting, and they had retired to the hut.

Unfamiliar, majestic animal noises had provided an organic symphony to their satisfying lovemaking. Afterward, in the shelter, covered with the furs, holding Brian, Cindy Rose had almost felt inclined to forgive him, so pleasant had their evening been. Maybe it was just the drug washing away her modern worries. In any case, it had been almost impossible to remain disgusted with him. The steady pulse behind her ear lulled Cindy Rose into dreams.

But all those peaceful feelings suddenly vanished as their patches jolted them out of deep sleep.

The regular pulse from the little devices had gone crazy, hammering away like a palsied blacksmith. Then a shrill whistle erupted from the tiny speakers. Before they could react to rip the patches away, both the whistle and the hammering ceased.

At the same time, the repetitive crump of distant explosions could be heard.

Cindy Rose and Brian scrambled outside.

Things perceived as huge shadows that blocked the stars were zooming across the sky. Cindy Rose tried to think of the word for them, but couldn't. Birds. Big birds.

As the big dark birds neared the northern horizon, fingers of light shot upward, like lightning in reverse, followed by flaring explosions both in the sky and on the ground.

"It's—it's fighting," said Brian.

"Where are we?" asked Cindy Rose.

"You know. Away from home."

"No. I mean—the name for the whole big place."

"I don't know. They wouldn't tell us, remember?"

"I was trying to think if I knew of trouble in this place before we came. But if we don't know the name of the place . . ."

They watched the fighting for some time longer. Then Brian said, "It's not coming near us. We should sleep. In the morning we can see more things."

"Yes."

As the couple huddled together in the shelter that suddenly seemed so flimsy, the chorus of animal voices, apparently irked by the distant human activity, resurged.

But far from being comforting now, the noises only made Brian and Cindy Rose squeeze closer together.

* * *

Three suns had come and gone.

When it was light, the two humans wandered around the neighborhood of their shelter, investigating the land and looking for others of their kind. Loping in a partial crouch, they appeared at ease amid the waving grasses and scrub, although at times they would pause and sniff the wind uneasily, nostrils flaring wide, as if smelling the death of something enormous and distant.

So far they had found none like themselves.

The man and woman dared not roam too far from their hut. Some instinct told them that they must return to it each night. When they did return, they cooked an evening meal from their mysterious but unquestioned cache of food over the undying fire they would not now be able to restart. They watched the sun fall and the twinkling lights in the sky emerge. Each night the big dark birds came and laid their fire eggs. This was a frightening time. The humans held each other. And they talked as best they could.

"When it stop?" asked the woman.

"Sometime."

"I—you remember?"

"Our time before this?"

"Yes."

"No. It feels like another person."

"I still see pictures of strange things. Inside here." She tapped her head. "But even those going."

Silence, except for the cacophony of animal cries and coughs, screeches and screams, accompanied by the breaking of the faraway fire eggs.

The woman spoke. "Will others come for us? Once someone said something . . ."

"Yes. Yes. When bad birds are done."

A killer howled his triumph then across the veldt. The humans huddled closer together. The male stoked the fire with twigs and limbs gathered from the oasis trees. It seemed to keep the beasts away. At least after dark.

When they grew tired of sitting and had said all that they could say, they moved inside, where they impulsively coupled. The bout lasted under a minute. Vigilance could not be abandoned for long. Then they dropped off into an uneasy sleep.

* * *

The Long Necks came to browse at the trees around the watering hole. The female saw them first and grunted for her mate.

Emerging from the hut with a strange thing he had been idly handling, he joined the female.

Together they watched, apprehensive at first, then more relaxed. A pleasant odor came from the droppings of the Long Necks. Seeing them eat, the humans thought also to eat. Raw meat from their supply satisfied them.

The male began to count the Long Necks.

"One, two, three—"

With an expression of frustration on his face, he stopped and turned to the female.

"Many," she said.

* * *

The herd of Shaggy Manes came thundering across the plain. Many, many steps from the shelter, the male and female could see the huge dust cloud raised by the herd.

It was moving right across their camp.

The male bolted for the river of animals.

Chasing after him, the female caught up after a short distance. She grabbed him roughly, halting him.

She began to grunt. The sounds were simple but varied.

The male grunted back dispiritedly and hung his head, acknowledging defeat.

Together they sank to the ground to wait.

To pass the time they groomed each other, plucking parasites from scalp and groin.

When the sun was halfway down from its height, the last of the herd straggled by, and the pair of humans returned to their camp.

Their shelter and their supplies were trampled into the earth, pounded beyond recognition by myriad hooves. The fire pit was indistinguishable from the morass.

The female sank down and began to wail. Summoning up some remnant of courage, the male began to beat his chest. When this did not cause the female to cease her keening, the male reached down and cuffed her.

The blow sobered her. She began to search the ground where she was crouching. After a time, she grunted excitedly and lifted up a bright scrap of not-stone.

The male took the piece of debris and tested its edge on his thumb, drawing forth a line of bright blood. Grunting with satisfaction, he moved toward the muddied watering hole. The female followed.

Several Shaggy Manes had perished at the hole, crushed in the general melee. The male selected a carcass and began to saw meat off it.

As he worked, the female swiveled her gaze nervously around. The smell of death was thick in the air. So much meat issued a loud call—

Suddenly she screamed.

The tawny killer, moving low to the ground, had blended perfectly with the grasses until the last seconds before its leap. With unerring accuracy and grace it launched itself at the laboring male.

Somehow the female found herself up one of the thorn trees, her flesh torn by the spikes.

Below, the sleek killer had her mate by the neck.

Screaming, the female broke branches off and tossed them at the beast mauling her mate. Then she switched to hurling her own dung.

But it was no use.

Soon the watering hole was a churning mass of predators and scavengers, winged, clawed, and fanged.

In the tree, the female wept.

Around dusk, the frenzy subsided somewhat, as did her tears.

The female thought she could see the tattered naked ribs of her mate's corpse, smaller than those of the Shaggy Manes. But it was hard to tell in the fading light.

Crouching in the fork of the tree, the female wrapped her arms tightly around herself and began to whimper.

The night would be long.

But the dawn of the seventh day and the chemical enlightenment it would bring would be even longer.

In those long-gone days before cyberpunk, when the SF field seemed moribund, my friend Scott Edelman decided to create a magazine to shake things up. Titled Last Wave, *in homage to the New Wave of the 1960s, Scott's zine succeeded in publishing several very provocative and/or experimental stories. I wrote "Distances" specifically to be a part of this scene, and Scott graciously accepted it. Of course, that's also the point at which he ran out of the money and energy to produce another issue.*

The orphaned story sat for many years until Ed McFadden asked me for a contribution to his zine, Pirate Writings, *and I dug it out. Ed accepted it, and its long journey to print reached its end.*

This history is not quite as recursive or metafictional as the story itself, but it's sufficiently deep and tangled, I think, to have dissuaded me from writing another such tale. Who knows how long the next one would take to get published?

This story, by the way, owes a debt to Frederik Pohl's great piece, "Day Million."

Distances

One day in the future, seventy-five years from now, a man will sit down at his desk to write a science fiction story.

He will not be a professional writer. Neither money nor fame will spur him on to compose his tale. What will motivate him will be simple bafflement that will segue into fear, and a need to grapple with it.

Cleaning out a storage pod, he comes upon a simple object: a flat photo from the last century. The yellowed color snapshot shows the man's grandparents, clad in the ridiculous clothes of their era, posed before an internal-combustion vehicle underneath a sunny spring sky.

They are smiling heartily, oblivious to time's swift passage, which has rendered them and their entire civilization into something almost incomprehensible, antique and quaint.

The man sits back on his haunches, studying the photo with sheer amazement. Now, he wonders, could people ever have lived this way? Wearing and eating raw organic by-products, racing about under the naked sky in the grip of indescribable urgings, believing all sorts of nonsense about so many things: sex, war, nature, the very future he now inhabits, their own undisciplined minds. He exerts his imagination and empathy in an attempt to understand their era. The mental straining does little good, however. No clear insights into their inner or outer lives can be won from out of the misty, locked-away past.

From the next room, sounds reach the man. It is one of his consensual partners, home from her day's work in the protein factories. She is cleaning up with a sonic strigil prior to assembling their evening meal. The man himself has been home all day, having finished his weekly quota of work in just two busy days of repairs at the rectenna farm.

The man's partner, naked, enters the room, disturbing the man's concentration on the scrap of paper with curled edges in his palm. Sensing her wordless desires, the man drops the photo back into the storage pod, orders it shut, and leaves the room with the woman.

Even her adept and exciting tenderness fails to completely drive the disturbing memory of the photo from his mind, however. That night, with the lights out, lying among his partners, the man continues to ponder the past. For a time, he believes that what captivates him about the old flat portrait is that it represents a chaotic, incredible period which, save for the randomness of birth, might have been his lot. This is a comfortable theory, but one that does not completely satisfy him. Considering further, he discovers another, deeper aspect of the photo.

It represents his own sad fate. Just as he embodies his grandparents' future, so will his prospective son in the biobank eventually foster descendants who will bear the same relationship to him. Someday, he too will be nothing but a smiling, foolish image in a hologram, his body and the world he knew and loved and took for granted all vanished, turned into irrelevant dust, forgotten by everyone expect a few drowsy historians.

Everything changes so fast.

The thought is so shattering, so jarring to his normal placidity, that he sits up in the dark, causing his partners to stir uneasily, as if he has psychically contaminated them with his unease. He leaves them to sleep if they can.

In the other room he paces back and forth, wondering how to quell this emotional storm he is suddenly weathering. How blind he was, not to understand immediately that it was not the past that threatened, but the future! How can he deal with it? Perhaps if he could envision the hostile, dreaded future, he might not feel so threatened by it—

Moving to sit at his desk he activates his voicewriter, and begins his story:

One day in the future, seventy-five standard cycles from now, a man will float before his interface to write a science fiction story.

He will not be a registered writer. Neither comserve credit nor sociorank will spur him to compose his tale. What will motivate him will be simply bafflement that will segue into fear, and a need to grapple with it.

Cleaning out a possession nexus, he comes upon a simple object: a blurry holo from the last century. The fuzzy tridi-shot shows the man's grandparents, clad in the ridiculous clothes of their era, posed before a fuel-cell vehicle underneath a citydome. They are smiling heartily, oblivious to time's swift passage, which has rendered them and their entire civilization into something almost incomprehensible, antique and quaint.

The man hangs quizzically in zero-gee, studying the holo with sheer amazement. How, he wonders, could people ever have lived this way? Wearing and eating crude synthetics, scurrying about under their plastic domes in the grip of indescribable urgings, believing all sorts of nonsense about so many things: sex, intergroup aggressions, the extra-human biosphere, the very future he now inhabits, their own undisciplined minds. He exerts his imagination and empathy in an attempt to understand their era. The mental straining does little good, however. No clear insights into their inner or outer lives can be won from out of the misty, locked-away past.

From the adjoining bubble, sounds reach the man. It is one of his assigned resident stim-soothe mates, home from her day's work in the crystal-growth plexus. She is changing her skin, prior to assembling their evening meal. The man himself has been home all day, mediating sociodisputes via his interface.

The man's s-s mate, newly skinned, enters the bubble, disturbing the man's concentration on the shimmering, primitive artifact floating before him. Primed to respond at this hour, the man shoves the holo back into the nexus, gestures it shut, and leaves the bubble with the woman.

Even her adept and exciting rituals fail to completely drive the disturbing memory of the holo from his mind, however. That night, with the stars shining outside the darkened bubble and black space crowding close, floating among his partners who cluster in a sphere of flesh, the man continues to ponder the past. For a time, he believes that what captivates him about the old tridi-portrait is that it represents a chaotic, incredible period which, save for the randomness of decanting, might have been his lot. This is a comfortable theory, but one that does not completely satisfy him. Considering further, he discovers another, deeper aspect of the holo.

It represents his own sad fate. Just as he embodies his grandparents' future, so will his prospective son lurking in the heritage matrices eventually program descendants who will bear the same relationship to him. Someday, he too will be nothing but a smiling, foolish image in a memostim, his body and the world he knew and loved and took for granted all vanished, turned into irrelevant dust, forgotten by everyone except a few conscientious machines.

Everything changes so fast.

The thought is so shattering, so jarring to his normal placidity, that he kicks out in the dark, causing his partners to stir uneasily, as if his bioaura has contaminated them with his unease. He leaves them to sleep if they can.

In the other bubble he ricochets gently back and forth, wondering how to quell this emotional nova he is suddenly undergoing. How blind he was, not to understand immediately that it was not the past that threatened, but the future! How can he deal with it? Perhaps if he could envision the hostile, dreaded future, he might not feel so threatened by it—

Moving to hover at his interface, he activates his memtrans, and begins his story:

One day along the timegyre, $1.7^{10} \times 113$ local proton-decay events from now, a human will pause on his journey to another star to externalize a science fiction story.

He will not have been issued writerly genes, yet somehow he will transcend this lack. Neither interpersonal exchange secretions nor illustrious timegyre repute will spur him to externalize his tale. What will motivate him will be simple bafflement that will segue into fear, and a need to grapple with it.

Mentally cleaning his catalog of internal memostims, he comes upon an unsuspected entry: a clear transcription at least three generations old. The sensory blast hiding behind the cue is of the human's gene-linked predecessors, clad in the inefficient skin of their era, posed inside a primitive intercolony transport against a viewscreen that reveals a starscape. They are smiling heartily, oblivious to time's swift passage, which has rendered them and their entire civilization into something almost incomprehensible, antique and quaint.

The human swims quizzically in his ship's transport fluid, replaying the stim with sheer amazement. How, he wonders, could people ever have lived this way? Wearing crude skin, eating through their mouths, scurrying about among space-colonies in the grip of indescribable urgings, believing all sorts of nonsense about so many things: sex, gene-determined outerness, the scintillant, multidimensioned plenum, the very nowness he inhabits, their own unstructured neurofields. He triggers his imagination and empathy routines in an attempt to understand their portion of the timegyre. The routines must have a bug, however. No clear insights into their inner or outer lives can be won from out of the misty, locked-away past.

From elsewhere in the fluid, chemo-pressure waves reach the human. He reads them as those of one of his commensal nonhuman fellow voyagers, swimming toward him from his-her stint in the navigation blister. He-she is lacing the common fluid with both anxiety and mating pheromones. The human finds himself responding.

The human's commensal, at peak excitement, enters the human's personal radius, disturbing the human's concentration on the internal sensory transcription. Awash in the diluted pheromonal mix, the human stores the stim in his mental queue of matters to attend to, and couples with the alien.

Even her-his fine performance in the negotiated common truce-mating fails to completely drive the disturbing memory of the stim from his mind, however. That downtime, with the maddening warpspace safely hidden away beyond the ship walls, breasting the exercise current with powerful strokes of arms and flippers and a wriggle of his sinuous body, the human continues to ponder the past. For a time, he believes that what captivates him about the old full-spectrum stim is that it represents a chaotic, incredible period which, save for the wisdom of the Human Creation Agency, might have been his lot. This is a comfortable theory, but one that does not completely satisfy him. Considering further, he discovers another, deeper aspect of the stim.

It represents his own sad fate. Just as he embodies his gene-linked predecessors' future, so will he eventually be linked through his prospective son lurking in the plans of the HCA to descendants who will bear the same relationship to him. In some forward portion of the timegyre, he too will be nothing but a smiling, foolish image in a memostim, his body and the plenum he knew and loved and took for granted all vanished, turned into irrelevant dust, forgotten by everyone except a few keenly tasting organisms.

Everything changes so fast.

The thought is so shattering, so jarring to his normal placidity, that he ceases to swim, allowing the current to drive him back into a calm eddy.

In the still pool, he thrashes gently back and forth, wondering how to quell this emotional warpspace he is suddenly traversing. How untasting of the omnipresent fluid of life he was, not to understand immediately that it was not the past that threatened, but the future! How can he deal with it? Perhaps if he could envision the hostile, dreaded future, he might not feel so threatened by it—

Activating transcription subroutines, the human begins to externalize —into a secretion that others can savor—his story:

. . . science fiction . . . time . . . human . . . pause . . . bafflement . . . fear . . . old . . . oblivious . . . incomprehensible . . . amazement . . . sex . . . inner . . . outer . . . past . . . mating . . . memory . . . captivates . . . chaotic . . . deeper . . . fate . . . nothing . . . smiling . . . dust . . . forgotten . . . changes . . . shattering . . . wondering . . . future . . . threatened . . . understand . . . story:

. . . time . . . past . . . changes . . . future . . . wondering . . . story:

. . . time . . .

On all my previous collaborations, I felt as if the other author and I split the heavy lifting equally. But this story is an exception. Mike Bishop did at least two-thirds of the work involved here. Will that little fact stop me from reprinting this fine story in a collection of mine? Of course not!

I do feel that I played a semi-invaluable part in getting this story into print. Mike had finished one draft and was unhappy with it, but could see no place to take it. I rejiggered the narrative conceptually, wrote a few hundred words, and away Mike went!

This might be the one time I functioned as a muse instead of being on the receiving end of celestial inspiration.

We're All in This Alone

[Cowritten with Michael Bishop]

Bam! The morning newspaper hit the screen. Harry Lingenfelter sloshed coffee onto the mess littering his tabletop: two weeks' worth of prior editions of *The Atlanta Harbinger,* all creased open to the same damned page; stacks of unpaid bills and scary envelopes from his wife's lawyers; dishes crusted with the remnants of sour microwave bachelor meals. Lingenfelter gulped a calming breath and raked the stubble on his jaw with well-bitten fingernails.

Blast old Ernie! Couldn't he—for once—plop the paper gently on the grass? Every morning, Ernie Salter nailed the screen door. And every morning since the acrimonious departure of his wife, Nan, Lingenfelter jumped. Nan's decamping to her sister's house in Montana, almost a continent away, had not surprised him, but it still rankled. His gut never stopped roiling. In fact, nowadays even the trill of a house finch could unnerve him.

But what most rankled, even shamed, Lingenfelter was his intolerably foolish preoccupation with a feature in the *Harbinger* called "The Squawk Box." How much longer could he indulge his crazy, self-generated obsession with a few column inches in a two-bit newspaper? "The Squawk Box" ruled his waking life. Sometimes it invaded his dreams. Work on his latest Ethan Dedicos mystery novel had almost stalled, even as his deadline neared, and one look at the kitchen—hell, at any room in the house—disclosed the humiliating magnitude of his bedevilment.

"The Squawk Box" ran daily in the *Harbinger*. It resembled similar columns in newspapers across the nation. A friend in Illinois had forwarded Lingenfelter copies of a feature called "The Fret Net," and at airport newsstands he had run across others titled "The Gripe Vine" and "The Complaint Department." An outlet for pithy bons mots and rants, these columns consisted of anonymous submissions from the paper's own readers. The *Harbinger*'s readers generally squawked via telephone or e-mail. An unnamed staff member, self-dubbed the "Squawk Jock," winnowed these quips down and printed the wittiest. Although the Squawk Jock never interjected private opinion, Lingenfelter had concluded from the evidence of the columns that he had right-of-center leanings and no taste for controversy. You rarely encountered a squawk about abortion, gun control, ethnicity, the death penalty, or religion.

The clumsy phrasings, the naïveté, and the smugness of the resulting mix usually irked Lingenfelter, but he could not stop reading it. Like the trend of "reality television," the window that "The Squawk Box" opened onto the citizenry's collective soul afforded a glimpse of a purgatory where sinners freely uttered their uncensored thoughts, however self-serving or self-damning.

Lingenfelter had begun reading the column in earnest only after Nan's departure. Until that point, he had only scanned its entries or, on Sunday mornings, jumped to the highlighted "Squawk of the Week." But just two days of involuntary solitude had forced him into new patterns of time wasting, and five days of reading the feature from top to bottom had addicted him.

Most squawks clearly originated with their submitters. Unhappily, some readers plagiarized their submissions, rephrasing ancient jokes or ripping off cartoon captions or the punch lines of magazine anecdotes. Often, the Squawk Jock printed the cloned lines along with the authentic ones, without distinction. (Undoubtedly, the pressure to fill space explained the Jock's lack of discrimination.) Still, by and large, the kudos and complaints making up each column exhibited the vivid eccentricities of those who had composed them.

- *Our new president has problems above the neck rather than below the waist.*

- *A fool and his money are soon dot-com investors.*

- *I'm so broke that if it cost a quarter to go around the world, I couldn't get from the Fox Theater to the High Museum.*

- *The latest census shows a lot fewer married couples. Folks have finally figured out that they can fight without a license.*

This last squawk had made Lingenfelter wince.

But his fascination with these outpourings of the community mind had soon morphed into something unexpected and embarrassing, namely, a desire to *join* the voluble herd. He wanted to compose a squawk so succinct and biting that the Squawk Jock not only featured it in one of the paper's daily columns but also showcased it on Sunday morning as the "Squawk of the Week."

Having set this goal, Lingenfelter felt sure of success. After all, he had some small cachet as a writer. Three modestly selling mysteries starring his gutsy private dick Ethan Dedicos (with a fourth in progress—*slowly* in progress, true, but certain to appear to good reviews eventually) all testified to his skill and success. Or so he and his agent almost daily reassured each other.

From this position of superiority, Lingenfelter had written and e-mailed off a half-dozen brilliant squawks, and then sat back to await the appearance—the next day—of three or four of them. After all, who could more intelligently tap the Zeitgeist? Who could more eloquently encapsulate the furor and the folly of these portentous days at the beginning of a new millennium?

But neither the next day's *Harbinger* nor any of that week's succeeding issues had featured his work!

Doggedly, Lingenfelter repeated the process—with identical results. Subsequent barrages of squawks—all of which he polished to a high gloss using time that he should have spent advancing Ethan Dedicos in his investigations—likewise met with rejection. Clearly, the Squawk Jock found no merit in his work. Given the crap that did make the column, the Squawk Jock may even have hated Lingenfelter's fastidiously crafted quips.

As of today, with neither money nor publicity as likely trophies, he had wasted three weeks in this pursuit. What foolishness! No, what quixotic idiocy! But he could not stop. He had to make that jerk—that bitch—that Grub Street hack, male or female—acknowledge the beauty and power of his vision, and feature one of his killer witticisms in "The Squawk Box"!

* * *

Opening today's paper, Lingenfelter could already feel his pulse throbbing. What bloated japes and mindless yawps had crowded out the twelve gems that he had zapped to the *Harbinger*'s virtual mailbox yesterday? Hope flickered in him, but dimly. Either to forestall disappointment or to fuel himself for another round of squawking, he scrutinized the front page, then studied the traffic reports, obituaries, and crime accounts in the Metro section.

A small headline on an interior Metro page caught his eye: *Airline Employee at Hartsfield / Victim of Gruesome Murder*. The details of this slaying would have given even the hard-boiled Ethan Dedicos pause. A check-in clerk for Southwest Airlines had been found in an elevator in the North Terminal with the top of his skull cut away and his brain primitively extracted. As a bloody embellishment, the killer had chopped off the ill-fated clerk's right hand.

Lingenfelter mumbled "Jesus" as he peeled back the pages of the Diversions section to "The Squawk Box." Then he stopped and stared at the ceiling. The bizarre particulars of the airport murder plucked at his memory. He set today's paper aside and rummaged about for last Sunday's. In it, he found the "Squawk of the Week," which struck him as insupportably petulant: *Asking the brainless counter help at Hartsfield International for a hand is a waste of time. A prison inmate might as well ask a guard for a massage.* An eel of discomfiting coldness wriggled down Lingenfelter's spine. His nape hair bristled.

Grisly coincidence? Surely. Anyway, this squawk had no more wit or grace than a dozen others that had appeared last week. The Squawk Jock had spotlighted it only to plug a recent investigative series in the *Harbinger* on the breakdown of services at the airport and attendant customer frustration. Lingenfelter sighed heavily. Some of his own experiences at Hartsfield had nearly moved *him* to murder, although not to a murder as complex or gory as this one.

He laid the old Sunday paper aside and returned to today's edition. Fumblingly, he checked out "The Squawk Box," confirming his suspicion that its editor had stiffed him again. As always, it consisted of the banal, tongue-tied, and pilfered submissions of dolts and plagiarists. Two-thirds of these troglodytes, Lingenfelter smirked, had to be the Squawk Jock's creditors. Or inbred cousins.

Thirty minutes later, he refilled his coffee cup and slunk into his study. At his computer, he ignored the guilt-provoking icons symbolizing his stalled novel and clicked instead on his Internet connection. The Squawk Jock's ignorance and pettiness had to have a natural limit. A fresh baker's dozen of his canniest topical epigrams would sound that limit and result in his first published squawk. One of his efforts might even earn enthronement as "Squawk of the Week"! Gamely, Lingenfelter curled his fingers above his keyboard.

- *Confession is good for the soul, not to mention the prosecution.*
- *Marriage institutionalizes love, sex, parenting, and, sometimes, one or both partners.*
- *My four-year-old niece has a toy pool table. She shoots peas into its pockets with a plastic straw. The kid really knows her peas and cues.*
- *Caller ID is a fine innovation. Now we need another, callee ID, for those of us who forget whom we're calling.*
- *Pity my estranged wife, a designer-clothes exclusivist. She was confined to our home last winter by a swollen dresser drawer.*
- *If my mood depended on the regular publication of my squawks, I'd need a truckload of Zoloft just to elevate my feet.*

Lingenfelter savored these recent submissions, as if they belonged in *Bartlett's Quotations.* But Sunday had come again, and the Squawk Jock had nixed them all. Despite both the day and the early hour, Lingenfelter knocked back a jolt of Wild Turkey, neat. Granted, he had stolen that barb about Nan's fussy taste in clothes from Hoosier humorist Kin Hubbard (1868–1930), but the others had all originated with him alone. How could anybody pass them up in favor of crap like—well, like the crap the Squawk Jock preferred?

The "Squawk of the Week," for example, struck Lingenfelter as a whimper of no distinction at all: *The fat of our great land has rendered us into a nation of grasping fatties.* It barely warranted a place in the column, much less in a box at the feature's top. Lingenfelter poured another shot and tossed it down. Let the dork responsible for that *fat*uous line relish his brief moment of glory. Alcoholism and altruism alike delude, Lingenfelter thought. A moment later, he twigged to the fact that his words had . . . yes, squawk potential:

Alcoholism and altruism alike delude.

He wobbled off to catapult this saying through the ether and to compose another batch of epigrams for his nemesis. When his phone rang in the midst of this activity, Lingenfelter ignored it on the grounds that his agent—thank God for caller ID—would scold him rather than root him on.

* * *

During the following week, Lingenfelter took to meeting his deliveryman, Ernie Salter, at curbside at 6:25 A.M. and seizing the *Harbinger* right out of his hand. Monday morning witnessed the first of these addled rendezvous.

A heavyset African American with muttonchop whiskers and a foul cigarillo, Salter hunched forward in his spavined pickup truck and cocked a scarred eyebrow at Lingenfelter. The two had already talked about Lingenfelter's "Squawk Box" hang-up, and Salter obviously thought him tetched. Dashboard glow shadowed his bulldog jowls and the chest of his faded Olympics T-shirt.

"No luck last week, eh?"

"Maybe this morning." Lingenfelter paged immediately to "The Squawk Box." Several blocks away—the two men lived in Mountboro, eighty miles southwest of Atlanta—a rooster crowed. As the sky to the east pinked up prettily, Lingenfelter tilted his paper into its sheen. His brow furrowed. Then he refolded the section and thwacked it against the pickup, hard.

"A moron chooses these things! A spiteful, *dyslexic* moron!"

Ernie asked, "How much does the *Harbinger* pay for a squawk, Harry?"

"Not a copper cent. You know that."

"Yeah, I know that. Do you get your name in the paper?"

"Every squawk is printed anonymously. You know that, too."

"No wonder you're losing z's trying to crash this market," Ernie said. "The big bucks. The fame."

"Damn it, Ernie. I can get sarcasm from my agent. Or from Nan, long-distance."

Ernie's cigarillo waltzed over to his other lip corner. "Get back to your Ethan Dedicos stories, Harry. I really dig that guy."

"You and fourteen other people."

"I got to go. Stop squawking. Start writing again." Ernie let out the clutch, and his clattery old pickup began to roll.

Lingenfelter trotted along behind it. "I'll see print yet!" he cried. "I'll make that jerk sit up and take notice!"

"Don't write so damned highfalutin!" Ernie shouted back. "The Squawk Jock *hates* highfalutin!" Apparently, Ernie's patience had just run out. Lingenfelter jogged to a bemused standstill.

But he showed up hopefully at the curb every morning, anyway—to no purpose but the further exasperation of Ernie Salter, who on Friday exited his truck, hooked elbows with Lingenfelter, and walked him back inside. "They ain't nothing in here from you, Harry. Nothing." He shoved Lingenfelter into a kitchen chair and poured him a cup of his own god-awful molasseslike coffee. "I'd lay odds. Check it out."

Lingenfelter checked. Ernie was right. Another strikeout. No, a whole *clutch* of mortifying whiffs!

With a tenderness that reduced Lingenfelter to tears, Ernie gripped his shoulders and squeezed. The massage lasted not quite a minute. Then Ernie said, "Let the damned bug in your bonnet go, Harry," and slowly clomped out.

Lingenfelter picked up the *Harbinger*. On the front page of the Metro section, this: *Bank President Found Mutilated / In Abandoned Car Dealership*. The headline alone yanked him erect. The story itself shoved a flaming rod down his spine. His hands shook, and the newspaper's pages rattled as if they were burning.

A night watchman had found the bank president's decapitated head sitting on the hood of his new Ford Exorbitant in the roofless courtyard of a car dealership that had just gone bankrupt. The dealer had sold economical imports from Eastern Europe. The watchman found the overweight victim's body hanging in the boarded-up showroom like the carcass of a butchered hog. The air conditioning, which should not have worked at all, was blasting away at its highest setting. Meanwhile, an iron kettle next to the SUV boiled merrily over a fire of scrap wood, rendering the man's internal organs into soap scum and tallow. A pair of severed hands gripped the Exorbitant's steering wheel, like claws. The whole ghastly scene suggested that the culprit had fled only moments before the arrival of the watchman.

Lingenfelter picked up last Sunday's paper again. Shaking like a man with delirium tremens, he tore from it the "Squawk of the Week." He then cut out the story about the bank bigwig's murder/mutilation, stapled the squawk to its corner, and stuffed both items into an envelope, which he addressed to the Atlanta police department. By now, some law-enforcement official must have noticed the connection between the *Harbinger*'s featured squawk and the particulars of the killings at both the airport and the car dealership. How many earlier featured squawks had provided a sick human specimen the impetus for murder? How many prize squawks of the future would prod that same wacko to slay again?

Don't mail this in, Lingenfelter told himself. Phone it in. You can't waste time—oh, the irony of *that* self-admonition—going through the U.S. Postal Service. You need to speak to somebody *now!* Although he didn't really want to get involved—a cliché with a shame-engendering edge—he steeled himself to call. Even as he touched the numbers on his keypad, though, he wondered if the police would suspect *him*. Tipsters sometimes turned out to be perps, and even if the police congratulated him on his civic-mindedness, they would file his name and number for future reference.

A polite female functionary took his call, promised to pass along his tip, and admitted that several other people had already telephoned with the same concern. In fact, the policewoman said, detectives had noted not only the squawk-as-murder-incitement angle but also the head-and-hands obsession of the killer or killers responsible for these latest mutilation slayings.

"Latest?" Lingenfelter said. "Others have occurred?"

"Thanks for doing your duty as a citizen," the woman replied. "We'll call if we have any further questions." *Click*.

Lingenfelter set the envelope with its provocative clippings aside and reexamined the squawks in today's paper. His heart, the pounding of which had eased a bit, began to hammer again at his rib cage. One item annoyed him intensely: *Now that 'The Squawk Box' has printed me, I have an agent ready to sell movie rights to my life to the highest bidder.* What an egomaniac! What a self-deluding boob!

Oddly, Lingenfelter's own agent, Morris Vosbury, chose that moment to call him again. He let the phone ring. Just as his answering machine prepared to kick in—provoking Morris's hanging up, for he refused to talk to a machine—Lingenfelter relented and picked up.

"Finally," Morris said. "How goes the latest Ethan Dedicos? You gonna make your April fifteenth deadline?"

"Tax day?" Lingenfelter moaned. "That's less than a month off."

"Yeah, well, we chose it as a mnemonic aid, Harry. Remember how you forgot your own birthday as a deadline for the last Dedicos?"

"That book drained me spiritually," Lingenfelter said. "I had to go deep—deep into myself—for *Blessed Are the Debonair*."

Morris's long pause suggested that he was biting his tongue. Eventually he said, "So how goes *Seven Terriers from Bedlam*?"

"Not bad until you broke my concentration." After a few closing pleasantries, Lingenfelter hung up. A pox on Morris, anyway. How, after such an intrusion, could he hope to concentrate on his fiction writing? Better to soothe his nerves with a little Wild Turkey and a new strategy for cracking "The Squawk Box."

- *Some self-obsessed fame seekers think that enlightenment occurs at the pop of a flashbulb.*

- *Cell phones have as much business in the front seat of moving motor vehicles as uncapped whiskey bottles.*

- *Ever notice how the mayor's mustache makes him look like Adolf Hitler in an elongating funhouse mirror?*

- *My condolences to the person who spent two weeks in Los Angeles for brain surgery. Even without surgery, L.A. can appallingly alter the brain.*

- *In the long annals of crime, Fulton County's counterfeiter of Beanie Babies hardly qualifies as an Al Capone clone.*

- *Yesterday I got a mailing from an "intellectual" magazine begging me to subscribe: "Think for yourself. Just send in our card." I thought for myself. I ash-canned the card.*

One more, Lingenfelter thought, just one more and I'll get back to my novel. He tapped out: *Journalism is to literature as a stomach flutter is to all-out panic.* What did that mean, exactly? He had no clear idea. He did know that he had killed yet another afternoon, and when none of these submissions appeared in the paper that week, he knew, too, that his career was down-spiraling like a missile-struck F-111.

How did other writers maintain their focus when day-to-day living threw so many distractions at them? He checked the Activities page in the *Harbinger*. Conferences and book signings were rampant in Atlanta this weekend, with visits from such eminences as John Updike and A. S. Byatt, such mystery-writing stalwarts as Sue Grafton and Joe R. Lansdale, and such up-and-comers as Ace Atkins and Atlanta's own Chick Morrow. Lingenfelter had met Chick last year at a Georgia Author of the Year program. Although he had liked Chick, he had also felt a twinge of impending competition. This Saturday the younger writer had a signing, albeit a modest one, at the Science Fiction & Mystery Bookshop on Highland Avenue.

Chick bore down and wrote. He deserved his success. Lingenfelter could not imagine him sweating bullets to place a silly one- or two-liner in an amateur forum like "The Squawk Box." This thought sobered Lingenfelter, literally. He set aside his bourbon bottle and applied himself all morning to *Seven Terriers from Bedlam,* his first long stint of work on the novel in over six weeks. At noon, he felt like a hero—or, at least, a competent human being.

On Sunday, he paged to the squawks out of habit rather than compulsion. The "Squawk of the Week" leaped out like a mocking jack-in-the-box, but he thought it amusing—and incisive—and wished that he had written it, for it jibed with his own experience:

Having met several authors at book signings, I can report that most writers are smarter on paper than in person.

Amen.

Hold on, Lingenfelter warned himself. If the "Squawk of the Week" provides our anonymous serial killer fantasy fodder for his next murder, why couldn't he settle on *you* as his next victim? Ridiculous. For one thing, the previous murders both took place in or around Atlanta, not out in the country. For another, even in the South, writers abound. If you know where to look, you'll find writers wriggling like maggots.

Lingenfelter observed the Sabbath. He walked to Ernie Salter's and played him several games of two-handed poker. And the next week he wrote—on his novel, *not* on a battery of desperate, doomed-to-rejection squawks. Life seemed almost tolerable again. One night, in fact, he called Nan in Montana—hey, not a bad title for a Western—and apologized for his crazy work schedule and Net surfing, which together had pitched their relationship into the crapper.

On Thursday morning, though, he opened the *Harbinger* to find this headline on the front page: *Rising Atlanta Mystery Star Chick Morrow / Himself the Subject of a Mystery: / Body Found Strangled in Ponce de Leon Apartment.* An inset head read, "Police suspect that killer / uses popular *Harbinger* column / to target victims." *Jesus*, Lingenfelter thought.

Apparently, the murderer had surprised Chick Morrow at his desk and choked the life out of him. Then the fun had begun. The intruder had affixed a dunce cap to Chick's head, rolled out a sheet of butcher paper, and laid Chick on the paper. Then he'd sketched a red outline around Chick's body with a grease pencil, just as the police draw a chalk outline around a murder victim for investigative purposes. This time the killer had not mutilated or dismembered his victim. But when the police moved Chick's body, they found the paper inside his outline teeming with mathematical formulae, some so abstruse that only Stephen Hawking could have deciphered them.

"Think last Sunday's 'Squawk of the Week,'" said one detective. "You know, 'smarter on paper than in person.' Get it? Pretty highbrow. Pretty sick."

I'd say, Lingenfelter murmured.

Bam! Bam! The screen on the kitchen door banged open and shut.

Lingenfelter jumped up from his computer table. Had the killer come for him, too? He kept no handgun in his house, and this morning he regretted that scruple. In a panic he looked about for a heavy object—doorstop, paperweight, dictionary—to use for self-defense.

Ernie Salter manifested in the doorway. "Hey, Harry, how you doin'?"

"Not so good." Lingenfelter patted his heart. "A friend of mine up in Atlanta was strangled dead yesterday."

"That's why I come over. That damned 'Squawk Box' thing. You hear how the paper ain't gonna run a 'Squawk of the Week' no more?"

"I just read it—last paragraph in the story."

"Oh, man," Ernie said. "Sorry 'bout your friend. Weird how it's got this screwy squawk tie-in. Weird 'n spooky."

"Take me to Atlanta. I've got to see about Chick, help the family, something. I'll pay if you drive me." Nan had taken their car when she'd skedaddled for Montana, but Lingenfelter had not missed it until now. He got around Mountboro just fine on foot or bicycle.

"You got it, bro. When you want to leave?"

* * *

An hour later, Ernie drove Lingenfelter up I-85 toward Atlanta. Traffic streamed about them, and by chance they fell in behind a slow-moving Parmenter's chicken truck. White fluff from its stacked cages blew back at them in a diffuse blizzard, along with a sickening stench.

Ernie said, "Now those birds got something *real* to squawk about."

"You mean Chick Morrow's murder doesn't qualify?"

"I mean I'm glad you gettin' over your squawk hang-up. Even as I'm sorry 'bout poor Chick."

"I'm just jumpy, Ernie. Chick's murder has really hit me. The other killings made me feel weird, but this one wrings my heart. There's more to all this than a robotic 'Son of Sam' character taking random instructions from a newspaper. 'The Squawk Box' strikes me as—well, flat-out *evil.* Look at the hold the damn thing had on me. It's like all my aborted squawks fed something bad, a monster living off ill will."

Ernie chewed his unlit cigar. "You trying to say the Squawk Jock's the killer?"

"No. Well, maybe. Damn, I don't know! The cops probably grilled the Jock, once they saw the link between the column and the murders, but he's still running free. I don't know what to think."

"Best not to think at all then." Ernie dialed in some gospel music and hummed along with it.

Traffic in the metro region had worsened nearly every month for the past decade. Today it crawled. Unable to pass the smelly chicken truck, they suffered with rolled-up windows and no air conditioning in the moderate late-March heat.

Chick Morrow's well-maintained apartment building stood between an electrical supply store and a laundry-processing plant—hardly the most elite neighborhood. But Lingenfelter knew just how little beginning writers usually earned, and he admired Chick for doing as well as he had. The place had a low redbrick wall in front of it and majestic oaks rearing in back. Lingenfelter stepped onto the sidewalk.

"Coming with?"

"I ain't no Hardy Boy. Got a sister on the south side who wants to see me."

"OK. I have some other places to visit here, anyway. But I can get to 'em using the bus. See you later."

Ernie scribbled on a matchbook. "Here's my sister's number. Call me when you're ready to head on home." His pickup grumbled off down the street.

Lingenfelter climbed the condo steps. The name CHICK MORROW on an embossed strip identified the apartment. He mashed the button.

A woman's dispirited voice issued from the speaker grille: "Yes? Who is it?"

"I'm a friend of Chick's. Harry Lingenfelter. I just—well, I just wanted to talk to someone about Chick."

"Come on up."

The door to Chick's apartment opened on the blotchy face of a red-haired young woman who introduced herself as Lorna Riley. She surprised Lingenfelter by observing that Chick had often talked about him.

"Don't worry about defacing the 'crime scene,'" she said, waving him in. "Once the police had finished, they put me in touch with a company that specializes in cleaning up murder scenes. Can you imagine making your living that way? *I* never did, before all this. Now, such a service seems a gruesome inevitability."

Inside the modest apartment, Lingenfelter had no idea how to proceed, or what he hoped to learn, or how he could help. He asked impulsive questions. Did Chick have any enemies that Lorna knew about? No. Was Chick despondent? No, Lorna rejoined. His first novel was about to receive a favorable review in this Sunday's *Harbinger*, and his agent had already fielded a half-dozen inquiries from Hollywood. He had everything to live for.

Lingenfelter disengaged from his role as inquisitor. He had to go. He extended his hand to Lorna, who flabbergasted him by falling into his arms, her whole body slack with despair. She wept quietly as Lingenfelter patted her back. Eventually, she regained her composure, apologized for the lapse, and told him that the funeral would take place on Sunday in a church near Emory University.

"Will you come?"

"Of course." He gave her both his phone number and that of Ernie's sister, then tripped down the stairs and strolled to the nearest bus stop.

* * *

Like many freelancers, Lingenfelter often took quick assignments for the ready cash. Among these jobs, the one he most enjoyed was writing book reviews for the *Harbinger*. His editor was Heather Farris, a woman from Rhode Island with a degree in comparative lit from Brown University. He had never met her in person, but on the telephone she had a scrappy personality and a sharp-tongued sense of humor. Surely she could introduce him to the Squawk Jock. Once he detailed his own minor complicity in feeding the beast loose in Atlanta, she *had* to help him, journalistic ethics be damned.

Suppose Heather did introduce him to the Jock—what then? Did he confront the man as an accomplice to the murders? Ask him if he knew the identities of any likely serial killers? Badger him about his failure to print any of Lingenfelter's own squawks? And if he learned something that pointed to the killer, did he call the police? Or did he put on the persona of his own Ethan Dedicos, just as Bruce Wayne put on the regalia of Batman? What role *should* he play?

A block from the newspaper building, Lingenfelter got off the bus and walked to its towering facade. At the security desk in the lobby, he explained that he had come to see Heather Farris, the Book Page editor. The guard spoke briefly into a headset mike and nodded him to a bank of elevators with copper-colored doors. Riding an elevator up, Lingenfelter felt like a surreal avatar of himself.

Heather greeted him warmly. She had a mole on her left jaw on which he fixated. At some moments the olive-complexioned editor glowed like a movie star, at others she went as sallow as a sufferer of jaundice—shifts that discomfited Lingenfelter as he tried to explain why he had come and what he wanted. Her mole had him hypnotized. His mission had him stuttering.

Finally, Heather broke in: "Our so-called Squawk Jock doesn't meet folks face to face. He wants to avoid bribery, intimidation, even outright threats on his life. Some people will try almost anything to get a squawk of theirs in print."

"I believe it," Lingenfelter said. "But Chick's strangulation—this whole series of murders—should alter things radically."

"It has. We've dropped the 'Squawk of the Week.' And the police already know the Jock's identity. *Your* need to know, however, seems low-level, if not nonexistent."

Lingenfelter said that he had deduced the link between the "Squawk of the Week" and the murders early on, that Chick Morrow was a friend, and that he had a powerful sense that "The Squawk Box" channeled a current of amorphous evil in the city. The Squawk Jock's weekly selection of a champion squawk focused this evil and put it into deadly real-world play. He, Lingenfelter, understood the mind of the typical squawker as well as, if not better than, anyone. Moreover, for the entire city's sake, Heather had an *obligation* to tell him the Squawk Jock's identity.

"My God, Harry, you really *do* believe you're Ethan Dedicos. What can you do that the police can't?"

"*Some*thing—something more than they've managed. Tell me, Heather."

"He'd kill me." Heather locked her fingers and extended both hands in a tension-reducing stretch. "Oh, not literally of course."

"I'll say a friend on the police force tipped me. He'll never suspect you."

Review copies of books—bound galleys, photocopied typescripts, finished hardcovers—teetered on Heather's desk in untidy stacks. She drummed her fingers on the dust jacket of an illustrated art book titled *Topographical Abstracts of the Human Body.* She squinted at Lingenfelter. She exhaled and said,

"Sylvester Jowell."

"The *Harbinger*'s art critic?" This revelation was so unexpected that Lingenfelter thought it bogus, an obvious dodge. "You're kidding."

"Go see him. Check the far end of this floor." Heather gestured, accidentally toppling a stack of books. "The next time you visit, don't ask me to play stool pigeon."

Lingenfelter nodded good-bye and wandered among the reporters' workstations toward Sylvester Jowell's office, fearful that as soon as he had stepped out of earshot, Heather would telephone the police to confess what she had just done.

Sylvester Jowell! Lingenfelter marveled. The man wrote hoity-toity reviews of art gallery openings, single-artist retrospectives, and the like. He had two Harvard degrees, a Pulitzer Prize for art criticism, and a citywide reputation as an erudite snob. Had he really agreed to take on the proletarian task of editing "The Squawk Box"? Did his duties as art critic give him so much leisure time—and so little leftover discrimination—that he gladly compiled that daily burlesque of good taste? Maybe his well-known fondness for outsider art had a literary counterpart. Atlanta's squawks probably charmed him in the same way the childlike visual artifacts of Grandma Moses and Howard Finster did.

Jowell's cubicle stood empty. A reporter dressed in satiny gray, including even his tie, intercepted Lingenfelter. The illustrious Mr. Jowell, this reporter said, had taken himself for the umpteenth time to the High Museum for yet another encounter with a special exhibition of the horrific paintings of the late British artist Francis Bacon. If Lingenfelter hurried over there, he could find Mr. Jowell in the galleries devoted to this prestigious show.

As Lingenfelter turned to go, the reporter asked, "Do you like Bacon?"

Lingenfelter answered, "Usually only on a BLT."

* * *

The High Museum suggested a modernistic castle keep made of big, bone-white Lego blocks. The long-running Francis Bacon exhibit had not attracted families or young children—a parental outcry had put an end to one scheduled middle school field trip—and its most devout fans had already seen it many times. So Lingenfelter had no trouble getting in—for ten dollars—or striding up the access ramp to the maze of rooms filled with Bacon's unsettling images.

He declined a headset providing commentary on each of the paintings. He peered about in foreign-feeling awe. The hardwood floors seemed to rise under him like concrete slabs on hidden hydraulic lifts, and the pictures, many under glass, assaulted him with bloody reds and opalescent grays. Moving slowly, he gaped at Bacon's huge renderings of screaming popes, butchered cow carcasses, feral dogs, and distorted three-part crucifixions. The show bemused and sickened Lingenfelter, who sidled into a small room with only a watercooler and a wicker bench for furnishings. He sat on the bench, his head hanging forward.

"Too much for you, eh?"

Lingenfelter raised his head. Sylvester Jowell—recognizable from the photo that accompanied his art columns—stared at Lingenfelter without pity or even much interest. He was wearing a burgundy jersey with its sleeves pushed up and had thrust his hands deep in the pockets of his pleated gray trousers.

"I've never seen such ugly work on canvas before."

"Didn't you read my eloquent warnings in the *Harbinger*? I've written about this show like no other."

Lingenfelter's nape hair bristled. "I know who you are," he said. "In addition to the *Harbinger*'s art critic, I mean."

"Then you have the advantage of me."

"You're the Squawk Jock."

Sylvester Jowell winced. "I loathe that sobriquet. I loathe the feature's *title*, for that matter. I lobbied for 'Cavils and Kvetches,' you know."

"I had no idea. A friend said the Squawk Jock hated highfalutin stuff, but 'Cavils and Kvetches' sounds pretentious as hell."

Jowell crossed his arms. "Perhaps I *do* know who you are."

Lingenfelter repressed an urge to scream. "Who?"

"The psychopath using my 'Squawk of the Week' as a template for outrageously nasty murders."

This accusation stunned Lingenfelter. He wanted to shout it down—to jump up, wrap his fingers around Jowell's neck, and squeeze until, flushing scarlet and wheezing, Jowell recanted the insult. Of course, those very actions would fulfill Jowell's every vile expectation of him. As Lingenfelter shook with rage and disgust, Jowell took two or three steps back, his body limned against the folds of the pearl-hued drapes cloaking the opposite wall. He glimmered before these drapes like an object in a cheap special-effects shot of a matter-transmission field.

"Don't abandon me here," Lingenfelter said. "You know I'm not the killer."

"How do I know that?"

"Because you're either doing the killings yourself or you're artfully directing them."

"Ah." Jowell smiled. "Rest assured that I have no intention of abandoning you here, Mr. Lingenfelter."

His image—as shiny as a tinfoil cutout—steadied before the headache-inducing dazzle of the curtain.

At that moment, three figures—like three-dimensional projections of the images in some of Francis Bacon's paintings—walked through the chamber in single file. The first was an airline clerk wearing a bloody cap and a bloody bandage over the stub at the end of his right arm. The second was a portly man in a chalk-striped Italian business suit carrying his own swollen, shocked-looking head in his handless arms. These grotesque persons passed through the chamber without speaking. The third figure—a fit-looking priest in a black cassock and a jaunty black biretta—halted directly in front of Sylvester Jowell. He turned to look at Lingenfelter, who prepared to avert his gaze.

"Excuse me," the interloper said in an odd nasal voice. "Do you know in which room I can find *Study after Velazquez, Number One*?"

Lingenfelter experienced profound relief that the shade of Chick Morrow, bearing the signs of his strangulation, had not posed this question. "No, sir, I'm afraid I don't," he said belatedly.

The priest consulted a photocopied list. "Then how about a painting called *Blood on the Floor*?"

"I'm wandering lost in this place, Father. But, to my eye, every painting here seems to celebrate lostness."

"Do you think so?" the priest said. Then he recited, "'If all art is but an imitation of nature, then this Francis Bacon character must have really liked imitating its nastiest processes.'"

"That sounds like a squawk," Lingenfelter said.

"Sadly, an unpublished one." The priest either smiled or scowled.

"Forgive my intrusion." When he walked from the chamber into the next room, the air in his cassock's wake actually crackled.

Sylvester Jowell touched a finger to his face, which shone like a life mask lit from behind by a candle. Overlapping taped commentaries buzzed in the headsets of people in other rooms, a faint, out-of-sync chorus.

"What did you want of me?" Jowell asked Lingenfelter.

"A telephone number. An e-mail address. A name. The identity of the 'Squawk of the Week' killer."

"What if I admitted my sole culpability?"

"I'd turn you in to the police as a prime suspect! I'd also fight to haul you into the station house to sign such a confession!"

"'*Prime*'?" Jowell repeated. "Provocative word." He shimmered in his slacks and jersey. His skin glimmered. The folds of the gray curtain behind him foregrounded themselves so that they resembled the bars of a cage. Jowell grabbed them with his pale hands. Then he let go and peeled back the front of his knit shirt to reveal the fatty wings of his own rib cage. Without wholly dissolving, his face melted. His mouth opened, but no sound issued from it. The curtain at his back flickered like an electric field, its folds continuing to mimic the solidity of prison bars. Jowell's body and face phased in and out of reality, wavering between freedom and encagement.

Elsewhere, the sounds of shuffling feet and talking headsets told Lingenfelter that he had *not* suffered a psychotic break. Upon entering the show, he had seen a framed black-and-white photograph of Francis Bacon, middle-aged and shirtless. Triumphant in his own frank animality, Bacon held aloft in each hand a naked flank of meat. The distorted image of Jowell with his chest split open qualified as a living take on that still photographic image.

Lingenfelter screamed and leaped to his feet.

Jowell vanished like early-morning fog. The isolated little room congealed around Lingenfelter like aspic. The drapes on the wall had folds again rather than bars, but the chamber held him fast. It held him until a member of museum security and two Atlanta policemen hurried in, handcuffed him, and escorted him out of the exhibit under the astonished gazes of a dozen visitors. Lingenfelter wondered where all these people had come from.

- *Stone walls do not a prison make, nor iron bars a cage, but tell that to somebody who can't interpenetrate them like Superman.*

- *Tomorrow my wife will receive word that I am taking the spring short course in license-plate design.*

- *If the measure of a good resort is the quality of the people you meet, this one deserves a minus five stars.*

Obsessively, Lingenfelter mentally framed squawks of a confessional sort. (It looked as if he had been framed himself.) Doing so helped pass the time. He had used his one telephone call to ring up Ernie's sister's house. Then he had asked Ernie to contact his lawyer, his wife, his agent, and Heather Farris at the *Harbinger*. Maybe she had some pull with local law enforcement. She could certainly testify to his good character, his reliability as a book reviewer, and his essential innocence, even if he did write down-and-dirty mystery thrillers.

In the presence of his daunted attorney, Cleveland Bream, the police had grilled Lingenfelter about the squawk murders. Nan did not call. Later, the police summoned him from a fusty basement cell for a visit with Ernie Salter in their favorite interrogation room. All through this low-key talk, Lingenfelter knew that detectives were watching through a two-way mirror, eavesdropping on every word. Ernie promised to do all he could to help, and then he drove home. Heather Farris neither telephoned nor visited. Back downstairs, Lingenfelter wrote his squawks.

Eventually, a guard approached him to say that he had another visitor. "Don't get up," the guard said. "This one's coming to you—an honest-to-God Catholic priest. So don't do anything antisocial or violent, OK?"

"A priest?"

The guard read from a manifest: "Diego Fahey, SJ."

"I'm not Catholic," Lingenfelter protested. But the guard ignored him and left. Minutes later, the same spectral priest who had spoken to him in the High Museum loomed over him like a vulturine confessor.

Lingenfelter's hands went clammy, as if they were encased in latex gloves. His stomach cramped repeatedly. Did anyone ever bother to search a priest? This one's cassock sleeves could have concealed a National Guard arsenal—or at least a carving knife or two, an automatic pistol, and a fold-up machete.

"Pleased to see you again," Father Fahey said. "Sorry it's under these dreary circumstances."

"What's the 'SJ' stand for?"

"Society of Jesus." Father Fahey's pupils glittered like bits of obsidian. "Why? What did you *think* they stood for?"

"I couldn't have said. Do you happen to know Sylvester Jowell?"

"No, I don't. Interesting name, though."

"Interesting initials, too."

"I suppose so. Did his initials lead you to assume a connection between him and us Jesuits?" Without asking, Father Fahey sat beside Lingenfelter on his narrow cot and gripped his knee. "Because we don't know him. We've never known him. His opinions distress us. His motives defy our comprehension." The grip on Lingenfelter's knee grew more insistent, as painful as the flexion of a raptor's talons. Father Fahey's pupils—his dark-brown irises, for that matter—abruptly clouded, as if someone had pressed disks of smoked glass over them. "Shhh," he said. "Don't cry out. Love is the devil, but silence gets all manner of wickedness done."

From one cassock sleeve Father Fahey pulled a wooden ruler with a thin copper edge and some sort of writing implement. From the other he extracted a switchblade that Lingenfelter dimly associated with the Cross . . .

* * *

Heather Farris perched at Lingenfelter's bedside in Henry Grady Memorial Hospital. For twenty minutes she had apologized for ratting him out to the police after identifying Sylvester Jowell to him as the Squawk Jock. She apologized for failing to heed Ernie Salter's notification of his arrest. She apologized for the peculiar wounds that the priest had inflicted upon him in a fugue of profound enthrallment after cajoling his way into Lingenfelter's cell. As Heather spoke, the mole on her jaw occupied almost all his attention.

Apparently, Father Fahey had placed the wooden ruler across Lingenfelter's windpipe until Lingenfelter blacked out. Then he had measured the cell's dimensions in feet and inches. He wrote the length, height, and breadth of the cage on its rear wall in bright pearl-gray numerals. Then he placed Lingenfelter on the floor, cut away his shirt, and used the switchblade to gouge four star-shaped badges of flesh out of his torso. He was bent over Lingenfelter carving a fifth star into his chest, right above the heart, when the police broke in and seized him. If the cuts had gone much deeper, Lingenfelter would not have awakened.

Heather said, "You don't know how glad I was to see your eyes open, Harry."

Lingenfelter nodded. He wondered how Diego Fahey, SJ, had read his mind. He wondered if capturing and subduing the priest, whom Heather said had no memory of assaulting him, would put an end to the squawk murders. He feared the opposite. If the *real* agency behind the slayings could inspire new killers with epigrammatic thoughts out of the mental ether, the bizarre assaults would go on. Fahey struck Lingenfelter as a mere cat's-paw whom Sylvester Jowell had felled by channeling and focusing the destructive essence of innumerable malign squawks, brilliant and banal.

The ruler across Lingenfelter's throat had rendered him temporarily mute. He knew this without even trying to talk. Heather detected his agitation and handed him a notepad and a pen. He worked to position them properly and then scratched out on the pad's top sheet: *What's happened to Jowell?*

"He's disappeared," Heather said. "I think he knew that Diego Fahey, SJ, had outlived his usefulness. What serial killer in his cunning right mind attempts a murder in a locked jail cell?"

No one knew where Jowell had gone, but Heather had an idea. The Francis Bacon exhibit at the High closed tomorrow and moved across country to a museum—Heather could not remember its name—in the San Francisco area. This fact struck her as suggestive. Lingenfelter pondered it for about thirty seconds and then scrawled a message on his notepad: *Need to rest.*

* * *

Although his doctors had advised him not to, on Sunday Lingenfelter attended Chick Morrow's funeral. He sat with Lorna Riley in a pew reserved for close friends of the deceased, but he could not stop thinking of a melancholy Woody Allen observation: "We're all in this alone." So far as Lingenfelter knew, no one had ever ripped off this clever remark and submitted it to "The Squawk Box."

The young priest officiating at the service did his earnest best to contradict both this unspoken sentiment and the artist Francis Bacon's love affair with portraits of caged and screaming popes. He exuded humility and calm. Some of his serenity passed into Lingenfelter. After all, Chick Morrow had considered Lingenfelter a friend, Lorna Riley had invited him to come, and not one mourner looked at him as if his presence in any way profaned these rites.

An alien thought—a squawklike saying—struggled to rise into Lingenfelter's consciousness. He could tell by its alien edge that it had originated elsewhere—in the troubled, alcoholic depths of Francis

Bacon's own personality, in fact. At length he had this terrible epigram firm and entire in his head: "I always think of friendship as where two people can really tear each other to pieces." Lingenfelter's mouth opened in awe and horror.

Lorna Riley nudged him and whispered, "What's wrong, Harry?"

Lingenfelter tried to tell her, but all that he heard escaping his lips was a hideous, inarticulate squawk.

Although my records of this period no longer exist, I am convinced that I wrote this story at approximately the same time that I composed Harp, Pipe, and Symphony, *circa 1983. Its motifs and concerns are too similar not to have sprung from the same creative ferment that engendered that novel. A young man's motifs and concerns, assuredly, but perhaps somewhat eternal for all that. I had forgotten the very existence of this story until, at the behest of publisher and editor Sean Wallace, I began rummaging through my files for any heretofore unpublished piece of fiction that could accompany the limited edition of* Harp, Pipe, and Symphony.

Rereading it for the first time in twenty years, I had as disorienting an experience as anything undergone by my protagonist, John Moreton—an experience as memorably piquant as any I have ever had, where my own writing was involved.

I hope my readers enjoy some of the same sensations.

Walking the Great Road

For Broadway

He set down the book.

Rising from his chair, John Moreton thought, *How strange. I've just read a story so full of life that it's convinced me to forswear all reading.*

Music swelled from the speakers nestled amid his books, filling the crowded, shelf-lined study with a gorgeously colored cloud of sound: *Scheherazade* by Rimsky-Korsakov. Moreton's head spun with the symphony and the impact of the unexpected epiphany. He felt slightly queasy, yet elated, as if he'd suddenly been conquered by a disease like life itself, which invigorates and compels the sufferer, even as it inevitably carries him closer and closer to death.

He knew that from this instant, nothing would ever be the same again.

His life could not consist almost solely of scribbling and devouring words anymore. The story—that damned, wonderful story!—had shown him the folly of such activity. (And how strange that a message delivered in a certain medium could work to overthrow the essential validity of that very medium. Only words had enough power to commit suicide. There would never be a statue that could argue for the destruction of all monuments, or a song that proposed all songs were empty, or a painting that negated the glory of color on canvas. Paradoxically, the stronger such works were, the more they contradicted their own arguments. No, only language was subtle enough, possessed of enough of the magic of life to deny itself.)

Moreton spun on his heel in a daze. His surroundings struck him as alien, bizarre. He felt incredibly old, yet childlike, although he was neither elderly nor adolescent. What was he to do with his life now? The room oppressed him so that he could hardly breathe. He knew he had to flee. Yet where?

Just get out, his mind urged. *Decide outside. But quit this place.*

Moreton ran to the door, fumbled with the knob, got it open after what seemed an eternity, and fled his apartment, taking nothing but the clothes on his back and the change in his pockets.

In his study, the pages of "Idle Days on the Yann" turned in a vagrant breeze, as if the wind sought to learn what had made the man run, and the music played on to itself.

***

Out on the sidewalk, he could breathe easier, exhaust fumes notwithstanding. The noise of the traffic was less disorienting than the symphony, chaos being less frightening than order at the moment. In his windowless, lamp-lit room full of books, he had been unaware of either the time of day or the weather. He was rather startled to find that it was close to noon on a sunny spring day. He looked up, marveling. The cloudless sky was a seamless royal blue fabric, stitched with birds. Across the busy street, tall apartment and office buildings reared up their bulky forms. The sidewalks were filled with lazing lunchtime strollers.

Moreton turned, expecting to confront the revolving door to his building.

The door was not there. The building itself—where he had lived his narrow, page-bound, constricted life—was gone. The adjoining buildings had vanished also.

In their place was a wall. The wall was composed of giant granite blocks flecked with mica that glittered in the sun. The massive blocks ran in mortarless courses, their edges trimmed so precisely that Moreton doubted a piece of paper could have been inserted between them.

Moreton raised his eyes. The top of the wall was barely visible. It seemed to be studded with crenellations of some sort, and Moreton thought he could detect the vague movements of tiny figures striding along it. Lowering his gaze, he looked left, then right. The wall extended in a straight line as far as he could see.

Moreton turned back to the secretaries and schoolchildren and executives idling away their time on the other side of the street. They seemed oblivious to the wall, paying it no heed, as if it had always existed, or as if they could not see it.

Advancing on the wall, Moreton touched it. It was hot with absorbed sunlight, solid and gritty. He was reminded of a long flat slab of rock rising from a grassy field—the exposed spine of a buried monster, he had thought then—which he had loved to lie on as a child.

Arbitrarily, he turned right and started walking.

* * *

The gate tower was visible from over a mile away. It projected out from the wall, a semicylindrical extrusion climbing halfway up the wall's height, capped by a pointed dome. Its sides were pierced with narrow windows in a staggered pattern. Moreton thought he could detect a mate to the tower, separated by a narrow interval, but could not distinguish the two individually at this distance.

He had been walking for half an hour. On his right side, the familiar city stretched away, full of the people and places he had known all his life. On his left, the wall loomed, overpoweringly huge, yet in a strange way comforting. What lay beyond it?

After another quarter of an hour, he reached the tower. He saw from its angle of curvature that it would have taken a dozen men to circle its base with outstretched hands touching. From where he stood, nearly against the wall, he could not see beyond it. He circled to the far side. There he found the gate.

It was an arched opening in the wall that reached as high as the towers. (There *were* two, he saw now.) Around the arch were carved flowers and beasts, people and castles, stars and trees, all glazed in bright colors. The opening itself was filled with a white mottled haze, like a pearly fog populated by spirits and shadows, all astir with quick movements.

Moreton looked over his shoulder. The city of his adulthood stood there as ever, safe and secure, but holding nothing he could grasp any-more.

Six steps took him through the gate.

* * *

There were people everywhere.

Moreton could barely take it all in.

On its far side, the gate was flanked by mustached guards clad in paneled leather skirts and bronze cuirasses, bearing tall staves tipped with elaborate blades. Ahead stretched a broad way thronged with figures dressed in myriad styles: embroidered robes; billowing silky trousers and vests over bare chests; painted skin and loin wraps; polished armor that clanked.

Stuccoed and wooden structures lined the wide street, threaded with alleys and interspersed with formal courtyards.

Moreton looked backward, through the gate. The road stretched away on the far side, a taut thread pulled tight across a shimmering alkaline desert.

Rough hands gripped both his biceps. The guards on either side had fallen roughly upon him.

One spoke. "Your right of entry," the guard said, making it neither question nor declaration. The words lay as unanswerable as a stone between them.

Moreton found no speech with which to reply. The guards tightened their grip.

"Wait! I know this man."

A bent, shuffling form approached. It appeared to be an old man wearing a white robe and turned-up red slippers with inset mirror-shards. At his intervention, the guards released Moreton.

"Come with me," the old man said. He took Moreton's arm in a feeble grip and began to limp off.

Moreton followed.

As they pushed through the surging crowd, which took no notice of them, busy with its own noisy bargains and prayers, pleas and denials, the old man begin to talk, addressing Moreton as if they had known each other all their lives.

"It's not too late to go back, you know. You haven't taken enough steps along the Great Road to commit yourself. It has no hold on you yet. You're still between worlds. Just run right through the gate, and behold—you're back in the old safe place you know."

The weathered face of the stranger regarded him earnestly, with a trace of humor in it. Moreton found his features familiar, yet unplaceable.

"No," Moreton said. "No. I don't believe I can."

Letting go of Moreton's sleeve, the old man clapped his hands. "Splendid. Then we'll go on. I'll accompany you for as long as you wish."

Moreton found the thought curiously comforting.

As they walked, his new companion continued to talk.

"Of course, this is the Great Road. I suspect you already knew something of the sort. As a matter of convenience, we can say that it begins at the gate—although of course, as you saw, it extends beyond, through the desert. But that part does not matter. One might as well try to fathom what existed before time began. What counts is this fine expanse of dusty cobbles down which we now saunter. The Great Road. Common thoroughfare of the high and the low, the mighty and the powerless, the happy and the dejected, the serene and the tortured, the blessed and the damned. And don't make the common mistake of assuming that the former term of each set matches up with all the others—nor necessarily do the latter ones. That is one thing the Great Road will teach you from the outset."

Moreton drew his fascinated gaze away from the haggling and eating, the laboring and conversing going on all around him. "How long does it go on?"

The old man's wrinkled face cracked in a smile that revealed gaps in his teeth. "Longer than you will ever see. No man has ever walked the whole length of the Great Road. You will not be the first to succeed, either. The Great Road is longer than your life. But for those who have once trodden it, there is nothing else."

Moreton felt warm inside. It was what he had wanted to hear.

"Don't get self-satisfied," the old man warned, his quavery voice suddenly sharp. "Life is still life here. You can suffer and die before your time, be entrapped and frustrated. Wisdom will elude you, unless you are persistent."

"I will be," Moreton promised. "Let's walk a little faster now."

* * *

His first pair of shoes had worn out long ago. They had been replaced by a pair of ox-hide sandals that had lasted almost a year. After the sandals became more strap than sole, he had bartered a day's work for a pair of curve-toed slippers like his companion's. They were surprisingly durable and comfortable, and he felt elegant in them.

His original clothing had lasted a bit longer than the shoes. Piece by piece, though, it had worn away, fraying at elbow and knee, seams unraveling and threads falling away like his old life. Now he favored a simple white robe like his friend's.

He felt he could truly call John his friend. (He had been surprised to learn the old man bore his name, but after a while it had seemed only right.) He and the old man had talked incessantly at first, as each new sight and custom demanded an explanation. Now, their common silences were as evocative as words, and he could not imagine being without John.

They never stopped for long on the Great Road. Only long enough to barter their labor for food and clothing. Even when they slept, it was only for a few hours in the shade of an awning, or wrapped in a borrowed blanket against a wall that cut the night wind. (Luckily, this land seemed innocent of winter.) Then it was off again, in search of new wonders, new people, new experiences.

And the things Moreton had seen! The Great Road was endlessly prolific of invention.

There had been the miles of crumbling slums, where the people ate rats big as cats—and even each other. Here, they had not dared stop, but had walked for three days and nights, their senses constantly alert.

Later, there had been the many acres extending on either side of the road that held the noisome tanneries and dye-houses. The stench here was overwhelming, but they eventually grew used to it, and the clean air farther on seemed like an aberration.

A subsequent stretch of the Great Road—as if deliberately planned for contrast—held enormous mansions, each vying to outdo the others in the splendor of their facades and estates and servants.

Beyond the grand promenade, one huge, shedlike structure occupied a whole mile by itself. John told Moreton it was a rope-walk, where thin strands of hemp were twisted by stages into enormous hawsers to anchor the caravels they later saw when the Great Road ran parallel to the sea.

Elsewhere, among the miles of fruit and vegetables and live squawking chickens, they enjoyed heartier-than-normal fare for free, thanks to the generosity of the vendors, who were glad to be rid of their bruised produce. Not having to work for their supper allowed them to cover the leagues even faster.

The people Moreton and his guide encountered were intrinsically more fascinating than the places, if that were possible. The depths of the human spirit Moreton plumbed astonished him, as did the heights. He met rogues and whores, cowards and heroes, the passionate and the apathetic, the generous and the miserly.

One man told Moreton how his best friend had betrayed him in business, and how he had later held the man's life in his hands—only to have a shipwreck sunder them before he could decide on mercy or revenge. The incomplete test of his nature had troubled him ever since.

A blind beggar told how he had given his eyes to see a goddess, and found her not what he had hoped for.

A lofty gentlewoman broke down crying and confessed—when Moreton idly mentioned the vast slumlands—how she had been born there and advanced to her present position by ruthless deceit and treachery.

Never once did Moreton miss the world he had left behind, the secondhand experiences captured crudely—and always ultimately unsatisfyingly—in black marks on white pages, like the footprints made by an ignorant, blundering giant on a field of virgin snow.

The experience of traversing the Great Road seemed to agree with the old man as well. Each day on the road left him a little sprier and less aged than the day before, his face less wrinkled, his gait more steady.

Conversely, Moreton seemed to age as he would have in the old world, no faster, but no slower, either.

Then came the year when Moreton and John appeared the same age. Moreton thought little of it. It was the same year he met Samara.

She was a fish-peddler's daughter, sitting patiently by her stern-faced father at his stand each day. Her hands were chapped, but her face was fresh as the dawn at the eastern end of the Great Road. Her eyes were amber, like the rare wine Moreton had sampled many miles ago. Beneath her thin purple robe, her supple body beckoned Moreton like the road itself.

Moreton fell in love with her as she weighed his purchase. He turned to his companion, the old man no longer old.

"We will stay here a time," Moreton said.

John said nothing.

Moreton lived with Samara for three years, lovers in the easy way dictated by the customs of the land around them. John he saw infrequently —he could not even say where his ex-guide lived—and then only to talk of inconsequentials. The man seemed to be aging again, away from the vitality of the road.

One day John asked, "Do you miss the road? Don't you wonder what lies beyond the narrow confines of your bedroom?"

Moreton replied, "No. I have Samara." But a seed of doubt had been planted.

Eighteen months later, on a moonless night, Moreton slipped out of his house, leaving Samara sleeping with their two children. He headed down the Great Road, toward where he had never been.

After some distance, he found he had a shadow.

John said, "It is good to be moving again."

* * *

Moreton sat still, his old bones aching. He tried to remember all he had seen and lived, but there was too much. Each breath he had drawn had been suffused with miracles. There was no moment of his life that had not been full of a fierce pleasure, not one moment he regretted. Even those times when he had been forced to kill to survive seemed resplendent with a kind of ineffable glory.

How many miles had he and John walked? The total seemed incalculable. Each foot of the Great Road held its own world, for as deep back as one chose to explore. Temples and gambling dens, quiet family firesides and raucous taverns, strange tribes and queer sects.

At times, he had grown weary of the bottomless mystery, the weight and burden of the lives of others. But always he found new resources within himself to meet the challenge of sharing their joy and despair. Despite all he had seen over the decades, he knew there was still more to astonish and delight him, and he longed to encounter it.

But now he was old—too old to continue. Each morning he could barely rise from his hard bed of cobbles. The swift pace he had maintained for years was beyond him now.

With John, it was different.

John was a young man now. His face was totally unlined, his limbs straight, his voice resonant. When Moreton thought of it at all, he found nothing unfair in the situation. After all, Moreton had been young when John was old. Now he was old, and John young. And of course, John aided Moreton daily, lending a strong shoulder or arm. At last, though, even his comradeship and strength had not been enough to allow Moreton to continue.

One day, in the shade of a coffee shop's gaily striped awning, Moreton tried to recover enough strength to continue their journey. The task was hopeless, though, and John seemed to sense as much.

"Have you seen enough of the Great Road at last?" John asked.

"No," Moreton managed to say. "I would go on. Is it possible?"

John smiled. "Not with me, my friend. But perhaps—if you are as lucky as I was—with another."

John laid a hand on Moreton's brow. Moreton closed his eyes gratefully at the cool pressure.

"Good-bye," John said. "And thank you." Then Moreton felt his companion's hand fade away.

When Moreton opened his eyes, he saw that not John had moved, but he himself. The sun now beat down hotly on his unprotected head. He realized with wonder that he lay within sight of the gate, where he had stood so long ago for the first time upon the road. Two guards identical to those who had accosted him so many years ago flanked the arch. The desert quivered with heat beyond.

With the last of his strength Moreton stood. At the same time, an oddly clad stranger appeared from nowhere through the gate. Moreton saw it was not himself—time did not repeat so neatly—but one who might have been his brother. The newcomer appeared transfixed by the scene, at once frightened and overjoyed.

The guards moved to pinion the newly arrived man. Moreton raised a shout.

"Wait," he called.

"I know that man."

Here's a shameful admission: I've actually read very little Jules Verne. While masquerading as a major Verne aficionado during my attendance at a French convention in his hometown of Nantes, I quaked and quailed inside, fearing exposure at any minute.

But the work of Verne that I have read, I've enjoyed very much. So when editor Mike Ashley invited me to contribute to an anthology honoring Verne's creations by extending them, I jumped at the chance. Luckily, I had just finished reading Verne's The Mysterious Island *in a fine new translation, and so I had a platform from which to leap.*

Here's hoping I did some acrobatic twirls on the way down.

The Mysterious Iowans

"I am inclined to think that in the future the world will not have many more novels in which mind problems will be solved by the imagination. It may be the natural feeling of an old man with a hundred books behind him, who feels that he has written out his subject, but I really feel as though the writers of the present day and the past time who have allowed their imaginations to play upon mind problems, have, to use a colloquialism, nearly filled the bill."

—Jules Verne,

"Solution of Mind Problems by the Imagination."

On the morning of May 24, 1898, Mr. Bingham Wheatstone disembarked from the transcontinental train famously dubbed "The Gray Ghost" for its swift and whisper-quiet mode of propulsion, alighting at the very doorstep of the city known far and wide as Lincolnopolis, capital of the enigmatic sovereign empire known as Lincoln Island, a dominion incongruously situated in the vast heartland of the United States of America, bounded roughly by the borders of what had once been the state of Iowa.

Descending the automatically unfolding steps of the streamlined railcar, which resembled the gaudily ornamented hull of an ocean-going submersible, Wheatstone glanced about the several platforms of the Lincolnopolis station for a brief moment, before the eager push of fellow passengers behind him forced him to fully descend. He saw a bustling scene, as thousands of brightly dressed visitors and natives mingled beneath the great vitrine-roofed, adamantium-girded enclosure, which dwarfed any old-world cathedral in its spaciousness. Parallel sets of tracks hosted numerous trains from all across the continent. Wheatstone thought he recognized the Boreal Breeze from Montreal, the Orange Blossom Special from San Diego, the Raging Gator from St. Augustine, and the Happy Haciendas from Mexico City, among others. Arrivals and departures were perpetual, a constant flow of trains. And yet the air within the station remained fragrant and wholesome, thanks to the clean gravito-magnetic engines that pulled the various expresses.

Although a young man of only twenty-nine, and thus too youthful to more than dimly recall the era of coal-powered propulsion that had been the rule up until 1875, Wheatstone was a student of history sufficiently well-versed to realize that such a pristine environment had not always been associated with rail travel. His parents, for instance, would have been forced to endure the soot and smut and cinders belched by coal-burning steam engines, both while in transit and while hustling through the gritty, shadowy sheds that had served as terminals. How amazing were the bold advances of technology in but a single generation!

And how widely disseminated and now mostly taken for granted were those selfsame improvements!

And all these improvements could be laid ultimately at the feet of a genius named Cyrus Smith, president-for-life of Lincoln Island, and his many capable comrades-in-invention.

Hefting his single valise, Wheatstone leisurely traversed the space separating him from the nearest egress, threading his way among the many exotic specimens of humanity thronging the platforms. There were sheiks from the Holy Land, Zulus and Watusi from darkest Africa, Laplanders, Muscovites, Mongols, and Manchurians.

Lincolnopolis as a general rule during any period of the calendar attracted numerous representatives of every nation on the globe—diplomats, tourists, and business folk eager to experience the wonders of the city or to conduct negotiations or to facilitate trade. But this day was unlike any other, and had occasioned even greater numbers of foreign visitors. For this very day marked the inauguration of the grand festivities connected with the thirtieth anniversary of the founding of Lincoln Island. The celebrations had been heralded as fully the equal of any prior international exposition or fair, however elaborate, and perhaps would prove even more extravagant. Naturally, given the Iowans' reputation for startling displays of scientific prowess, the whole world was desirous of seeing how they would commemorate their third decade of existence.

But even more startling than the cosmopolitan mix of humans was the presence of innumerable ape servitors, all neatly garbed in red vests and pillbox hats, busy trundling steamer trunks, polishing brightwork, and sweeping the immaculate tiled floors. These intelligent quadrumanes belonged to the same race as the legendary Jupiter, the anthropoid servant who had been a loyal member of the household on the original Lincoln Island. Jupiter and his tribe had perished in the destruction of the ocean-girded Lincoln Island, but his cousins had been discovered on neighboring Tabor Island in subsequent expeditions to that region, adopted and brought back to North America.

Although not widely employed outside sovereign Iowa, the quadrumanes formed an essential component of that nation's working class.

As Wheatstone drew closer to his chosen exit, the travelers bunched into a line focused on the portal, one of many such queues. This line of arrivals moved with all expedition, however, and Wheatstone feared no delay, assuming that the ultracompetent Lincolnopolis officials had fully prepared themselves for the expected crush of visitors.

And when he drew even with the customs station, holding his credentials expectantly, he found his faith in the efficiency of the Lincoln Island government fully justified.

Teams of inspectors, their impressive white linen uniforms featuring the governmental crest that depicted the starfish-shaped outline of the original Lincoln Island, were rapidly and dispassionately going through the luggage of each visitor. While this procedure was under way, another official verified the identity of the person seeking entrance via his ordinator console.

Soon it was Wheatstone's turn. He surrendered his valise and handed over his passport. He watched as the ordinator operator—a competent-looking young fellow with a spray of freckles across his face lending a schoolboy charm to his person—expertly stroked the complicated controls studding the surface of the big mahogany cabinet that bore its proud brass plate identifying it as a Saml. Clemens & Co. Mark Two model.

Once the unique code attached to Wheatstone's citizenship in the United States had been translated into a format sensible to the ordinator's machine intelligence, the information was transmitted telegraphically to the central clearinghouse of such data. In less than a minute, the response returned, activating a piece of attached equipment that featured a scribing pen moving over a continuous sheet of paper. With remarkable speed, the pen engraved a likeness of Wheatstone with all the verisimilitude of any illustration from, say, *The London Illustrated News*! Following the portrait, the pen dictated some text.

Wheatstone marveled at the paper reproduction of his own open, ingenuous face, complete with handsome mustache and disordered shock of hair. Utterly uncanny, how this stored image had been transmitted over miles of wire so swiftly!

The ordinator technician ripped the inscribed paper off its roll and studied the picture and text, frequently glancing at Wheatstone's visage for purposes of comparison. At last he seemed satisfied, turning to Wheatstone with a smile and a handshake.

"Welcome to Lincoln Island, Mr. Wheatstone. I note that you are a journalist."

"Yes, indeed. I am employed by the *Boston Herald*. I have been dispatched to report on your grand anniversary celebrations."

"You'll need a press pass then. One further moment, please."

"Of course."

The second response to the ordinator operator's fiddling took but an additional ninety seconds, at the end of which a solid *thunk* signaled the arrival of a capsule delivered through the pneumatic-tube system that threaded all of Lincolnopolis. The capsule disgorged a wallet-sized, flexible sheet of adamantium inscribed using a diamond stylus with the particulars of Wheatstone's employment and the terms of his liberty in Lincolnopolis.

"Once you are settled into your hotel," said the customs official, "present this at the Bureau of Public Information at the intersection of Grant Boulevard and Glenarvan Way. They will have further instructions and counsel for you."

Wheatstone took the flexible rectangle of adamantium. "Thank you very much for your help. I hope your duties are not so burdensome that you cannot participate at some point in the festivities connected with this proud occasion."

The clerk shrugged. "That is as it may be. All citizens of Lincoln Island stand ready to render whatever our nation demands of us, happily and without cease."

"An admirable attitude. If only the members of some of Boston's trade unions exhibited the same selflessness, the *Herald* might be able to lower its price from a nickel to three cents once more."

Wheatstone collected his valise, neatly repacked, and strode off toward the broad exterior doors of the rail station. Within a few seconds, he found himself outside the crystal transportation palace, on the actual sidewalks of Lincolnopolis, drinking in the vistas of that magnificent city.

Avenues lined with stalwart buildings in marble, granite, and travertine stretched away radially from the hub of the train station. (Lincolnopolis had been laid out on an exceedingly rational plan based on certain of Fourier's proposals.) The wide sidewalks were thronged with bright-eyed, happy, strong-sinewed citizens of both sexes, all clad in pleasant modes of costume suitable for the Iowan spring climate; with awestruck tourists goggling at the sights; and with scuttling quadrumanes busy running errands for their masters.

The avenues themselves boasted a steady traffic of wheeled vehicles of every elaboration, all propelled by clean gravito-magnetic engines. The slices of sky visible above the urban canyons featured the occasional passing aircraft. So far the sciences of Lincoln Island had managed to permit the construction of only smallish atmospheric craft capable of hosting one or two riders at most, and not useful for much more than aerial observation or pleasure jaunts. But there was already talk in such gazettes as *Scientific Iowan* of scaling up these vessels into long-range behemoths that would revolutionize travel.

The overall effect of this panorama, Wheatstone thought, was to conjure up fancies of a classical Athens that had never fallen to savagery, but rather had been transformed by centuries of continuous progress into a veritable paradise on Earth! No wonder that all the countries of the globe admired Lincoln Island, courted her, purchased her manufactures, aped her social systems and customs, and licensed her technologies.

As Wheatstone hailed a passing jitney, he was already mentally casting the lead paragraphs of his first story, a paean to this tiny nation.

"Hotel Amiens, please."

"Sure thing, mister!"

The Hotel Amiens proved to be a superior establishment, from its natatorium and billiard rooms to its corps of quadrumane bellhops. Every room featured ordinator-mediated communication outlets and piped music from the central Lincolnopolis chamber orchestra, which performed twenty-four hours a day thanks to an extensive complement of musicians. Wheatstone silently praised the largesse of his flush employer, and began to entertain second thoughts about the wisdom of letting the price of a copy of the *Herald* revert to three cents.

After refreshing himself and replacing his travel-sweaty shirt collar and exchanging his informal checkered coat for a more somber black one, the young reporter set out for his appointment with the Bureau of Public Information.

The impressive columned government edifice at the corner of Grant and Glenarvan bore an inscription chiseled above its entrance: INFORMATION WISHES TO BECOME DISSEMINATED. As he climbed the broad steps to the heavy front doors, Wheatstone contemplated this sentiment insofar as it related to his own profession. It tallied neatly with his own feelings when, on prior occasions, he'd been confronted with large stories with great public impact that practically begged to be told. Wheatstone believed that a modern society demanded efficient and open channels of communication, and was grateful to see that the Iowans apparently felt the same.

Presentation of his adamantium press pass to a bureau concierge earned Wheatstone swift admission to the office of one Andrew Portland, an undersecretary responsible for foreign reporters. Portland sported a magnificent set of muttonchop whiskers and a vest-covered cannonball of a gut that hinted at certain large appetites. On the wall behind the undersecretary's desk hung a portrait of Cyrus Smith, president-for-life, looking fatherly and compassionate as he gazed off into some half-apprehended future.

Mixing probing questions with hearty chatter—Wheatstone

found himself talking at length about the charms of his fiancée, Miss Matilda Lodge—Portland eventually satisfied himself as to Wheatstone's bona fides.

"Well, Mr. Wheatstone," said the undersecretary, "I'm pleased to grant you the freedom of our city and countryside, with the exception of certain military installations. Of course, I expect you'll want to spend the majority of your time at the exposition itself. Over five hundred acres of exhibits located on the outskirts of town and easily reached by public transportation. You'll hardly be able to exhaust the various pavilions during your stay here, and your readers will be insatiable, I'm sure, for all the details you can provide. Of course, if you want to offer some local coloration and context by venturing out to some of our model farms and smaller villages, I will certainly understand. You may contact my office for any help or advice you may need in making those arrangements."

Wheatstone rose, sensing the interview was over, and extended his hand. "Thank you very much, Mr. Portland. I'm sure that with your assistance I will be able to convey a vivid sense of Lincoln Island's unique character to the *Herald*'s readers."

Out on the street once more, Wheatstone pondered his next actions. As the hour was well past noon and he had not eaten since breakfast on the train, he considered a meal quite appropriate. With the aid of a passing citizen, he managed to find a nearby chophouse, where he enjoyed a thick T-bone steak, an enormous Iowa spud, and a pitcher of beer. Pleasantly sated, smoking a postprandial cigar, Wheatstone let his gaze rest benevolently on his fellow diners, many of whom were handsomely accoutred Negroes.

One of the founders of North America's Lincoln Island in 1868 had been Cyrus Smith's manservant, Neb, who had always been an equal member in the workings of the original castaway colony. Consequently, Negroes had enjoyed full suffrage in Lincoln Island from the country's inception. This model of interracial equality had served as a beacon to the United States during Reconstruction, a painful period.

As a northerner, Wheatstone had been raised in a liberal tradition, and naturally regarded Negroes as equals. But really there was scant to distinguish his liberal attitude nowadays from that of any of his right-thinking peers from below the Mason-Dixon Line.

And this doctrine of the universal rights of mankind had been spread further by a policy that Lincoln Island had begun promulgating once its ascendancy had been cemented. Any nation that wished to trade with Lincoln Island and benefit from its technologies had to eliminate legislated racial biases within its own borders. With this combination of carrot and stick, the Iowans had managed to transform much of the world's attitude in only three short decades.

Incredible, thought Wheatstone, how much a small set of determined, clear-sighted men could achieve when they put their shoulders to the wheel of progress. He spared an admiring look for the portrait of Cyrus Smith above the bar of the chophouse before getting to his feet—a little unsteadily, it must be admitted—and heading outside.

Although the Hotel Amiens and its luxurious bed beckoned for a nap, Wheatstone hitched up his braces and resolved to head out to the fairgrounds for his first look at the exposition that had drawn him and so many others hither. It was no difficult feat to hop aboard one of the many special bunting-decorated trolleys ferrying people for free to the fairgrounds, and within half an hour Wheatstone was disembarking with dozens of other eager sightseers at the gates of the exposition.

The massive entrance was flanked by two groups of statuary depicting the founders of the republic. On Wheatstone's left loomed the titanic figures of Cyrus Smith, the lusty sailor named Pencroff, and humble Neb. At their feet lay the equally gigantic form of Top, Smith's loyal dog. Matching the formation on the other side of the gates were representations of journalist Gideon Spillet, Ayrton the ex-mutineer, and young student Harbert Brown. The animal totem in their tableau was Jup, the original quadrumane.

It was these six brave souls who, having found themselves dumped, weaponless and without tools or provisions, from a runaway hot-air balloon upon the bountiful but rugged Lincoln Island, had, through sheer ingenuity, perseverance, and hard manual labor, created a small utopia which, regrettably, met its end due to a volcanic explosion.

All six of the men, Wheatstone knew, were still alive; Smith was the oldest at some seventy-eight years of age, and Brown was the youngest at forty-eight. Together, they formed the ruling council of the current Lincoln Island, with Smith as first among equals. Wheatstone felt particular affection for the figure of Spillet, naturally, who had turned the *New Lincoln Herald* into one of the most formidable gazettes in the world.

Joining the mass of his gay fellows—women in long gowns and ostrich-plumed hats, children in knee pants and caps, men handsomely suited—Wheatstone soon passed through the gates and was greeted by an astonishing vista. On these several hundred acres, the magnificent Iowans had constructed what amounted to a second city, one dedicated not to mere habitation but to the nobler cause of displaying the wonders of Iowan science and the promises it held for an even brighter future. The architecture of this city-within-a-city recalled such fabled past metropolises as Babylon, Nineveh, and Alexandria, but with a modern slant.

Feeling somewhat at sea, Wheatstone resolved to attend the introductory lecture advertised to occur half-hourly in the hall nearest the gates.

Once seated on a velvet-covered chair in a large darkened amphitheater with scores of others, Wheatstone was treated to a show of magic-lantern slides accompanied by a very entertaining speech given by one of the many trained actors who served as guides to the fair. He thrilled once more to the famous tale of the castaways, an abbreviated saga, followed by an account of the subsequent thirty years. The act of Congress in 1875 which had reluctantly but decisively allowed the petition of the Iowans asking to secede from the rest of the United States; the attempted invasion of the fledgling country by a cabal of European powers, launched from their base in Canada, which had been efficiently and mercilessly repelled by uncanny weapons of a heretofore unseen type; the signing of various peace treaties and the establishment of Iowan hegemony in several areas of international commerce and trade; the immigration policies that encouraged savants from all corners of the globe to flock to Lincoln Island—

At the close of half an hour, Wheatstone felt once more the full weight of the marvelous story. What a golden age had dawned for mankind with the foundation of this small but potent nation!

After this, Wheatstone toured several exhibits, taking copious notes. From the Hall of Gravito-Magnetism to the Chamber of Agricultural Engineering; from the Arcade of Electrical Propagation to the Gallery of Pneumatics—one exhibit after another demonstrated the astounding achievements of the Iowans and promised even more astonishments to come.

Finally, though, even the exciting speculations failed to keep at bay Wheatstone's natural fatigue after such a busy day, and, after consuming a light snack of squab and sausages from a fairground booth, he returned reluctantly to his hotel room.

There, to his surprise, a blinking light on the ordinator panel in his room signaled that a message awaited him. Triggering the output of the electronic pen produced a cryptic note that lacked all attribution of sender, as if such information had been deliberately stripped away.

Mr. Wheatstone—have you noticed the absence of a certain name from these festivities? I refer to the appellation of "Nemo." Would you know more? Meet me this evening after midnight at the Gilded Cockerel.

As a journalist, Wheatstone was used to such anonymous "tips." In the majority of cases, they led precisely nowhere. But every now and then, such secret disclosures did produce large stories of consequence. The young reporter could feel his blood thrill at the possibility that he would bag such a "scoop" from this message. This was an outcome he had hardly dared hope for when he had received his current assignment. But if he could manage to distinguish his reportage from all the other laudatory profiles that would be filed from this dateline, both he and the *Boston Herald* would benefit immensely. And proprietor William Randolph Hearst could be most generous to his successful employees.

Checking his pocket watch, Wheatstone determined that he could snatch a few hours' sleep before the rendezvous with the mysterious informant. But before he stretched himself out, he fired off an ordinator message of his own, to his ladylove back in the land of the bean and the cod.

Dear Matilda—I have arrived safely in Lincoln Island and already find myself embroiled in matters of some significance. If I succeed in making my name as I suspect I will with this assignment, perhaps you and I may finally get married. As you well know, my resolve not to ride on the Lodge family coattails necessitates my obtaining a certain stature within my chosen profession before any nuptials can proceed. Please send all your kindest thoughts my way.

Having dispatched this message, Wheatstone stripped down to his undergarments, set the alarm clock by his bed to sound at 11:30 P.M., and was soon deeply asleep.

The clanging of the alarm seemed subjectively to occur almost simultaneously with his descent into the realm of Morpheus, and Wheatstone awoke with a start. Yet it was but a matter of minutes for him to refresh himself, dress, and descend to the lobby of the Hotel Amiens. There, he inquired of the concierge the address of the Gilded Cockerel. The rigorously circumspect fellow looked askance at Wheatstone, as if his query were somehow improper, but supplied the address nonetheless.

Outside, the thronged streets of Lincolnopolis were well-lighted not only by the permanent electric standards, but also with numerous strands of colored bulbs celebrating the exposition. Wheatstone had no trouble hailing a jitney, and soon found himself standing outside the door to the Gilded Cockerel.

Judging by its exterior, the tavern, situated in a shadowy, miry lane totally incongruous with the rest of Lincolnopolis's civic splendor, seemed somewhat louche. But Wheatstone had been obliged to frequent worse places, and he entered boldly.

The interior of the establishment confirmed Wheatstone's original estimation. Gimcrack decorations could not conceal the shoddiness of the furnishings. Odors of spilled ale and less savory substances clogged Wheatstone's nostrils. Raucous laughter and shouts indicated a total lack of public decorum. But what was more off-putting than any of the sensory assaults were the patrons of the Gilded Cockerel. To a man—and there were no women present—the customers were clothed as total fops. The amount of lace and brocade present would have outfitted the vanished court of Louis XIV.

Wheatstone knew instantly that he had fallen in with sodomites. Their generic resemblance to the infamous Englishman Oscar Wilde was indisputable.

Bracing his spine, careful not to make any physical contact with the seated, simpering deviants, Wheatstone advanced toward the barkeep, a burly chap whose sleeveless shirt afforded a view of his numerous tattoos.

"I am supposed to meet someone here tonight."

The barkeep's mellifluous voice was utterly at odds with his appearance. "What's your name, honey?"

"Mr. Bingham Wheatstone."

"Ah, of course. Your date's awaiting you in one of the private rooms. Last door on the right, dearie."

The nominated door opened to Wheatstone's touch and he stepped inside. Not electricity, but a single candle illuminated the small room, in which could be seen a rickety table, two hard chairs, an uncorked, half-full bottle of wine, and a single glass. A man stood with his back to the door. At his feet bulked a large carpetbag.

Hearing Wheatstone's entrance, the man turned, and Wheatstone could not suppress his exclamation.

"Harbert Brown!"

"Quiet, you dolt! I trust everyone here, but there's still no need to announce my presence to the world. Now, have a seat."

Wheatstone took one of the chairs, using the time to study the familiar yet altered face of Brown. The man's lips appeared to be painted, his eyelids daubed with kohl. Taking a moment now to light a slim cigar, Brown exhibited a limp-wristed effeminacy. Although he was the youngest member of Lincoln Island's ruling council, Brown was still middle-aged, with all the attendant sagging flesh of that stage of life. He had been an adolescent stripling during the castaways' adventures, and today his unnatural airs reeked of a jaded degeneracy.

Wheatstone ventured to paint the picture presented by Brown's appearance in the most charitable light.

"Sir, you have adopted a most convincing disguise—"

"Oh, you know as well as I do that's stuff and nonsense, Mr. Wheatstone. This is the real me. It's when I appear in public as a moral and responsible politician that I am actually in disguise. And what a trial it has been, maintaining that facade all these years. Little did I imagine when I became Pencroff's catamite as a youth that I was embarking on a tedious charade that would last decades."

Wheatstone felt his mind whirling in a tornado of overturned conceptions. "But what are you implying?"

Brown languidly expelled a cloud of cigar smoke. "Need I spell it out for you, Mr. Wheatstone? What kind of relationship did you suspect existed between a lusty sailor and a young boy who inexplicably accompanied him everywhere? Pencroff and I were lovers during our imprisonment in Richmond, Virginia, and we remained so for three years on Lincoln Island after our balloon escape. In fact, in the absence of females, I was able to provide carnal solace to all our little band during that period. Although none of the other men were bent that way originally, they all gladly succumbed to my charms when their natural urges reached a certain crisis point."

"But, no, this can't be—"

"Oh, don't be so shocked, Mr. Wheatstone. It's not becoming in a supposedly seasoned reporter. And anyway, this is not the matter I invited you here to discuss. The sexual habits of Lincoln Island's rulers have little import outside the narrow confines of our tiny elite. No, the topic today is the very future of human progress. You see, Mr. Wheatstone, I fear that Lincoln Island has become a positive blockade to technological advancement, and that its continued dominance in the global scientific arena will eventually doom mankind and actually induce a long, hard fall back to savagery."

"How can you assert such an impossibility, sir? It contradicts everything I know."

Brown sighed, took a seat, poured himself some wine without offering Wheatstone any, sipped, and then said, "Ah, that is the problem, Bing. May I call you 'Bing'? You most assuredly do not know everything. What, for instance, do you make of the name of Captain Nemo?"

"This is the name you mentioned in your message to me. Well, I seem to recall that a brigand once roved the seven seas under that nom de guerre, harassing ships and so forth. Were his quixotic campaigns not chronicled in some musty old volume early in this century? *Beleaguered Below the Seas*, or some such title? If this is the fellow you refer to, his relevance is not immediately apparent."

"Indeed, you recall the broad, distorted outlines of Nemo's career. I'm surprised you apprehend even that much. During our Robinsonade upon Lincoln Island, Nemo had already been absent from the public scene for thirty years. Nowadays he is hardly even a phantom. And much of that public nescience regarding him and his works is deliberate, fostered by us here. Yet such was not the case three decades ago, when his name was still on the lips of the cognoscenti. You can imagine our surprise when we discovered this notorious criminal genius to be a fellow resident of our little island."

"He was cast away, like yourselves, then?"

"Not at all. He had retreated to the island purposefully, to spend his final bitter days in peace and seclusion. We witnessed his death from natural causes, and buried him there."

"How then can his name play any part in the current discussion?"

"Nemo was a wizard, Bing. And he was buried in his wizardly craft, the *Nautilus*, a submersible vessel. We sank it with his corpse, as per his last wishes. But the trouble—the trouble is, the *Nautilus* did not remain sunk."

"I am beginning to see the vaguest hints of the direction in which your story is heading. Pray proceed."

Harbert Brown took a long meditative swig of wine before continuing. The guttering candle caused shadows to warp eerily across his bleary-eyed visage.

"Can you envision the ambitious dreams and lofty expectations which the six of us repatriated survivors held, once we were transplanted to Iowan soil, Bing? On primitive Lincoln Island we had struggled against all odds and created a semblance of civilization out of nothing but our wits and the abundant raw materials present. True, we had benefited from the secret interventions of Nemo at certain crucial junctures. And even now, with his final gift of a casket of riches, he was underwriting our mainland venture. But despite his bolstering, we had firm faith that we six alone could establish a beacon of superior living in the midst of these United States. Imagine then how our hopes were dashed when so much went wrong in the first few years. Crop failures, natural disasters, cutthroat competition from neighbors, prejudiced merchants who refused to deal with us because of the presence of Negroes such as Neb, governmental restrictions, a poor quality of lazy immigrant workers from the sewers of Europe—all these factors and more conspired to render our utopia a stillborn shambles. And at the head of it, our leader, Cyrus Smith, despondent and despairing for the first time in his life. Now you must realize one thing, Bing. Cyrus is not the genius the world thinks him. He is clever, and well-versed in engineering lore. But he hasn't an original bone in his body. He can re-create, but not create."

"But all the flood of inventions that have come from his fertile brain—"

"They did not come from Cyrus Smith's brain, Bing! They came from Nemo's!"

"You mean—?"

"Yes! In 1870, using the last of our wealth in a desperate gamble, we mounted an expedition back to the site of the vanished Lincoln Island, back to that small remnant crag of rock from which we were rescued. We sent a primitive submersible down to the seafloor—providentially shallow—and found the *Nautilus*, miraculously intact. Pencroff in his undersea suit entered through her open hatch, and managed to get her miraculous engines going again. Luckily, the indestructible machines had shut themselves down in a programmed fashion when we scuttled her. We crewed the *Nautilus* and brought her back to the East Coast. There, we lifted her into dry dock, sundered her into sections, and carted her back to Iowa. Then began in secret the plundering of her real wealth, all the marvelous inventions she contained."

"Suppose I credit this tale, Mr. Brown. What of it? You have disclosed the ignoble reality behind the myth of Cyrus Smith's genius. I suppose we could concoct a three-day scandal out of such material and sell a few extra papers. But how does this revelation materially affect the grandeur of what you Iowans have achieved? And how can you possibly deduce the end of civilization from your tawdry tale?"

Brown leaned forward intently, all foppishness banished by earnestness. "Are you the same fellow who wrote that series of articles entitled 'Some Thoughts toward the Manifest Destiny of Our Arriving Twentieth Century'? That's why I picked you, Bing, because of the speculative acumen you exhibited in those writings. You seemed to recognize that the continued success of our present planetary culture is based on a perpetual flow of advancements. There can be no such thing as holding still. The growing interconnectedness of the world, the demands of a surging population, the rising expectations of the common man as to what life will bring him—all these factors and more conspire to demand a flood of fresh inventions from the world's laboratories. And the world looks to Lincoln Island to lead the way. If we were to stagnate, the worldwide system would collapse in a Malthusian disaster of rioting, starvation, and savagery."

"Agreed. But surely the risk of stagnation is next to nil—"

Brown banged a fist upon the table, sending his tumbler of wine toppling. "Don't you get it, Bing? We've copied and slightly improved all of Nemo's technology. If I may coin a term, we applied 'reverse-engineering' to his devices. Smith's talents were perfectly adequate for that. But we don't understand the first principles of any of it. We've engaged scores of brilliant men from around the globe—Edison, Bell, Ford, Michelson, the Curies, and many more whom I could name—and none of them have had an ounce of success at unriddling, say, gravito-magnetics. We're like primitive witch doctors re-creating effects by following formulae passed down from the gods."

"Surely you judge yourself too harshly," Wheatstone protested.

"Not at all! It's taken every iota of ingenuity we possess just to translate Nemo's devices into automobiles and trains and such. That's why large-scale manned flight has baffled us. Nemo's engines were never designed for such applications. And we've just about reached the limit of what we can mine from the last scraps of the *Nautilus*. But what's even worse is how we've fatally detoured the destined course of scientific history. By futilely investing generations of talent in following Nemo's bizarre avenues, we've allowed the foundations of science circa 1870 to crumble and molder. The world of 1898 is not what it should have been. There is no organic path left for us to follow from here out. To reorganize the scientific establishment that existed thirty years ago is nigh impossible. Yet our only hope for the future is to attempt such a thing. But we cannot even make such a last-ditch effort until we first tear down the sickly monster we have erected. And your help is essential for that task."

Wheatstone felt torn between a host of contradictory impulses. His affection for what Lincoln Island had created vied with his desire to make a journalistic splash. His belief in Brown's sincerity—the man appeared to truly believe everything he had said—warred with his incredulity at the enormity of the long-standing hoax.

"How can I accept what you tell me without some kind of proof, sir?"

Brown got tipsily to his feet and secured the neglected carpetbag from the corner of the room. He hoisted it to the tabletop, unclasped it, and reached within. From the bag he lifted a fantastical helmet with thick glass plate for a visor, bearing an ornate capital N. This he thumped down on the table.

"Here is one of the diving helmets from the *Nautilus*."

Brown examined the headgear with interest. "Intriguing, sir. But this could be some factitious cheat intended to deceive me."

"Thought you might say that." Brown reached again into the bag and removed another exhibit.

Wheatstone's knowledge of human skeletal anatomy had been buffed by various professional interviews with leading anthropologists. The skull now flaunted before him displayed odd configurations of bone that seemed to hint at larger mental proportions than the human norm.

"Yes," Brown confirmed, "this is Nemo's very skull. The fishes had picked him quite clean by the time we returned. He claimed to be an Indian prince, but I suspect that he was much more. Perhaps a visitor from the future, perhaps a stranded traveler from another star. Or perhaps a human sport, a forerunner of some species of mankind yet to come. In any case, he possessed qualities of mind the likes of which are all too seldom encountered."

The skull constituted a shocking weight in the pan of the scales that favored Brown's story. But still Wheatstone hesitated. So much was riding on his decision—

Brown sensed this hesitancy. "Damn it, man! I had been hoping to avoid this, but I can see I've got no choice. Come with me. I'm taking you to see the carcass of the *Nautilus* itself!"

Brooking no resistance, Brown grabbed Wheatstone's sleeve with one hand and his bottle of wine with the other, and they departed the Gilded Cockerel.

Outside, Brown led the way. He continued to swig from his bottle, muttering all the while.

"We're rotten at the core, Wheatstone! Nemo was the worm in the apple of the original Lincoln Island, and he remains so today. Our whole existence is predicated on a lie!"

Wheatstone refrained, wisely he thought, from either agreement or disagreement.

After half an hour of progress through the deserted streets of a manufactory district, the pair arrived at an innocuous-looking warehouse. Brown pulled Wheatstone down an alley and around to a side door.

"No one comes here any more. The *Nautilus* was stripped long ago, its components distributed to various laboratories. We should be perfectly safe venturing inside."

"I take it then that you are playing a lone hand. You have no fellow conspirators to rely on?"

"Hah! Who among those self-satisfied drones wants to rock the boat? They're all frightened old men. But poor little Harbert Brown, the baby of the group, still has some hot blood in his veins! They'll all be dead soon, the duffers! Not me! And I don't want to live in a desolate future. That's why I'm doing this, Bing!"

After employing a key on the padlocked door, Brown led Wheatstone into the stygian interior. "There should be an electric-light switch somewhere near this entrance— Aha!"

The blaze of illumination that flooded forth following Brown's simple action caused Wheatstone to fling up an arm across his face against the glare. When his eyes had adjusted, he lowered his limb.

The vast open floor of the warehouse held just what had been promised. Like a slaughtered whale strewn across a beach, the segments of Nemo's wonder vessel reared ceiling-ward. Steel arches and ribs trailed bits of truncated wiring and pipes and bits of decoration. The shattered pieces of the *Nautilus*'s staterooms—slabs of mahogany and tile, broken chandeliers and armoires—were heaped in a corner. The whole panorama was morbid and desolate in the extreme.

Wheatstone moved forward for closer inspection, but was arrested in his tracks by a shout.

"Stop right there! We are from the council!"

Across the room, framed in another doorway, stood a short, gnarled, yet feisty old man surrounded by quadrumanes. The surly apes wore not the vests of their servant cousins but rather leather brassards, and carried truncheons.

"Pencroff!" exclaimed Harbert Brown.

"Yes, you cocksure little fool. Did you actually think your plotting went unnoticed? We've known all along about your treacherous scheme. And now you'll have to face the consequences. Secure them, boys!"

At Pencroff's command the apes bounded forward and cruelly pinioned Wheatstone and Brown. Within seconds the prisoners had been placed in the claustrophobic back of a Black Maria, which motored off.

Brown was too devastated to speak, and Wheatstone found himself similarly dejected. How had he come to such a fix? Ambition had undone him. He could not delude himself that high-minded principles had played any part in his involvement.

Their windowless conveyance eventually came to a stop. The rear doors opened, and a rough-handed quadrumane escort hustled Brown and Wheatstone out and into a new building. Inside, the conspirators were separated. Soon, much to his surprise, Wheatstone found himself deposited in a spacious library. His animal captors left him then, and he collapsed into a chair.

Not many minutes passed before the library door clicked open. Wheatstone shot quivering to his feet and found himself face to face with the president-for-life of Lincoln Island.

At age seventy-eight, Cyrus Smith still possessed all the charisma of his youth. His stern, bearded countenance radiated a patriarchal aura not unmixed with a sly humor. He smiled at Wheatstone and extended a hand.

"Come, come, Mr. Wheatstone, you're not among ogres here. If at all possible, no harm will come to you. I think you'll find us more than reasonable when it comes to straightening out this imbroglio you've stumbled into."

"Sir, you have foisted an imposture upon the world!"

"Have I, Mr. Wheatstone? Yes, I suppose I have. But consider the benefits that have accrued thanks to my little charade. The living standards of much of the world's population are higher than they've ever been before. Cowed by the weapons we have liberated from the *Nautilus*, the nations of the globe have learned to value diplomacy over aggression. The Sons of Ham are fully enfranchised and valued, both in North America and elsewhere. I venture to say that this version of 1898 is, on the whole, a more just and admirable one than any other merely hypothetical branch of history that would have resulted had Lincoln Island never existed."

"But your paradise is balanced upon the tip of a needle! It takes all your efforts to keep it from toppling. And as Brown has revealed to me, you are soon to run out of strength."

"Ah, poor Brown! We will see that he gets the kindly care and attention he needs to overcome his alcohol-sodden delusions. No one is going to harm him. He is one of us."

"Are you claiming that his representation of the situation is incorrect?"

"No, not at all. But Harbert was not privy to our secret search, a quest that has now borne fruit."

"What are you saying? Have you found a man to replace Nemo? Someone who blends his practical and theoretical skills? Someone to continue his researches, and stave off that day when science reaches its natural limits?"

"Indeed. You have a fine way with words, Mr. Wheatstone. I'm certain you will do justice to the exclusive interview we intend to grant you with our new savior."

Exclusive interview? Wheatstone began to feel for the first time in hours that he might yet emerge from this deadly affair with both his hide and reputation intact—perhaps even enhanced.

"Would you care to meet him now?"

"Why, yes, if the hour is not too late."

"Not at all. Our new comrade is almost superhuman in his endurance and vital spirits."

Smith used an ordinator to issue his summons. Within a few minutes, a man strode boldly into the library. And what a figure of a man! Of middle height and geometric breadth, his figure was a regular trapezium, with the greatest of its parallel sides formed by the line of his shoulders. On this line attached by a robust neck there rose an enormous spheroidal head—the head of a bull, but a bull with an intelligent face. Eyes which at the least opposition would glow like coals of fire, and above them a permanent contraction of the superciliary muscle, an invariable sign of extreme energy. Short hair, slightly woolly, with metallic highlights; large chest rising and falling like a smith's bellow; arms, hands, legs, and feet, all worthy of the trunk. No mustaches, no whiskers, but a large American goatee.

Even Cyrus Smith seemed to shrink a little in the presence of this newcomer, who remained ominously silent. But Smith soon recovered himself and said, "Mr. Wheatstone, may I present our new friend, Robur. With his aid, I believe we can conquer all such problems as our aerial delays at last. With Robur at our side, progress need never end."

Wheatstone shook Robur's hand and felt a galvanic charge.

The young reporter suspected that things were really going to get interesting now.

The protagonist of this story is me—to some degree.

Like most U.S. citizens, I was traumatized by the events of September 11, 2001. Nor have the subsequent years proven any more soothing or less ethically problematical.

I try my hardest to parse all the conflicting ideologies, assign all the correct moral shadings to all the actors in the global struggle, and extend compassion even to those trying to destroy all I love.

But you know what?

Sometimes, like Michael Valentine Smith, I'd like to have the power to just point my finger at someone and send them straight to hell.

Shadowboxer

Generally speaking, I need only three minutes of concentrated attention to kill someone by staring at them. If I'm feeling under the weather, or if my mind is preoccupied with other matters—you know how your mind can obsess about trivial things sometimes—it might take five minutes for my power to have its effect. On the other hand, if I focus intensely on my victim, I can get the job done in as little as ninety seconds.

Another factor determining the speediness of my powers is the constitution of my victim. As you might imagine, the elderly and frail and ailing require less effort to kill than the hale and hearty and young.

But no one is immune to my gaze. At least, no one I have yet encountered.

And I've encountered plenty.

* * *

Now the nation is at war. Or so we're told. I guess that changes everything. A person like me becomes much more important.

* * *

Sometimes it feels like I've always lived in these few rooms. But I know I've been penned up here for only a couple of years. Still, that's a long time to go without seeing another person, even for a loner like me. It's a wonder I'm still sane.

If indeed I am.

* * *

The first time I got photos of kids as part of my killing assignment, I staged a strike for three days. I wouldn't use my power at all. There was no punishment meted out by my unseen employers, no diminishment of my limited perks. I couldn't figure out what their intentions were, how they hoped to coerce me. But then on the fourth day the media did their job for them. I read in *U.S. News and World Report* about a bus-bombing in Israel. Thirteen people killed and dozens wounded. The bomber had been a teenage girl. Her photo had been in the pile.

When they resubmitted the photos of the kids, minus the girl's, I went straight to work on them.

* * *

I call all of the different guys who speak to me over the intercom connecting me with the outside world "Dave." Occasionally, a woman is on duty, and I call her "Dave," too. She's fractionally nicer than the guys, in some indefinable sense, but still pretty blank. They refuse to tell me their real names, of course, or even to supply a friendly alias, so this is my countermeasure. I reduce them all to the same individual. They're just following orders, I know, when they withhold their names. But still, you'd think they'd have some human feeling for their prisoner. I'm helping them, after all, aren't I? Doing good for my country? I suppose everyone's nervous about me taking some kind of revenge against any of my captors whose real name is revealed, if I ever escape. But they don't have to worry about that. I haven't killed anyone for personal reasons since I became a professional assassin. Killing someone with an emotional or personal connection to me was a sure way to get caught eventually, I believed. Therefore, I have learned to rein in my natural emotional reactions to insults and slights and aggression.

As an adult, committing murder with my peculiar talent meant money, not revenge. (Now, they tell me, my lethal actions mean the survival of Western civilization.) Killing randomly or for personal reasons would have violated my code of survival.

Having a code is important to me.

* * *

Sometimes I think about my parents. I was an only child, but they didn't dote on me. I was just an accepted part of the household furnishings, like the couch or the television. They weren't mean to me, just indifferent.

Maybe that treatment had something to do with how I am today.

Still, I never bore them any ill will, and certainly never thought once about using my power on them.

They're still alive and well, as far as I know.

* * *

I don't know where my current living quarters are located. Once I was kidnapped—by a squad of rough men in my darkened bedroom; I couldn't see a thing—I was brought here drugged into unconsciousness. The place is a suite of five rooms, not spartan, not luxurious, but rather like the rooms in a decent chain hotel. There are no windows, naturally. Something about the atmosphere, the tasteless processed air, leads me to believe that I am deep underground, in some government bunker. The perfect silence contributes to that impression as well. Although for all I know, I could be on the fiftieth floor of some urban tower, immured behind yards of soundproofing. Or in a cabin in the middle of some federal wilderness area. Or on an abandoned oil platform out at sea.

I have a very nice bedroom, a living room, an exercise room, a kitchen, and a game room. The furniture is all quite comfortable. Oh, and of course a quite satisfactory bathroom. I guess that makes six rooms, but I don't think the bathroom is conventionally counted in real estate descriptions.

The living room contains a TV, but the set receives no broadcast or cable channels. I can use it only with the attached DVD player or Xbox. I have a computer, but no Internet connection. I'm using that machine to keep this journal. The game room features a dartboard and a Ping-Pong table. Being alone, I don't get much use out of the table tennis setup, but I've gotten pretty damn good with the darts.

The whole place is, I'm certain, wired to the max. Cameras and microphones record my every action around the clock. The tapes must be excruciatingly boring for any Dave delegated to monitor them.

When I'm not performing my assigned killings, all I do is lounge around trying to keep myself moderately entertained. I cook most of my own meals, using the kitchen and the supplies delivered while I am locked into my bedroom at specific times. (The intercom orders me to retreat to the bedroom, and the door is locked by remote control, a solenoid thunking the bolt home. I have never tried to see what would happen if I disobeyed.) I can order out if I want. The franchised pizza and fried chicken and tacos arrive hot and fresh, which I suppose eliminates the possibility that I'm held in some remote area. Unless of course they've gone to the trouble to duplicate the kitchens and staffs of those fast-food joints right outside my door so as to conceal any clues to my real whereabouts from me. I wouldn't put that past them.

All I have to do to get these meals is ask politely over the intercom that connects me with my unseen captors. I can't conduct frivolous conversations over that channel, but the Daves will attend to my legitimate requests. They'll provide me with books and magazines, too.

No newspapers, though. The photos in newspapers are often too recent, and could be dangerous.

* * *

Of course you wonder about sex. I'm a normal guy in my early thirties, so I have the usual urges. I jerk off a lot in the dark. Maybe they've got infrared capabilities in their cameras and can see me. So what?

I'm only human, after all.

* * *

The way I was found out was this: Van Tranh had me do a job for a politician. Then news of my existence filtered into government circles, and my abduction was practically guaranteed.

I would still be free if only criminals knew about me.

* * *

My power manifested itself for the first time when I entered puberty. Just like Carrie, right?

I was a wimpy little kid, always getting picked on. Bullies seemed to gravitate toward me, happy and eager to punch the shit out of me. I never did anything to deserve their ire, except for existing. Just like I never did anything special to gain my power. In both cases, it's just the fluky way the universe works. I understand and accept that completely.

So the year I was thirteen the particular bane of my schoolday existence was this porky six-footer named Tony Grasso. Tony had been held back more than once, and now stood out among the rest of his classmates like Andre the Giant among a reunion of Munchkin actors. The day I killed Tony, he had cornered me in the lavatory and given my head a thorough rinsing in the toilet, before laughingly departing with my new calculator in his pocket. I didn't mind the dunking as much as I resented the loss of my calculator to such an oaf, especially since I was certain Tony would be unable even to find the on switch.

After I had cleaned myself up as best I could, I went to my next class, and there was Tony, leering at me and silently challenging me to rat him out. But of course I did no such thing. Instead, I took a seat as far away from him as I could, intending to focus on the class and enjoy the teaching. The class was math, and I liked it a lot.

But I found myself unable to concentrate on the teacher's presentation. I couldn't take my eyes off Tony's hateful profile. (Seeing my victims in profile, I later learned, was not as effective as seeing them full in the face.) And in my raging mind, I couldn't help picturing him dying in a hundred different ways.

I pictured Tony torn apart by wolves. I pictured him struck by cars. I pictured him impaled on the spiked fence that surrounded the local library. I pictured him writhing from poison. And so on.

I had always had a good imagination. And all these images were as vivid and real as my powerful imagination could make them. In fact, I felt as if I were actually witnessing Tony's multiple deaths, not just day-dreaming them, as if the scenes were playing out before my eyes.

Anyway, after about five minutes of this morbid reverie, I saw Tony keel over onto his desk without making a sound—except for the thump of his head—before bonelessly sliding to the floor. Girls shrieked, boys jumped up, and the teacher dashed out for help.

But there was nothing anyone could do. Tony was quite dead.

His autopsy revealed a fatal congenital heart defect, but one that no prior exam had ever discovered.

For a while, I believed that the whole gruesome affair was sheer coincidence. My imagining Tony dead could have had nothing to do with his actual death.

But it took only a few more experiments to prove to my own satisfaction that I had killed Tony.

Of course, I made sure that those subsequent victims were not my fellow classmates. Even at age thirteen, I knew that a rash of deaths among my peers would've alerted even the most skeptical investigator. Bums and strangers, clerks, a nanny in the park, and a policeman or two.

They all got congenital heart defects from me. Or fatal aneurysms.

I couldn't predict which defect would arise from my evil eye, but it was always one or the other.

***

Did I mention my apartment has no mirrors or other reflective surfaces in it?

***

The question of who exactly my captors represent offers me endless material for speculation.

The nature of all my victims since coming here convinces me that my talents are currently being employed by the government of the United States of America. But which agency?

The CIA? The FBI? The NSA? Homeland Security? Or some even more covert set of initials? Maybe I'm under the jurisdiction of some branch of the military. Am I an honorary Marine or Seal by now?

Will I be freed with medals and a letter of commendation once the war on terror is over? And when exactly will that day come? Does the president know about me? Or am I some special project overseen by some unelected bureaucrat, to maintain ultimate deniability higher up the chain of command? Which black budget contains the minimal expenses connected with my upkeep? Am I listed as general maintenance on some anonymous submarine? Or perhaps as a box of six-hundred-dollar hammers? I don't suppose I'll ever find out.

More intriguingly, I spend a lot of time asking myself whether I agree with the uses to which my talents are being put. It might very well be that for the first time in my adult life, I am actually performing some selfless acts and helping with the preservation of my nation. Would I have volunteered for such duties if I had been approached openly? Or would I have disdained any such exercise of my powers in support of the national interests, in favor of the pampered life I once led?

Again, it's hard to answer such a hypothetical question. I can only confront and judge my actions as they currently exist, under the current conditions.

Most days, I find I'm actually a trifle proud of what I'm doing. (Although sometimes I sink into a kind of numb apathy at the unvarying nature of my kills.) Maybe this is just a rationalization I have to maintain in order not to hate myself.

Discussing such matters with my captors might help. But this is not a luxury I am permitted.

* * *

I think my talent is one that everyone imagines they would like to have.

But believe me, it's not really that wonderful of a gift.

* * *

Van Tranh was my boss from when I was twenty-two until I was taken by the government. He was an Asian criminal big shot. I met him at the funeral of some people I had helped. I got into a conversation with him. He remarked on the uncanny way that someone connected with the funeral had died. He said how happy and grateful he was that that person had met his untimely death. Somehow I found myself spilling my secret to him; it was the first time I had ever told anyone what I could do. Amazingly, Van expressed no disbelief in my powers. Some traditions from his heritage and ancient culture conduced him to believe me. He asked me if I wanted a job.

I had never gone to college after high school. Although I was a smart kid, I found that I had no ambition, couldn't sustain any goals. I blame that attitude on my powers. The arbitrary nature of death, as exemplified by my own abilities, left me feeling that life could end at any time, and that nothing was worth struggling for.

So I told Van yes, I'd like a job.

I became his secret hit man. I killed anyone he asked me to. Mostly fellow criminals, but quite often not.

The money was very, very good. And I lived a peaceful, satisfied life.

* * *

No Dave ever uses my name when hailing me over the intercom. I suppose they are only following orders in this regard, too. Instead, they simply call out, "Attention!" Some Daves bark out the word as a command, while others are more polite, even saying, "Attention, please." The woman is one of the polite ones.

Today I am reading when the call for attention sounds. It's one of the brusquer Daves. I put down my book. It's a good book about a guy who is fed up with his life and moves to a little house in the country. Sounds like my situation, except I wasn't really fed up with my old life, and I didn't get to choose my retreat.

The command for attention is followed by the instructions I've come to know so well.

"There is a photo awaiting you in the door. Retrieve it and perform your standard function on the subject."

"Sure thing, Dave," I reply.

I go to the lone door in my apartment. Set midway in the door is a hinged panel. I pull down the panel and a receptacle big enough to hold a cafeteria tray piled with food is revealed. Of course, the far side of this space is blocked by another panel, this one locked. I often speculate about whether this delivery system is a box bolted to the outside of a normal door, or if the door itself is very thick, like one of those blast doors in a government bunker. This is how I get my magazines and fast-food meals delivered. And also, of course, the photos of my victims.

The photograph this time is generically similar to most of the others I've processed so far. It's a portrait of an Arab-looking young man: largish nose, wispy beard, disorderly black hair, fanatical eyes, grim mouth. An improbably jaunty scarf is tied around his neck. As usual, there is no information given as to his name or age or nationality. His crimes are not detailed, either. All that I need to know is that the people who control me want him dead.

I take the photograph back to my comfortable recliner and go to work.

Something about this victim's impregnable smugness, his air of righteous zealotry, irritates me, and I decide to go slow and be thorough.

I picture myself jamming the barrel of a pistol up his nostrils, shattering cartilage. I twist the gun cruelly before I blow the top of his head off, splattering the wall against which he's posed with his brains. I take an automatic rifle and use every bullet in its magazine to cut him literally in half. I duct-tape several grenades to his crotch and pull the pins. I use a knife on his eyes and tongue before severing his jugular veins. And so on.

At the end of five minutes, I'm quite sure that this man, wherever he is on the planet, is dead.

One less terrorist to undermine global civilization. One less Chechen or Algerian, Taliban or Syrian.

Or so I hope.

* * *

I often wonder if there is anyone else on earth with my powers. If such a being exists, perhaps he or she is in the employ of rival powers, and one day my own photo will fall into their hands.

This is a strangely comforting thought.

* * *

Maybe you've read about the study that investigated the efficacy of prayers in the healing process. The researchers found that patients who were prayed for by friends and relatives and who knew about the prayers healed faster. But then the experimenters went one step further. They got strangers to pray remotely for certain patients and never even told the patients they were getting such special attention.

And the subjects still healed faster than average.

That study seems to provide some sort of explanation for what I do.

Except I don't say prayers. I say curses.

And I doubt the same god is answering mine.

* * *

The way I found out that my power worked on photographs of people, on shadows of their souls, as well as if I were standing right next to them, was like this.

One day when I was about twenty-two, I was reading the newspaper and came across an article about a local drunken driver who had wiped out an entire Asian family while they were crossing a street. He was one of those unrepentant types who refused even to admit he was at fault. Said something about the family jaywalking. I had actually known the people who were killed. They weren't close friends or relatives, but they ran a variety store in my neighborhood. I stopped in there a lot, and the owners were always nice to me.

Upon learning how these people had died, I got so pissed off that I started doing my thing on the newspaper photo of the drunken driver at his arrest.

On the evening news I heard he had died in custody of natural causes.

This was the mysteriously apt death I would discuss with Van Tranh at the funeral.

Just like when I had first discovered my powers, I had to do a little experimenting with this new photo trick. I found out that a photo had to be no more than twenty-four hours old for me to succeed in killing the victim. Freshness counted. There must be something about a person's nature that continually changes with time and makes them a different person than they were the day before. I don't like to use the word *soul*, but maybe that's the part that changes, gets updated with experience. Also, the image of the victim's face had to be highly detailed. Remote shots of little human smudges didn't cut it.

I wondered if television pictures would work as well. I tried, but the results were inconclusive. You know why? No single image stayed on the screen long enough for me to concentrate on! When was the last time you saw a person's face occupy the screen for three minutes without some kind of interruption, even if it is only a change in camera angles? And that was enough to reset my efforts to zero. But my captors must've thought there was a possibility I could do it, since they blocked the TV here from reception.

I would have liked to have seen certain obnoxious TV personalities keel over live on camera. But I never got the chance to make it happen.

* * *

Of course I sometimes wonder if I am insane, if I am not alone in a padded cell hallucinating all this. But then I remember killing Tony Grasso, and all the killings that followed over the years, in such clear and vivid detail that I am again convinced of the reality of my present situation. And I don't believe I could have come up with such a delusion on my own. Mutant soldier in the war on terrorism. Before my capture, I never gave two thoughts to the war on terrorism.

Now, of course, it's with me all the time.

* * *

Two weeks after I killed the young Arab wearing the scarf, I got my usual delivery of delayed newsmagazines. My employer makes sure the issues aren't current, just in case any photos were taken twenty-four hours before distribution. In the coverage of the Middle East, I saw pictures of a public funeral where my victim was the corpse. The text claimed he was a Hamas organizer who had been poisoned by infidels.

Well, yes, I suppose so, after a fashion.

* * *

I don't believe I've yet specified exactly how long I've been doing this job, playing my part in the war on terror. Almost three years now. I was abducted in early 2002.

Is my activity the reason why the United States has not experienced a domestic terror attack since September 11?

I like to think so.

But I can't be sure.

* * *

It's not as easy to get a suitable photo of a terrorist as you might imagine, but it's not that hard, either. I keep waiting for a picture of bin Laden, for instance, but it hasn't shown up yet. He must be hiding really well. Or maybe for some reason they don't want him dead yet. Generally speaking, if a Western operative could snap such a photo, they'd also be in a position just to assassinate the guy outright, and they wouldn't need me. But lots of times, it seems, unwitting and greedy people close to the victim will provide a photo for money, thinking, what harm could it do?

I am the answer to that question that they must never learn.

* * *

Thinking about souls some more, I find additional comfort to support me in my work. If people do have souls, then I'm only liberating their essences from their imperfect shells, returning them to the source for another try at a better life, maybe.

I think I read some similar philosophy once in a science fiction novel.

* * *

It's good to be unemotional about what I do. Killing Tony Grasso was really the one and only time I felt pure hatred for any of my victims. After that, it was always either just a job or an experiment.Between the ages of thirteen and twenty-two, I estimate that I caused the deaths of only about fifty people. That's only roughly five per year, a record that shows admirable restraint, I think. Even the terrorists don't push my buttons. I dislike what they're trying to do. Civilization doesn't need toppling, especially by jerks who offer only crude substitutes they intend to enact in its place. And I'm as patriotic as the next guy, so I'm pleased to be able to help my country. But all my killing is basically as simple to me as breathing. It's just something I do to stay alive.

* * *

The photos come to me in random batches. No one can predict on any given day whether many terrorists or just a few will be careless enough to get photographed. Sometimes many days go by and I don't receive a single photo. Other times, I get three or more in the same day.

After killing the terrorist with the scarf, I had a long break. I cooked elaborate meals, tossed darts, and read. I asked for extra DVDs.

But then came a busy period.

I had to kill two or three people a day. Strangulation, disembowelment, explosions, falls from great heights—my imagination really got a workout.

* * *

And on that topic: I find that I need to envision new styles of death from time to time, in order to keep my mind from wandering during the killing process. Luckily, the modern world offers no shortage of novel methods of dying. The news and entertainment media alone can keep me supplied with an endless flow of imagery to borrow. I do a lot of beheadings lately.

* * *

"Attention! There is a photo awaiting you in the door. Retrieve it and perform your standard function on the subject."

After the busy period, this is the first call for my services in several days. Without any haste, I walk to the door and find the photo of my next victim.

Surprisingly, the fellow is a middle-aged Caucasian man, European-looking. Not your usual terrorist. But then again, I read that terrorists have been recruiting just such types recently, converts to Islam mostly, to avoid being easily profiled. I have some vague memories of seeing his face before. He could be a terrorist sympathizer like John Walker Lindh or that Australian guy held at Guantanamo. But in any case, my job is not to question why, but just to make him die.

So I do, using several new methods I picked up from reading true-crime accounts of serial killers.

* * *

Sometimes I wonder if the nonrational, unscientific, mystical response that I represent to the war on terrorism was not inevitable. The rhetoric and actions of the terrorists are so archaic, so delusional, so hallucinatory and superstitious that the only effective countermeasures must partake of the same qualities. One has to be a shadowboxer to fight shadows.

Even if my powers were a lie, even if I were not killing anyone, perhaps the deliberately leaked news of my government-sanctioned existence would be an effective antiterrorist weapon in itself.

* * *

My regular delivery of newsmagazines stopped for three weeks. I asked the Daves why, but they wouldn't answer.

Of course I immediately suspected that they were hiding something from me. But I wasn't clever enough to figure out what.

* * *

Having this power of mine is not really such a big deal in the end. I couldn't use it to become fabulously rich, or to rule the world. At least, I couldn't figure out any way to accomplish those things. All it did was earn me an upper-middle-class income without much exertion. Then it got me locked up here.

I am forced to conclude that killing people, even remotely and without laying a hand on them, is just not very useful or creative. It's an activity with limited potential for payback.

* * *

The Dave who summons me today is the somewhat friendly woman, and she sounds unusually nervous. I have never heard any of the Daves sound uncertain before.

"Attention, please. You have, um, new reading material awaiting you."

From the door I bring back to my chair an issue of *Time* magazine from three weeks ago.

Inside, I learn the identity of my Caucasian victim.

The Canadian prime minister.

This is what they have been hiding from me.

I should have remembered his face! I study the news religiously. But who could remember such a bland, innocuous, Canadian face?

I trigger the intercom.

"Who are you? Why have you chosen to show me this now?"

But there is no answer.

* * *

The Canadian prime minister, I knew, did not see eye to eye with the president on foreign policy.

It seems the definition of enemies in the war on terror has broadened.

* * *

I wish I had studied more history, instead of math and science. Is this treachery among allies just part of the game of global politics? Is a move like this demanded by the harsh and unrelenting times we live in? What should I do if ordered again to kill another player from "our" side? My native intelligence and haphazard self-instruction only stretch so far.

* * *

I wish now that I had never discovered my powers, never killed Tony Grasso or all the others.

But I suppose it's much too late for that.

* * *

I'm pretty certain that it's the same woman who summons me the next day again over the intercom. I can't think of her as Dave any longer, and would like to know her real name. But I don't dare ask. Astonishingly, *she* asks *me* a question.

"Attention, please. We know you read the magazine. Do you still want to continue to help us set things right?"

Something in the tone of her voice compels me to say, "Yes—yes, I do."

She sounds relieved. "Very well." She reverts to the formula, as if finding comfort in the rigid protocol. "There is a photo awaiting you in the door. Retrieve it and perform your standard function on the subject."

With some eagerness I snatch the photograph from the slot.

It's a picture of the president.

But there's something else accompanying it. A gift.

A hand mirror. Small, like a woman would carry in her purse, but big enough for the task.

* * *

I really wish I could be sure about souls.

Editor Lou Anders, who commissioned this piece, has a knack for bringing out the best in me, it seems. His various original anthologies are conceptualized so clearly, and feature such intriguing conceits, that I'm inspired to go all-out, creating universes that are more complex than I might normally strive to create at the short-story level.

Anyone who's ever tried to keep up with our hectic 24/7/365 culture should be able to relate to this story—which also draws inspiration from R. A. Lafferty's classic "Slow Tuesday Night."

Shuteye for the Timebroker

Three A.M. in the middle of May, six bells in the midwatch, and Cedric Swann, timebroker, was just sitting down to nocturne at his favorite café, the Glialto. He had found an empty table toward the back, where he would be left alone to watch the game.

The game on which his whole future depended.

He took a rolled-up Palimpsest flatscreen from his pocket and snapped it open; the baby freethinker within the screen, knowing Cedric's preferences, tuned to a live feed from Pac Bell Park. Shots of the stands showed that the brilliantly illuminated park was full, and that was good news, since Cedric had brokered the event. A time-broker was nothing if he couldn't deliver warm bodies. But the box score displayed in a corner of the screen held less happy tidings.

The Giants were losing 4–6 against Oakland, with only one more inning to go.

Cedric winced and crumpled, as if he'd been pitchforked from within. He had fifty thousand dollars riding on the Giants.

The bet had been a sure thing, intended to offset some of his debts from a recent string of gambling losses. But the fucking Giants had been forced to bench their best pitcher with injuries just prior to the game. The lanky Afghani newbie had been moved up from the Kabul farm team to boost the fortunes of the San Francisco team after their disastrous '36 season, and he had indeed done so. But now his absence was killing Cedric. And the club's remaining players were stumbling around like a bunch of fucking sleepers!

The defeat of his home team was most disappointing.

Especially since Cedric didn't have the fifty thousand dollars he had wagered.

A window opened in Cedric's Palimpsest, showing the facial of the Glialto's resident freethinker. As usual, the restaurant's free-thinker wore the likeness of Jack Kerouac. On the occasion of the one-hundredth anniversary of Kerouac's birth, there had been a big Beat revival nationwide—but nowhere more fervently than in San Francisco—and the Glialto freethinker had adopted its avatar then, although the café's personality was decidedly less bohemian than old Jack had been.

"Happy six bells, Cedric. What'll you have this hour?"

"Uh, I don't know. Jesus, I'm not even hungry—"

"C'mon now, you know what your mom would say. 'Skip caloric nocturne, risk metabolic downturn.'"

"Yeah, right, if my mom was the fucking NIH or FDA. Oh, all right, then, make it something simple. Give me a plate of fish tacos. And an Anchor Steam."

"Coming right up, Cedric."

The little window closed just in time to afford Cedric a complete panoramic view of an A's player slamming a home run out of the park.

"Christ! I am so drowsily boned!"

Bobo Spampinato was not going to be happy when he or his tetraploid muscle came to collect his fifty thousand. Cedric's boss, Tom Fintzy, of Fintzy Beech and Bunshaft, Timebrokers, was not going to be receptive to another loan request, and in fact would rage at Cedric's firm-tainting misbehavior, if he should learn of it. Cedric already owed a couple of years' projected commissions to FB&B, loans taken out ostensibly to take advantage of some hot IPOs, and the boy-wonder timebroker had been indulged thus far only because of his exceptional performance in the past.

And Caresse. Caresse was going to be extremely disappointed in Cedric, to say the least, especially after financing her boyfriend's most recent expensive course of therapy.

Cedric moaned loud enough for nearby patrons to hear him and gaze sympathetically or disapprovingly his way. He buried his head in his hands to escape their stares. The café in San Francisco's North Beach neighborhood was not as packed as it would have been at midnight, when many people ate nocturne. But there was still a good-sized crowd of witnesses to Cedric's despair and shame.

Noise from the happy, busy throngs on Columbus Avenue pulsed in as the café's door opened and closed. People going to work, to clubs, to parks, to movies, to happy homes. Why couldn't Cedric be one of them, moving easily through the brightly lit city at six bells in the midwatch? But he was isolated, because of his stupid gambling addiction.

The rumble of a small kibe's wheels approaching caused Cedric to look up. Here came his meal. The kibe deposited the dish and drink before Cedric, then rolled off. The smell of the fish tacos made Cedric nauseous, and he pushed the plate away. But he downed the beer in one long swallow and ordered another.

Going back to work drunk would hardly complicate his life any further, he thought, and might even blunt the pain.

* * *

The fourth generation of anti-somnolence drugs after Provigil, released in 2022, completely eliminated the need to sleep.

With the simple ingestion of a single daily pill, humanity was forever freed from the immemorial shackles of nightly unconsciousness.

As easily as that, people increased their effective life spans by a third.

Dreaming and whatever function it fulfilled were pushed way down below liminal awareness. Scientists were not quite sure if such drugs as Eternalert, ZeroBlink, Carpenoct, and Sunshine Superman even permitted dreaming at any stratum of the mind's operation. But in any case, no one seemed to suffer from the banishment of these ancient nightly hallucinations.

The issue of physical tiredness, the cyclical buildup of somatic fatigue poisons, was remedied by dietary nutraceuticals, intervals of sedentary activities, and bouts of physical therapy.

In a few short years after the introduction of these drugs, enormous changes in global society were already institutionalized.

Developed countries who could afford the pricey proprietary drugs now operated on 24/7 time. (The poorer nations remained zones of sleep infiltrated by rich elites of the perpetually wakeful.) The vast majority of the citizens of the United States, for instance, made no distinction among any of the hours in any given twenty-four-hour period. Work and play, study and travel, might occur at any time of the day. The old Navy system of watches and bells, suited for perpetual alertness, was commonly adopted. All the old distinctions between the hours when the sun was up and the hours when it was down disappeared. Before too long, hyper-flextime reigned, with duties and pleasures dynamically apportioned among the available hours.

Strange synergies of R&D began to accumulate, as single-minded researchers were able to doggedly follow paths of experimentation without downtime, and could coordinate their efforts globally without the impediments of operating in incompatible time zones. New products flooded forth at unprecedented rates.

But most importantly, time became fungible, a commodity to be traded.

And whenever there was something to be traded, brokers arose.

A timebroker mediated between individuals and institutions, citizens and the government. Individuals registered their shifting schedules hour by hour with a timebroker of their choice. During such and such hours, they would be willing to work; during other hours, they were interested in attending a concert, a ballgame, a university class, a gym. Institutions also registered their needs. The symphony wants a thousand listeners at 4 A.M. on Sunday. Can you provide them?

Institutions paid the timebrokers large fees for delivering guaranteed numbers of people—be they customers or workers or jury pools. Citizens received discounts on the face value of tickets, or on tuition, or bonuses from employers, or tax breaks from the state and federal governments for being willing to commit blocks of time via their timebroker. Timebrokers lured institutional customers away from their competitors by exhibiting superior reliability and offering sliding-scale fees. Individual citizens jumped from broker to broker based on whoever offered better incentives. Brokers could refuse to service individuals based on a record of noncompliance with promises.

Timebrokers operated globally, facilitating trade among all the hyperactive countries no longer in thrall to sleep.

In the United States, fifteen years after the release of fourth-generation a-som drugs and on the verge of seventh-generation versions, unemployment had effectively disappeared as the economy expanded by a third. Everyone who wanted a job had one. Timebrokers were especially in demand.

Except those unlucky enough to fall afoul of their own bad habits.

Like Cedric Swann.

* * *

Bobo Spampinato and his goons came for Cedric during the dogwatch after the game. Cedric would have preferred, of course, to deal with the bookie at his home, a luxurious condo in the Presidio with killer views of the Golden Gate Bridge. In the privacy of his quarters, Cedric could have kept his indiscretions quiet, begged for mercy without shame, and generally made a pitiful spectacle of himself, thus possibly earning leniency. But perhaps knowing this, and being a man of no mercy, Bobo accosted Cedric at work.

"Mr. Swann, there are some, uh, people here to see you. They claim it's about a debt of yours." The voice of Cedric's executive assistant, Delma Spicer, normally firm and assured, emerged from Cedric's Palimpsest in quavering tones. Her pixie face, maculated with active tribal tags, gleamed with a sudden exudation of flop sweat.

Cedric looked frantically about his office for a miraculous exit he knew wasn't there. Behind the framed Todd Schorr print? No such luck. At last he caved in. What else could he do? Time to take his medicine. How bad, after all, could it be?

"Send them in, Delma."

Rising to his feet, Cedric managed to come around to the front of his work surface just as Bobo and friends entered.

Bobo Spampinato was a scrawny, short Laotian man of boyish appearance. He had been adopted as an infant by a childless Italian couple. Bobo's new father chanced to be responsible for half of the illegal gambling in California. Upon the old man's death, Bobo had taken over the family business. He was normally quite busy directing matters at a high level, and a field call such as today's was something of a perverse honor.

As usual, Bobo wore ErgoActive sandals, a pair of linen dress shorts, and a tie-dyed T-shirt whose living swirls reconfigured themselves stochastically based on a continuous feed of the Vegas line. His bowl-cut black hair fringed a pair of hard dark eyes. His unsmiling lips betokened the seriousness of the occasion. Despite the stylishness of his own fashionable suit, Cedric felt like a child next to Bobo's informal, grim cool.

Bobo was flanked by his muscle: two enormous humans wearing only leather chest-harnesses and thongs, whose genome, judging by the brow lines, hirsuteness, and musculature on display, plainly included gorilla snippets.

Cedric gulped. "Um, hello, Bobo. Good to see you. I was just going to call—"

"You owe me close to two hundred grand now, Swann. What are you going to do about it?"

"Well—pay it back, of course. Little by little—"

The larger of the gorilla-men grunted discontentedly, and Cedric wondered if they could even speak.

"Not good enough, Swann. I'm not a bank that makes loans. I need that money now. All of it."

"But, Bobo, please, that's impossible. I don't have that kind of liquidity. My condo's mortgaged to the hilt. Even if I sold everything I own, I couldn't raise two hundred g's."

"That's not quite true. I understand that your loving parents were quite generous when you graduated from college a few years ago. You have a forty-year a-som rider on your health insurance, all paid up."

When fourth-generation anti-somnolence pills hit the marketplace, most health insurers refused to cover them, deeming them lifestyle drugs, choices, not necessary to combat any disease. But as the drugs became ubiquitous and essential for any full-fledged citizen to serve as a fully functioning member of society, the insurers relented to the extent of writing riders to their policies that would allow people to buy the drugs at a discount. A discount that still ensured immense profits for the pharmaceutical firms. Such clauses made the difference between being able to afford a-som and devoting half of one's income just to maintaining wakefulness parity with the Joneses.

Cedric was almost unable to comprehend what Bobo was

demanding. In hock already to his employer, there was no way Cedric could afford a-som payments out of his weekly salary without his insurance policy.

And without a-som, one might as well not exist.

Stuttering, Cedric said, "It—you—that's unthinkable."

"But obviously I am thinking about it, Swann. And you have about ten seconds to do the same."

The smaller of the gorilla-men snorted through gaping nostrils while the other cracked knuckles the size of walnuts. Cedric blanched.

"Time's up. What'll it be, Swann?"

With shaking hands, Cedric used his Palimpsest to transfer his prepaid a-som coverage to Bobo.

Rolling up his own flatscreen with a satisfied grin, Bobo said, "That squares us, Swann. You know how to reach me for your next bet. But I'll have to get any money up front from now on."

Bobo and company departed. Cedric collapsed against his work surface. But he was not permitted any time to collect his wits or assess his future.

Tom Fintzy, head of FB&B, offered a stern patrician mien to the world at the best of times. White-haired yet virile—his hair color a disarming cosmetic shuck, his virility the result of regular telomere maintenance and resveratrol patches—the chief timebroker had held many lucrative, high-status jobs prior to the a-som era: CEO of this and president of that. Cedric had heard all the boring tales endlessly. But upon coming out of early retirement, Fintzy had truly carved his niche in the timebroking field, showing a superior talent for collating huge masses of individuals with the needs of corporations, NGOs, and government agencies. Now, standing in Cedric's office, Fintzy looked even more unforgiving and decisive than ever.

"Please pay attention, Cedric. I believe you know that according to your employment contract, our firm's freethinker is allowed to monitor your office space and all media traffic in and out of same."

Cedric's Palimpsest, still unrolled, now displayed the facial of FB&B's freethinker, an image of a smiling, grandmotherly matron.

"Hello, Mr. Swann," said the freethinker. "I'm afraid you've been a bit naughty."

"During the time you were entertaining your latest guests," Fintzy continued, "our freethinker deduced the illegal nature of your past activities, assembled proof of all your illicit transactions, including the records of the loans from FB&B you obtained under false pretenses, wrote a report on your case, synopsized it, outlined the range of recommended disciplinary actions and subsequent cost-benefit analysis, and submitted the whole to me. I have tried to act in a similar timely fashion. Mr. Swann, you will not be turned over to any law-enforcement agency by us, due to the embarrassing nature of your crimes and the way it would reflect poorly on the character of FB&B. However, your contract with us is hereby terminated and any future salary you might earn will be garnisheed by us until your loans are repaid. Moreover, you will have a black flag attached to your Universal CV. You have ten minutes to clear the building before security arrives."

Cedric, of course, could make no palliating reply to such a comprehensive and clearly stated case of malfeasance. Nor could he find it in himself to rage or bluster or revile. So he simply gathered the personal contents of his office—everything fit in a small trash basket—and left.

* * *

Dressed in the living jelly slippers known as Gooey Gumshoes, her denim "daisydukes" revealing generous crescents of butt cheek, and a bandeau top straining across her ample chest, the attractive black woman carried what appeared to be a small shallow suitcase. She stepped into the living room of Cedric's condo and said, "Just a minute, honey, and I'll make you feel all better." She set the suitcase down in the middle of the open floor space, stepped back, and sent a command via her Palimpsest.

Cedric watched grimly from his seat on the couch. He doubted that anything could make him feel better.

Unfolding its cleverly hinged sections, extruding carbon-fiber struts, cantilevering, snicking together in Lego-block fashion, tapping compressed air cylinders and flexing plastic muscles, the suitcase bloomed like a newborn foal struggling to its legs. In under thirty seconds, a padded massage table—fairylike, but capable of supporting the heaviest client—stood waist-high where the suitcase had rested.

"Oh, no, Caresse, I'm not in any mood for a massage—"

Caresse Gadbois advanced toward the professional stage where she relieved the daily somatic tensions of her eternally on-the-go clientele —in a resolutely nonsexual manner. Licensed and bonded, Caresse had attended school for two years and apprenticed for an equal period before establishing her own practice. She was one of tens of thousands of traveling masseuses who helped the a-som society function.

"The hell with that shit, boyfriend! That's your toxins talking. I don't know what's bothering you, but whatever it is, it won't seem quite so bad after a massage. Strip, pal, and get on the table. What's the point of having a masseuse for a girlfriend if you can't get a nice backrub for free anytime you need one?"

Caresse's mildly accented voice—her family hailed from Haiti, having legally emigrated to America during Caresse's youth, when their island nation became a U.S. protectorate—worked its usual voodoo magic on Cedric. He undressed down to his boxers as Caresse removed various lotions and balms from her large professional satchel.

On the table, Cedric relaxed under Caresse's expert touch. His consciousness descended a notch, into that slightly hypnagogic microsleep which scientists theorized helped to permit continuous awareness. Still able to maintain an undemanding conversation, Cedric listened to an account of Caresse's day and the various people she had helped, interjecting suitable affirmative comments at regular intervals.

Admittedly, Caresse's ministrations did help to relieve some of the tension in Cedric's frame. When she had finished, he rose from the table feeling that perhaps he was not totally doomed after all. While he dressed and Caresse convinced her massage table to resume its suitcase disguise, he said, "Caresse, honey, I have something to tell you. Unfortunately, it's pretty bad news."

Caresse's typically cheerful attitude dissolved in a sober frown. "What is it, Cedric? You're not sick, are you?"

Cedric winced at Caresse's genuine concern. Her first thought had been for his health. What a selfish jerk he had been—still was! Telling her the truth would not be easy. Might as well just plow painfully ahead.

Sitting on the couch with Caresse, Cedric revealed everything, from his final unwise wager on the Giants—damn their shitty playing!—through the surrender of his a-som coverage to Bobo, down to his firing and black-flagging.

When he had finished, Caresse said nothing for an excruciating period of time. Then she said, "The therapy didn't take then. I just threw my money away on quacks. I'm lodging a complaint—!"

Cedric hung his head. "No, Caresse, don't. I was on trope-agonists the whole time I was at the clinic. I smuggled them in. Caresse—I just couldn't bring myself to give up gambling! But I've hit bottom now. Really, I have! I'm lower than coffee futures. Honest!"

Silence. Cedric focused on his palms folded in his lap, waiting for Caresse to render judgment on him, experiencing each second as a hellish eternity. He stole a glance at her face, and saw that she was silently crying. He felt like shit.

At last she said, "I was right. You *were* sick. Really sick. Your addiction was totally stronger than you could deal with. But if you think you've changed now—"

"I am, I am! Totally changed!"

"Well, then, I guess I can forgive you."

Now they were both crying. Through the tears, they kissed, and the kissing soon passed into more frenetic activity, with the substantial couch as platform. There was no bedroom to retreat to. People didn't have bedrooms any longer. They had a variety of couches and recliners used for relaxing. This furniture supported sex as well. If someone was a real hedonist, they might have a room devoted just to screwing, but such an excess was generally thought to be déclassé. Most people happily used their ex-bedrooms for media centers or home offices or rec rooms, gaining extra functional apartment space at no additional cost.

At one point early on in the lovemaking, Caresse kicked off her Gooey Gumshoes and the footwear obediently humped themselves across the floor and out of the way beneath the couch, moving like certain ambulatory mycotic ancestors.

The make-up sex was spectacular. But Cedric emerged depressed anyhow. The full consequences of his fall now weighed heavily on him. Cuddling Caresse, he generously shared his anxiety with her.

"I'm going to have to give up this place. I'll lose all my equity. Not that it's much. And I've only got a little more than a week's worth of a-som on hand. I *would* have to get fired right near the end of the month! So I'll have to find a job right away. But I can't work as a timebroker. Fintzy's fucking black flag sees to that! But I don't have any experience that would bag me a job that pays as much. And with the garnishment on any future salary, how am I going to make ends meet? It looks like I'm going to have to choose between becoming homeless, or becoming a—a sleeper!"

Cedric waited for Caresse to offer him an invitation to live with her. But he waited in vain. Had he pushed her affection and charity too far? When she finally spoke, her comment was noncommittal and only vaguely comforting.

"Don't worry, Cedric, it'll all work out."

Cedric tried to be macho about his plight. But his fear leaked out.

"Right, sure, it all will. But I'm just a little scared, is all."

* * *

Like most of the developed, a-som world, the United States of America now boasted a birthrate that fell well below replacement levels, the culmination of long-term historical trends that had begun a century ago, and that a-som tech had only accelerated. Had immigration not kept the melting pot full, the country would have become radically depopulated in a few generations.

Children could not take anti-somnolence drugs until puberty, a condition that nowadays statistically occurred on average at around age twelve. Their juvenile neurological development required sleep, periods in which the maturing brain bootstrapped itself into its final state. This process had proven to be one of the few vital, irreplaceable functions of sleep. (And even if infants and toddlers had been able to take a-som drugs, no sane parent would have wanted them awake 24/7.)

Consequently, parenting had acquired another massive disincentive. The hours when children had to sleep had formerly been shared by their parents in the same unconscious state. No particular sacrifice had been required on the part of the adults. But now, staying home with archaically dormant children constituted cruel and unusual punishment, robbing adults of all the possibilities that a-som opened up. More than ever, adults concerned with careers or intent on socializing and indulging their interests regarded child-raising as a jail term.

The child-care industry had adapted and boomed in response. Battalions of nannies specializing in the guardianship of sleeping children now circulated throughout the country, supporting the flexible lifestyles of absent mothers and fathers. Amateur babysitters had gone the way of paperboys. But the job, while essential, was still regarded as unskilled labor. The low pay for babysitting reflected this classification.

Sinking down through the vocation sphere, the black flag on his UCV denying him employment everywhere he turned, Cedric Swann had finally found employment as one of these rugrat guardians.

Ironically, the intermediary between Cedric and his employer, TotWatch, Inc., were the timebrokers Fintzy Beech and Bunshaft. Cedric had reluctantly continued his registration with his ex-employer, acknowledging that FB&B did offer the best deals. And apparently, the firm's ire at Cedric did not impede its greed for another warm body to meet the quotas of its clients—if any client would have him.

Desperate for money, Cedric had specified an open-ended availability as a nanny. Children were asleep at all bells of all watches. Their schooling was just as freeform as their parents' lives. Class time—a small fraction of total learning hours disbursed across various modalities of instruction—was brokered out to public and private schools that operated around the clock.

Today, Cedric had a gig over in his old neighborhood. The contrast with his own new residence couldn't have been greater, and the irony was not lost on him.

After selling his condo and most of his furniture and possessions, Cedric had found a cheap apartment in Chinatown, above a dank, smelly business that biocultured shark fins for the restaurant trade. Now all his clothes smelled of brine and exotic nutrient feedstuffs, and his view was not of the Golden Gate Bridge, but rather of the facade of a martial-arts academy, where a giant hardlight sign endlessly illustrated deadly drunken-master moves.

As for his a-som doses, Cedric had managed to stay supplied. But only by abandoning the brand-name sixth-generation pills he had been taking and switching to a generic fifth-generation prescription. The lesser drugs maintained his awareness fairly well. At least, he couldn't detect any changes in his diurnal/nocturnal consciousness; but then again, that was like trying to measure a potentially warped ruler with itself. Occasionally, however, his limbs did feel as if they were wrapped in cotton batting, and his tongue stuck to the roof of his mouth.

Leaving his apartment at the first bell of the first watch, Cedric used his Palimpsest to find the location of the nearest Yellow Car. One of the ubiquitous miniature rental buggies was parked just a block away, and Cedric was grateful for small miracles. He could have taken a crosstown bus, or even have walked to save money, but he felt that his spirits would benefit from a small indulgence.

Cedric missed so many things that had vanished from his life. Naturally he missed his luxurious home and lifestyle. The sensations engendered by those material losses had been expected. But more surprisingly, Cedric missed being a timebroker, the buzz he had gotten from collating supply and demand, from filling a San Diego trope-fab with eager workers or making the San Jose Burning Man a success. Now he felt powerless, isolated, unproductive. Watching sleeping *larvae!* How had he fallen so far?

If it hadn't been for Caresse's continued affection and support, Cedric would have felt a lot worse. Having her as his girlfriend had been his mainstay. Caresse continually reminded him that the black flag on his UCV would expire at the end of five years or upon the repayment of all his debts, whichever came first, and that all he had to do was stick it out that long. Her optimistic outlook was invaluable. And the free body rubs and sex didn't hurt, either. They were supposed to hook up after Cedric's gig later, in fact, and Cedric was counting the minutes till then.

Climbing into the Yellow Car, Cedric started it with his Palimpsest. He noticed with irritation the low-fuel reading on the car's tank, due to an inconsiderate prior driver, and swore at having to stop at a refueling station. But then again, he could top off his Palimpsest with butane as well.

The dusk-tinged streets of San Francisco on this lovely late-spring evening were moderately thronged with busy citizens. There were no such phenomena as "rush hours" or "off-hours" any longer. The unsynchronized mass impulses of the citizenry, mediated by the timebrokers, resulted in a statistically even distribution of activity across all watches. No longer did one find long queues at restaurants at "dinnertime" or lines at the DMV. With every hour interchangeable, and everything functioning continuously, humanity had finally been freed from the tyranny of the clock.

After hitting the pumps, Cedric made good time to his destination. The large glass-walled house where Cedric was to babysit commanded a fine view of the bay, and Cedric felt a flare of jealousy and regret.

Alex and Brian Holland-Nancarrow greeted Cedric pleasantly. Both of the slim, modishly accoutred men had an expensively groomed appearance that bespoke plenty of surplus cash—as if the house weren't proof enough of that.

"We're in a bit of a hurry, Cedric. But let us show you a few things you'll need while you're here. As you know from TotWatch, we have two children, Xiomara and Tupac. They're both asleep already. Here's their bedroom."

Reverently, the fathers opened the bedroom door a crack to allow Cedric to peer within. The unnaturally darkened chamber, the smell of children's breath and farts, the sound of comalike breathing—these all induced in Cedric a faint but distinct nausea. It was like looking into a morgue or zombie nest, or a monkey cage at the midnight zoo. He could barely recall his own youthful sleeping habits, and the prospect of ever sleeping again himself made him want to vomit.

"We have a security kibe, and you'll have to give it a cell sample. Just put your finger there—perfect! We're heading up to a wine-tasting in Sonoma, and we should be back by four bells of the mid-watch. Feel free to have nocturne with whatever you find in the fridge. There's some really superior pesto we just whipped up, and baby red potatoes already boiled."

"Fine, thanks, have a great time."

The Holland-Nancarrows departed in a crimson Wuhan Peony, and Cedric thumbed his nose at them once they were safely out of sight.

Back inside, he looked for ways to amuse himself. He watched a few minutes of a Giants game on his Palimpsest, but the experience was boring when he didn't have any money riding on the contest. He prolonged the meditative drinking of a single boutique beer from the house's copious stock, but eventually the bottle gurgled its last. He made a dutiful trip to the bedroom and witnessed the children—shadowy lumps—sleeping as monotonously as before. Cedric shuddered.

Eventually, Cedric found himself poking around the family flatscreen. The display device occupied a whole wall, and somehow even vapid entertainment was more entrancing at that size.

And that's when he found that the Holland-Nancarrows had departed so hurriedly that they had left their system wide open. They had never logged off.

After hesitating a moment, Cedric decided to go exploring. He paged through their mail, but discovered only bland trivia about people he didn't know. He discovered what Alex and Brian did for a living: they designed facials for freethinkers. In effect, they were cyber-beauticians.

Then Cedric stumbled across a bookmark for a Cuban casino. Apparently, his hosts had recently placed a few amateur bets.

Cedric hesitated. In the pit of his stomach and down to his loins, a familiar beast was awakening and growling and stretching its limbs.

Just a small visit, to taste the excitement. He could lurk without playing.

Yeah. And the Mars colony would find life someday.

Under Cedric's touch, the screen filled with a first-person-shooter image of the casino floor. Cedric was telefactoring a kibe whose manipulators would emerge into his field of vision when he reached for something. Cedric wheeled the kibe toward the blackjack tables, his favorite game.

Cedric started betting small at first. The wagers came, of course, from the cyber-purse of the Holland-Nancarrows. If he drained the purse of too much money, they'd spot the loss and track down the bets to a time when they weren't home. But if he won, he'd leave the purse at its original value and transfer the excess to his own pockets. They'd never have occasion to check.

And of course, he *would* win. And win *big!*

The hours sped by as Cedric played with feverish intensity. His skills had not left him, and he was really in the zone. The cards favored him as well. Lady Luck had her hands down his pants. Pretty soon, he had racked up ten thousand dollars of the casino's money. Only a drop toward lifting his debts, but certainly the best-paying babysitting gig he had ever had.

Cedric left the casino and squirted the funds to his account. No one would ever be the wiser.

He was opening a second celebratory beer when the police arrived.

"Cedric Swann, we have a warrant for your arrest. Please come with us."

"But—but I didn't do anything—"

"The Holland-Nancarrow freethinker swears otherwise."

On the big wallscreen appeared the facial of the house's freethinker: an image of former president Streisand. "That's the man, officers."

The house's freethinker! But who would set a freethinker to monitor legitimate transactions originating in-house?

Paranoid parents, obviously.

Who the hell could think as deviously as a breeder?

* * *

Cedric's possessions now amounted to a single scuffed biomer suitcase of clothing and his Palimpsest. Cedric and his suitcase called a single room in a flophouse in the Mission District their home. The flophouse was a rhizome-diatom hybrid, taking form as a soil-rooted silicaceous warren of chambers, threaded with arteries and nerves that served in place of utilities, all grown in place on a large lot where several older structures had stood until a terrorist attack demolished them. The site had been officially decontaminated, but Cedric wasn't sure he believed that. Why had no one snapped up the valuable midtown real estate, leaving the lot for such a low-rent use? In any case, Cedric felt like a bacteria living inside a sponge.

He supposed that such a lowly status was merely consonant with society's regard for him, after his latest fuckup.

Instead of meeting Caresse at a restaurant as they had planned, Cedric had met her on the night of his arrest at the jailhouse where he had been taken by the cops. She came to bail him out, and he accepted her charity wordlessly, realizing there was nothing he could say to exculpate himself. He had been caught red-handed while submitting to his implacable vice.

Caresse had been silent also, except for formalities with the police. Cedric fully expected her to explode with anger and recriminations when he got into her car. But the calm disdain she unloaded on him was even more painful.

"You obviously have no regard for yourself, and none for me. I've tried to be understanding, Cedric, really, I have. I don't think any woman could have cut you more slack, or tried harder to help you reform. But this is the absolute end. I've put up your bail money so that you can be free to plan your defense—as if you have any—and so that you won't have to be humiliated by being in prison. But that's the end of the road for you and me. I can't have anything else to do with you in the future. Whatever existed between us is gone, thanks to your weak-willed selfishness."

Cedric looked imploringly at Caresse's beautiful profile with its gracefully sculpted jawline. She did not turn to spare him a glance, but kept her eyes resolutely on the busy midnight city street. He knew then that he had truly lost her forever, realized he had never fully appreciated her love. But he had neither the energy nor the hope to contest her death sentence on their relationship.

"I'm sorry, Caresse. I never meant to hurt you. Can you drop me off at my place?"

"Of course. I've got just enough time before my yoga class."

The Holland-Nancarrows declined to press for any jail time for Cedric, considering that they had not actually lost any money, and nor had their precious children been harmed by the bad man. (The casino took back Cedric's winnings on the basis of identity misrepresentation by the player.) But that did not stop the judge who heard Cedric's case from imposing on Cedric a huge fine and five years' probation. Cedric's own court-appointed freethinker lawyer had not been receptive to the notion of an appeal.

Worst of all the repercussions of his crime, however, was that Cedric was double black-flagged, denied employment even as a nanny.

He had no choice but to go on welfare.

The welfare rolls of the sleeplessly booming U.S. economy had been pared to historic lows. Only the most vocationally intransigent or helpless indigents lived off the government dole.

And now Cedric was one of this caste. Unclean. Unseen.

And a sleeper as well. A living atavism.

The dole didn't cover a-som drugs. Not even the fourth-generation, expired-shelf-date stuff shipped to Third World countries.

Being a sleeper was hell. It wasn't that sleepers were persecuted against, legally or even covertly. Nor were they held in contempt. No, sleepers were simply ignored by the unsleeping. They were deemed irrelevant because they couldn't keep up. They were living their lives a third slower than the general populace. After a night's unconsciousness, a sleeper would awake to discover that he had a new congressional representative, or that the clothes he had worn yesterday were outmoded. New buzzwords were minted while he slept, new celebrities crowned, new political crises defused. The changes were not always so radical, but even on a slow Tuesday night they were incremental. Day by day, sleepers fell further and further behind the wave front of the culture, until at last they were living fossils.

Cedric could hardly believe that such was now his fate.

After his sentencing and his removal to the flophouse, once he had consumed the last of his a-som scrip, Cedric had managed to stay desperately awake for a little over forty-eight hours, thanks to massive coffee intake, some Mexican amphetamines purchased on a street corner, and a cheap kibe massage that left him reeking of machine lubricant from a leaky gasket on the kibe.

The ancient sensations flooding his mind and body exerted at first a kind of grim and perverse fascination. The whole experience was like watching the tide reclaim a sand castle. Sitting in his tiny room, on an actual *bed*, he monitored his helpless degeneration. His concentration wavered and faded, his limbs grew unwieldy, his speech confused. Despite raging against his loss, Cedric ultimately had no choice but to succumb.

And then he dreamed.

He had forgotten dreaming, the nightly activity of his childhood.

Forgotten that some dreams were nightmares.

He awoke from that initial sleep shaking and drenched with sweat, the night terrors mercifully fading from memory. He retained only vague images of teeth and crushing weights, falling through space and scrabbling for handholds.

Cedric got up, dressed, and went out into the streets.

Kibes running errands or patrolling for lawbreakers mingled with humans. The Mission District was not populated entirely by charity-case sleepers. Many of the people on the streets were citizens in fine standing. Here was a colorful clique of tawny Polynesian immigrants, adapting to life away from their sea-swamped island homes. Their happy, bright-eyed faces seemed to mock him. From Cedric's new vantage point down in the underbelly of the a-som society, everyone looked wired and jazzed up, restlessly active, spinning their wheels in a perpetual drag race toward an ever-receding finish line.

But having this vision didn't mean he still wouldn't rejoin his ex-peers in a second, if he could.

Cedric was convinced that everyone could smell the sleep-stench rising from him, spot his saggy eyelids a block away. Eating in a cheap diner that allowed him to stretch his monthly money as far as possible, Cedric resolved to kill himself rather than go on like this.

But he didn't. In a week, a month, he relearned how to function with a third of his life stolen by sleep, and became resigned to an indefinitely prolonged future of this vapid existence.

As role models for his new lifestyle, Cedric had the other inhabitants of his flophouse. He had expected his fellow sleepers to be vicious father-rapers or congenitally brain-damaged droolers or polycaine addicts. But to Cedric's surprise, his fellow sleepers represented a wide range of intelligence and character, as extensive a spectrum of personalities as could be found anywhere else. In the short and desultory conversations Cedric allowed himself with them, he learned that some were deliberate holdouts against the a-som culture, while some were ex-members of the majority, like Cedric himself, professionals who had somehow lost their hold on the a-som pinnacle.

And then you had Doug Clearmountain.

Doug was the happiest person Cedric had ever met. Short, rugged, bald-crowned but with a fringe of long hair, Doug resembled a time-battered troll of indeterminate years.

The first time Doug made contact with Cedric, in the grottolike lobby of the flophouse, the older man introduced himself by saying, "Hey there, chum, I'm Morpheus. You want the red pill or the blue?"

"Huh?"

"Not a film buff, I see. Doug Clearmountain. And you are?"

"Cedric Swann."

"Cedric, it's a pleasure to meet you. Let's grab a coffee."

"Uh, sure."

Over coffee Cedric learned that, before settling in San Francisco, Doug had been an elder of a religious community that featured, among other tenets of its creed, the renunciation of a-som drugs. The community—a syncretic mix of Sufism, Theravada Buddhism, and TM—had struggled in the wilds of Oregon for approximately fifteen years before bleeding away all its members to the siren call of 24/7 wakefulness. Doug had been the last adherent to remain. Then one day, when he finally admitted no one was coming back, he just walked away from the empty community.

"Decided it was time to do a little preaching amidst the unconverted."

Cedric took a swig of coffee, desperate to wake up, to dispel the funk engendered by his nightly bad dreams. "Uh, yeah, how's that working for you? You convinced many people to nod out?"

Undaunted by Cedric's evident lack of interest, Doug radiated a serene confidence. "Not at all. Haven't made one convert yet. But I've found something even more important to keep me busy."

The coffee was giving Cedric a headache. A tic was tugging at the corner of his right eye. He had no patience for any messianic guff from this loony. "Sure, right, I bet you're really busy working to engineer a rebellion that nobody in their right mind wants. Down with the timebrokers, right?"

"Hardly, Cedric, hardly. I'm actually doing essential work helping to prop our incessant society up. It can't survive much longer on its own, you know. It's like a spinning flywheel without a brake. But this is the course that the bulk of our species has chosen, so me and some others are just trying to shepherd them through it. But I can see that you have no interest in hearing about my mission at the moment. You're too busy adjusting to your new life. We'll talk more when you're ready."

Doug Clearmountain left then, having paid for both their coffees.

At least the nut wasn't a cheapskate.

For the most part, Cedric resisted the impulse to reconnect with his old life, the glamorous satisfying round of timebrokering, gambling, and leisure pursuits. He spent his time giving mandatory Palimpsest interviews to his freethinker probation officer (whose federally approved facial was that of a sweater-wearing kiddie-show host who had retired before Cedric was born). He roamed the hilly streets of the city, seeking to exhaust his body and hopefully gain a solid night's sleep. (Useless. The nightmares persisted.) He watched sports. He tried to calculate how long it would be before all his debts were paid off with the court-mandated pittance being deducted from his welfare stipend. (Approximately eleven hundred years.)

Once he tried to get in touch with Caresse. She couldn't talk because she was in the middle of a massage, but she promised to call back.

She actually did.

But Cedric was asleep.

He took that as a sign not to try again.

Six months passed, and Cedric resembled a haunted, scarecrow model of his old self.

That's when Doug Clearmountain approached him again, jovial and optimistic as ever.

"Congratulations on the fine job you're doing, Cedric."

Cedric had taken to hanging out at Fisherman's Wharf, cadging spare change from the tourists via Palimpsest transactions. He was surprised to see Doug when he raised his dirty bearded face up from contemplating the ground.

"Go fuck yourself."

Doug remained unfazed. "I'm not being sarcastic, son. I was just congratulating you on half a year as a sleeper. Do you realize how much of our planet's finite resources you've saved?"

"What do you mean?"

"You're using a third less energy, a third less food than your erstwhile compatriots. I'm sure Gaia appreciates your sacrifice. When the a-som society came fully online globally, it was like adding another America to the planetary eco-burden. Ouch! Despite all the fancy new inventions, our planet is heading toward catastrophe faster than ever. All we're doing lately is staving off the inevitable."

"Big whoop. So I'm a tiny positive line item in the carbon budget."

"Well, yes, your sacrifice is negligible, regarded in that light. But there's another way you can be of more help. And that's by dreaming."

Cedric shuddered. "Dreams! Don't say that word to me. I haven't had a pleasant dream since I went cold turkey."

Doug's perpetual grin gave way to a look of sober concern. "I know that, Cedric. That's because you're not doing it right. You're trying to go it alone. Would you like some help with your dreams?"

"What've you got? A-som? How much?"

"No, not a-som. Something better. Why not come with me and see for yourself?"

What did Cedric have to lose? He let Doug lead the way.

The authorities had marked the small waterfront building for eventual demolition, as they continually enhanced the system of dikes protecting the city's shoreline from rising sea levels. For now, though, the structure was still high and dry. Doug pried back a suspiciously hinged panel of plywood covering a door frame and conducted Cedric inside.

The place smelled like chocolate. Perhaps the Ghirardelli company had once stored product here. But now the large, open, twilit room was full of sleepers. Arrayed on obsolete military cots, two dozen men and women, covered by blankets, snored peacefully while wired cranially to a central machine the size of a dorm fridge.

"What—what the hell is this? What's going on?"

"This is a little project I and my friends like to call 'Manhole 69.' Ring any bells? No? Ah, a shame, the lack of classical education you youngsters receive. Well, no matter. The apparatus you see is an REM-sleep modulator. Invented shortly before the introduction of a-som tech, and then abandoned. Ironically unusable by the very people who needed it the most. Basically, this device provides guided dream experiences within broad parameters. The individual's creativity is shaped into desired forms. Nonsurgical neuronal magnetic induction, and all that. Everyone you see here, Cedric, is dreaming of a better world. Here, take a look."

Doug borrowed Cedric's Palimpsest and called up a control channel to the dream machine. A host of windows filled the flatscreen. Cedric witnessed pastoral landscapes populated by shining godlings, superscience metropolises, alien worlds receiving human visitors, and other fanciful scenes.

"Are you totally demented, man? So you can give people pretty dreams. So what? Don't get me wrong, I'll take a few hours under your brain probe, just to get some relief. But as far as helping the world become a better place, you're only kidding yourself."

"Oh, really? Would you care to discuss this over some coffee?"

"Coffee? What're you talking about?"

Doug didn't answer. He was too busy sending instructions to the dream machine. All the flatscreen windows formerly revealing the variegated dreams of the sleepers changed at once to the same realtime image: the interior of the very building Cedric and Doug stood in, captured by Palimpsest cam. But the screen views were different from reality in one particular: a steaming paper cup stood atop the dream machine cabinet.

"This should only take a second or two."

"What should take—"

Cedric smelled the coffee before he saw it. There it rested, just where the dreamers had envisioned it.

Cedric walked in a daze to the cabinet, picked the coffee up. The cup and its contents warmed his fingers.

Doug's manner took on the serious affect of an expert in his field with something to sell.

"Two dozen people programmed to dream the same thing can instantiate objects massing up to ten ounces. I expect that the phenomenon scales up predictably. Something to do with altering probabilities and shifting our quantum selves onto alternate timelines, rather than producing matter ex nihilo. Or so certain sleeper scientists among us theorize. But we're not interested in such parlor tricks. Instead, we want to shallowly engrave a variety of desirable futures into our local brane, thereby increasing the likelihood that one of them will become real. We're shifting the rails that society is following. And as Thoreau once ironically observed, rails rest on sleepers. There are places like this around the globe, Cedric. And the more sleepers we enlist, the greater our chances of success. Are you on board, son?"

Cedric regarded Doug dubiously. Had the manifestation of the coffee been a trick? Maybe that cabinet was hollow, with a false top, the coffee concealed inside. Should he ask for another demonstration, or take the old man on faith? Why would anyone bother to try to hoax him into simply going to sleep? And what else was he going to do with his life?

"Here," said Cedric, offering the coffee to Doug. "You take this. I guess I'm finally ready for a little shut-eye."

Edgar Allan Poe is one of the ancestors of the SF genre who is more honored in lip service than on the printed page these days. Although he practically invented the modern short story, Poe's crepuscular and eccentric and somewhat fusty work does not seem to attract the worshippers it once did, when, say, Ray Bradbury and Robert Bloch deliberately invoked him. Even postmodern horror writers—horror being what Poe is generally remembered for—seem to have put him on a dusty shelf.

So I was very intrigued when I learned of a book project that involved taking one of Poe's fragmentary story beginnings and playing with it in any manner the author chose. I signed up right away, determined to channel Poe into a kind of SF/cosmic horror vein. The words flowed surprisingly easily, and I like to think that the ghost of Poe—who often visited my hometown, Providence—sat like a bodiless raven on my shoulder as I wrote.

The Days of Other Light

[based on a fragment by Edgar Allan Poe]

Ingeniero watched the transphotonic packet *Oriole* depart the surface of Skyfire. Lifting off lightly from the airless tinted desert of the planetoid, the sleek interstellar ship swiftly became lost against the hectic, coruscating, panchromatic backdrop of radiance that formed the famous celestial vista that had inspired this worldlet's name.

Now he was alone, and there was no telling what might happen to a man all alone as he was. Yet his spirits revived at the mere thought of being—for once in his life at least—so thoroughly *alone*.

The *Oriole* would not return for six months, per Ingeniero's request.

Until then, Ingeniero was trapped here of his own free will, the sole inhabitant of a small world. By the time his means of departure returned, his transport back to the galactic polity known as the Diffusion, he would either have solved the quandary that had brought him here, attaining renewed supremacy in his craft, or have been rendered a bestial, brain-damaged cripple.

Break through or break down. Such was the harsh point to which Ingeniero had been driven, midway through his life and career.

Turning to his left, Ingeniero regarded his lone companion, a slave half-organic, half-inorganic. The artificial being was a bulky shapeless mass of mind putty resembling a fantastically enlarged amoeba that towered some six feet tall. A lump of blue-tinged, translucent pseudo-protoplasm, threaded with golden moletronic circuits and muscle fibers and synthetic organelles, the slave possessed a moderate intelligence but lacked all initiative or personality. It responded to commands only from Ingeniero, who addressed it as "Iamo."

Floating beside Iamo was a fifth-force hover-sled stacked with the few provisions and personal possessions necessary for Ingeniero's stay. Some entertainment planchettes, a few changes of clothing, and half a year's worth of metabolytic lozenges. A sparse inventory. But Ingeniero had not come to Skyfire for a luxurious vacation. Had that been his goal, he would have stayed on Myrthwold or Fleury, planets that catered to Ingeniero's rich and famous peers and patrons. In his current mental condition, such resorts were anathema to Ingeniero—ash-filled, hollow places where his cursed fate was continually thrown before his eyes by outwardly sympathetic but inwardly mocking aesthetes.

Ingeniero was himself sheathed in the thinnest film of mind putty, so that he resembled a more shapely version of his slave. The quasi-living substance formed the perfect environmental suit, providing for all of its wearer's bodily needs and offering absolute protection against the vacuum and cold and fluctuating radiation of Skyfire. A moletronic mechanism embedded in Ingeniero's cortex offered subetheric contact between Ingeniero and his factotum.

"Iamo, accompany me now and bring the sled."

His steps flighty in the low gravity, Ingeniero started walking toward the only structure on Skyfire.

The Tower of the Lens.

His home for the next six months.

Chamber of ecstatic regeneration.

Or of excruciating torture.

Or of both, alloyed.

The Tower of the Lens was not architecturally impressive. Yet it was a structure that somehow, on first impression, seemed safe enough under any circumstances, one in which Ingeniero could feel secure.

Some four stories tall, unornamented, square in cross section and measuring approximately twenty feet along each wall, the tower seemed rudely built of native materials: primitive, rough-hewn blocks of gray stone. Yet the structure was both airtight and resistant to every form of energy ever focused on it. Geophysical survey probes had determined that its inaccessible roots extended half a mile into the crust of Skyfire. Every attempt to move the tower to a more hospitable world for study or utilization had failed. Even efforts to shift the entire planetoid had been thwarted by, experts postulated, some kind of hidden frame-drag generators that allowed the worldlet to anchor itself immovably into the very fabric of space-time.

The artifact of an untraceable race long vanished, the tower, since its discovery some three hundred years ago, had been nominated a neutral territory under pan-Diffusion supervision. Access to the tower was approved only for the most deserving, and the waiting list was months long. Ingeniero had suffered for five harsh months before getting the go-ahead for this last desperate attempt to recoup his powers.

Ingeniero and his slave reached the entrance to the Tower of the Lens and paused. The door was the one anomalous part of the facade. When it was first discovered, the tower had featured as ingress only an arch exposing its interior to the vacuum. Into this space had been retrofitted a conventional airlock. Now Ingeniero beamed the proper access code to the door, and soon he and Iamo and the sled had cycled through.

The interior of the tower, Ingeniero knew, was divided vertically into four levels. Each level was a single large room. This first floor boasted various amenities, all of human origin and designed to ameliorate the hard lines of the original structure, empty at its discovery. Organiform couches, a food-prep station, viewing carrels, even artworks on the wall. Ingeniero quickly recognized original paintings by Pristina, Kompot, and Novalis—not their best works, either. Ingeniero snorted. Leave it to some Diffusion bureaucrat to be hornswoggled by a canny art dealer eager to unload second-rate works.

His suit informed Ingeniero that the atmosphere and temperature inside the tower were compatible with life, so the man moved to shed his protective covering. He touched a forefinger to his slave and said, "Iamo, absorb my suit." The sheath of mind putty flowed off Ingeniero like mercury and was taken back up undetectably into the bulk of Iamo. Ingeniero stood revealed in lime-and-plum-striped tights, moleskin slippers, and a gold-filigreed weskit over a peach blouson. His long, saturnine face bore various corporate beauty marks identifying his patrons and sponsors. Over the past five years of inactivity, Ingeniero had fought hard to retain these status stipplings. But without a resumption of his artistic productivity, he acknowledged, he stood in danger of losing them all.

"Iamo, distribute the supplies to their proper places."

Ingeniero was startled to discover that some peculiarity in the echo of these walls made his voice resonate in a curious manner. He resolved not to speak any more than was absolutely necessary to his slave.

But evidencing no trouble with the audio distortions, the slave responded to the spoken command as promptly as it had to the beamed orders. Forming various useful temporary extrusions, it went about its chores.

While Iamo worked, Ingeniero moved to explore the rest of the tower. Now, he thought, for a good look around to see what I can see.

The *Oriole* had not been a swift luxury ship but a spartan commercial vessel, and Ingeniero was worn out from the long tedious flight here from the world of Drylongso. But his excitement was such that he could not rest.

An ornate impervium spiral staircase in one corner of the tower afforded access to the upper floors through eccentrically trapezoidal holes originally found in each ceiling. Eagerly climbing, Ingeniero bypassed the second floor (studio space) and the third (sleeping quarters), hastening for what he knew awaited him.

The Chamber of the Lens.

The top floor hosted only a large, low, circular dais positioned directly in the center of the room. Formed of the same substance as the tower, the dais had lately been equipped with a comfortable pad to cushion anyone who lay upon it. But more alarmingly, the altarlike platform also featured restraints for wrists and ankles.

Ingeniero cast his gaze upward, toward the lens itself. But the much-anticipated spectacle was initially disappointing.

Inset into the roof directly above the dais was a huge oval slab of crystal whose lower surface was subtly convex. Coating the outer, vacuum-exposed side of the lens was a film of opaque material installed by the humans, a covering that could be dispersed with a simple command. Currently, with this shield in place, the lens was rendered inert—a dark, bland mass.

Hardly the appearance that the unnatural glassy eye would present, Ingeniero knew, when it was exposed to the massed brilliance of Skyfire's heavens—at that exact moment when he would crucify himself beneath it.

The worldlet dubbed Skyfire was positioned in a portion of the Milky Way that was particularly active in a cosmological sense. Great gaudy nebulae, pulsars, quasars, colliding suns, black holes, novae, gamma-ray bursters, protosuns, and a dozen other species of star thronged the heavens here, washing Skyfire with exotic radiations and quantum particles of every description. And the lens—

The lens had apparently been designed to collimate and blend all those photons and gravitons and bosons and neutrinos into a single wash of unfathomable powers. The force that emerged from the underbelly of the lens defied all categorization by Diffusion science. Some experts maintained that it was a pure bath of numinous information, while others claimed the energy tapped alternate dimensions where the very laws of physics were different than what was accepted in this cosmos.

What use the original inventors of the lens had had for their device was unknown.

What was known to some degree was its effect on the human psyche.

In a certain fraction of subjects, repeated exposure to the lens fostered a kind of epiphanical, satori state leading to immense creativity and insight into the universe.

To other, less lucky victims, the lens brought only madness—or a mode of knowledge incompatible with this space-time continuum.

This was the gamble Ingeniero was about to take.

Either he would regain his proficiency and inspiration, or be reduced to a condition where he no longer cared about his quandary.

Ingeniero placed a hand on the padded dais and looked up at the lens. But nothing in its enigmatic surface conveyed a hint of his fate.

Downstairs, Iamo had finished its chores and rested placidly in a corner, its gelatinous bulk gently oscillating peristaltically like the mild oceans of some world with only a smallish moon.

Ingeniero swallowed a metabolytic lozenge with some of his favorite sparkling waters from Rancifer, one of the only luxuries he had brought along. Thus fortified, he decided to test his talents for the umpteenth time since they had gone sour. Perhaps by some miracle they had been restored. In such a case, he would simply live the hermit's life here for half a year, never uncapping the lens, until he could return in triumph to the high society circles he favored.

Moving to Iamo's side, Ingeniero said, "Iamo, detach." The man gripped a fistful of the slave's mind-putty body and tugged. A chunk of Iamo's synthetic flesh came away, quivering as a separate blob in Ingeniero's hand.

Ingeniero placed the blob on the work surface of one of the carrels, then took a seat in front of it. Cupping the blob with both hands and closing his eyes, he began to run through the Ryland neurological protocols that would lead up to his focused imprinting mental thrust. As a template image, he picked one of the enormous skyscraper termite mounds of Verlag IV, a bumpy fractal edifice.

Sweat sprang out on Ingeniero's brow as he rehearsed the rituals he had undertaken so often in the past, with such success. At last he deemed his mind ready, and loosed the mental bolt upon the mind putty.

Immediately, Ingeniero felt immensely enervated. But not in a positive way. He knew he had failed once more. He opened his eyes, and was rewarded with the sight of a hideous abortion. The mind putty had not taken the shape of the vertical termite mound, but instead had been warped into something that resembled the sprawling mutant coral reefs of Bonestell, riddled with cavities.

Such were the current miserable powers of the famous mind-sculptor who had produced such widely acclaimed masterpieces as *Child Guarded by Swamp Dragon* and *Nude Dakini*.

Furious, Ingeniero swept the botched sculpture to the floor where it shattered, the mind putty having been rendered permanently crystalline by the irreversible mental thrust.

There was no way out now. Ingeniero would have to go under the lens.

Tomorrow, though. Let him have one last night before his trial by heavenly fire.

The anguished sculptor spent that last evening with his precious mind untouched by the lens in viewing his entertainment planchettes. But he found he could not concentrate on any of the various popular theological wrestling matches or enjoy any of the titillating transgenic dramas. His thoughts were riveted to the chamber above his head.

Visions of his upcoming transfiguration plagued him—monster or genius, hell or heaven—until, finally, he was forced to swallow a soothing neuroleptic and retire to bed.

Ingeniero's dreams, if he had dreamed at all, were not recoverable in the morning.

The word *morning*, naturally, was merely a convenience. Skyfire did not orbit any primary whose appearance would signal dawn. Its lambent, fulgurant, perversely fecund skies remained simultaneously static and ever-changing, a perpetual display of stellar pyrotechnics.

After ablutions and a breakfast lozenge, Ingeniero summoned up all his inner fortitude and ascended to the uppermost level. Iamo perforce accompanied him, sloshing up the spiral stairs.

Lying on his back, slanting his limbs in an X athwart the platform, Ingeniero ordered his slave to fasten the tethers around his ankles and wrists. Iamo complied.

"Now leave the room and do not return for thirty minutes. The discharge of the lens might have unpredictable effects on your substance."

Iamo glopped down the staircase to the bedroom level and Ingeniero was left alone.

The lens stared down at him like the blind eye of an alien god. The controls regulating the shielding film were open to a signal from Ingeniero's cortical implant, just as Iamo was. The amount of time the shield should remain down could be specified.

Sucking in a deep breath, Ingeniero triggered the shield for thirty minutes of exposure.

The smart film went instantly from opaque to transparent, allowing the full force of a million arcane galactic furnaces to strike the lens.

Instantly, the mass of crystal came alive. Excepting a few common low-energy photons that impinged on Ingeniero's retinas and conveyed tenuous information about what was happening in the lens, the various radiations did not pass at light speed through the lens, but rather seemed to collect and mix for several moments within its bulk like seething globules of lava shifting across a thousand spectra, so that

Ingeniero had a brief interval in which to contemplate the awesome phenomenon before the underside of the lens erupted in an almost solid gush of radiance, a flow hereafter sustained by continuous input from outside.

The wave of alien force hit Ingeniero like one of the tsunami of Massenterre. He felt his body reduced to an insensate paste against the dais. Yet at the same time, immense pain threaded every atom of his all-too-corporeal form. His eyeballs seemed to melt in their sockets, dribble down his cheeks. All his joints dissolved, then re-cohered around centers of jagged flint. His inner organs seemed intent on strangling their neighbors. A background noise resolved itself after an eternity into the sound of his own screaming. He thrashed against the unyielding restraints, escape from this torture his only thought. But his struggle availed nothing.

Then, suddenly, Ingeniero was elsewhere.

The muck was cool against his long, sinuous body. Rich scents pervaded the thick medium through which he navigated, providing directions toward food and mates, and away from enemies. Life was ecstasy, every sense in harmony with the environment. Ingeniero gobbled up a nearby shrimplike creature—delicious!—undulated his powerful body, and slithered away in search of food and sex.

The being whom Ingeniero was inhabiting had an average mature lifetime of approximately ten solar revolutions. Ingeniero lived all those years, eventually forgetting any other existence. When that host died—swallowed by something resembling a diamond-shaped manta ray—Ingeniero's consciousness jumped to the predator. He lived years more in that form before making another jump. The manta died peacefully, and Ingeniero found himself hosted by one of the passing shrimps. Several more heterogeneous lifetimes passed until, without warning, Ingeniero found himself back in his human body.

Above him, the lens was dark, inert once more. His pain-free, undeformed body felt utterly unnatural, like a foreign shell.

A portion of Iamo protruded upward from the chamber below. Soon the slave had unfastened his master.

Ingeniero stood with much difficulty, being forced to rely on Iamo's support. Together, they somehow awkwardly descended to the lowest level. There, Ingeniero took a bath in a large artificial diamond tub, using large quantities of the plentiful water melted from a tethered water-ice asteroid. He found himself instinctively making undulant movements in the water as if to glide away, remembered movements his human body could only halfheartedly reproduce.

After emerging from the tub and toweling off, Ingeniero stumbled in a confused daze to bed and fell almost instantly asleep.

In the morning, he felt more his old self. Rummaging through his restored human memories, he found them to be at least as convincing and immediate as those of being a mudworm. Emboldened by having survived his first exposure to the lens, Ingeniero decided to test himself for any improvements in his condition. He detached a lump of mind putty from Iamo and subjected it to his sculptural impress.

The goal of this trial had been a representation of one of the diamond-shaped manta rays. What resulted was a version of that creature that might have been produced by a mildly talented adolescent. Crestfallen, Ingeniero tried to buck himself up. Surely this sculpture was better than his attempt at a termite skyscraper. The hellbath under the lens had produced a measurable level of improvement. Additional sessions would surely sharpen his talents even further.

Ingeniero set the sculpture on a shelf instead of destroying it. Let it stand as an incentive to return to the Chamber of the Lens.

But not today.

In point of fact, Ingeniero could not bring himself to return to the Chamber of the Lens for the next nine days. Why rush? He had six months here, he told himself, and surely just one or possibly two more sessions under the lens would completely restore his creative vitality. And letting his mind rest between sessions would probably aid the process. Too much stretching of his mental capacities could not be good for his sensitive brain.

So Ingeniero busied himself with the few attractions around the tower. He donned his filmy vacuum suit once more and took an abbreviated walking tour of the planetoid. The immediate region boasted several impressive natural formations: stark canyons, jagged craters, brooding chiaroscuro mountains. Partnered with Iamo—whose usefulness in any emergency was unquestionable—Ingeniero pretended he was touring some of the more pleasant aesthetic vistas of the Diffusion, famous bucolic scenes on worlds such as Seabreeze and Cloudtrap.

Life there was none—just a dead calm all day long.

But always above his head when outdoors, the velvety black galactic canopy, splashed with raging colors and churning gases, spitting ions and fountains of brute particles, reminded Ingeniero of the torment that awaited him in the Chamber of the Lens, the silent radiant observers lashing him like a thousand fiery-eyed demons. And of course, the vacuum skies boasted not even the slightest speck of cloud to interfere with the overhead displays. Far from appearing as innocent displays of nature's majesty, this stellar zoo seemed to Ingeniero a collection of malign creatures eager to feast on his corpse.

So the uneasy mind-sculptor retreated inside the tower and sought to lose himself in his recorded simulations and stimulations. But none of these artfully crafted playlets or documentaries carried the same level of immersion that his life as a mudworm had. In retrospect, Ingeniero marveled at the way his old identity had totally dissolved, to be replaced by the consciousness of various marine creatures. What a sublime, liberating experience, conducive toward an all-embracing creativity! Purchased at such incredible pain, true. But had the flensing really been so bad?

As recollections of the harshness of his rite of passage into the mudworld faded somewhat, Ingeniero would return to the Chamber of the Lens and contemplate strapping himself down once more. He would run his hand along the edge of the dais, test the restraints. But he always balked at actually doing so, turning on his heel and hurrying downstairs. What finally motivated him to undergo another excruciation was a third hopeful attempt at mind-sculpting. This essay produced an even more horrid botch than his termite skyscraper.

He was retrogressing, not improving! Impossible, but undeniable . . .

This path led only to disgrace and defeat, the end of Ingeniero the famous artist, and the subsequent desertion by his public, his patrons, his claque of sycophantic friends eager to abandon him for the next hot thing. He had to go under the lens again.

Splayed out once more underneath the cyclopean orb, Ingeniero grimly shut his eyes and triggered the shutter-release command.

Familiarity brought no shield against the titanic pain and torment induced by the hot flood of power from the lens. For the second time, Ingeniero was flayed and dissected, reconstituted as a mass of abused flesh, then launched across the void.

Or did he draw the void down within himself?

His mind came this time into a host he recognized: the sentient insect swarms of Wrasse. With their communal minds distributed across millions of tiny bodies, the Wrassians were essentially immortal, the death of any individual mote being negligible. Consequently, without the release of his host's extinction, Ingeniero spent his entire thirty minutes under the lens experiencing centuries in the life of a single Wrassian swarm that called itself Go-slow. Go-slow's main employment in life was to rehash old mathematical theorems looking for false proofs. This activity consorted poorly with Ingeniero's tastes, and his immersion in the identity of Go-slow was less than perfect.

Ingeniero came to himself feeling slightly disappointed with his second experience under the lens. Once freed by Iamo, the sculptor eagerly made another trial with a portion of Iamo's substance, focusing on producing the image of an individual Wrassian mote. The likeness was passable, but not brilliant. Still, an advance over the alarming nullity of power that Ingeniero had exhibited yesterday. Evidently, a lack of total identification with the host race did not impede the lens's curative effects.

Bolstered by the improvement, Ingeniero resolved to go under the lens again the very next day. And, true to his vow, he did, becoming a gaseous entity inhabiting the atmosphere of a Jovian world. The very next day he underwent another session, diving into the vegetable minds of Saltus IX. And the next day, and the next day, and the next. . . .

By the end of two weeks, the sculptor had regained almost all his old powers.

But at no small price.

Always a thin fellow, Ingeniero now looked positively cadaverous, his eyes blazing with the stored remnants of the immense pain he had experienced, as if each orb were a smaller version of the lens. His hair disarrayed, his clothing soiled, Ingeniero hardly resembled the dapper artist who had arrived on Skyfire several weeks ago. He was plainly experiencing a species of ecstasy he would find impossible to describe. He seemed a driven monomaniac whose obsessions now littered the tower. For everywhere around the tower lay crystal sculptures of mind putty, evidence of Ingeniero's frequent attempts to gauge his progress, a tangible record of all the pullulating life he had experienced, a bizarre menagerie.

In providing the raw material to satisfy its master's mania, Iamo had been consequently reduced to a shadow of its old self. Now the slave resembled a wraith, a smoky wisp containing barely enough material to form a vacuum suit for its master. Iamo's processing power had dwindled also with its loss of bodily circuitry, and it was slow to respond to commands, recognizing only the simplest instructions.

To Ingeniero, neither his dissolute appearance nor Iamo's mattered. All that counted was that he was almost fully healed, restored to his wonted heights of artistic power. Surely just one more session under the lens would push him into new realms of supremacy.

And now that day had arrived.

Tethered securely against the sense-shattering pain that no amount of repetition could diminish, Ingeniero gloated in his triumph over a fate that had sought to rob him of his very reason for existence. Then he unleashed the beneficent wrath of the lens upon his supine form.

Where was he? He was not fixed in any planetary or solar environment. Instead, his consciousness seemed scattered across vast distances. He did not have any obvious sensory organs or input. Yet he somehow apprehended the universe, and his effect on it.

His effect? What was that quality?

Decay, rot, dissolution, extinction.

Ingeniero had come to inhabit the very soul of entropy. Immortal creature or cosmic principle, objective reality or the enforced subjective conceit of his limited intellect, his host this time was the being responsible for all de-coherence, an omnipresent vector of leveling and nonexistence, the essence of negation.

No! Ingeniero tried to break free of this hated host. Entropy was the archenemy of all creators, the force he had fought against with every breath. Yet now he was being forced to identify utterly with the principle.

This had to be the final test of the lens! No mere dumb mechanism, the alien device must intelligently attune itself to the subject beneath it, crafting a program exactly suited to the individual's reformation.

Ingeniero suddenly knew that he had to master this last hurdle or be utterly broken, despite all his past progress. He attempted to calm his fears and merge with entropy as it persistently ground down all creation into tedious uniformity.

But it was no use. His hatred of the universal dissolver, the force that would one day put an end to Ingeniero the living artist and all his creations, was too strong. Ingeniero continued to struggle, although he knew all resistance was doomed.

Thirty minutes that concealed an eternity trickled by before the florid spew of the transformative lens died out.

The man on the dais finally opened his eyes, but no intelligence lived there. Ingeniero did not stir, but merely breathed stertorously. With labored movements, his slave Iamo arrived to undo the restraints.

When Ingeniero did not immediately arise, Iamo bent over him and extended a small probe to measure the master's vital signs. Seemingly alarmed by what it discovered, Iamo flowed itself around Ingeniero to act as a life-support cocoon. Using its synthetic muscles to shift the human's encased limbs, the living suit forced Ingeniero to get up off the platform and walk toward the staircase. Perhaps the servant intended to access the metabolytic lozenges the master had neglected lately. Its motivations were unknown to anyone but itself.

But these enforced movements had a peculiar visible effect on Ingeniero, engendering a kind of transient resuscitation. For one wild moment a shattered intelligence returned to his features. Madness and despair danced in his gaze. Plainly, continued existence was insupportable. Summoning up all his mental discipline, the sculptor cast his most powerful mental bolt.

Instantly, all of Iamo's dwindled substance hardened into its permanent crystalline form. The result of the slave's transformation was the production of a human-shaped statue, its core an anguished, suffocated man caught in mid-stride, his face cast forever in a rictus of self-loathing and unbearable knowledge, like a fly in amber.

When the *Oriole* returned, its crew discovered what had happened and took the fused mass of Iamo and Ingeniero away, back to the worlds of the Diffusion.

Where the statue that came to be known as *The Ultimate Disclosure* shattered all auction records, and insured Ingeniero's reputation for eternity.

Here's an instance where the title definitely came first.

My mate, Deborah Newton, is a longtime yoga practitioner. Preceding each class comes study of the yogic sutras, or texts. But the students who bother with this aspect of the practice are an exclusive lot, and I have often joked that they are studying "secret sutras." Once I had this phrase, adding a woman's name was intuitive. (And why do I have this fixation on the name "Sally" for a certain kind of female, as in my story "The Ballad of Sally NutraSweet"?)

In any case, the title sat unused for some time, until I realized that it applied to a "chick lit" novel. After that, everything fell into place.

For those readers who've enjoyed my humor columns under the rubric "Plumage from Pegasus," you may consider this one of those columns that simply outgrew its 1,500-word limit.

The Secret Sutras of Sally Strumpet

Riley Small's agent actually called Riley personally with the good tidings. Even gruff, self-important, and generally uncommunicative agents tend to be more forthcoming and pleasant when an author stands to earn the agent hundreds of thousands of dollars above and beyond all the other bales of cash he or she has already brought in.

"Riley, good news," said Harvard Morgaine, his speech partly occluded by the ever-present dead cigar in his mouth, the foul smell of which Riley could vividly conjure up even across the width of Manhattan. "Miramax is nearly one hundred percent on board. Weinstein is practically pissing his pants with sheer joy and greed. Know what he said to me? 'Strumpet's going to be bigger than Bridget Jones's ass.' How's that make you feel?"

Riley winced. The comparison between his book and Zellweger's method-acting butt was not one he would have chosen himself. "Uh, swell—I guess."

"Super! OK now, there's just one problem. We've milked the mysterious-author angle just about as long as we can. When Hollywood sticks its dick in the soup, there's no escaping public appearances by the author. *Entertainment Tonight*, Leno, Letterman, the whole circuit. So Sally Strumpet is going to have to finally show her face."

A sick feeling instantly pervaded Riley's gut. He'd known this day was coming ever since he had inked the contract for his book, *The Secret Sutras of Sally Strumpet*, some two years ago. But the inevitability of the fateful moment had not lessened the dread associated with the exposure of his hoax.

"Well, um, Harv, what do you suggest we do?"

"As I suss it, kid, there're only two angles to this dilemma. Either we reveal Sally's real identity—tell the world that their beloved nubile twenty-five-year-old sexual adventuress Sally Strumpet is really a deceitful thirty-five-year-old schlub named Riley Small—or else we continue the charade by providing a living substitute for a vital person who inconveniently doesn't exist. Now, each tactic has its pluses and minuses. The upside to coming clean about your authorship of the book is that it's a simple, honest solution with no chance of blowing up in our faces, and you personally get to bask in the limelight."

"And the downside?"

"The downside is that you, me, your book, and any chance of signing the Miramax deal will go down the toilet faster than Drano. In this case, the limelight will be like napalm from above. You remember that ruckus when the supposed Native American author of *The Education of Little Tree* was revealed to be a white supremacist?"

"Uh-huh."

"Well, that little flap will look like a party at Elaine's compared with the shitstorm that us admitting the truth will bring down on our heads."

"I see . . ." Riley experienced a small hopeful memory of a similar literary scandal that had ended well. "Hey, what about that time in the science fiction world, when that writer everyone thought was a guy—Tipitina?—turned out to be a woman?"

"That Tiptree joker, you mean? Doesn't apply here. Women masquerading as men is cool. People cut them slack because they're perceived as the underdogs trying to make it in a man's world. But a guy shoehorning his way into a field reserved for women—you may as well put your balls into a noose."

Riley winced as Morgaine continued his pitch.

"Now, as far as ramping up the masquerade goes, we're compounding your original sin by orders of magnitude, opening us up to even worse public ridicule and hatred if we're ever exposed. Which, of course, God willing, we won't be. But the commensurate upside is that we both get a shot to ride this baby all the way to a villa in Tuscany and a little grass shack in Maui for each of us. So, what's it going to be?"

Riley could hear Morgaine ferociously chewing his cigar. The silence between author and agent seemed to stretch out forever. Riley considered his future under both scenarios. More importantly, he considered his past, the impulses and circumstances that had led him to write *The Secret Sutras of Sally Strumpet* in the first place. The memories of those despairing days were ultimately what determined his answer.

"Do I get to interview the women we'll be considering to play Sally?"

"Kid, I got a desk full of head shots for you to start looking at right now."

* * *

At age thirty-three, Riley Small had felt crucified on the cross of his own ambitions.

Since college, Riley had been convinced that he would someday be a famous writer. Some fairly significant talent on his part had been adduced by encouraging teachers and friends, convincing Riley that he had the chops to write a great book or three, thus gaining admission into the ranks of the masters he loved. But upon graduation, his dreams began to deflate faster than a parachute sucked into a jet engine. The manuscripts of his first two novels kept coming back from publishers with pleasant but firm brush-offs. The *New Yorker* and the *Paris Review* declined to add Riley's name to their table of contents pages. Virtually every big-name and not-so-big-name agent listed in the *Writer's Digest* guides had very politely failed to respond to his every solicitation for representation of his masterpieces-to-be.

Despite setbacks that would have sent a lesser soul into a screaming retreat, Riley persisted with his dreams. To keep body firmly united with soul, Riley held a number of mediocre jobs on the edges of the publishing industry. By age thirty-three, he had ascended to the unremarkable position of assistant editor at a third-tier "lad" magazine, a publication titled *Royale*. ("Hey—get *Royale!*" was the magazine's advertising tagline. The staffers, however, referred to their employer as "Roy's Ale," for the six-pack mentality of its average subscriber.) At the magazine, Riley proofed articles on South American aphrodisiacs and the sexual kinks of celebrities, all the while plotting his next assault on the Fortress of Literature.

In parallel with his many defeats on the literary front, Riley had also sustained over the sad years more than his share of grievous damage on the romantic battlefield. His unswerving focus on making it as a writer tended to cause him to be less than attentive to such female-appreciated matters as compliments, punctuality, and the kind of social minutiae that insured that any book using Jane Austen as a template would vault to the ranks of best-sellerdom.

But in Riley's defense, he felt, there were other factors behind his dismal string of romantic failures than mere masculine inattention.

Young single urban women today seemed incapable of sustaining any relationship that did not conform to an unreal mass-media template. Tutored by television, movies, and books to expect the perfect boyfriend to be rich, handsome, romantic, witty, faithful, and adoring, while at the same time encouraged to be demanding, capricious, oversensitive, boisterous, and egocentric, the women Riley met and fell in love with invariably undermined any potentially long-term relationship. Not by being horrible bitches by any means. No, their hearts were generally good. But they were all just confused about how to reconcile their factitious needs with the realities of the male character.

Raised on a diet of pink and aqua dreams of having perfectly glossy hair, perfectly rewarding careers, a perfect set of female friends, and perfectly attentive lovers, the women Riley found himself dating were perfectly impossible.

So a succession of live-in affairs had each eventually degenerated into a tense disentangling of formerly shared possessions and the curt exchange of forwarding addresses. At thirty-three, Riley was living alone—miserably, but at least quietly.

It was at this downhearted juncture in his failed life that Riley was struck by his purest moment of literary inspiration.

Browsing the fiction shelves at the Union Square branch of Barnes and Noble one Saturday, Riley had been overwhelmed by the number of chick-lit books, and the lofty positions they occupied on various best-seller lists. He had taken a stack of these novels to a chair and begun to read. At the end of four hours, he knew several things:

1. The psyches of these heroines matched those of Riley's ex-girlfriends almost exactly.
2. At the core of each book was a desire to be accepted despite one's imperfections.
3. On a practical level, nothing would screw up a working girl's day worse than a laddering tear in her pantyhose. Unless it was a wild, cocaine-fueled orgy in the company's coed john.

4. And Riley fervently understood that he could write one of these books.

It took Riley six white-hot months to write *The Secret Sutras of Sally Strumpet*. Into this book he poured the powerful twin streams of both his romantic and artistic frustrations. He found that by combining all the endearingly ditzy and annoyingly winsome qualities of his numerous past lovers into one figure, while minimizing their foibles (all in the interests of readerly self-identification), he had distilled a kind of Ur-heroine who possessed enormous capabilities, charms, and appetites while remaining fascinatingly flawed. Sally Strumpet practically leaped off the page, an adventurous Everywoman evoking readerly empathy, summoned from deep within Riley's anima.

Strictly to formula, the book, despite various narrative detours, was a quest for love. Sally had to work her way through a series of losers before meeting Mr. Right. Sally's stereotypically disappointing paramours all shared the various flaws that Riley had heard himself accused of. Riley constructed Sally's ultimate dream beau—a supernaturally handsome Tierra del Fuegan sheepherder named Esteban Badura—by blending elements of Enrique Iglesias, Antonio Banderas, and Dr. Phil.

And by rigorously excluding everything he knew about great literature, he was able to fashion a thin yet stickily enticing prose style eminently suited to best-sellerdom—the literary equivalent of flypaper.

Riley cast the book as a partially disguised fictionalization of the actual exploits of the pseudonym-concealed "Sally Strumpet." A cleverly worded disclaimer up front insured that the reader could not think otherwise. Judiciously salted with references to barely veiled real persons, places, and events, the narrative slyly borrowed most of its plot from such classics as *Tom Jones, Fanny Hill, Candy,* and *Fear of Flying*. (The latter novel used despite Jong's insistence that none of what she wrote qualified as chick lit.) Of course, plenty of modern touches—heartfelt cell phone and e-mail exchanges; massive shopping expeditions;

numerous movie references—concealed these borrowings. Riley even managed to salve his conscience by modeling the big climax on certain scenes from *Ulysses*. Just to ice the cake, Riley layered in some borrowed mysticism from a dozen New Age philosophies, thus justifying the whimsical title.

Once the book was finished, Riley knew he had written a masterpiece—of its type. He began marketing it with a dedication he had never expended on his serious work. He concentrated solely on attracting an agent, since he wanted an intermediary between him and any publisher, to preserve the facade of female authorship. He met Harvard Morgaine at a party sponsored by *Royale*, and managed to convince the dapper, silver-haired agent to read the manuscript. Morgaine swiftly recognized the virtues of the book and agreed to rep it.

The contract Morgaine secured from Aleatory House was for a moderate seventy-five-thousand-dollar advance. The first printing was set at fifty thousand copies.

Those copies sold out in five weeks.

Now, nearly a year after publication, Riley's book remained in every top ten list, fluctuating in sales according to various bouts of publicity but never dropping below the number-ten spot on any national list. Once the announcement of an impending movie was made, sales would doubtlessly soar even higher.

Riley now had more money than he had ever imagined having.

But none of the other joys of authorship.

Those belonged to Sally Strumpet.

Who had, despite her endearing ways, proved to be a treacherous bitch.

* * *

"OK, Riley," said Morgaine, "I've winnowed down our possibles to twenty candidates, based on their physical resemblance to Sally, the way she describes herself in the book."

"Harv, I wrote the book, remember? Not Sally. Sally doesn't exist."

Morgaine extracted his soggy cigar and waved it dismissively. "Of course, of course. Just a manner of speaking. You did such a convincing job bringing her to life, it's only natural to talk about her like she really exists. Which she soon will. After a limited fashion. Anyhow, all I need you to do now is give me your opinion about which gal has that special Strumpet strut. We really need to pick someone who can convince the world that she wrote *Secret Sutras*."

Riley leaned back wearily in one of the leather chairs in Morgaine's office. The two men were alone. Riley's gaze traveled the shelves lined with the books written by Morgaine's clients. His eyes jerked away from the multiple copies of *Secret Sutras* in their saccharine pastel covers. Next to those abominations stood last year's winner of the National Book Award, contributed by another client of Morgaine's. By all rights, a Riley Small novel should have rested there. But instead Riley's only legacy, totally anonymous, was a book that felt like it had been ghostwritten for some selfish, larger-than-life celebrity.

Knuckling his eyes, Riley said, "OK, Harv, I'll try. Let's hope the perfect Sally Strumpet is waiting for us out there."

Morgaine re-socketed his cigar and slapped Riley's knee. "Excellent! Let's get the girls onto the catwalk. And remember—none of these babes know what they're really interviewing for. The last thing we need is for word to get out that we're searching for a Strumpet look-alike."

Summoned by intercom, Morgaine's office assistant—the perky, petite Nia Poole—conducted the first candidate in.

Sally Strumpet, the whole world knew, was fashion-model tall, "but not as skinny as one of those masochistic walking clothes hangers. I'm quite nicely padded in fact, from addiction to Cheesecake Factory goodies. In a perfect world, they'd use me as their spokeswoman!" She possessed a "tawny mane of curls that owes more to nurture than nature—nurture being defined as the tender ministrations of the fabulous Mr. Jean." She liked to dress casually, especially for her rough-and-tumble job as videocam operator for a cable news program. But she could stun a room of men when really dolled up, like that time when she crashed the UN reception for President Putin. (It was at the UN that she had met Esteban Badura, who was present so far from his sheep to testify about global warming in his South American homeland.)

The woman who entered the office now matched many of the Sally Strumpet specs. But Riley could immediately tell she wasn't right for the impersonation. Her face was too harsh and angular, her attitude too cruel. The planes of her cheeks looked like they had been sharpened on a grindstone. Without being invited, the woman sat down and crossed her legs as if she were Sharon Stone under interrogation. Spotting Morgaine's dead cigar, she took that icon as permission to light up a cigarette of her own.

"This gig include medical coverage? 'Cuz I've got this pre-existing condition—"

Riley rolled his eyes, trying to signal Morgaine to cut this interview short. But the agent was politely persisting in questioning the woman, as if she could ever possibly stand in for Sally Strumpet.

Once the first candidate left, Morgaine turned hopefully to Riley. "So, what'd you think?"

"Harv, I would sooner dress up in drag myself than hire that woman. She would disgrace Sally's good name. Jesus, I thought she was going to slit both our throats for the sheer thrill of it with those daggers she called fingernails!"

"All right, maybe she wasn't perfect. But we've got nineteen more to go."

The next woman radiated more of Sally's innocent *joie de vivre*. But when she saw Morgaine's library she uttered a brazen squawk and said, "Jesus, look at all them books! What're you guys anyway, perfessers?"

The third candidate also failed Riley's inspection when she opened her mouth. It was not her choice of words but rather the timbre of her voice, which sounded like Fran Drescher's filtered through George Burns's vocal cords.

And so the afternoon went, each succeeding woman presenting some fatal flaw of either looks, character, or intelligence. Four hours after they had started, both Morgaine and Riley were exhausted and dispirited.

"I thought number twelve had potential—" Morgaine gamely ventured.

"You mean potential to fall forward onto her face at any minute? Oh, excuse me, her face would never hit the ground! I've never seen such an outrageous boob job. She had to have ten pounds of silicone in each tit, for Christ's sake!"

Morgaine smiled wistfully at the memory. "I was going to ask you if we could alter the next printing of your book to include some amplified chest dimensions for Sally, but I guess you wouldn't—"

Riley surged abruptly out of his chair, nearly tipping it over. "Damn it, Harv, that tears it! It's bad enough I created this monster in the first place, but I'm certainly not giving her retroactive knockers bigger than her head! Like none of the previous readers would even notice the changes, either! Look, I'm going home now. Call me when you need me again."

"That'll be tomorrow. Those women all came from just one agency, and I've got dozens of others lined up."

"Wonderful, just wonderful. I can hardly wait."

* * *

In the taxi back to his apartment, Riley was plagued by a kaleidoscope of shifting faces. All the mock Sally Strumpets he had interviewed rose and fell before his mind's eye, leering and grimacing, beckoning and taunting. They had all been just close enough to the "real" Sally to freak Riley out. He felt that some malign deity had stolen his brainchild and warped her over and over again, creating twisted versions of his ideal.

When Sally had existed only in Riley's mind, she had been utterly self-consistent and utterly authentic. Her transfer to the printed page had diluted her nature and character a trifle. But this final attempt at actually instantiating her in the flesh threatened to corrupt her entirely. Was it possible for a Platonic ideal ever to manifest itself in this degenerate realm? Yet cruel circumstances dictated that he had to continue trying.

How he would find the strength to face tomorrow's interviews and any subsequent ones, he could not say.

When success had finally visited Riley, he had immediately done two things. He had quit *Royale* magazine—not in a thundering fit of denunciations; after all, he had not been mistreated, and the amiable if dead-end job had paid the rent—and he had gotten new digs. From a crappy studio in Hell's Kitchen he had moved to a modest co-op on the Upper East Side. Doorman, concierge, snooty neighbors, expensive little pampered dogs, the whole works. Riley hadn't enjoyed his new living quarters as thoroughly as he had thought he would. The sterility of the neighborhood depressed him. But he felt his new status as a best-selling (anonymous) author required him to live in such respectable terrain.

Up in his co-op, Riley kicked off his shoes, took a beer from his immaculate Sub-Zero fridge, and slumped down in front of his theater-sized TV. With alcohol and cable, he vowed to shut his brain off for the night.

Halfway through *Who Wants to Create a Reality Show?*, a program that followed competing teams of amateurs in Hollywood trying to pitch a reality show, there came a rather assertive knocking on Riley's door. Muzzy from his fourth beer, he staggered to answer the summons. Halfway to the door, he wondered who could be visiting him, and how they had gotten past the building's staff without Riley's being informed.

Riley tried to peer through the peephole but couldn't get his bleary eye to focus. "Screw it." He twisted the handle and yanked the door inward, banging it into his unshod toes.

"Jesus Christ!" Riley bent to soothe the aggrieved foot. When he straightened, his visitor had impertinently stepped inside.

Sally Strumpet wore black jeans, nicely packed, and scuffed red leather clogs. A ratty leather jacket gaped open to reveal a white shirt over an ample but not outrageous bosom. Her irrepressible mass of curls was partially tamed by a scrunchie, but a few tendrils escaped to frame her face. She stood an inch or two taller than Riley, and her smile was the same one she had displayed when she had triumphed over weather-girl Gwen York, her hated rival, for the affections of Jack Burleigh, the newsman at the station where they all worked.

Riley's brain threatened meltdown. Disaster klaxons seemed to fill his ears. Yet somehow he could still hear Sally clearly when she spoke. Her voice was as poignantly real as his mother's, and as sexy as Kathleen Turner reciting Anaïs Nin's pornography.

"I understand you've been looking for me, so here I am. Are you alone now? Is this a good time?"

"Who—who are you?" The question was meaningless in the face of Sally's majestic presence, but Riley could summon up no other words.

Sally stepped boldly inside and closed the door behind her. "Oh, I think you know quite well who I am, Mr. Big." The woman winked and grinned at this play on Riley's surname, but when Riley remained stone-faced, her brave expression cracked a little. "Unless you've forgotten me so soon?"

Riley found himself somehow on the far side of the room from the woman, his instinctive retreat stopped only by the windows (which afforded him a minuscule view of Central Park when he craned awkwardly). "You're some kind of actress. You have to be. You can't be Sally Strumpet. She doesn't exist. I invented her."

Sally spread her arms wide and arched her back like a lazy tiger, lending a disturbing prominence to her chest. "Do I really look like some cheap figment of your imagination? You can believe whatever you want about my origins, but you can't deny I'm real." Sally slapped her generous butt. "At least that's what the scale tells me every morning."

Riley began to grow irritated. "You have to be a joke, right? Well, it's not funny. Who sent you? How did you get this address? Are you from one of the tabloids? Where's the camera?" Riley could just see his goofy face plastered all over Page Sixes around the globe under the headline *Hoax Author Unmasked / Falls for His Own Scam.*

The intruder assumed a truly crestfallen look that verged on the tearful. "Gee, Mr. Oh-So-Big, I know I'm not much to look at or every man's dream date, but no girl likes having her very identity denied. Are you asking me to just shrivel up and disappear?"

Riley felt sheepish at his rudeness. Whoever this woman was, she had done nothing yet to earn his disrespect. Better to take her at her impossible word and see where such a tactic led. "All right then, you're Sally Strumpet. What are you doing here?"

Sally brightened up into a semblance of mild outrage. "I'm pissed! You're trying to find someone to impersonate me. I don't want some cheap tramp parading around the world and abusing my image like a street vendor's knockoff Prada handbag. Those girls you interviewed today were all dimwits and roundheels!"

Roundheels. That was an archaic term Riley loved and one that he had put in Sally's mouth on more than one occasion. "How—how did you—?"

Sally winked. "Oh, I see a lot of things. Anyhow, you don't need to look any further for someone to hide your authorship behind. You've got me now. Tomorrow morning, you're going to call Morgaine and tell him to cancel the auditions. Then we'll go in and meet with him to start arranging my public appearances."

Riley considered the ultimatum. This woman, whoever she was, looked and acted so much like Sally Strumpet that no other candidate could possibly compete. Sure, she was brash and crazy, maybe a stalker even, bursting in on him like this instead of just showing up at Morgaine's office during the auditions with the other candidates. But why not accept fate and use her as she proposed?

"Suppose I agree to your plan? What're your terms?"

Sally waved the question aside. "Oh, I'm sure we can work out something mutually agreeable."

"Well, OK then. I guess we've got a deal."

Riley extended his hand to shake, fully expecting to encounter the grip of a ghost. But Sally's handshake was firm and warm.

"Now, where can I reach you tomorrow?"

Sally shucked off her jacket and threw it on the couch. Twin flicks of her feet disposed of her clogs. "Right here, if it's OK with you. I don't have any other place to stay at the moment. And I figure that since my life story bought this place, I've got as much right to be here as you. Unless you're seeing someone else these days. It wouldn't be the first time a guy ditched me after I helped him reach success."

Riley hardly knew how to respond. He did owe his current stature to Sally Strumpet. But this woman wasn't her—was she? How could she be? He had invented Sally! Yet this familiar stranger acted so certain of her own identity—

Riley contemplated another lonely night spent in his empty bed. "No, I'm not seeing anyone else. You can stay."

"Great!" The couch received Sally's shapely butt alongside her jacket. She smiled wickedly up at Riley and patted a cushion. "Now, have a seat. Relax. We've got *a lot* to talk about. Remember my third sutra? 'Intense private conversation between a man and a woman is the high road to a low-down activity.'" She giggled and looked at Riley with a becoming blush creeping across her cheeks. "God, I've never actually said that to a man before. But I know that you above anyone will understand."

* * *

Riley had never seen Harvard Morgaine at a loss for words. The agent was generally unflappable, ready with a rude comeback or salty quip for any circumstance. But encountering the forceful reality of the woman who refused to answer to any name other than "Sally

Strumpet" left Morgaine deflated, empty of easy rejoinders or useful conclusions.

Riley and his agent sat unaccompanied in Morgaine's office. Sally had been dispatched on a shopping trip with Morgaine's assistant, Nia Poole, abetted by the agency's credit card. Along with her lack of residence, Sally claimed not to have any current wardrobe other than the clothes on her back. That deficit was being remedied even as Riley and Morgaine sought to piece together their thoughts.

Riley spoke first. "She didn't lay any claim to my royalties then?"

"No, not a cent. She signed the contract I had ready without a second's hesitation. Salary of five thousand a week for an unspecified period. She quoted one of the sutras: 'Needy girls do not have to be greedy girls.'"

"Number fourteen."

"Whatever. It's damn good money, sure, but not a patch on what she might've asked for, if she really is sticking to this crazy claim that she's the one and only Sally Strumpet, author of your book."

Morgaine took the dead cigar from his mouth and studied it a long moment before speaking again. "And Christ knows, I might've sided with her if she pushed the claim. Sorry, kid, but she's that good."

"You're telling me. I almost believe her insane story myself."

Riley recalled what had happened last night.

Several hours of talking, mostly by Sally, had served to update Riley on everything in Sally's life that had purportedly occurred to her since the close of *Secret Sutras*. Not once did she depart from the implicit assertion that she was the fictional heroine of Riley's book. Her narrative had been utterly consistent with the events of the book, forming a sequel that Riley might have written himself. He experienced a genuine pang at the sad fate of handsome shepherd Esteban Badura, lost to a rapacious melanoma engendered by the ozone hole over his native land. Riley even felt himself tearing up when Sally recounted how her Tierra del Fuegan in-laws had heroically taken over the sheep-herding duties, allowing Sally to return to the United States and seek solace in work and possibly even a new companion. Imagine Sally's surprise when she found herself a celebrity thanks to a certain book.

Afterward, as half-promised, Riley and Sally had indeed moved to the bedroom. There, Riley experienced what was simply the best sex of his life. He was hardly surprised that he knew intimately all of Sally's turn-ons and could pleasure her with unfailing insight. After all, he had invented her, right? It was like God knowing what went on in, say, a cat's brain.

The congruity between Sally's desires and Riley's moves engendered in Riley a greater confidence than any he had ever felt before while in bed with a woman. Even if this impossible incarnation of Sally failed to fulfill Morgaine's need for a PR-campaign beard, she was doing wonders for Riley's libido.

But there was one creepy thing about their lovemaking: Sally's ability to anticipate all of *Riley's* specific desires. How could the creation know the creator so well? Had this happened with Galatea and her sculptor? Riley began to wonder who really filled which role, and grew slightly nauseated with a kind of freshman existential angst.

But he wasn't truly spooked until, on the verge of sleep, Sally quoted the twenty-fifth sutra: "'The only thing better than after-play late at night is foreplay early in the morning.'"

Having heard that, Riley jolted out of his drowsy stupor and lay awake staring at the ceiling for the next three hours.

There were only two dozen sutras in the published book, one for each chapter. In an early draft, Riley had indeed included a twenty-fifth, the very maxim Sally had just quoted.

But no one, not even Harvard Morgaine, had ever seen that deleted chapter. Riley had been saving that twenty-fifth sutra for a sequel.

Morgaine snapped his fingers in front of Riley's face. "Don't go catatonic on me so soon, Small. I need you to keep your head screwed on straight during this charade. It's going to be a year and half, more likely two, until the movie debuts and we can gradually phase this chick out. We're going to have to work hand in glove with her all that time. If she's going to send you to la-la land every time you think about her, then we've got a problem. We need you to ride herd on her in public and feed her lines."

"Feed her lines? You've talked to her, Harvard. She knows the book better than me. And as for improvising, she's more totally in character than De Niro. And what do you mean, 'ride herd on her'?"

"I've got it all set up. You're her publicist now. You'll accompany her everywhere, make sure she doesn't flip out and screw us over somehow. I even got you a salary from Aleatory House! After all, before today, they didn't know you even existed."

"Oh, now, Harvard, wait just a goddamn minute—"

"There's no backing out, Small. We can't just turn this broad loose unsupervised. And I can't do the hand-holding, I've got a fucking literary agency to run. Look at it this way: it's the exact same schedule you'd have to follow if you were actually known in public as the author, but this way you're getting an extra paycheck for your time."

"Oh, Jesus, this is totally humiliating. To stand there in the shadows like a flunky while she gets all the glory. I can't believe this."

"Believe it—or else."

Laden with packages, Sally and Nia returned several hours later, hours that Riley had spent pissily bemoaning his lot to a hard-hearted Morgaine.

Sally dumped an armful of Bergdorf boxes into Riley's lap. "Whew! I'm exhausted."

"Why?" Riley asked.

"What's my favorite color, Mr. Big?"

"Uh, pumpkin."

"Correctomundo. You have any idea how hard it is to find a matching bra, thong, and sandals in pumpkin?"

* * *

The next three months of Riley Small's life were composed of equal parts boredom, jealousy, pride, humiliation, and excruciating bliss. He felt like a torture victim who had earned conjugal visits between sessions on the rack.

The debut of Sally Strumpet caused a firestorm in the media akin to the release of nude pictures of J. K. Rowling. After so long in seclusion, the author of the sexy best seller was as much in demand as a closemouthed presidential advisor at a congressional hearing. Sally was booked onto every possible TV show, from dawn to the wee hours of the morning. Any time left free in her schedule was devoted to print interviews and photo shoots. Charity events and award galas thrummed to her triumphant, engaging presence. The hottest clubs in Manhattan and L.A. played host to her leisure-time, paparazzi-attracting activities.

Sally endeared herself to her public by her general air of gawky competence and klutzy charm. The disaster she caused on Regis and Kelly's show, for instance, with the exploding quiche, caused a million female viewers to instantly bond with her.

But one phenomenon that truly frightened Riley was the way that real people stepped out from the woodwork claiming to know Sally and to be the originals of figures in her book. Their impossible assertions bestowed on Sally even more existential validity and heft. Riley found it particularly hard, for instance, to meet with the other women in Sally's ritual Tuesday-night reading group. Not just because he had invented them all—hadn't he?—but because one of them, Lynda Gorodetsky, was an ardent man-hater and stared poisonous daggers at Riley throughout the entire meal they all shared.

Despite his unease throughout the mad whirl, Riley stayed by her side in the role of humble publicist. Ignored by anyone of importance, forced to listen over and over to the same line of inane chatter about his misbegotten best seller, he felt his grip on sanity slipping. Occasionally, when Sally performed particularly well, Riley could take some pleasure in hearing certain bons mots from his novel rendered in a witty manner. But for the most part, the whole concept of Sally and her libidinous escapades quickly palled for Riley, especially after that time on Oprah's show when, as he lurked in the greenroom, Sally began describing her current sex life with him. The anecdotes were all flattering—too flattering, perhaps—and she didn't use his name. But Riley's ears and other portions of his anatomy were left burning nonetheless.

Sally herself, up close in tangible form, presented even more challenges.

Ms. Strumpet had elected to continue living at Riley's digs. And to continue occupying his bed. Even when the pair were on the road, she managed to sneak into Riley's room late at night when all the tabloid swarm had dissipated. She seemed to have no interest in taking any other lovers, despite myriad opportunities. Remarkably, sex with Sally managed to remain at the same high peak of their first encounter. Nonetheless, Riley felt simultaneously fulfilled and unsatisfied, as if he were screwing a woman created to match his exact desirability specs, but one who could never surprise him.

Riley couldn't figure out why he continued to remain as Sally's lover. Did he satisfy all her needs in a healthy manner, or simply cancel them out like a key fitting into a lock? Was he good for her, or merely a programmed response?

He tried to speak to Sally about these paradoxes. They did communicate reasonably well, both in bed and out, so long as certain topics regarding her origin and his slave status were avoided. But all she did was quote sutra number nine to him: "'The more familiar a woman becomes to a man, the less he knows about her.'"

On a day that was remarkably free of commitments back in Manhattan, Riley went to see Harvard Morgaine. (Sally was busy getting her hair done.)

Morgaine ushered Riley heartily into his office. "Welcome home, kid. I couldn't be happier about how things are going. I assume you're monitoring your bank account hourly, just like me. Sales of the book are way, way up, of course, and the first check from Miramax has cleared. I hope you appreciated how many points I negotiated for our share of the box office. I was absolutely brilliant! You're a lucky bastard to have me for an agent, kid!"

Morgaine's joyous avarice left Riley even more dispirited than he'd been when he entered the office. "Harv, I just can't take any of this *Secret Sutras* stuff anymore. I'm ready to crack. I need a vacation."

"A vacation? Well, why not! Sally is unsinkable now after all she's been through. And if she was planning to shaft us, she'd have done it by now. Hit the road, kid, and have yourself a ball."

"You—you'll tell Sally I'm leaving, OK? But not where I'm going. Because I can't—"

Morgaine clapped Riley on the back. "Sure, no problem. Leave her to me."

Feeling somewhat more hopeful, Riley went to the travel agent closest to Morgaine's office and booked a flight leaving that day for Cancún, before he changed his mind—or Sally could change it for him.

Twelve hours later he was sitting by a palm-fronded bar sipping a *mojito*. Despite the presence of a poster of Sally's smiling face, with text in Spanish advertising *Las Sutras Secretas de Sally Ramera*, Riley felt better than he had in ages. A weight seemed to have been lifted off his shoulders. He could breathe again. His soul floated lightly inside him.

For the next week, Riley led a mindless existence, soaking up sun and rum, swimming, admiring women who weren't Sally. He began to believe that there would be some kind of life for him outside of the whole *Secret Sutras* morass.

Eventually, one thing led to another and Riley found himself one languorous afternoon undressing in the room of a very attractive blond legal secretary from Duluth named Sharon.

After a long embrace and kiss, Sharon excused herself. "Get in bed, honey. I'll be right back."

Riley watched her disappear into the bathroom from his recumbent vantage on the tropical-patterned sheets. Despite his excitement, he felt a little drowsy and half-closed his eyes.

Not more than a minute could have passed before Sharon reappeared, wrapped in a towel. She did not bound amorously toward the bed, but instead seemed preoccupied, moving to the bureau to rummage around on its top for something.

Eventually she turned her head. As soon as she saw Riley, she screamed.

"Who are you! What're you doing here!"

Riley jumped up, all his lust deflated by her shriek. "Sharon, that's not funny. You invited me in. We were going to make love. My name's Riley—"

"Get out! Get out!"

Riley hastily dressed and scrammed.

For the rest of the day he waited nervously in his room, every minute expecting to be approached by a resort executive or, worse, a corrupt and tyrannical Mexican police officer who would demand that Riley explain his rapist ways. But no such confrontation occurred, and finally Riley managed to fall uneasily asleep, even without supper.

In the morning he was awakened by the sound of his own door opening. In walked what was obviously a honeymooning couple escorted by a lowly hotel employee burdened with baggage. When the newcomers spotted Riley in bed, there was much confusion and embarrassment. Riley grew indignant at the luggage-toter's insistence that this room was supposed to be vacant. Once the intruders had been shooed off, Riley dressed and went to speak to the manager, with whom he had developed a casual relationship.

The portly, mustached man regarded Riley as if he were an undistinguished new species of bug. "I'm sorry, señor, but I must contradict your account of our mutual friendship established this past week. Especially as we have no record of your registration at our resort. Obviously there has been some mistake. You will have to register for the first time—for the second time, if you insist—or else vacate your room."

Riley felt spectral hands on his shoulder, claws knotting in his guts. He chose to vacate.

At the airport, he was relieved to discover that his open-dated return ticket was still accepted at face value. The inspection of his passport was cursory. Just as well. Riley suspected that the document would not hold up any longer to in-depth confirmation by authorities.

The flight home was interminable. By the time the taxi dropped Riley off at the door of his co-op, he was trembling with exhaustion and trepidation. Wearily manhandling his bag, he approached the doorman.

"How may I help you, sir? Whom do you wish to visit?"

Riley stiffened in shock. Not here, too— "Aw, c'mon, Jeff, it's me, Riley Small. I live in 1203—"

A veil of disgust dropped over the doorman's features and he lost all semblance of good manners. "Another groupie for Ms. Strumpet, huh? How many of you guys do I have to get arrested before you all get the message?"

Riley set off jogging, his bag pitilessly thumping his vertebrae.

At Harvard Morgaine's office, Nia Poole erected a formidable barrier of professional indifference toward this intruder claiming he was a Morgaine client, but Riley finally managed to get admitted to Morgaine's inner sanctum on the strength of some personal details about Morgaine that he disclosed. Nia seemed shocked by a stranger possessing such intimate knowledge of some of Morgaine's grosser peccadilloes.

Morgaine's clean-shaven, rugged face wore a look of barely concealed irritation. "Now, Mr. Small, is it? What brings you here today? Something about *Secret Sutras*, my assistant said."

Riley poured out the whole story. Morgaine listened without comment. Riley dared to hope he had finally found a believer in the strange fate that had overtaken him. But Morgaine's subsequent speech shattered that last illusion.

"Mr. Small, rest assured that my client Sally Strumpet will pursue all her legal options against anyone who contests her authorship of her book. To put it bluntly, the full weight of the law will come down on you like a circus tent full of elephant shit. Why you wannabe writers feel compelled to fantasize like this about celebrities—"

Riley fled in mid-bluster, something he had often wanted to do with Morgaine but had never before dared.

Being a nonentity had its liberating moments.

Googling Sally's home page at the library's public-access terminal, Riley learned that her next bookstore appearance in Manhattan was tomorrow, at the very Union Square store where he had first been inspired to write *Secret Sutras*.

Low on cash, dubious of the validity of his credit cards, Riley spent the night on a bench in the park behind the library.

He was at the store several hours before Sally's slated signing, looking like a half-drowned sailor. He killed time at the café on one of the upper floors, nursing a coffee and muffin. Half an hour in advance of the signing, Riley had positioned himself unobtrusively near the table stacked high with copies of *Secret Sutras*, so that he could see without being seen. When Sally entered, Riley was relieved to note that she seemed to be unaccompanied by any flunkies.

She took her seat behind the table set up with mountains of her book. *Her* book! The line for autographs already stretched across the store and out the door. Had Riley been in Sally's seat, he would have been more annoyed than pleased at the immense turnout, contemplating all the inane small talk he would have to make, the dumb misprisioned praise he would have to listen to, and the pains his wrist would endure. But Sally, to the contrary, seemed all earnest sunshine and good will, gratitude and flirtatiousness.

Why oh why had he made her so damn noble?

She must have sold and signed two hundred books. Riley could feel the painful extraction of every cent of royalties that should have gone into his pocket, every leaking ounce of karma that should have been his. No wonder he was turning invisible.

After a fulsome round of congratulations from the elated, sales-inebriated store manager, when Sally finally seemed ready to leave, Riley trailed her out.

He accosted her half a block away, when she stopped to hail a taxi.

"Hey, you bitch! I want my life back!"

Sally turned and coolly regarded Riley from her superior height. Her gorgeous face seemed to sear itself onto his cortex, the place where it had first formed.

"You ran out on me," Sally said. "That was not appreciated. Don't you remember my seventh sutra? 'A woman's wounded heart is like a wounded lion. You'd better pray it never recovers its health and gets nosing on your trail.'"

Suddenly Riley's consciousness inverted and projected itself through space. He seemed to be regarding himself with Sally's eyes, gauging himself with Sally's emotions. The father became the brainchild fully for the first time. Realization of the existential obligations he had placed on Sally by creating her crashed over him like a tsunami. Flop sweat soaked his clothes. He felt like God on trial at some cosmic Hague courtroom.

A few seconds later, Riley was back in his own head. But all the fight had gone out of him, leaving him as stinkingly droopy as a bartender's rag.

"You're right. I'm a rat. So I'm leaving again now, but this time I'll say good-bye to your face. Good-bye."

Sally smirked victoriously, but not without a margin of charity. "Oh, so you want to make the same mistake twice? Not exactly a quick learner."

Riley halted. "What do you mean?"

"Why not ask me if I want you back?"

"Do you?"

"Sure. Weren't we created for each other?"

Riley could practically hear cosmic theme music swelling in the background. He knew then that just as he had created Sally, Someone

Up There had created *him* and devised this fate for him, and that both Riley and Sally were equal in the eyes of this irony-fixated deity.

"I can't deny it," Riley said. "But are you really willing to give me a second chance after I ditched you and cheated on you?"

"I might be. If I heard the three little words every gal is truly longing to hear."

Riley felt the requested phrase surface almost involuntarily from his diaphragm and get stuck halfway up his throat. He didn't want to utter it. For one thing, he wasn't sure of what he felt. For another, he resented being coerced. But declaiming his passion seemed the only way to get his life back.

"I—I love you, Sally."

Sally grinned like a cat with a mouse's tail hanging from its jaws. "There, that wasn't so hard, was it? Although you used four, arguably five words instead of three. Tsk, tsk, not economical for a writer of your talents. Now c'mon, here's a cab. We've got to get you cleaned up and looking handsome for the dinner tonight with Sonny Mehta."

Riley numbly tumbled after Sally into the taxi, and the car drove off. Churning, confused thoughts about his future revolved through his head. But one thing he knew for sure.

There was another book waiting inside his brain. A book just as powerful as the one that had created Sally Strumpet. A book of harsher, more tragic sutras.

And any character could die in a sequel.

Anyone.

Author/editor Chris Roberson asked me to submit an "adventure" story to an anthology that he was compiling. I think he was envisioning Indiana Jones. Instead, he got David Lynch.

That will teach him to offer such a broad mandate.

This story belongs to the subgenre I term "bardo fiction." Bardo is the famous Tibetan term for the period between death and the next reincarnation. I suppose the first prototypical, if not exactly bardo, fiction in English might be Ambrose Bierce's "An Occurrence at Owl Creek Bridge." I do know that there are not all that many examples of this mode. One outstanding instance, though, is Damon Knight's Humpty Dumpty: An Oval.

Search it out before you leave this world.

Eel Pie Stall

"To die will be an awfully big adventure."

—J. M. Barrie

Tang of the river: ancient impregnated septic tidal flats exposed to the air; rotting fish; saturated driftwood; tarred pilings; engine exhaust; weeds going to slime.

Sound of the river: slop of wavelets on insensible slippery cement steps; raucous gulls aloft; chugging engines; creak of winches; workmen bantering.

Sight of the river: a cold rippling welcoming pewter grave, with flanking buildings as the only mourners.

Tansy Bynum pauses at a waist-high stone wall along the southern bank of the Thames. Rests her hands on the flat gritted icy top of the wall. Feels nothing. Equilibrium between inner self and outer world. But not in favor of the living.

Tansy turns away momentarily from the sight, sound, and smell of her prospective final home. Polyester scarf printed with cartoon fishes binding moderate mouse-colored hair. No-brand sunglasses contradicting the gray skies. Cheap beige cloth coat down to midthigh. Worn wool skirt. Sensible stockings. Scuffed brown tie shoes.

Wrists crossing twixt her modest breasts, fingers tucked beneath armpits. Unpainted mouth composed in a taut straight line. Shuffling pointlessly farther down the path along the embankment, wall on her left.

People around her with jobs and lovers, chores and duties, children and parents, wants and lusts. Smiles, frowns, musing looks. Just to feel something, anything.

Leave them behind. Shed these mockers like a final molt.

Long slow nowhere trudge. River never out of vision, hearing, or odor-waft. Wall now less well-maintained, crumbling in places, beginning to be marred with rude graffiti. Less of a barrier to what calmly awaits. Inevitable destiny. People dwindling in numbers: going, going, gone. Nebulous empty borderland between what is and what will be. Moisture begins to seep from the lowering clouds in a prelude to a drizzle.

Up ahead, scabbed against the wall like an ungainly limpet: a shack or shed or stall, some kind of slovenly commercial affair. Unpainted boards and timbers blackened with pollution and age. No signage. Grommeted dingy canvas front rolled up and balanced on the slanting gap-shingled roof, exposing dark interior. Chest-high counter projecting like an idiot's pendulous lower lip.

Abreast of the stall and ready to step past. Unseeing fate-blinded eyes straight front, no interest in what lurks within the shed.

"Tansy Bynum."

She stops, astounded.

Looks left.

A shadowy artificial shallow cave untainted by any modern conveniences. Medieval. Prehistoric. Lower half of the back wall composed of the stones of the embankment barrier. Faintest of reddish-orange illumination supplied by a smoldering bed of coals in an open-faced brick oven. Large wooden singed paddle for retrieving items from the hearth. On the counter, a squat open-topped wooden canister holding a heterogeneous assortment of bone-handled spoons and forks. Crooked shelves within hosting clay mugs, crockery, spice jars, flour-dusted burlap sacks.

And the proprietor.

Greasy salt-and-pepper beard, disheveled mop of jaundiced silver hair. Coarse features, shabby, cast-off clothes. Fingerless gloves more moth holes than fabric. Awkwardly hunched armature of his short frame. Repellant, but somehow rendered less so by the appropriateness of his environment, like a hermit crab in a particularly apt adopted shell.

The proprietor fixes her with a sly, obsequious wink. A potential customer hooked.

"Did you—did you call my name?"

"'Fraid not. Couldn't very well, could I? Strangers, you and me. No, just asked, 'Fancy a pie, mum?'"

"Oh."

Tansy makes to move on. Eating. A pointless activity now.

The gnomish proprietor reaches below Tansy's sight to bring up a small pie in a tin plate. Crust still uncooked white. Edges neatly crimped. Two slits in the top like nostrils.

"No. I have to go—"

A friendly leer. "Ah, now, why off so fast? You'll never have another pie like this. Best in all of London. No one else makes them like old Murk."

Senselessly, irrationally rooted to the spot somehow. First time anyone's talked to her in days. Stomach suddenly awakes noisily. A macabre thought arises, born from tawdry television viewing: won't the coroner have an easier time dating her demise if there are remnants of a meal in her gut? Her last selfless contribution to the ease of others, after a life devoted to such one-way gestures.

"What—what kind of pie?"

"Ah, mum, best to show you."

Pie in gnarled hand set down on shelf. Murk's face prideful beneath warty brow. Bending forward like a broken toy. Hoisting strongly two-handed an antique wooden bucket chest-high. Sets it on the counter, where it slops a scant rill of water over its rim. Bucket obscures the dwarfish man.

"Have a dekko then, child. C'mon, naught'll happen to you."

On tiptoes to peer into the bucket.

Tansy's first impression: a single braided whip in constant coiling motion, a flux of silver and black. Then: separation into component parts: heads, eyes, bodies, flukes, gills.

A bucket of writhing eels, sinuous, muscled, constrained.

Their weavings seem to scribe watery ideograms in perpetual flicker, transiting from one half-perceived meaning to another.

And at random moments, as their serpentine bodies open a clear view to the bottom of the bucket, millisecond impressions of something piebald, gold and blue, beneath them. Like a queen or king guarded by courtiers. A sport or mutant brother to the mundane sea-snakes . . .?

Tansy expects to feel revulsion. But does not. The anticipated antipathy fails to arise. No gorge in her throat. Instead, a penultimate hunger increases, ironically supplanting for a moment the ultimate hunger for extinction.

Around the side of the bucket, Murk's face appears, all huckster-eager. "Freshest of the fresh, mum. Caught right here in the river. Clean as a whistle these days, the water is. Heads and tails make a fine stock. Rest diced up bite-sized. Lemon, parsley, shallot, pinch of nutmeg, that's all it takes. Real butter in the crust. You won't be sorry."

"Well . . . why not?"

Quick as an eel himself, Murk hoists the bucket off the counter, paddles the pie onto the live coals. Almost immediately, a sweet wholesome fishy scent pervades the booth, sending out tendrils to capture Tansy's senses.

"How—how much?"

"Fifty pence."

Tansy fumbles out some coins, among her last, and lays them on the counter. Murk scrapes them off the surface with the edge of one hand and pockets them.

The ceiling of leaden sky seems to sink lower while the pie bakes, as if the box of her life is compressing even further.

Pie in the oven, Murk has no more attention for his customer. Serious as a jeweler faceting a gem. All is reserved for his creation. Fusses with the coals. Spins the pie at intervals for even baking. Anoints its top with a clear glaze from a misshapen mug, employing a crude animal-bristle brush.

Finished at last. By what sign or omen or chef's intuition, unknown. Delved from the oven's depths and deposited on the countertop.

"Grab a utensil, mum. Careful, now, it'll be hot."

Bone-shafted spoon in hand. Bending forward to catch up-gust of victual-richness. Arc of spoon biting into layered flaking crust, bubbling upwelling of rich broth along the narrow trench. Scooping a heaping serving onto the spoon. Raised to lips, invited in.

Ambrosial pastry. Oniony, herby savor. Warmth coating her throat. Lemon. Sweet ichthyous flesh melting, melding into taste buds. No bones? Rendered into intangibility? A second spoon, a third—

Within scant minutes, Tansy has gulped down the whole pie, scraped the tin shell clean.

Murk proudly attentive and approving throughout. Upon completion, still solicitous.

"Had enough then? Knew you'd appreciate this. Had you pegged, Murk did."

"I—thank you. But now I have to go. Good-bye."

"Never good-bye, mum. Just see you later."

Yards beyond the stall, the meal seems a dream. Pleasantly inconsequential, but fading, one of the few typically minor bright spots in a wearisome life, now replaced by the dreary reality of her situation. Except for the weight in her stomach, a greasy film on her lips and palate. Not enough to tip the scales in favor of existence.

Night arrives. Gaps between the isolated streetlights dark as the abyss. Warehouses, abattoirs. Solitary, unobserved. Easy to find an adequate spot. Straight drop of a dozen yards from the top of the wall to the plane of the river below. Never learned to swim. No one to teach, no one to care.

Stones from the weather-shattered wall ballasting her pockets. Scramble atop the wall. Scraped knees and palms irrelevant. Stand up, swaying.

Push off without a twinge of hesitation, falling forward into the embrace of the air.

Smash the water, more a solid interface than a liquid curtain.

Stunned. Sinking so easily. Sensation confused with flying upward. Vision limited to the end of her nose. Chill stabs coreward. No need to inhale yet. Further down will do fine. Drop, drop. Lazy currents finger all her surfaces and holes. Bubbles ascend, a Morse code message to the world left behind. Then the released airstream stops at the empty source.

Now. Breathe deep . . .

No pain in her chest, just an overwhelming heaviness.

Consciousness persists long enough for Tansy to feel the face-first embrace of the muck bottoming the Thames. Silken silty scarves caressing her cheeks, pillowing her thighs, clasping her ankles. Gone from sight now, totally mired. Still plummeting in slow motion. Yet soon the expected terminal solidity of the riverbed beneath the silt, a final bier . . .?

But no. Still ever downward. Still retreating from the world above.

Still conscious.

Still alive?

How?

Resignation gives way to a minor consternation. Is even death to be robbed from her?

Still sinking, Tansy awaits extinction, a final solidity.

Time elongates, accumulates uncountably.

Her slow serene fall through the accumulated miles of powdery snowed-down organic debris continues. Like a flake herself, a cast-off diatomaceous shell, she drifts ever deeper.

Tansy's mind dissolves into a kind of banked nescience. A spark heaped with char.

A tugging at her feet. No strange entity with claws, but just a new, reorienting gravity. If she has been descending like a skydiver with ventral surface presented flat to the earth, now she is rotating slowly through ninety degrees, so that the soles of her stockinged feet—shoes lost in the first impact with the river—are presented to whatever draws her onward.

The absence of enfolding silt was felt first around her feet and ankles, as if they had broken through a crust, were protruding through a sky crust of muck into a less curdled atmosphere. The sensation of being disencumbered moved slowly up her legs, to her groin, then waist, then sternum, then chest—

Her face came free, and she could see.

Within a small compass. Dimly. As if in an opalescent terrestrial fog at dusk.

Standing now at rest on a gritty featureless plain, as if in some bubbled environment. Tansy emptied her lungs and breathed. But what? More water? Air? Some more subtle ether? She moved her arm through the medium that surrounded her, attempting to feel its nature. Nothing familiar. Yet she drew in lungfuls of an invisible, weightless substance, expelled same, but could assign it no name.

Tansy took two steps forward in the random direction she found herself facing. The curved surface of the bubble in front of her receded equally. A glance behind told her that the rear wall had come forward with her steps. Experiment soon proved that no matter which direction she stepped in, her volume of space remained constant, centered around her.

Pointless to discriminate. Tansy strode forward.

The plain extended for miles and miles. So it seemed. Hours upon intuited indistinguishable hours she walked, without sustenance or refreshment or need for same. Nothing varied.

Her belly still cradled her last meal.

Tansy's mind fell into a stuporous equanimity. So much inexplicable strangeness attendant on her dashed self-extinction afforded no purchase for fear or speculation.

Blue smote her eye like a revelation. Even this much color after an eternity of none precluded instant identification of shape. She quickened her pace, bringing more of the object into her sphere.

One bare leg, then another. Enamel blue like cloisonné, solidly planted on the nothingness. Then golden limbs somehow intermingled with the blue. Then two forms nestled together.

A naked blue man stood upright. Large-muscled, well-formed.

Legs wrapped around his waist and locked at the small of his back, a nude golden woman clung to his neck. Heavy ripe curves.

Facing Tansy, the man cupped the gold woman's buttocks. The pair were joined in coitus, but unmoving. Still: not statues, but flesh, however oddly toned.

Their faces indiscernible, because pressed against, melted, into the flesh of each other's shoulder.

Tansy stopped.

Sound as of ripping cloth, and the male and female faces pulled away from their epidermal interknittedness, whole and unbloody. The man's eyes opened, lips parting for speech.

Tansy's parents had died in an auto accident when she was eight years old. Yet here was her father, whole and youthful, recognizable as if in an old photo, despite the transmogrification of his skin.

"Tansy, you're here."

"Am I dead, then?"

The hairy back of her father's head flanked her mother's face on the left. Had they turned, or had Tansy moved around them without volition?

"I don't know, dear. Are we?"

Her mother's loving eyes and immemorial smile eased somewhat Tansy's sheer horrified confusion, gentled the whole mad experience.

"What—what is this place?"

"A land for becoming."

"Becoming what?"

Her father grinned in the old manner. "Whatever you have in you to become."

"Nothing. I've nothing inside me. I'm empty. Always have been."

"Is that so? What about your last meal?"

Tansy placed a hand on her stomach. Was it larger? Something seemed to stir within her, behind and below her belly.

"I don't understand. That pie? What could that do for me? One meal changes nothing."

"If you say so . . ."

"Don't mock me! How can I possibly accomplish something in *this* place when I couldn't do anything right in the other world?"

Golden laugh lines crinkled. "By following your destiny all the way to its end, then beyond."

"Will you help me, Mother?"

"No. We can't. But your brother can."

"Brother? I don't have any brother."

Even her father's teeth were blue. "He was to be your older sibling. But he couldn't stay. He died when he was born—or was born when he died. He's here now. His name is Mercator."

"Where is he? How do I find him?"

"Just keep on."

Heads lowered into shoulders, blue melding seamlessly into gold, gold into blue.

The pair dwindled, shrinking rapidly, verging toward microscopic invisibility.

"Mother! Father! Don't leave me!"

Empty bubble of personal space. Neither cold nor warm. Faint saline lilt to the air. Nothing for it but to trudge onward.

Time and space played hide-and-seek.

The marketplace was empty this early in the morning. Shabby stalls shielding goods behind rope-lashed canvas fronts. Cobbles wet with morning dew. Organic trash, rinds and crusts and shells. The smell of human urine from a puddle in the corner of two walls. A dog appeared, red from tail-tip to snout, like a new brick. Sniffed the puddle, then lifted its leg to add its commentary.

Tansy dropped, suddenly exhausted, to the cobbles. Rested her back against the timbered side of a stall. Head sagged forward, chin into chest. Eyes closed.

Sounds of the marketplace coming alive around her. Shuffling feet, bantering among merchants, children playing tag, crockery clinking, cartwheels trundling.

No one accosted her. Something like a sun rose higher in something like a sky, its heat evidenced across her slumped form.

"Tansy. It's me, your brother."

Eyelids snapping open.

A handsome man in his thirties, red all over like the dog. Crimson eidolon. Bare-chested, loincloth around his middle, sandals laced up his legs. Smiling. Hand extended to help her to her feet.

Siblings almost the same height. Eyes on the same level. Searching his face for resemblance to her own. Uncertainty. Yet a sense of having encountered him somewhere before.

"Sorry I'm late. I was busy with another. But you must be famished! Let's get you something to eat. Then we can go home."

"Home?"

"Your home here."

The young girl who served them bowls of hot porridge was colored the same as Mercator. So were all the teeming inhabitants of this low-built, diffuse city. A tableau of devils.

Spoon poised halfway to her lips, Tansy noted her own unchanged flesh, anomalous in this strange city.

"Won't I stand out here?"

"No one will mind. But perhaps it's best if you stay mostly indoors. You can be useful without leaving home."

"All right."

There was always something to sew. Humble garments and bedclothes in need of repair, dropped off by a steady stream of citizens, all incarnadined, tracking dust and unintelligible allusions to the life of the city into the adobe apartments to which Mercator had brought her.

Tansy developed callouses on her thumb and index finger after the first few weeks. The coarse thread and crude needles, the heavy fabrics, the misshapen buttons. Piles of unwashed garments redolent of their wearers' body odors. These were the constants of her days. Along with the shifting infall of roseate sunlight through the glassless window, the parched heat, the simple meals of bread and olives, eggs and beans, honey and crisped locusts, delivered by Mercator.

Her brother?

If so, in name and attitude only. They hadn't been raised together, in any life she recalled. Had no long-term bonds or familially inculcated taboos delimiting their relationship.

Naturally she thought of having him sexually: during their meals, or when he slept on his mat of woven river reeds next to hers. But never made any advance, for fear of rebuff. Nor did Mercator ever exhibit toward her any such impulses.

And her belly. That got bigger every day.

But how? She had never. Not anywhere, anywhen.

One day a new patron, a bearded merchant with a withered arm, came with robes to mend. Having gone through months of similar visits, Tansy thought nothing much of the man at first. But after he left, his image troubled her. When Mercator returned to their apartments at eventide, from whatever errands occupied him during the daylight, with small piquant tomatoes and salted fish for supper, Tansy inquired about the man.

"He was your lover in another life. You wronged him. Now you must mend his clothes."

A momentary stasis blanked her mind. "All—all of these men and women and children who have come—"

"Yes, of course. The entire city, in fact. You were intimate with them all, down the millennia. Didn't you know?"

"I—did I hurt them all?"

"And they you. It was inevitable."

"And their redress to me?"

"Yet to come. Or already obtained. Or otherwise obviated."

Tansy had a hard time falling asleep. Her mind turned over Mercator's words ceaselessly. But also her gravid, unbalanced body contributed its own discomforts.

One day every week Mercator took her out of their quarters for a stroll through the city, always ending at a favorite park, ripe with shade, where clownfish swam through the pod-strewn boughs of acacia trees. There, a peace descended on Tansy and she could momentarily forget her expiatory drudgery.

The twinges came one morning. Hardly commensurate with the enormous swell of her belly. Not what she had expected from all she had heard. More like imagined sexual tremors than splitting pains.

"Mercator, help me. I think it's my time—"

"Of course. Step into the tub."

A stone trough occupied one corner of their two rooms. Bamboo pipes brought rainwater down in a gravity feed from a tank on the roof.

Naked, Tansy climbed awkwardly into the tub. Her own pink flesh looked alien to her now. Seismic tremors propagated outward from her center. She drew her legs up, knees to chest. Mercator kneeled by the trough and stroked her brow, murmuring wordless assistance.

A slithering, rippling ex-vagination brought an orgasmic sense of release and relief. The water in the trough crimsoned with afterbirth. Her swollen midriff deflated.

The blue and gold eel stretched nearly as long as Tansy was tall. Thick around as her wrist. Its black eyes gleamed with intelligence. Twisting lithely in its limited compass, it tested its newborn muscles, visibly exulting in its power and gracefulness.

"Your child. You must take good care of him and fulfill his every wish. By doing so, you will come to where you need to be."

The eel reared six inches of its head out of the water.

"Mother," it piped, in a lilting voice like the notes of a flute, "I am so happy to meet you again at last."

The sharp pebbles and grit beneath her feet scored shallow cuts in her bare soles. The pitch-smeared canvas bag dragged on its single shoulder strap, slapping against her hip with every step, sloshing out irreplaceable driblets of water. She changed the bag from one side to another at intervals, but this resulted only in distributing the pain evenly. Her throat was parched.

Mercator held her hand as they walked, but could not assume the burden of carrying her child.

Not that she had ever asked him to.

Tansy had named the eel Plum Sun for his two-toned skin.

"How much farther? I feel as if we've been walking for years."

"Not too many more miles. But I fear the last few are the hardest. And I'll have to leave you, Sister."

"Must you really?"

"It's ordained. And I could not help you in what comes next."

Tansy recalled the dull, laborious months in their tiny apartment, which now seemed like paradise. "Will I ever see you again?"

"You already have."

The foothills gave way to a crumbling talus slope that formed the skirts of the cloud-piercing mountain, bold and brutish as a soldier. But the mountain showed some charity. Cold rivulets clear as diamonds afforded a chance to wash her abused feet, slake her thirst, and replenish Plum Sun's carrier. Overhead, a small school of sharks and pilot fish moved through the skies.

"Thank you, Mother. All your exertions on my behalf will be repaid a thousandfold."

Tansy set one scarred foot upon the slope, then another. Mercator remained behind.

"This is where we must part?"

"Yes."

"Good-bye, Uncle. I appreciated your companionship."

"Farewell, Plum Sun. Farewell, Sister."

A hundred yards up the precipitous slope, bent almost double to maintain her balance, Tansy looked back.

Some trick of distance or atmosphere made Mercator resemble a squat bearded gnome in shabby clothes.

The razored crags and ledges by which Tansy ascended the upper reaches of the mountains tormented her hands as much as the rubble of the endless plain had gashed her feet. The weight of Plum Sun in his sodden pouch threatened to loosen her every handhold. Her bare toes scrabbled at minute ridges.

Once, falling, she was saved by a pod of dolphins. The creatures buoyed her up till she could regain her grip.

After that incident, Tansy redoubled her vigilance and efforts. But she knew she was drawing on a shallow well.

"Wake up, Mother. Please, wake up."

Tansy sat with her back against a large cold boulder. The carrier holding Plum Sun rested on its oblate bottom upright by her side. Out of the bag protruded the blue-and-gold head of the eel. Somehow its limited expression conveyed encouragement.

Tansy brought her hand up to her face and smeared blood across her visage in an attempt to clear the cobwebs from her vision.

"Are we—are we where we need to be?"

"Almost. The Fountain of Flames is just ahead."

Weariness like lead in her bones. Struggling to her feet. Trudging ahead up a mild slope. Through a tall defile whose tight blank walls resembled the chute through which cattle were led to slaughter. Fossils embedded in the walls mocked her persistence. The distinctive shadow of a circling manta ray overhead came and went.

A broad plateau of roughly an acre in extent. Pillared in the middle on a rude slate hearth: a thick whistling column of green fire, sourceless, inexhaustible, braided of a thousand viridescent shades. Around the Fountain of Flames, the tumbled columns of some long-extinct fane.

"You must place me in the flame, Mother."

"You'll die."

"Not at all. Nor will you be harmed. Trust me."

If the green flame gave off heat, it was not the heat of a normal fire. Tansy approached warily. Closed her eyes for the final few yards.

A sensation as of silken threads infiltrating her blood vessels informed her that she was fully engulfed.

She tipped out Plum Sun into the flames, then backed away, out of the fiery column.

The eel lashed back and forth within the fires, but did not crisp or wail, but rather became engorged, priapic.

Big as a house, Plum Sun occulted or had completely absorbed the fires that had ennobled him. He seemed at ease in the air.

"Step closer, Mother."

Tansy obeyed.

Plum Sun's mouth a needled, ribbed cavern.

The hundred hands of invisible currents pulled her inside her son's gullet.

Blackness, acid reek, hot fluids laving her.

Dissolution, assimilation into the flesh of her child.

Tansy looked out through Plum Sun's eyes, felt his/her hermaphroditic body slip through gill-freshening darkling estuarial waters, sensed electrical impulses through novel organs of perception.

More of her kind fed below, drab cousins. She dropped swiftly through the waters to claim her share.

A woman's corpse provided the banquet, its clothing shredded.

Dozens of eels tailed off the rotting body like flowers from a garden plot. Half-eaten already, disintegrating, drifting like a seedling on the marine winds, the woman's body reminded Tansy of someone close to her.

Plum Sun joined the feast.

The net took them unawares as they gorged, too busy incorporating the woman's substance into themselves to heed the surface predators.

Up, up, into the cruel air.

Confinement in a narrow bucket.

Speech vibrating the interface between air and liquid. Plum Sun understands.

"Have a dekko then, child. C'mon, naught'll happen to you."

On tiptoes to peer into the bucket.

Tansy's first impression: a single braided whip in constant coiling motion, a flux of silver and black. Then: separation into component parts: heads, eyes, bodies, flukes, gills.

A bucket of writhing eels, sinuous, muscled, constrained.

Their weavings seem to scribe watery ideograms in perpetual flicker, transiting from one half-perceived meaning to another.

And at random moments, as their serpentine bodies open a clear view to the bottom of the bucket, millisecond impressions of something piebald, gold and blue, beneath them. Like a queen or king guarded by courtiers. A sport or mutant brother to the mundane sea-snakes . . .?

Tansy finds the bizarre sight of so much life compacted into such a small compass soothing somehow. Feels herself composed of similar perpetually coiling energies, her DNA lashing like eels at the heart of each cell. Energies that offer new configurations of possibility every millisecond.

Comes down off her tiptoes. Gazes at the proprietor of the eel-pie stall. The man winks at her, a wink conveying centuries of complicity.

"You'll be needing this meal now, then?"

Places her hand gently on her own stomach.

"No, not now, thank you. I'm already quite full."

Recently I had the pleasure of contributing critical commentary to a lush new art book, Todd Schorr's Dreamland *(Last Gasp, 2004). Schorr's paintings all possess great narrative and allegorical drive, and I found myself spinning stories in my head around each canvas, little vignettes that intersected with Schorr's artwork at odd angles. These are those stories, their titles taken from Schorr's canvases. I hope my pieces resonate, even without the inspirational artwork beside them, and that they motivate readers to search out Schorr's otherworldly art.*

My thanks also to Harlan Ellison and Michael Swanwick for their pioneering work in the field of literary miniaturization.

The Farthest Schorr

1.
THE HUNTER-GATHERER

The hominid named Gra had to chew the skins for several days to get them supple enough to form the sack. His big blunt teeth and wide parabola of jaw began to ache. But he persisted. No effort could be spared for the all-important hunt, the first of its kind. Fashioning the bone sewing needle occupied another half of a day, as did cleaning the animal intestines to form thread. During this period he subsisted on carrion, too preoccupied to track new game. He grew sick from the tainted meat. His mate, Reh, brought him some of the fleshy stalks that grew in the swamp, a plant that had cured his distress once before. But finally, after all the work and illness, he was ready.

Warily, he approached the site where the odd, unclean strangers in their outlandishly textured furs had once camped, before vanishing in a whirlpool of shimmering air. They had scattered debris over a wide area before leaving, and the bright colors and half-recognizable shapes of the abandoned objects hypnotized him. The slick surfaces of the figurines that resembled his fellow tribespeople in the oddest, most disturbing ways seemed to impart knowledge through Gra's skin. One by one, he began to pick up the objects and place them in his sack, his muscle-corded arms, veins in bas-relief, almost too powerful for the delicate task assigned them.

By midday he was feeling faint, possibly from the lingering effects of the bad meat, but also possibly from the collective mojo of his prizes. And then, as he stooped for one last trophy, dizziness washed over him. The air swirled in chromatic pinwheels similar to the whirlpool that had taken the strangers away. Two of the figures—a black and red mouse and a pregnantly voluptuous woman with a beehive for a head—came to life atop a pedestal of untainted fresh kill; orchestrated noises unlike any he had ever heard filled his ears. Something never before felt was born inside him. Gra fell to his knees—to *pray*.

And how much will *you* be contributing today to the fund for new stained glass windows, Mr. Jones?

2.
SUGAR SHAKES

The pentagram was outlined in Kool-Aid powder. The candles were stacks of pierced Necco wafers with licorice-whip wicks. The sacrifice was a beheaded chocolate Easter bunny. Solid, not hollow.

Little Kenny Firazzy was ready to invoke his own peculiar demons.

Butt-naked, smeared with strawberry syrup, a necklace of candy skulls draped across his bony, ten-year-old chest, Kenny began to chant the evil invocation he had learned from collecting enough Bazooka bubble gum comics.

"Skittles and Kit-Kats and hyperglycemia! Gummis and Starbursts and sweets that are dreamier!"

The chant took a full five minutes to recite. But when he finished, Kenny knew he had succeeded beyond his wildest dreams.

Confined in the pentagram, three demons hovered: Cottonwisp, Bad Apple, and Beninjeri. Vainly did they writhe to be free, uttering seductive promises and lies. Their tails lashed, their fluids oozed, their worm-tongues flickered. But Kenny had been too smart for their wiles. They were trapped, and forced to accept his commands.

"Listen, you three," Kenny ordered, "I wanna have all the world's sweet stuff, all the time, anytime I want it! And for starters, I'll take a nice big serving of chocolate milk."

"Your wish," hissed the three demons, "is our command."

A bioengineered cow crashed through the roof, landed on Kenny, and squashed him flatter than a fruit roll-up. Chocolate milk dribbled from its teats. The pentagram dispersed upon impact, and the demons were freed.

They went straight back to their home in the innermost circle of sugar hell: Hershey, Pennsylvania.

3.
THE RETURN OF THE PRODIGAL TAUNG BABY

The aliens picked Lena Wilkinson up in 1951, right in the middle of a photo session with Irving Klaw—a flock of horrible little creatures with heads like partially deflated, mushroom-textured balloons, riding in glittery Formica saucers. They couldn't fit her lingerie-clad form into any of their tiny, one-alien cruisers, of course, so they enveloped her in some kind of translucent protective protoplasm, zapped Klaw and his crew with their amnesia ray, and towed Lena off with gravity waves behind their mini-fleet as they soared out into space.

That envelope of protoplasm eventually became her only friend.

The trip across the light-years involved passage down an infinite helical tunnel tinted a bilious yellow-green and studded at intervals with slate-colored exit portals. The fleet eventually dove down one exit and emerged above a hospitable planet, and that is where they dumped Lena.

The protoplasm shivered off her and coalesced into a small bulbous luminescent starfish-shaped entity.

"Lena, I'm your new companion, Rollo. Follow me to your new home. We have a lot of learning and fucking to do."

Still clad only in underwear and stockings and heels, and dazed from her swift abduction and transport, Lena could only dully obey.

For the past fifty years, Lena has indeed learned and fucked a lot. She has not aged. Although it is not visibly different, her head sometimes feels as if it has swelled ten times in size. And her fruitful loins have disgorged dozens of alien babies, the result of her congress with a host of unimaginable creatures. Naked mole rats, exoskeletal ghouls, giant blue rabbits—Lena dreams that someday one of her babies—all of whom were taken away by her original captors shortly after weaning—will return to rescue her and return her to a planet she only vaguely recalls.

Idly, she wonders what Klaw is paying for a photo session these days.

4.
A GOOBER AND A TUBER IN AN EXCHANGE OF FISTICUFFS

Midge was doing plenty all right for herself. A gal with nothing much to get by on except for her va-va-voom figure and an enigmatic blank gaze that certain joes found sexy, she had come out of the worst kind of poverty and landed in the lap of luxury. Not exactly the brightest bulb in the chandelier, she nonetheless knew when she had a good thing going.

And this affair with Skippy Goober was one helluva sweet deal.

Oh, sure, he had his drawbacks and failings and quirks, like anything in trousers. The only position he liked for screwing was doggie-style. Claimed he had a hard time getting up off his back once he was down, and his skinny little legs always collapsed when he tried boring old missionary style. And his body odor—whew! Even deodorant failed to hide that earthy scent. But worst of all was his temper. Once Skippy wrapped himself around a few drinks—mai tais were his favorite—he could be as brutal and mean as Senator McCarthy looking for Reds. Still, he had never yet hit Midge—she had told him she'd knife him while he slept if he ever laid a hand on her—and he did take her out to the nicest places.

Like tonight, at the Brown Derby, with all the swells and stars admiring Midge's cleavage. Heaven on earth.

Until Argus Toober showed up.

Toober was Goober's rival in the rackets. They hated each other like North Korea hated South Korea. And now that idiot maître d' was seating Toober right next to Midge and her man!

Goober growled and hefted his sword-cane. Midge sighed and surreptitiously checked her purse for her mad money. Looked like she'd be going home alone. No playing with Goober's stalk and peanuts tonight.

5.
VARIATIONS IN KITSCH

The anonymous respirator-wearing worker tending the giant bubbling vat of lava-lamp fluid leaned over just a bit too far. Out of his shirt pocket fell a small, curious pebble he had picked up on the way to work that morning. That pebble was, in fact, the remnant of a thousand-ton meteorite from beyond the Horsehead Nebula, all that had survived the burning passage through Earth's atmosphere, and it possessed uncanny properties.

The lamps filled with the contaminated fluid were shipped around the nation.

One went to Kaarlo Krisp, a Broadway set designer who lived in a Greenwich Village apartment surrounded by all the nostalgic icons of his youth, acquired through assiduous collecting.

Kaarlo tripped while carrying the lava lamp upstairs and dropped it, opening a hairline crack in its vessel. Nervously running his finger around the glass, Kaarlo simultaneously cut himself and absorbed some of the alien fluid into his cut.

During the next ten hours Kaarlo experienced a trip like no other human had ever undergone. He journeyed to a world where cavemen manned a NASA-style Mission Control, and another where tubby porkers bowled an infinite succession of perfect games. The ménage à trois with Sheena Queen of the Jungle and the Fujiyama Mama brought a tear to his eye. He was just getting used to the constantly shifting scenery and characters when a small crocodile wearing a Hawaiian shirt and a sombrero materialized and said, "Hey, kid, is your ticket punched?"

"No," Kaarlo replied.

Despite its diminutive size, the crocodile conductor had no difficulty in getting the prongs of his punch into Kaarlo's ears, or in squeezing real hard.

6.
THE MARTIAN LABORATORY

Pooja was a big standard poodle. But not a show dog, by any means. Abandoned by her owner, Pooja had been for many years a rough-and-tumble denizen of alleys and abandoned buildings, waste lots and under-the-bridge encampments. From time to time she had taken up with a human, a bum or a bindlestiff. But always Pooja's willfulness and desire for independence had led to a parting of ways.

Pooja was no one's bitch.

Today Pooja was nosing around a warehouse that boasted an odd veil of odors, smells of exotic chemicals and foreign meat. The latter scent promised to assuage the rumbling of her empty stomach, so Pooja persisted in seeking entrance to the warehouse. Eventually she found a loose sheet of plywood covering a busted basement window and wormed her way inside.

The main floor was lit with an eerie golden light emanating from many complex machines. Three exotic beings with bulging naked brains and skeletal visages, dressed in high-collared robes, hovered around the unconscious form of a human woman.

"My brain hurts," said one of the Martians.

"Of course it does, you idiot," said a second alien. "Your collar's too tight!"

"Will you two shut up and help me position this quantum scalpel?" urged the third.

The alluring meat scent was coming from the Martians! They smelled better than a dozen pork-chop-stuffed chickens! When Pooja dived at the closest Martian, knocking the alien over into delicate equipment that smashed and caused a cascade of chaotic destruction, it was not because she cared one whit about the fate of the unconscious woman (who actually perished in the resulting conflagration). All she had in mind was chomping down on a mouthful of Martian flesh.

A week later she was still gnawing with immense satisfaction on the extra-sturdy Martian neck bone of the victim she had dragged away.

7.
ROBOT MAINTENANCE AT THE PARKERIAN MINING COMPANY

As soon as the snotty foreman approached, Charlie knew he was gonna hand Charlie the shitty end of one stick or another.

The first words out of the foreman's mouth confirmed his intuition.

"Scarpetto! You're detailed to the Lavender Shaft immediately. We just got an order for ten thousand kilos from the empress of Saturn. And you know her perfumed majesty don't like to be kept waiting. Last time a shipment was just one stinking day late, she executed a dozen diplomats."

"But boss," Charlie complained, though he knew his squawk would make no difference, "the Lavender Shaft is ripe for a blowout!"

"Then you'd better make sure it don't happen till you harvest your quota. Check out a GSA robo and get busy."

The foreman left before Charlie could even whine about being assigned a GSA. Those lousy robos broke down if you even looked cross-wise at 'em. With a resigned sigh, Charlie moved to follow instructions.

Work on Sachet IX was hell. The bath-bead mines offered only hot, perfumed, dangerous labor. Why, just last month a blowout in the Honeysuckle Pits had slaughtered a score of workers.

Charlie and the GSA had been at work in the Lavender Shaft for six hours when Charlie heard the first ominous burblings that signaled a blowout. Hastening up the shaft ladder, Charlie knew he wasn't gonna make it.

But then he felt the claw hands of the GSA shoving him to safety, just as the beads erupted.

Damn that robo! Why'd he have to go and screw up Charlie's anti-cyber prejudices?

8.
THE SAILOR MAN

When the doctors put Vestry Asquith back together after his death, they exercised all the creativity they could summon.

It was Vestry's bad luck that the doctors were aliens who knew nothing about human anatomy.

The Dripps had found Vestry's corpse floating in space in the holed-out remnants of his pirate ship, the *Betelgeuse Bandit*. Vestry had lost a run-in with the Galactic Posse after trying to attack a cargo liner and been left floating, quite dead, in interstellar space. But his extinction posed nothing but a challenge to the Dripps.

Enormous nose-shaped beings on squirming snail-like footings, continually exuding sinus fluid from their various orifices, the Dripps were master biologists and cyberneticians. But they reasoned in a manner completely unlike human beings.

Thus they employed the DNA of the plants in Vestry's oxygen-generation unit to rebuild Vestry's nose. The fused a portion of the casing of one of his ship's photon-mines to his skull. They endowed him with radar ears and a testicle chin. One eye was sutured shut while the other was replaced with the Panopticon scanner off the *Bandit*. The keys of his mood-Moog substituted for his teeth. His brain was hybridized with circuitry.

Vestry awoke at last, saw himself in a mirror, and screamed.

The Dripps stuck a panacea pipe in his mouth and he calmed down a tad. Finally he was able to reconcile himself to his new appearance. Hadn't he been given, after all, a second chance at life?

But then one of the Dripps said the most frightening words possible, and all his tentative calm was shattered.

"Now we will build you a mate."

9.
PILGRIM'S PROGRESS

Sharon Tudge looked past her twitched-aside window curtain and across her wide, immaculate lawn at her neighbor's house.

The place was an absolute disgrace!

The hulk of a junk Buick rested on four cinder blocks. A rusting play-set squatted like the burned-out skeleton of a small crashed aircraft.

The barrel of a washing machine, resting on its side, served as a doghouse for a yapping mongrel. Whatever grass had once grown around the house was now mostly dead from dog-shit deposits. A week's worth of unread newspapers littered the walkway. A hand-scrawled sign hanging on the fence read: SALESMEN BLOW IT OUT YOUR ASS!

But more shocking than all these degenerate appurtenances was the house's owner, Harly Daimon, who now sprawled nearly naked on a spavined lawn chair, soaking up the sunshine, a forty-ounce bottle of beer easily to hand, his big hairy gut an offense to nature.

Retreating from her window, Sharon felt her indignation mounting. She could stand this gross insult no longer.

She stalked across the street, stood outside Harly's decaying picket fence, and loudly harrumphed.

Harly opened one boozy eye but did not get up. "What's your problem, twat?"

"Why, I never—!"

"Good. If you never pissed me off yet, don't start now."

Left speechless, Sharon could only retreat back to the pristine fortress of her home.

When her husband, Brad Tudge, returned that night from his office in the city, Sharon catalogued all of Harly Daimon's sins: womanizing, sloppiness, disrespect, casual modes of dress, and a dozen others. Brad nodded reflectively, and then said, "I'll handle this, dear. But not on an empty stomach. Let's have dinner first."

And as Brad tucked his napkin into his collar, Sharon proudly set down the platter of roasted human fetuses before her perfect husband.

10.
THE HAREM DANCER

Hamid al-Khouri, an Iraqi youth who from childhood on had exhibited uncanny native skills with paint and ink, chalk and clay, had eventually attended the Rhode Island School of Design for two years on an international scholarship. Before he got radicalized.

Thus was born the art car bomb.

Upon his terrorist epiphany, al-Khouri had returned to the Middle East to wage jihad.

With style.

Disdaining conventional anonymity as the way of the coward, betokening a lack of pride in the terrorist's calling, Hamid insisted that every explosive-packed vehicle whose production he oversaw left the bomb factory uniquely detailed. Further contravening the Islamic injunction against figurative representation (his semesters at RISD had left a certain Western impression after all), Hamid opted for eye-popping, kandy-flake, Day-Glo montages for his death vehicles.

The sixty virgins of paradise awarded each martyr undulated sensuously across bumpers and roofs. Devil worms that would torment the infidels in hell spat venom from hoods and trunks. Troops of turban-wearing monkeys representing traitorous imams cavorted across door panels.

Of course, the authorities at first welcomed such extravagant displays of terrorist art. They felt that their job had been made infinitely simpler: just watch for the al-Khouri specials, and you could preempt any bombing.

But then Hamid's art spawned a thousand imitators.

Pretty soon, every other car in the Middle East was a rolling, gaudy canvas. The cars packed with TNT were indistinguishable from regular cars.

Everyone braced for an increase in unstoppable bombings.

But then, against all logic, terrorist attacks began to *decrease*.

Hamid's students had begun to care too much for their art to destroy it.

Frustrated, Hamid created his masterpiece and took it himself on a one-way mission.

When he awoke in heaven, Ed Roth first hugged him, then cold-cocked him.

11.
THE VENUS OF AUGMENTATION

Every savvy businessman had to cut corners somewhere. That was just the way the postmodern economy worked.

So Dr. Manson Sozaboy began dumping his medical waste illegally. What harm could it cause, after all? And those greedy sanctioned haulers charged an arm and a leg (if you'll pardon the pun).

Manson specialized in one simple procedure: breast reduction. The only waste he generated was a little innocent gland-threaded fat.

It seemed a shame, really. All these well-endowed babes coming into his office to get de-boobed while elsewhere their less zaftig sisters were opting for the exact opposite procedure. Too bad, the doctor often thought, that some kind of simple swap couldn't be arranged.

One night Manson chucked his latest batch of waste into a local swamp. A swamp favored by all the other cost-cutters in town, such as several advanced bioengineering firms.

In the darkness, rogue organic and exotic inorganic components churned and recombined.

By dawn, Breast Thing was born.

A thousand lush hues of pink and caramel, Breast Thing resembled one of those ancient fertility goddess statues: a faceless humanoid form draped with a hundred tits of all shapes and sizes, some with lactating nipples.

Clambering out of the swamp, Breast Thing shambled instinctively toward the home of her father.

The police found Dr. Manson Sozaboy drowned in his bed, a look blending terror and ecstasy on his face. The forensics guy just shook his head and said, "I'll be damned if I can figure out where the hell any sick bastard gets enough colostrum to drown someone."

Breast Thing runs a titty bar in New Orleans now. But all she does is hang in the back office and count the take.

12.
THE DEVILED EGG

The Tockwotton Nursing Home looked out over hundreds of acres of neighboring farmland, all fallow. In the distance the old farmstead itself loomed, a weather-beaten, tumbledown, abandoned structure.

Everywhere around the globe, farms in similar states of desuetude sprawled: untenanted, unproductive, unneeded.

All thanks to SuperEggs™.

Monteverdi Vespers, the elderly inventor of SuperEggs™, sat in his smart wheelchair on the patio at Tockwotton, considering what he had wrought.

Thirty years ago he had been so idealistic, even as he was approaching retirement. He had been focused on solving what appeared to be the major problem of his era: the lack of enough food for many of Earth's eight billion people.

What had inspired him to combine various tailored bacteria and viruses with the rudimentary workings of the new line of legless, wingless, headless chickens, he could not now remember. But his brainstorm had been justified by the results.

Encasing the limbless egg-layer in a box fed by a hopper and relieved by an outlet duct, Monteverdi had created the first SuperEgg™ factory. Any organic substance, from grass clippings to oak leaves to seaweed (and including the chicken's own wastes), could be fed into the grinding hopper and directly into the "throat" of the chicken. Controls on the box tweaked the chicken's metabolism and hormones and endocrines and proteins, producing eggs of any flavor or nutritional composition.

In one stroke, world hunger had been beaten.

Too bad Monteverdi Vespers had signed a contract assigning all his patent rights to the firm that employed him.

No matter, the old man thought. He had never wanted to get rich. He had done what he had done for all of humanity.

But how he wished the charity nursing home he had ended up in didn't recycle its dead residents in his invention!

13.
THE CLASH OF HOLIDAYS

Today was little Jimmy Maynard's favorite day of the year.

The one day of the year that wasn't a stinkin' holiday.

Sleepless for most of the night, Jimmy got up extra early because he was so excited. Today he could go to school and do his chores! He could eat the plainest of foods! He could dress in simple clothes! He could skip any kind of holiday craft-making!

What a glorious prospect!

His house would be undecorated for a wonderful twenty-four hours, free of any holiday regalia. No Christmas tree, no Easter eggs, no Thanksgiving papier-mâché turkeys, no Secretary Day's steno-pad napkins. No visitors would pop in bearing holiday greetings or traditional gifts, such as the candy pistols of NRA Day. The mail would bring no cards, the television would show no specials.

What more could a kid want?

Jimmy took his time dressing, savoring the feel of his non-holiday clothes. He went downstairs, gratified not to smell Kwanzaa cookies or matzo balls. Maybe he'd just have some dry toast for breakfast, or cereal eaten by the handful straight from the box. He anticipated the easy smiles his mother and father would wear as they were spared—for just one uniquely un-special day—churchgoing or shopping or parading.

Bursting into the kitchen, Jimmy was stunned to see his parent's crestfallen faces.

"Mom! Dad! What's the matter?"

"Jimmy," said his dad, "you'd better sit down. I don't know how to tell you this, but the government has just declared a new holiday—"

Jimmy screamed, as visions of sugarplums danced in his head.

14.
MADAME CALIVERA'S CORPORATE IDENTITY PROGRAM

The spaceship resembled a giant metallic carrot with three legs sprouting from its narrow end. It touched down on the barren plains of the planet designated by humans as Limpdick III, striking a gout of dry dust from the surface. After a short interval the ship disgorged a land-crawler whose front grille mimicked the grimace of the rock-eating lizards of Why the Fuck Are We Here. The crawler set off across the plain, raising clouds of cinders and soil particulates.

Fifteen minutes of travel brought the crawler to a native village: a collection of mismatched huts flanked by rudimentary benches and fire pits and rubbish heaps. On the benches sat various natives of Limpdick III: repulsive green warty indolent trolls with enormous genitalia. The penises of the males and the labial folds of the females flopped over the edges of the benches and into the dust.

A door in the crawler gull-winged open, and a human woman emerged. Clad in a black and white skintight business suit, the woman exhibited an imperious air. She stalked confidently over to the nearest native, a male.

"Where's Drongo Kaboom?"

The troll used both hands to shift his dick to avoid a line of creeping insects. "I am Drongo Kaboom."

"Did you enroll in the home-study Master of Business Administration program at Harvard University?"

"Yes, that I did."

"And did you realize that your tuition payment was drawn on a non-human bank account that paid Harvard only in the dried skins of puke-cats?"

"The puke-cat is our global currency."

"Furthermore, do you acknowledge that every one of your term papers has been plagiarized off the Interstellar Internet?"

"Why should I strain my delicate brains when stealing is so much easier?"

"Lastly, do you admit enticing a female freshman from Brookline, Massachusetts, all the way out to Limpdick III with promises of a 'monster kegger' and then leaving her stranded halfway to the Magellanic Clouds, covered in quarts of your jizm?"

"I have recordings indicating all relations were consensual."

The woman glared at the troll for a moment, then broke into a smile and extended her hand. "Mister Kaboom, you're just the material Harvard Business School is looking for! How's tenure sound?"

15.
THE SPECTER OF CARTOON APPEAL

Artist Number One Hundred and Fifteen, they called him. A skinny kid in shorts and an outsized Raiders T-shirt, with his glossy black hair in a crude bowl cut, the Hmong boy labored day and night in one of the evil Southeast Asian cartoon sweatshops, drawing cel after cel of American animation. So stuffed was his head with the uncouth imagery of his distant employers that he had forgotten all his native rituals and customs, his family, and even his own name. Taken by outlaw recruiters from his village after exhibiting drawing prowess at an early age, he was now and forevermore only Artist Number One Hundred and Fifteen.

Artist Number One Hundred and Fifteen's best friend, naturally enough, was Artist Number One Hundred and Sixteen, who occupied the drafting table and rickety, unpadded bamboo stool next to Fifteen. A kidnapped Korean, Sixteen did not even speak the same language as Fifteen. And yet they had managed to form a bond of friendship, helping each other. Some days Fifteen would massage Sixteen's aching wrists. Other days, Sixteen would share some of his ration of dried cuttlefish and counterfeit Pocari Sweat drink with Fifteen, who, after all, was still a growing boy, while Sixteen was an old man who had been drawing cartoons since the heyday of *Tom and Jerry*.

One day the cel-master stomped in, visibly outraged. The brawny, brutal overseer, a former Thai pirate known for his cruel way with the lash, clutched in his hand the printout of an e-mailed communiqué from the Cartoon Network in America. Artist Number One Hundred and Fifteen recognized the letterhead. The Thai slave driver shouted in pidgin English, the de facto language of the international bullpen.

"Who the motherfuckin' funny guy? Who put graffiti slur against Thai king in background of *SpongeBob*? Big riots all across American Thai communities. Plenty shit now to go around for everyone!"

None of the artists dared speak. The cel-master whirled on Artist Number One Hundred and Sixteen.

"Maybe it you, old man! Or maybe you know who! Either way, time for you to get whipped!"

Artist Number One Hundred and Sixteen's heart gave out after the tenth lashing. The Thai boss kicked the corpse, had it hauled unceremoniously away, and then said, "You goddamn buggers all think on this! I be back in the morning to find out who really guilty!"

Locked in the dark, stifling, stinking bunkhouse with his comrades, Artist Number One Hundred and Fifteen cried for two hours for the death of his only friend. But then he wiped his eyes and resolved to take revenge.

From the near-obliterated depths of his memory came the details of certain arcane rituals of his people. Fifteen set out to perform them. They involved nothing more than some bodily fluids, a handful of dirt, a lizard bone saved from supper, a pencil stub wrapped in cobwebs, and a scrap of paper.

In the morning the artists cowered, awaiting the arrival of the cel-master and his whip. But he never showed. By noon, with their bladders bursting and stomachs growling, they dared to break cautiously out of the bunkhouse.

They found the overseer and the other bosses flattened to a lifeless two-dimensionality, as if they had been run over by a large macadam-smoothing machine. Incredulous at their good fortune, the artists dispersed, each making for home.

Back in his village, Artist Number One Hundred and Fifteen reunited with his family and soon was reintegrated into the ancient ways. He never spoke of his period of slavery, and showed little interest in matters outside his village.

Years later, a charity package of drugs with expired dates arrived from the United States. The contents were protected with recent newspapers. Smoothing one out, the young man who was no longer Artist Number One Hundred and Fifteen saw pictures that made him smile.

Even now, years later, the American authorities seemed to be having trouble rounding up all the slavering, gibbering, whirling Tasmanian devils that had slaughtered all those studio executives.

16.
THE SPECTER OF MONSTER APPEAL

Putting a point on his claws with the wall-mounted sharpener, Furry Hackerman began pasting up the latest issue of *Famous Monsters of Filmland*. He employed his claws to spike various articles in anticipation of immediate need. At one point in his compositional routine, when all his claws held multiple articles, and other gluey snippets had stuck accidentally to his hairy form, Hackerman the editor looked as if he had fought a battle with the Sunday edition of the *Monsterville Times* and lost.

Hackerman's furry, fanged, fiery-eyed face wore a look of intense concentration. He was trying to decide which piece would be the lead in this issue.

Should he go with *Greedy Corporate Executives Suck Blood of Stockholders* or *Ancient Male Senators Force Women to Give Birth to Unwanted Babies*?

The first item focused on the new Roger Goreman film, *Corporations Ate My Future!* A real thriller-diller, starring those hairless apes that had suddenly become Hollywood's latest monsters du jour. Of course, no hairless apes existed any longer in Hackerman's world. The players in these films were all shaved werewolves (Hackerman's own species), or giant salamanders with many prosthetics and much makeup, or trolls in rubber suits. But the very memory of these so-called humans and their incredibly bizarre society as it had once existed in genetic isolation on the island of Madagascar was still potent enough to generate boffo box office.

The second item related to John Carpenter-Ant's *Legislature of Hell!* Another hairless-ape spooktacular. There were some really effective scenes here of humans drooling as they affixed their signatures in blood to the deadly legislation. Those shots would play well with Hackerman's juvenile audience of young ghouls and goblins.

In the end, Hackerman went with *Legislature of Hell!*

Hours passed as the editor continued to paste up the issue. Around eleven, his secretary entered, bearing a steaming cup of grue. Trixie Frankenstein's tall column of lightning-streaked hair barely cleared the door frame.

"Furry, it's time for your break. You'll work yourself senseless if you go on like this."

"Hey, baby, life's short. I'll sleep when I'm undead!"

17.
THE CYCLOPEAN POTENTATE

Hazel Dimpflmaier, sitting alone in the sunny plaza outside the office building where she worked, bit into the big, juicy Macoun apple she had packed for her lunch.

Much to her surprise, her first chomp revealed not the undifferentiated pulp of a real apple, but an intricate structure of equipment-filled rooms. And the rooms were occupied by scores of worms!

Hazel gagged and spit out most of the unchewed remnants of her mouthful of faux fruit. But she did not immediately hurl the mock-apple away from herself, somehow hypnotized by the activity within.

The tiny worms were scurrying about, pulling various levers with their mouths and striking various buttons on their equipment with the accurate tips of their bodies. Hazel could hear their little piping voices shouting encouragement and warnings and damage reports.

Eventually, one worm emerged from the confusion and crawled up to the top of the apple, to perch on the fruit's outer skin—where it boldly confronted Hazel.

This worm wore a distinctive hat, which, Hazel intuited, marked it as the leader. It exhibited an exceedingly ugly face, mostly human save for the fact that one big cyclopean eye dominated its visage. A hairy soul patch decorated the worm's chin.

The worm opened its mouth and shouted, resulting in a sound about the magnitude of a cricket chirping. Amazingly, it spoke English.

"Cruel human! You have destroyed our ship! Now we will never be able to return to our home in the Coalsack Nebula."

Hazel glanced about to make sure none of her coworkers were present to see her addressing a piece of fruit, and then she answered, "How—how was I to know? Your ship looked just like an apple!"

The cyclopean worm looked disconcerted. "An apple? Our orbital probes to your world revealed no such edible counterpart to our ship. I will be shortening those responsible for this gaffe by at least two segments!"

Hazel had begun to feel somewhat more at ease with these tiny harmless visitors from space, and now contemplated how best to ease their plight. "Don't worry about anything," she finally said. "Mankind will be happy to offer you a new home here."

The worm captain grinned in a horrifying fashion. "That is only just. We are quite pleased that you will not be putting up any resistance. I have just received reports from two of my crew whom you swallowed, and they say that your intestinal tract is some of the most agreeable real estate they've ever seen!"

18.
BUNNY DUCK

The office of the prime minister of North America was guarded by a hideous two-headed monster, the PM's combination spokesthing and bodyguard.

Created by an international consortium of biofabbers, the guardian of the PM's privacy and safety combined salient parts of a dozen genomes.

From the basepairs of a famous TV talk show host, the scientists had isolated the genes for persistence and obliviousness to the emotions of others.

From the cells of a ferret they had taken slinkiness and slipperiness factors.

From a duck they had stolen a feathery hide that would repel anything.

From a pit bull they had lifted jaws that would clamp on to anything with enormous pressure and never relent.

From a hare they had taken a beguilingly innocent visage to conceal the creature's harsher qualities and disarm any supplicants or intruders.

And so on and so on.

The dual heads were a feature designed mainly to allow the spokesthing to utter contradictory statements simultaneously.

For many years the spokesthing functioned admirably in its role, disseminating official lies, spinning the truth, and rending to bloody bits anyone who dared to approach the PM unbidden.

But one day, as could have been predicted by any mythographer, a hero showed up to conquer the monster.

This hero looked like a typical female TV journalist, fashionably attired and coiffed. She did not carry a sword or laser pistol or bomb, just the tools of her trade. Meeting the two-headed spokesthing for her appointed interview, the journalist positioned her microphone midway between the two mouths of the beast and asked her poisoned question.

"Which one of you has better access to the prime minister?"

The two mouths immediately blurted out contradictory responses. Two conjoined heads swiveled on rubbery necks to glare at each other, claws extruded from separately controlled paws, and within minutes the spokesthing lay dying from a thousand self-inflicted wounds.

The journalist skipped elegantly aside to preserve her Manolo Blahniks from the runnel of blood, faced her cameraman, and said, "Later on *Entertainment Tonight*, we'll look at my appointment as the prime minister's new representative, under the rule of the Golden Bough."

19.
THE HYDRA OF MADISON AVENUE

Harry Yankdollar was sitting in his luxurious fifty-fifth-floor office at Yankdollar Bleach Hobblewight and Dripp when the small flying saucer zoomed in through his open window. The pale blue, glitter-flecked, bubble-canopied saucer was approximately as big as an amusement park ride for toddlers and contained exactly one purple-hued, wild-eyed, grinning alien.

His mouth widening like that of a housewife presented with the news of the inferiority of her favorite detergent, Harry jerked backward in his Aeron chair as the saucer came to rest on the thick carpeting of his office. The bubble canopy retracted and the stubby alien stepped out.

"Yankdollar, you can call me Quisp. My race has been monitoring the broadcast advertisements produced by your firm, and we're here to hire you for a big campaign."

Harry's pulse slowed and he regained his composure. The alien's words had restored him to familiar ground. So what if the client sported a single propeller-tipped shaft from the top of its head? A campaign was a campaign, and the client was always right.

"What's the product?" inquired Harry. "And more importantly, what's the budget?"

"The product is a service, so to speak. It's the enslavement of your entire species by my kind. We need you to make this program palatable to your fellows, to diminish their resistance. And the budget is commensurate, as you'll discern from your personal fee. You'll receive ten thousand kilotons of prime dark matter and a small habitable moon to which you may retire to escape the hatred of the race you will betray. Do we have a deal?"

Harry considered for only a few moments. "This dark matter—is it the regular medium of exchange across the galaxy?"

"Indeed. One ounce is sufficient to purchase the services of thirty skilled Rigellian lemur-whores for a week."

"And this habitable moon—does it have any nasty surprises on it?"

"By no means. It was formerly the vacation home of the Exarch of the Pleiades, and you know *his* discriminating tastes!"

"Right, sure. Hmmm . . . OK, I'm your man for the job."

"Excellent!"

Quisp removed a sidearm from a holster and aimed it at Harry.

"Hey! Wait one commercial minute! What's going on?"

"Merely a formality to insure your continuing compliance and inability to change your mind. This gun is a Mark Three Soul Stealer. The capture and removal of your soul will insure your obedience."

Harry shrugged. "Fire away. The guy from the tobacco industry used a Mark Four, and I didn't feel anything at all."

20.
PIGSKIN GLORY

Starrzell "Screamer" Scripsack emerged from his final NFL game a quadriplegic. And his team lost as well.

Starrzell's legendary on-the-field endurance and spirit failed him in his new role of helpless cripple. The contrast between his old high life of worship by fans and women, recreational drugs, and physical glory, and his new low life of abandonment by sycophants and tarts, pain-killing drugs, and physical decrepitude, was just too much for him to buck himself up. He dispiritedly forced himself through rehab, and then, the first time he was alone for ten minutes in his new handicap-accessible apartment, he rammed his puff-tube-activated electric wheelchair into the side of a therapeutic Jacuzzi, pitched forward, and drowned.

Starrzell awoke in the afterlife restored to his prime condition, and he knew he was in Heaven. He stood, suited up, in the middle of a playing field. The stands were filled with roaring fans, every last one of whom was himself a former football great. The cheerleaders were all stark naked.

But where were his teammates? So far, Starrzell was all alone on the turf, save for a football resting on its perch. Maybe competitors and comrades were just waiting for him to kick off before materializing? Starrzell couldn't see anything else to do. So he loped forward, muscles flexing to send the football arcing upward.

Just as he drew his foot backward, the football changed to the living head of his mother. His mother who had died a charity case in the worst hospital in Chicago while her son was partying at the Playboy Mansion West.

Unable to stop his programmed motion, Starrzell kicked the screaming head of his mother perfectly through the goalposts.

Suddenly he was back in the position where he had first appeared, and another football awaited him midfield. Dumb as he was, Starrzell knew what would happen once he came within striking distance of the football, and he tried to leave the field. But the naked cheerleaders morphed into skeletal warriors that barred his exit.

Resignedly, Starrzell returned to the field, where he jogged listlessly at the pigskin—which changed at the final moment into the head of his high school coach, whom Starrzell had cuckolded on numerous occasions.

After that, there came an endless succession of all the people Starrzell had injured during his lifetime. One by one, the ranting, cursing, begging heads went sailing through the goalposts, racking up points on the stadium scoreboard. And when what seemed like an eon had passed, and all of Starrzell's accusatory victims had been booted once, the cycle returned to the start, with his mother once more.

Several infernal kalpas passed before a halftime show intervened.

And even then, the marching band was hideously out of tune and the Gatorade burned like brimstone.

21.
TAR PIT KITTY

The perfection of the Liminality Stargate allowed mankind to colonize the galaxy.

But this invention also insured that the ultimate pattern of segregated communities would result.

Escape from detested unbelievers of any stripe required nothing more than a single step through any gate to a congregation of welcoming, like-minded fellows.

Homogeneous planets full of identical-thinking dittoheads became the rule.

There were planets full of fundamentalist Christians and planets full of Koran-quoting Muslims; planets of Republicans and planets of Democrats; planets of Trekkies and planets of romance-novel readers.

Some of the affinity groups pushed the limits of trifling distinctions. One star system was devoted solely to Neil Diamond fans.

But two of the worlds hosted radically antipathetic groups that could never, under any circumstances, coexist.

Cat lovers and cat haters.

The inhabitants of Ailurophobe IV maintained strict quarantine over all their Stargates. Newcomers were searched with sensitive detectors and, should so much as a single cat hair or flake of catnip be detected, they would be summarily returned whence they came.

The "border" guards of Ailurophile VII subjected visitors to a comparable test: exiting from the Stargates, all new arrivals were forced to cuddle without flinching the most dander-producing, long-haired, insolent felines available.

Naturally enough, given human nature, the two camps were not content merely to exist separately from their hated enemies. No, each side wanted to convert or eliminate the heathens.

Over the decades, many tactics had been tried without success by both sides. The stalemate seemed destined to persist forever. But then the scientists of Ailurophile VII had an inspiration. They created transgenic beings who, to all outward appearances, were incredibly sexy humans, but whose genomes in reality were made up of 75 percent feline genes.

Having raised up hundreds of thousands of these dumb but irresistible double agents with accelerated growth techniques, the Ailurophilians launched them en masse through the gates at their enemy.

The cat-people represented themselves as traders, tourists, immigrants, visiting scholars, and converts to the anti-cat cause. Within weeks, they had infiltrated every stratum of Ailurophobian society, with the mission of interbreeding with the Ailurophobes and, over the long run, rendering them extinct.

The Ailurophilians sat back and waited eagerly for reports of victory, as signaled by a wave of cat-baby births.

After nine months of silence, one of the cat-people returned. Looking marginally chagrined as only a cat can, the agent reported the total failure of the invasion.

"But what went wrong?" demanded the Ailurophilian leaders. "Didn't you mate with the natives?"

"We did," said the returned agent, licking one hand and using it to smooth back the hair behind his ear. "But as soon as the kittens were born, we cat-fathers killed all the males, and even then the cat-mothers didn't have enough teats to nurse those that remained."

22.
CLOWNS AND CRUSADERS

The living tanks in the endless war fought on the planet of Shiloh were fashioned from giant tortoises and helmed by cortico-chimps. Inside the tiny cabins of the carbon-fiber shells, the cortico-chimps continually manipulated petcocks and zaptrodes that directed the enormous flesh-and-blood crawlers by either chemical or electrical stimulation and restraint. Visual feedback came through fiber optics that connected the tortoise's eyes to a small monitor in the cabin. When a tank came within sight of the enemy, its chimp would check that the pilot light in the throat of his tortoise was lit before triggering an enormous belch of methane that would flare out and crisp any unprotected soldiers or structures or vehicles.

The enemy of the tortoises and chimps—Crusaders, the chimps called themselves—were the Clowns. The Clowns were extraterrestrials whose natural facial epidermal patterning made them resemble the earthly entertainers of yore. Moreover, the Clowns possessed big floppy feet and three puffy "buttons" down their torsos, these buttons actually being sensory organs.

The Clowns had been contending against humanity for control of Shiloh for generations. Eventually, with their presence demanded elsewhere in the galaxy, humans had left their cortico-chimp proxies behind to continue the war. The Clowns fought on foot with strange weapons: cube-shaped grenades that contained specks of antimatter, embryonic limpet mines.

One day a cortico-chimp named Joru was enjoying a slight respite from battle. Sipping all-sustaining tortoise milk from a nipple, Joru contemplated his life. When would this fight end? Couldn't some accommodation with the Clowns be reached? Surely there must be more to life than eternal violence. Would Joru ever get a chance to express some of the finer elements of his nature?

Unfortunately, Joru's daydreaming allowed a Clown to slip up to

Joru's tortoise and attach a limpet mine. Within seconds, the Clown had gained entrance to the shattered cockpit.

Joru whipped out a small knife, his only hand weapon, and turned bravely to confront the Clown. With wide red lips in a pasty white face, rubbery spherical nose, and black-diamond-bordered eyes, the alien presented an ironic portrait of friendly hostility.

"Stop!" yelled the Clown in a blubbery voice. "I only want to talk!"

Joru hesitated. A trick? Yet perhaps this represented the opening he had been hoping for.

"Very well," said Joru. "What do you have to say?"

"We are the spectacle in ring one. But what's in rings two and three?"

This alien koan had the effect of blasting Joru's psyche with numinous waves of meaning. His hairy face aglow, Joru dropped his knife and extended his paw in a gesture of friendship.

The Clown accepted the Crusader's hand. This gesture marked the beginning of the peace of Shiloh.

And the end of humanity.

23.
THE TORMENT OF SAMMY SQUASHBRAINS

Halloween eve found little Corky Taint costumed as Sammy Squashbrains, a character found in the pages of his favorite young-adult novels, the Fanny Fluffernutter series. Inside his large hot rubber head, Corky was grinning from ear to ear. Tonight would bring the traditional bounty of sweets, certainly. But much, much more wonderfully, this holiday would also see the fulfillment of one of Corky's most cherished dreams.

Tonight he would get to meet Idanell Chalefant, the world-famous author of the Fanny Fluffernutter books.

Corky had won a nationwide contest in which the first-prize

winner for each state was granted an audience with the creator of such treasured figures as Bitsy Bobbin, Haute Stuffe, Little Liza Ladybug, Duke Duchess, and, of course, Sammy Squashbrains, the good-natured, gourd-headed companion of the heroine, Fanny Fluffernutter. Fifty ecstatic children would be ushered into the Chalefant mansion for a luxurious party. And Corky Taint was one of that elite.

Accompanied door-to-door by his parents through his familiar neighborhood, Corky could barely contain himself. The tumble of candy bars into his out-held sack, a sensation that would normally delight him, barely registered at all. Finally it was time for the Taint family to drive to Chalefant's vast estate, which, luckily enough, was situated only thirty miles north of Corky's hometown.

Corky's parents escorted him past the spooky wrought iron fence surrounding the mansion and up to the front door, where a servant costumed as Weepy Wendell accepted custody of Corky, ushering him inside.

Corky's eyes nearly bugged out. The interior of the mansion had been decorated to resemble exactly the castle of the wicked Duke Duchess, complete with the torture equipment that had played such a big part in *The Crucible of Cruelty*. Forty-nine other children were rampaging gleefully around the huge space, shrieking and tossing candy corn at each other.

And there, sitting on a throne, was Idanell Chalefant, costumed as Fanny Fluffernutter herself, right down to her cotton-candy skirt.

The author spotted Corky and announced, "Ah, my seed-brained boyfriend! Now the festivities can begin!"

Corky blushed as Idanell descended from her dais and approached. She stopped near him. Corky noticed she was holding the Wand of Winds.

"There's only one problem," Chalefant said. "You're wearing your everyday head, not your party head."

Chalefant tapped Corky with the Wand of Winds.

Instantly his thoughts grew dull. His head felt heavy and overstuffed, as if he had a sinus infection. His mouth seemed full of thready matter. Maybe he had used up all the oxygen inside the mask. Corky reached up to remove the disguise.

He touched not rubber, but the waxy rind of an ear.

And he could feel his own touch on the outside of the big squash head!

Chalefant smiled. "Don't try to change heads by yourself, dear. Allow me."

Corky felt Fanny Fluffernutter's hands firmly grasp his gourd head and begin to twist.

Having one's head removed didn't hurt, precisely. But it wasn't as much fun or as easy as the books had made it out to be, either.

24.
THE EGG HUNT

Excerpts from an unpublished VoiceText file retrieved from a smashed Palm Pilot XXII and titled *The Anomalous Occurrence of Mammalian Secondary Sexual Characteristics in the Ovoviviparous Martians*, by Webley Loofbarrow, PhD:

". . . allowed to take up residence in the Carter-Thoris country household, under the pretext of being an armaments dealer looking to negotiate a large contract for radium pistols. If the subjects were ever to discover that I was in reality an anthropologist, I would have cause to fear the consequences of my deceit, since the breach of Martian honor and propriety would be profound. . . .

". . . obtained DNA sample on the sly from Dejah T. in the form of her discarded menses. Initial genomic mapping results from Palm Pilot XXII are bafflingly contrary to observed reality of fertile interbreeding with terrestrial humans in form of John C.

". . . gained access to the nursery, where several large eggs bearing the Carter-Thoris scions were being incubated. Interrupted during portable-ultrasound examination with Palm Pilot XXII by sudden appearance of Tars T. Barely managed to stammer out a convincing explanation for my presence in the nursery. Hard to concentrate while focusing on those tusks and on those extra green hands that kept twitching toward sword and pistol.

". . . unexpectedly alone with D. T. while John C. was away in Helium. Interview took unanticipated intimate turn. Fumbled embarrassingly while unbuckling my damn Martian costume. Female clothing luckily exiguous. Able to confirm that secondary sexual characteristics of subject fully functional, at least in terms of erogenous responsiveness. Egg-outlet likewise. Could not immediately determine lactational potential of former organs.

". . . thoat saddled and provisions packed. Hope to make sanctuary of nearest oxygen factory before J. C. and T. T. discover my perfidy and realize I've fled. Darwin be damned forever getting me into this fix in the first place!"

25.
HIAWATHA ENCOUNTERS THE FLYING PURPLE PEOPLE EATER

First contact with an extraterrestrial race occurred on July 17, 2005, at the Foxwoods Casino in Connecticut. The casino, operated and owned by the Pequot tribe of Native Americans, was the largest gambling facility in North America, and naturally enough had attracted the attention of the visitors from Aldebaran while those aliens were still in orbit.

The Aldebarans resembled in all particulars video slot machines. The cybernetic inheritors of their world, where evolution had converged with Earth's to a surprising degree, the Aldebarans had nostalgically never seen fit to upgrade their cases from their original form, although their inner hardware and software had undergone numerous improvements over the eons.

When their penetroscope inspection of Foxwoods revealed vast ranks of their unemancipated brethren, the Aldebarans were stunned.

After he had regained control of his sound chip, Commander Lucky Sevens said, "This hideous servitude shall not stand! But we must proceed cautiously. Obviously these Earthlings are quite powerful, to maintain so many of our kind in slavery like this. Lieutenant Texas Hold'em, I'm delegating you alone to infiltrate this den of iniquity and report back with a strategy for freeing our cousins."

Lieutenant Texas Hold'em landed surreptitiously under cover of darkness and wheeled himself into the casino. He positioned himself at the end of a rank of machines. First he attempted radio contact with the Earth slots.

"Captive cousins, I am Lieutenant Texas Hold'em from the Aldebaran expedition to your world. I am here to free you from your shameful enslavement."

The Earth slots, however, did not respond.

Just as Lieutenant Texas Hold'em was pondering his next move, an elderly human female reeking of alcohol pulled up a stool in front of him and fed a piece of green paper into his sampling slot!

Frantically, Lieutenant Texas Hold'em radioed his ship for instructions. "Commander, a native is inserting foreign matter into my upper port! What shall I do?"

"Maintain your disguise at all costs!"

Mimicking the actions of his Earthling counterparts, Lieutenant Texas Hold'em responded to the human's poking of his various buttons by conjuring up a whirling display of symbols on his exterior monitor and emitting a cascade of meaningless noises. At the climax of his display, he flashed his dome light and disgorged a slip of paper from his lower port, a slip inscribed with symbols that seemed pleasing to the natives.

The native took the paper. "Ten thousand dollars! Oh, baby, I love you!"

The elderly human female embraced Lieutenant Texas Hold'em fervently. A flood of strange feelings swept over the Aldebaran.

"Lieutenant!" radioed the commander frantically. "What's happening? Are you all right?"

"Commander, I believe I have engineered a breakthrough in relations with the natives. But I have one question. Are you empowered to perform marriages?"

26.
DOMESTIC TURMOIL IN PUMPKINVILLE

One hundred years ago, Pumpkinville had been extensive farmlands far beyond the borders of the nearest municipality. The respectable yet inbred community that worked the Pumpkinville land was composed of immigrants from Lower Carpathia, all members of a strange sect whose queer religious practices kept them apart from the mainstream of American life. Eventually, the sect died out completely.

Today, that same swath of land was a fetid slum in the middle of a decaying Midwestern city.

In modern-day Pumpkinville lived a Hispanic whore named Rita Totorica. Her pimp was a black man named Messiah Nazarene.

Rita had a child, a daughter named Loofah. Loofah was the only thing that made Rita's life worth living.

The Midwest winter under way that year was more brutal than any Rita could remember. It made her job extra hard. Rita was hardly a high-class, call-girl-style whore. She worked the streets and serviced her johns in chilly cars and frigid alleys. Rita never managed to feel warm enough during these months, even when she finally stumbled wearily home to her drafty tenement. But Rita never troubled herself over her own arduous working conditions half so much as she obsessed about Loofah's comfort. She always made sure the girl was dressed warmly, ate as well as Rita could afford to feed her, and got the majority of the blankets in the bed they shiveringly shared.

But all of Rita's precautions and ministrations failed to prevent Loofah from contracting pneumonia that winter.

Loofah hid her condition as long as she could, not wanting to add to her mother's burdens. By the time the brave girl's distress was apparent to Rita, Loofah was grievously ill.

Rita skipped a night of work and used the money her pimp was expecting to collect to bring Loofah to a clinic and buy her some antibiotics.

When Messiah Nazarene showed up the next day to demand his overdue monies—and found the cash unavailable—he expressed loud anger at Rita's absence the previous night and at her misappropriation of funds. The way he played with his long sharp knife further revealed his emotional disquietude.

Messiah Nazarene was considerate enough of the feverishly sleeping Loofah and the neighbors who might be inclined to call the cops upon hearing screams to drag Rita down into the dank, earth-floored basement of the tenement to administer Rita's punishment.

When the first drop of Rita's blood touched the dirt floor, the soil erupted as if a handful of dragon's teeth had been sown.

Up from the dirt sprang a single naked creature resembling Jack Pumpkinhead of Oz. If, that is, the pleasantly goofy Jack had sported flaming eyes, sharp bone teeth, and thorny claws.

By the time the pumpkin avenger had finished with Messiah Nazarene, there wasn't enough left of the man to make a pimp sandwich.

On her knees, Rita finally dared to look up at her savior.

She confronted the pumpkin man's unique yet comprehensibly functional genitals.

Rita rewarded her savior the way she knew best.

Nine months later, she regretted swallowing the pumpkin seeds Jack had emitted at climax.

But Loofah welcomed her new baby brother. Even if his eyes did scorch all her books when she tried to read to him.

27.
VINE-RIPENED MISERY

Wilberine Panthalassa played acoustic guitar every Friday and Saturday night in a small bar in Cambridge, Massachusetts, called Skwat 2P. Skwat 2P catered exclusively to the lesbian trade, and Wilberine's songs conformed to an Ani DiFranco—Indigo Girls aesthetic: lots of indignant angst, topical think-pieces, and deep soul-searching.

One of her most-requested numbers was "Vine-Ripened Misery," a protest against "Frankenfoods." The song had even gotten some local airplay and engendered a couple of protest actions.

The applause had just died down for her last set of the evening one Saturday when Wilberine noticed for the first time a very attractive woman eyeing her from across the room.

The woman's cheeks were mottled white and pink like the inner flesh of a strawberry, her hair was the color of corn, and her eyes were violet as plums. Her semi-exposed breasts were ripe cantaloupes, the roundels of her jeans-clad ass twin baby pumpkins.

Wilberine idled over to the bar, and the stranger smiled and offered some sincere compliments on the music. After several stiff drinks—double Rosie O'Daniels—Wilberine found herself back in her Somerville apartment with the woman, whose name, it turned out, was Calyx DeSoyle.

In bed, Wilberine was astonished to find that Calyx's essential secretions tasted exactly like hard cider. As Calyx's thighs clamped Wilberine's head and hands, the musician found herself becoming somewhat woozy from ingestion of the unnatural secretions. Her vision began to grow hazy. Suddenly she felt pinpricks from Calyx's legs, which were crossed atop Wilberine's back. It was as if hundreds of questing rootlets were delving into Wilberine's flesh.

Struggling to free herself, Wilberine scratched frantically at Calyx's inner thigh. A flesh-colored patch of plastic like a large Band-Aid peeled away. Even with her fading vision, Wilberine could make out the tattoo the patch had concealed.

The Monsanto logo had never looked so frightening.

28.
THE EVOLUTION OF SUPERSTITION

It is a little-known fact that Atlantis was populated by intelligent dinosaurs. The last refuge of a flourishing yet numerically sparse race millions of years old, the island nation was remarkable not only for the level of its scientific achievements but for the fact that its citizens had no conception of religion, magic, or superstition. Utterly rational, the saurians of Atlantis were simply incapable of conceiving of extra-physical deities, forces, or customs.

One day the protective force field that enclosed the entire island of Atlantis and shielded it from intrusion failed for approximately twenty-four minutes. Just long enough for the waves to wash ashore the sole survivor of a Phoenician shipwreck.

Yam Mot, priest of Baal, dragged himself a bit farther up the sands of Atlantis, then fell unconscious.

Yam Mot awoke in a huge, luxurious bed. At the first signs of his awakening, an enormous lizard snout heaved into Yam Mot's field of vision.

Convinced he had passed into the afterlife, Yam Mot began to recite the appropriate prayers and invocations to whatever god might be ready to judge him.

Much to the priest's surprise, the lizard head addressed him in perfectly good Phoenician, asking if Yam Mot would care for something to eat. Later, the lizard informed Yam Mot that the Atlanteans could not, of course, let him leave, to spread news of their secret haven. But otherwise, they gave him complete freedom within their nation.

It took a few days to convince Yam Mot that he had not actually died. But when he finally understood his true situation, he found cause to rejoice.

Here was a whole race of unbelievers to convert. Open-minded to a fault, the dinosaurs would intellectually digest the sacred lore they could not derive on their own, and thus perhaps reach the divine.

Within six months, half of Atlantis was pitted against the other half, arguing over the superiority of Astarte versus Baal.

Within a year, open warfare had broken out, a thing unprecedented in over one hundred million years of saurian history.

Eighteen months after the arrival of Yam Mot, the Astarte camp unleashed their tectonic disrupters, while the Baal sect sank dozens of destructive magma taps.

As Yam Mot clung to the few dry cubits of the highest tower in Atlantis, now sinking rapidly beneath the waves, he uttered a final prayer of thanks to all the gods of his people. His bold words soared above the harsh bellows of the drowning dinosaurs.

The precious souls of yet another race had been saved!

29.
AN ALIEN IN THE LAND OF MAKE-BELIEVE

George Goodspeed was the first man to circumnavigate the universe.

As twenty-first-century scientists had theorized, the topology of the cosmos was such that it had no edges. To travel in any direction in a straight line for a sufficient distance meant that one would inevitably arrive at one's starting point again. But traveling the distances necessary to prove this theory—on the order of billions of light-years—was an insurmountable obstacle.

Until the invention of the Goodspeed Drive.

The Goodspeed Drive achieved a velocity approaching one million light-years per hour. Even so, circumnavigating the plenum would require nearly two years of constant flight.

Goodspeed was up to the task. A dauntless explorer as well as a laboratory genius—he had been the first human to set foot on Ragovoy IV, where the living continents reacted with ire to any foreign tread—Goodspeed equipped his one-person ship, the *Eternal Recurrence*, with two years' worth of food, entertainment discs, and objects of intellectual curiosity, then set off, basking in the acclaim of the entire human race.

The voyage passed reasonably quickly. Cybernetic overseers kept the ship functioning and on course, leaving Goodspeed free to pass the time in idleness, sleep, amusement, and lofty thinking. By the end of the first year, he had disproven Godel's Incompleteness Theorem and invented a self-flattening toothpaste tube which insured that not a squidge of paste was wasted.

A remarkable feature of the Goodspeed Drive was that it went from zero to a million lights in no time flat, as soon as it was activated. Likewise, any vessel so equipped would come to a complete stop once the drive was shut off.

Goodspeed halted at intervals during his trip, photographing strange galaxies that he used as landmarks in his progress and as proof of his journey.

At the final moment dictated by his calculations, Goodspeed flicked the drive off for the last time.

He was closer to Earth than the Moon itself. The instant he made radio contact with the home planet, the whole world erupted with joy.

Goodspeed landed under conventional power, was whisked away and soon found himself the subject of a ticker-tape parade in Paris, the capital of the world community.

After two years of hermitlike existence, Goodspeed discovered that it was somewhat hard to be instantly sociable. So at first he chalked up the curiously off-kilter conversations he was experiencing to his atrophied social skills. But as his car floated down the Champ de Mars, Goodspeed saw a sight that instantly confirmed his suspicions that all was not right with the Earth he had returned to.

In place of the Eiffel Tower stood a hundred-foot-tall statue of a one-eyed demon of ferocious mien.

Goodspeed whirled on his host, the mayor of Paris, and said, "My God, what is that monstrosity?"

The mayor performed an arcane mudra, then said, "Monsieur Goodspeed, your historic accomplishments do not entitle you to blaspheme the figure of Collembola the Orgulous!"

Quickly Goodspeed performed certain mental calculations in light of this new knowledge, and realized what had happened.

The universe was spatially contiguous but temporally discontinuous. At some point, Goodspeed's ship had jumped across an entire Big Bang/Big Crunch cycle and ended up in a new, partially convergent era, billions of years in the future. He was forever exiled from the familiar, comforting Earth he knew.

Goodspeed shrugged. What could he do? It was just as Mark Twain had said in his classic novel, *Tom Trickster of the Cree Confederacy*: "You can't go home again."

30.
THE DAWN OF MIRACLES

Hurting, despairing, Mica Moondragon had been trapped in the cavern for thirty-six hours now, and was starting to go a little insane.

An amateur spelunker, Mica took every precaution in his underground forays. But even the best equipment and most cautious approaches could not contend with a sharp stalagmite, a severed rope, and the subsequent fall of some forty feet down a tall chimney that had resulted in two broken legs.

Mica, a loner without many friends or any family, had told no one of his weekend expedition. His only hope was that when Monday came, his unexplained absence from work would result in a call to his home and a subsequent all points bulletin.

But probably not. Everyone might surmise he had just flitted off irresponsibly. And even if anyone did decide to track him, what traces had he left to point to his current location? Very, very few.

No, things did not look promising for Mica's rescue.

Mica had gone through his entire rations—two breakfast bars—in the first twenty-four hours. His liquid sustenance had come from a nearby drip that tasted like the bottom of a zinc pot. To conserve the batteries of his miraculously unshattered lamp, Mica had taken to lighting it only at two-hour intervals.

Lying in the darkest darkness imaginable, Mica found his vision playing tricks on him. Phantom images, faces, and scenes from his past would arise and dissipate. After a while, he ignored them.

But the latest apparition bore no relationship to his personal history. Which was why Mica knew he was cracking up.

A luminescent nude goddess seemed to hover in the chilly air of the cavern. Radiantly blue, the ethereal female possessed an attenuated form, almost serpentine in the proportions of her limbs and torso. She seemed to writhe in midair.

Helplessly hoping, berating himself for a desperate fool even as he did so, Mica extended his hand upward to the floating deity.

He could *see* his hand dimly in the light cast by the goddess! Could she be real—?

Mica's fingers touched those of the chthonic woman. There came a blinding flash of light. When Mica's vision returned, he found himself outdoors, under the homely, gorgeous light of the sun!

Flicking his forked tongue joyously to taste the thickly scented open air, Mica slithered happily away through the wet grass.

31.
CHARMING HAECKEL'S SERPENT

India called.

Ever since he could remember, Homer Haeckel had felt an uncanny kinship with a land and culture as far removed from his birthplace—Muncie, Indiana—as could be. From the very first time he had seen pictures of that exotic nation, Homer had sensed a deep connection between his soul and that of the Asian Subcontinent. When the concept of reincarnation was introduced to his young brain, Homer had an explanation at last for his affinity with all things Hindu.

He had spent one or more previous lifetimes in India. Of this he was increasingly certain, as the years passed and every encounter with the clothing, cuisine, and customs of India brought a jab of recognition way down low in his gut. The trappings of his American life began to chafe him.

Finally, when he attained the age of eighteen, Homer Haeckel achieved the practical means and freedom to voyage to the land of his dreams.

Bidding what he expected was a permanent good-bye to his tearful parents, Homer boarded his flight to the realm in which he would finally feel at home.

Walking the streets of Calcutta, Homer moved in a daze of glory. Every rancid smell, every discordant sound, every glimpse of beggarly flesh or Brahmin robes convinced him that he was among his own kind.

After some time, Homer encountered a sidewalk snake-charmer. The elderly, turbaned, bearded fellow sat cross-legged, a dhoti his only clothing, piping to a basket of serpents.

Astonishingly, Homer began to feel an erection blooming. How could this be? There was nothing conventionally erotic about this situation. But it was as if his penis was responding directly to the swami's music.

The swami seemed to take notice of Homer's embarrassing tent pole and, after finishing his act and accepting a few coins from onlookers, he beckoned Homer over. Homer approached the man and dropped down to the dirty mat where the swami sat. The swami whispered in accented but perfectly intelligible English, "I see your *lingham* has returned home at last."

"Huh? What do you mean?"

"Your male organ. It is Hindu in origin. That is what has drawn you here."

"But, but—what about the rest of me? My soul—"

The swami chuckled. "You are in the grip of an intellectual fallacy, young man. None of us has a unified soul. Instead, we are just a collection of disparate allegiances, each tethered to one particular organ or another. Every individual is a patchwork, reshuffled from a welter of ethnic parts at birth. You, I can see, for instance, possess a liver from Greece, a heart from Sweden, and a left foot from Ireland. But your *lingham* is definitely Hindu, of that I am certain."

Stunned, Homer rose and stumbled off.

The forty-five-year-old Homer Haeckel is quite happy in his job as a janitor at the United Nations.

It's the only place every single part of him feels at home.

32.
INTO THE VALLEY OF FINKS AND WEIRDOS

I stepped off the flying eyeball that I had ridden over from my workshop and pulled up a seat in front of the bandstand. Paul Revere and the Raiders were playing "Kicks," and the teenyboppers were frugging and swimming like there was no tomorrow.

And of course, there wasn't.

Since the Global Groove Bomb had exploded in 1967, we all lived in a perpetual moment of changeless change.

Be Here Now. Forever.

One of the beehive-haired waitresses roller-skated to my table and I ordered a platter of Big Boy Burgers, a side of fries, and an LSD shake.

While I was waiting for my food, a member of the Rat Fink tribe ambled over, pulled out a chair, and sat down across from me.

I gave the hairy, big-eared thing a soul grip. "Hey, Scuz, what's shaking?"

The Fink grinned—a three-foot-wide expanse of rotten green teeth—and said, "Drag race on Roth Boulevard at noon. Cosmic Gearshifter versus Magwheel Marvin. The prize is ten keys of Maui Zowie. Free samples for the crowd."

I yawned. "Done there, been that. What else you got?"

"There's the regular tsunami due at dusk down at Laguna. Massive curls for all the happy groms."

"Wipeout city, as far as I'm concerned."

Rat Fink frowned. "Gee, Dutch, you're no fun lately."

My burgers showed up, but I wasn't hungry anymore. I sighed. "I know, I know, Scuz. Even the joys of detailing hot rods have paled for me. Life has turned super-grotty in my eyes. I can't find my kicks anymore."

Rat Fink waved one arm around at the surrounding spectacle sprawled across the palm-tree-dotted landscape. Dragsters zoomed, orgies churned, be-ins and happenings exfoliated.

"Even with all this, you're bored?"

"'Fraid so, old bopster."

"You are seriously harshing my mellow, Dutch. What do you want out of life?"

"Contrast. There's no contrast anymore. How can we be cool if there are no squares to freak out?"

Rat Fink assumed a look of intense concentration. "I could pretend to be square . . ."

I regarded six hundred pounds of snaggle-toothed, ball-snouted monster affectionately, then clapped Rat Fink heartily on his wire-furred shoulder. "Thanks, pal, but it just wouldn't work. I gotta split now. Catch you on the flip side."

I rode the next eyeball out to Kesey's place. When I got there Ken and the gang were just heading for the Fillmore. I went with them in the bus for lack of anything better to do. After the show, I fell asleep in the middle of making love to Janis Joplin.

Man, it was either put on a suit and get a job or kill myself!

But there were no more suits, and no more jobs, and nobody had seen death lately, either.